Calaf and Ishmael

CALAF AND ISHMAEL

A TALE OF TURANDOT

Deak Wooten

ISBN: 1542785685
ISBN 13: 9781542785686

The English translations of the Greek poems "Oh soul, torn by unbearable concerns" by Archilochus and "Ode to Aphrodite" by Sappho are copyright Nikolaos A. Ioannidis and are used with permission.

The English translation of passages from Giacomo Puccini's opera *Turandot*, Italian libretto by Giuseppe Adami and Renato Simoni, are from the booklet accompanying the 1972 Decca recording of Joan Sutherland, Luciano Pavarotti, and Montserrat Caballe with the London Philharmonic Orchestra, Zubin Mehta conducting. The English translator is not identified. The Italian libretto of *Turandot* is copyright 1926 by G. Ricordi & Co.

The Persian carpet on the cover is at the Carpet Museum of Iran in Tehran.

Maps by Pease Press Cartography, San Francisco, California.

Author photograph by Jack Fitzsimmons.

To Rick Callison
who believed

TABLE OF CONTENTS

Acknowledgements

I BEGAN WRITING *CALAF AND ISHMAEL* in October 2011 soon after my first novel *Eyes of the Stag* was published. Recognizing that I was tackling a significantly more ambitious project, I attended classes given by novelist Sara Houghteling through Stanford University's Continuing Studies Program. Sara's instruction, critiques, and encouragement set me on a positive path at a critical time in the story's creation.

In the first class with Sara I met Daniel Nazer, Cheryl Pon, and Samantha Rajaram. Five years later our monthly meetings to share and evaluate each other's work continue to provide a supportive and frank environment for each of us to grow as authors. I am grateful beyond words for their support and friendship.

Thank you to my beta readers, Walter Gendell, Minda Lucero, Mary O'Tousa, and Judy Wagner. Their insightful and honest feedback encouraged me and made *Calaf and Ishmael* a better story.

My editor William Boggess challenged me over and over, and struggling with his feedback was difficult at times. But I could not be more pleased with the final result.

In important respects, there is no *Calaf and Ishmael* without Rick Callison. Rick was there when the story's first ideas began to form. Over the next five plus years, Rick became my sounding board during many a long lunch as I grappled with the novel's plot, characters, historical context, and underlying themes. He lifted a glass in my excited moments and was a hand on the shoulder through the discouraged ones.

And a special thank you to my husband Paul Takayanagi. His love and support gave *Calaf and Ishmael* a nurturing environment within which to grow.

History and *Calaf and Ishmael*

Calaf and Ishmael unfolds over forty-five years during the 3rd century CE in the Roman, Persian (modern day Iran) and the Kushan (modern day Pakistan) Empires. While references to Roman and Persian rulers and events are based on historical fact, those relating to the 3rd century Kushans and the Kingdom of Tur arise solely from the imagination of the author, who has also taken the liberty of moving the events of Giacomo Puccini's opera *Turandot* from China's Imperial City to Kanishka the Great's *City of Men,* Peshawar.

The postscript's story of Puccini's intention for the *Turandot* libretto is also the author's creation.

The World of *Calaf and Ishmael*

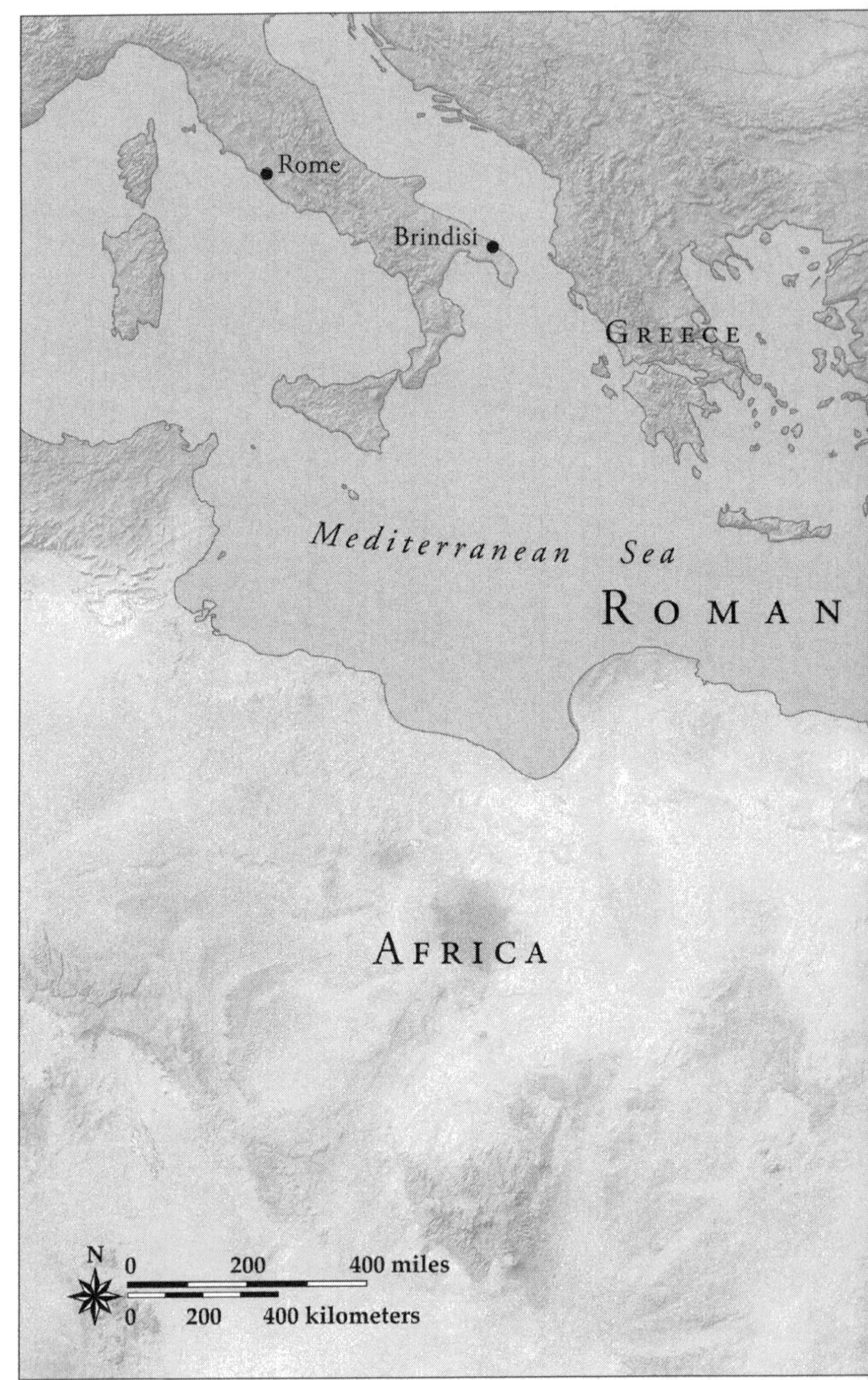
Rome
Brindisi
Greece
Mediterranean Sea
Roman
Africa
N
0 200 400 miles
0 200 400 kilometers

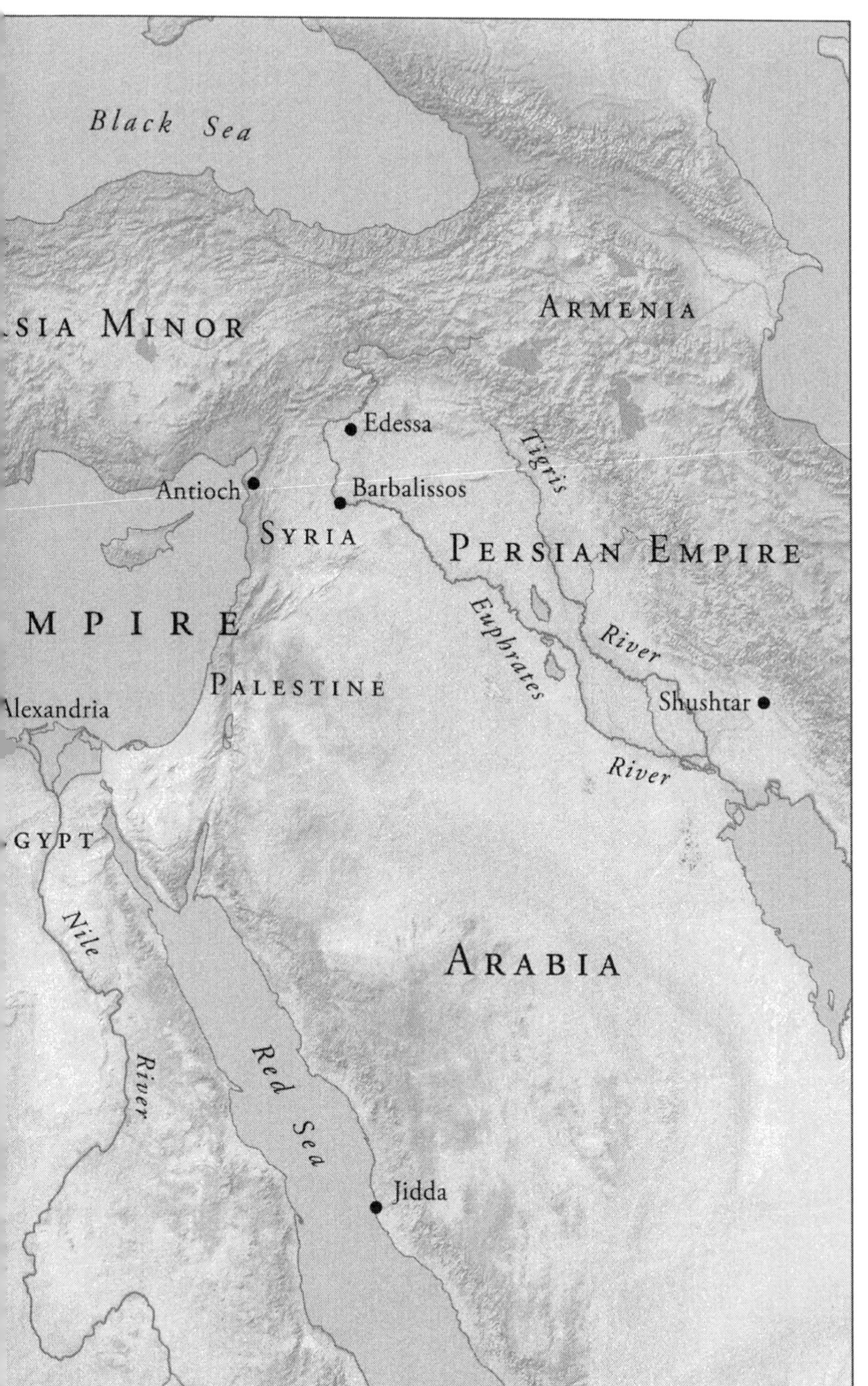

Black Sea
sia Minor
Armenia
Edessa
Tigris
Antioch
Barbalissos
Syria
Persian Empire
mpire
Euphrates
River
Palestine
Shushtar
lexandria
River
gypt
Nile
Arabia
River
Red Sea
Jidda

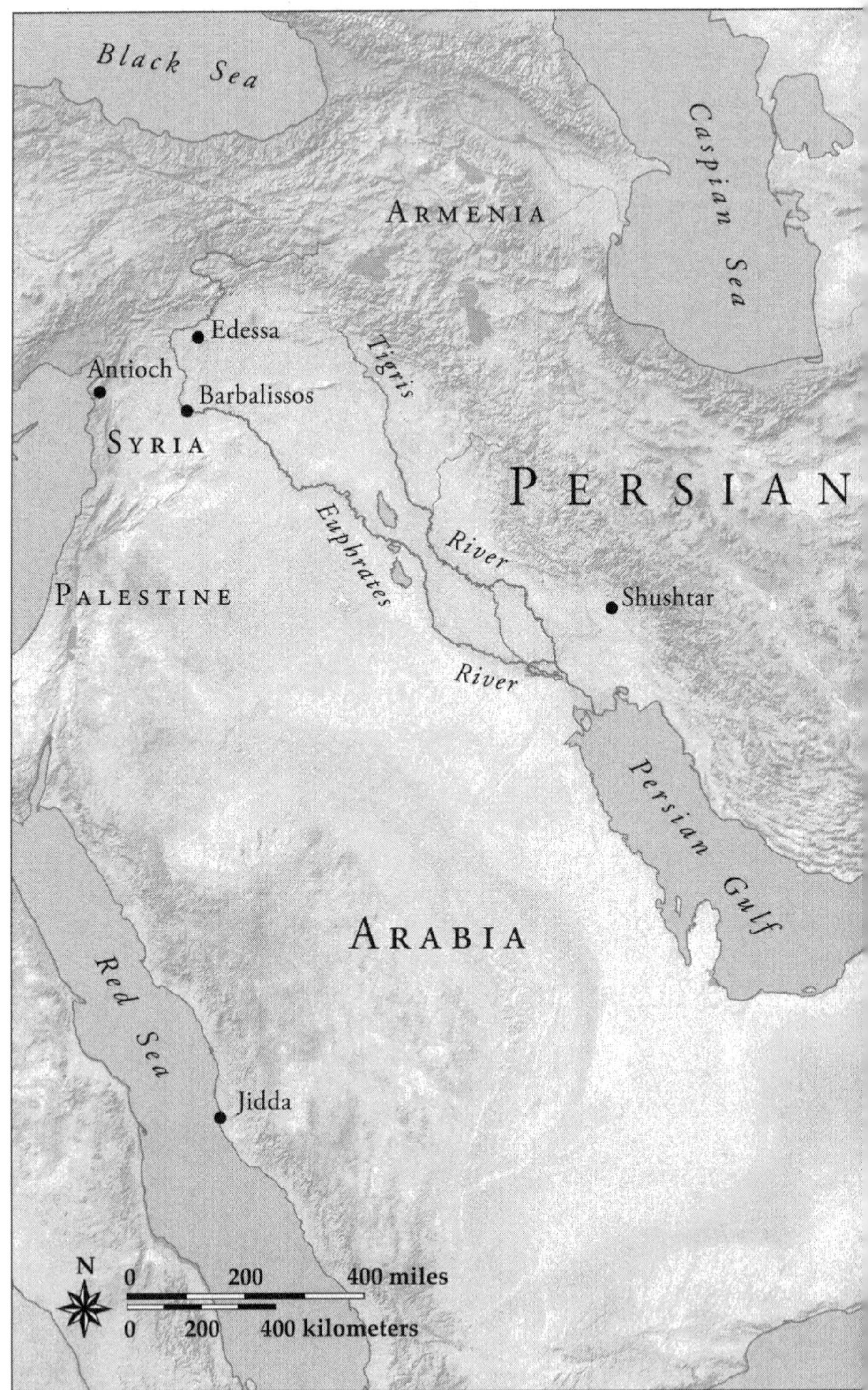
Black Sea
Caspian Sea
Armenia
Edessa
Antioch
Barbalissos
Tigris
Syria
PERSIAN
Euphrates
River
River
Palestine
Shushtar
Persian Gulf
Arabia
Red Sea
Jidda
N
0
200
400 miles
0
200
400 kilometers

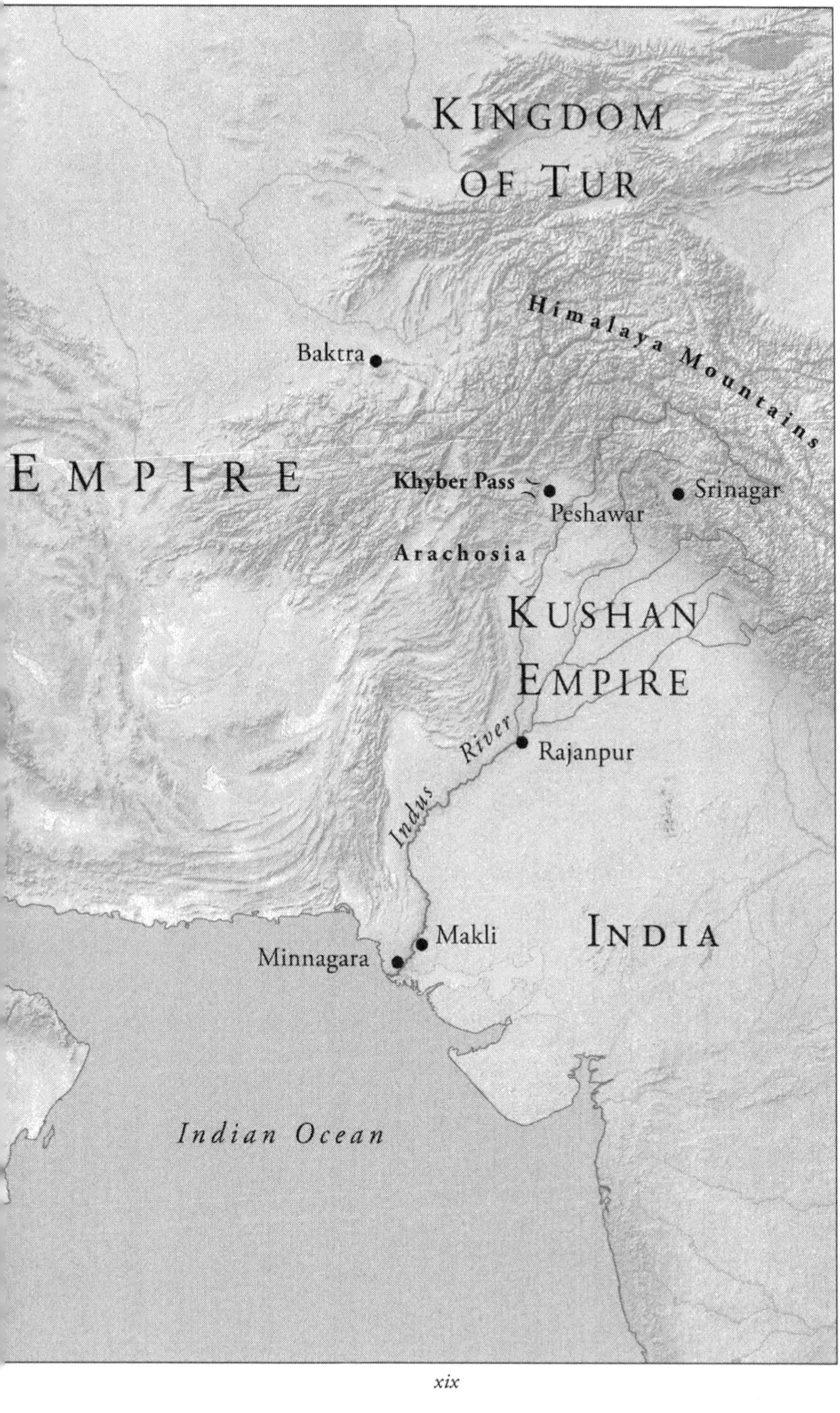

KINGDOM OF TUR

Himalaya Mountains

Baktra

EMPIRE

Khyber Pass

Peshawar

Srinagar

Arachosia

KUSHAN EMPIRE

Indus River

Rajanpur

Makli

Minnagara

INDIA

Indian Ocean

PROLOGUE

Only If You Survive This Day

215 CE

Prologue

Peshawar

One moment astride the stallion, the next aloft, then slammed on his back with the wind knocked out him, Timur rolled away from the pounding hooves. A hand yanked his arm, helping him scramble to his feet.

"Did you see that?" he yelled over the cheers of the horse market crowd as his best friend Yousef steadied him.

Sanjar rushed up, his innocent face beaming with excitement. "Unbelievable! You flew so high!"

Yousef snapped disapprovingly, "What, have you decided to ascend the throne on a litter?"

Waving at the crush of people his bodyguards restrained, Timur said, "Yousef, they loved it. They love me!"

"They love their future emperor."

"There's a difference?"

"Don't get arrogant."

Timur punched Yousef's shoulder. "Never with you at my side."

The Mongolian horse merchant slipped between them. "You like, my prince? His sire carried a great warrior in battle. Born to be yours."

Yousef pulled Timur aside. "Nozar wants him."

Sanjar added, "And his father's agreed."

"What's Nozar to me? Next week I'll be sixteen and his ruler." An eagle swooped low above the horse market, casting its shadow over them. With a broad smile Timur said, "See, an omen."

Sanjar scoffed, “It’s just an eagle.”

Timur playfully grabbed a fistful of Sanjar’s thick, curly hair. Sanjar laughed and slapped Timur’s hand away.

Yousef said, “There are other fine horses.”

“You worry too much,” Timur replied. “If Nozar wanted him, he should’ve gotten here earlier.” He called out to the merchant, “Deliver the horse to the palace stables.”

The captain of his bodyguards stepped up. “My prince, the regent awaits.”

Timur leaned into Yousef’s ear. “Soon old Rodmehr will wait for me.”

For much of the year Peshawar’s buildings of sunbaked clay gave the city the same drab earthy color of its high desert surroundings, but in spring wildflowers invaded open plots, orchid trees graced public squares with pink, violet and white, and great bushes of jasmine filled the air with their heavy scent. Spring also brought the great *Holi* market when the narrow, winding streets would erupt into an artist’s palette as merchants filled them with their wares, covering them with canopies of bright colors.

Timur’s guards opened a path through the crush of people passing through the Khyber Gate into the city’s massive entry. A distant throbbing of drums greeted their ears.

Timur leaned into Yousef and grumbled, “Hear that? Rodmehr forces me to sit and listen to him drone on and on while everyone is celebrating *Holi*.”

“He’s only concerned for your safety,” Yousef said. “The crowd can become unruly.” Nodding toward the guards, he added, “Anyway, what choice do you have?”

At that moment Sanjar tugged on Timur’s arm. “There’s the eagle again.” The great bird glided in wide circles above the royal palace, winter home to the Kushan ruler.

Timur winked at Yousef. "There's always a choice." Then pointing at the sky, he shouted, "Look!"

When the guards stared into the sky to see what caught their charge's attention, Timur bolted into the nearest side street, followed by his two friends, leaving a wake of overturned merchandise and angry merchants. They raced through the maze of narrow streets, slowing only when they lost the bodyguards. Slipping into a deserted alley, they paused to catch their breaths, only to find their pursuers had outfoxed them, appearing at both ends of the passage.

"Fun's over," called the captain.

Yousef nudged Timur toward an open second floor window.

As the bodyguards closed in, Yousef and Sanjar hoisted the prince within a hand's reach of the opening. Timur lunged, grasping the sill with a triumphant cry. The guards' shouts and his friends' laughter followed him as he tumbled into a darkened room heavy with the scent of sage incense. Out of breath he lunged for the door, stumbled, and fell to his knees. A hot draft crossed his face. Incense stung his eyes as silence enveloped him. Dizzy, he reeled as a vision emerged from the darkness. He saw himself kneeling at his father's bedside, holding his lifeless hand, staring at his ashen face and blood-soaked tunic. Once again, he heard General Rodmehr's plea that he come away so the priests could prepare the emperor's body for the funeral rites.

A voice slipped into his vision. "You see your dead father."

He jerked his head toward the sound. His eyes, now damp with tears, searched the room's dimness. A woman dressed in black knelt on the floor, an unrolled parchment between them.

"Who are you?" Timur asked.

"Who I am is unimportant. What matters is that the heavens have long foretold our meeting." Slowly she traced a finger over the parchment's astrological symbols. "Know this, Timur, son of Vasudeva, descendant of Kanishka the Great, villainy surrounds you. Today's sun rose upon a prince. It will set upon an emperor bathed in blood."

A chill ran down Timur's spine. An astrologer had foretold his father's death, which had kindled his fascination with astrology, much to the irritation of General Rodmehr, who believed an emperor must rule by verifiable truth and intellect and leave the delusions of the supernatural to the priests and their gullible followers.

"Am I this emperor?"

"Impressive, my prince. You grasp the nuances of prophesy."

"Answer me, am I?" he demanded.

"Only if you survive this day."

Outside the room heavy footfalls approached. Timur cleared his head with a shake and rushed to the window. Giving an exaggerated bow, he said, "You tell a good tale, my lady," then swung a leg over the sill, his friends on the ground yelling for him to hurry.

The woman asked, "Are they Yousef and Sanjar?"

"How did you know?"

She lowered her face as the room's door flew open and the bodyguards charged in. With an exultant grin Timur saluted and dropped back into the alley away from their curses.

"What took you so long?" Yousef asked.

"Crazy woman spouting crazier stories. Let's get out of here."

The cool of morning had long vanished, and the sun's harsh blaze enveloped every corner of the great public square, now writhing with flailing arms and leaping bodies. Revelers in various states of undress threw colored powders and jasmine-scented water into the air with euphoric abandon. Drums throbbed and unintelligible cries of bhang-induced jubilation celebrated *Holi,* Lord Krishna's festival of colors that rejoiced in winter's end and welcomed spring's fertility.

Timur and his companions rushed into the square, plunging into the melee. As wafts of cannabis surrounded them, a woman whose white dress was soaked transparent, draped her arms around the prince and planted her lips on his. With a laugh Timur broke the embrace, and she threw herself at a delighted Yousef. Timur waved at two army cadet friends. The bare-chested youths pushed through the crowd.

"I can't believe you're here," shouted one over the din.

"Escape your guards again?" laughed the other.

They lifted Timur onto their shoulders and paraded him about the square. With the crowd surging about them, an ecstatic Timur waved and cheered as he was engulfed in a dust storm of pinks, blues, and yellows and drenched in waters of good fortune. Finally, Yousef and Sanjar pulled him down and led him through the crowd to the square's central fountain. Timur kicked away his sandals and pulled off his now soaked and color-stained tunic and trousers. Clad only in a loincloth, he led his companions into the mass of men and boys shoving, splashing, and playing in the fountain's water. Sanjar jumped on Timur's back, causing them both to collapse in hysterical laughter into the shallow water.

Yousef grabbed Timur's arm. "They're here!"

The bodyguards pushed through the colorful deluge. On hands and knees Timur scrambled around and between legs, and then leaping from the fountain, he careened through the frenzied crowd. Once away from the square, he escaped with ease, and soon found himself, laughing and breathless, racing into a secluded courtyard that led into the royal palace.

Timur bent forward, one hand on his knee, the other holding onto his unraveling, water-soaked loincloth. A hand grabbed his shoulder, and he almost fell as he was spun about. Regaining his balance, he expected to find a grinning Yousef or one of his guards. Instead he stared into the face of an enraged Nozar. His high spirits vanished. The strange woman. The incense. The vision of his dead father. *Only if you survive this day.*

Nozar was the oldest son of a lesser noble in the Kushan court. A year older than Timur, broad of chest and taller by a head, he and his notorious temper tyrannized the boys in the palace, unleashing his frustration upon them over any wrong, real or imagined. Given his size and strength, even the palace guards were intimidated by his fury. Timur hoped the bully knew better than to harm his prince, but Nozar held onto his shoulder, pressing his thick, stubby fingers deep into the tender flesh around Timur's clavicle.

"That horse is mine!" Nozar's hot spittle struck his mouth and chin.

Yousef and Sanjar appeared and grabbed Nozar's arms, struggling to pull him away.

"He's your prince! Don't be a fool!" Yousef cried.

Nozar yanked himself free but stood motionless, his dark face contorted and teeth clenched. Timur stepped back, one hand holding his loose loincloth, the other kneading his sore shoulder.

"No one needs to know," Yousef said. His eyes darted to Timur. "Right?"

Timur nodded as his mind raced. *Hold firm—demand respect.* "But he must apologize." Yousef shook his head and mouthed *No.*

"Apologize?" Nozar bellowed. "Apologize to you? You stole my horse!"

Do not show fear. "It's an open market. The horse was for sale so I bought it."

"Everyone knew I wanted it."

"Then you should have—"

Nozar shoved him in the chest. Timur landed on his back on the stone pathway, his loincloth falling away. Yousef and Sanjar managed to hold Nozar back as Timur scrambled naked to his feet.

Sanjar became frantic. "He's the prince. You can't—"

Yousef broke in, "Nozar, think of your family." Then to Timur he said, "Go now, leave."

"No!" Nozar charged forward. Timur stumbled but kept his balance as he fled into the palace. Nozar grabbed a handful of stones and threw them. "Coward!" he howled, beginning to give chase.

"Bastard!" Yousef yelled.

Hearing his friend's cry, Timur turned and watched him lunge for Nozar legs, bringing the bully to his knees. Sanjar leapt onto Nozar's back, bringing them all to the ground. As Nozar thrashed beneath them, he continued screaming "Coward!" Soldiers poured into the courtyard and pulled them apart. Yousef and Sanjar did not resist as they were led into the palace, but it took six soldiers to subdue Nozar, his shouts fading as they dragged him away.

Timur clambered up the stairway to the second level. Breathless, ears ringing with Nozar's rage, heart close to bursting from his chest, toes bleeding from slamming into the stone steps below, he tripped on the final step and landed on his hands and knees, his wrist taking the full force of his fall. He cried out and rolled onto his back, eyes closed tightly against the pain radiating up his forearm. Groaning, he grabbed his elbow and rocked on the stone floor. His breath and heartbeat slowed. With calmness came a memory.

He and Yousef were ten when they became lost in the tunnels under Peshawar's eastern wall, dug during the Persian siege thirty years earlier, giving the city access to water and supplies that were crucial to victory. When the searchers found them, Yousef was comforting a crying, frightened Timur. Afterwards, standing before his father and General Rodmehr, his father said to him, 'All men experience fear, but a ruler must never show it.' As he left his father's chamber, Timur overheard Rodmehr remark, 'Words aren't enough, my lord. If he were mine—' Timur's father cut him off, 'He is not yours, General.' But a few months later a Persian assassin killed him, and General Rodmehr became Timur's guardian and regent, assuming control of the empire until Timur came of age at sixteen.

Timur stopped rocking. Stillness enveloped him, the silence shouting his weakness, now as visible as his naked flight. Last year's army cadet training proved he matched most in strength, and surrounded by the other cadets and filled with the excitement of simulated combat his courage was never questioned. And yet he fled Nozar's wrath rather than face him, panic inexplicably consuming all else.

The scrape of a poorly healed foot against the stone floor announced General Rodmehr's approach. Timur remained supine, eyes closed tightly against the world around him.

"Get up."

Once standing Timur looked at the floor then toward the arched openings overlooking the courtyard, anywhere but Rodmehr's face.

"Look at me."

Timur jerked, his eyes locked on Rodmehr's. Slightly shorter than Timur, the general did not blink. Sweat stung Timur's eyes and ran down his bare chest, back and legs. He could see down the corridor. Soldiers stood at the far end, backs to him, spears at their sides. *Only if you survive this day.*

Rodmehr thrust a folded tunic at him. "Cover yourself."

The general moved to an arched opening and looked toward the distant Khyber Pass, its outline visible through the hot afternoon haze. A lone eagle soared in the distance.

"You hate me, do you not?" Rodmehr asked.

"I dare not—"

Rodmehr swung about. "He dares not. An emperor in but a few days and what? He dares not? By the gods, if you're made of sterner stuff than that, you'd better begin showing it or you will never be emperor."

"The throne is mine by birth. No one can deny me."

"Don't be a fool. What happened just now will make your enemies bold. Fear is what they must feel in your presence, but now"—Rodmehr grabbed Timur's chin and forced Timur to look him in the eyes—"all they will see is your cowardice."

"But surely we can tell them—"

"What? Just a game you boys were playing? That you didn't really run away in fear? Oh, yes, we could do that, and everyone will dutifully nod in agreement, especially those who oppose you. But that boy's cries of 'Coward' are already echoing throughout Peshawar, casting doubts on any story we tell, doubts that will only fester and grow. You must act quickly—in your own name—to dispel any hint of weakness." Rodmehr gave Timur no time to respond. "Come with me."

The general walked down the corridor and into an anteroom. A massive tapestry hung from the far wall, depicting the decisive victory of Timur's ancestor Kanishka the Great. Rodmehr sat at one end of a large divan covered in blue silk embroidered with griffins, symbols of Kushan royal might. The prince hesitated at the anteroom entrance, silhouetted against the brightness of the corridor behind him.

"You are right to pause. Consider what you do next to be your first decision as ruler of the Kushan Empire. You may decide to walk away, but I will take that as a sign that you no longer require my services and will resign as regent. The head of the council will be delighted to take my place, as he often disagrees with my decisions. He is no friend of yours, but if you survive to take—and keep—the crown, you can remove him, or anyone for that matter, from the court."

If I survive? The old man goes too far. Timur spun around, ready to bolt.

"Please, my prince, a moment more. You know this tapestry?"

Timur turned and once again faced the general. "Of course, I do."

"Then you remember that your ancestor took the throne by overthrowing the rightful emperor in a civil war that almost destroyed the empire. Fortunately, the Bactrians and Persians were too busy trying to destroy each other to take advantage of our disintegration. But today we would not be so fortunate. The Bactrian king has built a strong army that he'd love to test against one of his neighbors, while the Persians are too occupied with their own internal squabbles to effectively counter a Bactrian invasion if we were to fall into civil war."

"Civil war? What are you talking about?"

"Your father's brothers are dead. You are his only son, the only one who can keep your dynasty alive. Without you in command the country will turn on itself, with lesser men fighting to take the throne."

"All this because I refused to fight Nozar over a stupid horse?"

"No, all this because you shrink from being who you must be to lead your people. If you want to save your throne, enter this room. If not, leave. If you enter, you agree to do exactly what I tell you—exactly how I tell you. These are my terms. I guarantee nothing—except that if you do nothing, you won't survive to see the civil war that will be your legacy."

Timur hesitated. For the past six years he had watched General Rodmehr manipulate the Kushan court, bending it to his will, loving the power that being regent gave him. Surely he had no intention of resigning. *If Yousef were here, he'd see through the old man's tricks just like he always does.*

Rodmehr often counseled him to listen first then act, so he would play the general's game for the moment. He stepped into the dim anteroom.

"You choose wisely. For your father's sake, it would have pained me to desert you at such a critical time."

"Enough!"

"Ah, some backbone at last. I expect if I ask you again whether you hate me, your reply will be different."

"Taunt me again and I leave."

"Leave? I think not."

"Don't tell me—"

"Leave and you will be destroyed. Do as I instruct, or I will be forced to stand aside and watch your enemies take you down."

"And dishonor your promise to my father?" Timur asked.

"All will agree that I did the best I could by your father as your regent. Yes, he sired a comely son, robust, athletic and strong, fit in appearance to be a great warrior and ruler. But am I to blame that this son is weak-willed? That a mere ruffian can intimidate him?"

Timur lunged but before he could strike, the general was off the divan and seized his wrist. They stood locked together, the only sound Timur's rapid breathing. Rodmehr relaxed his grip. Timur stood down, yanking his wrist free of the general's grasp.

"Anger serves you well. Something you'd be wise to remember."

"You speak treason, old man."

"I speak the truth. You freely entered this room and by doing so agreed to do what I tell you. Is that not so?"

"I agreed to nothing."

"Ah, but my words were clear, were they not?"

"You said nothing about betraying me. You play at deception."

"No, I protect the empire. An attack on you is an attack on the realm and must be dealt with quickly, ruthlessly, and without mercy. This incident is even more monstrous in its brazen attempt to cast you as anything but the strong, forceful leader that you must be. This you will demonstrate by ordering the executions of the three who attacked you."

"Three?" It was as if the ground were opening beneath his feet, threatening to swallow him. "But Yousef and Sanjar—they tried to stop Nozar."

"And they failed, making them complicit. If any guard failed you as they did, he would face the same punishment."

"No! Yousef is my best friend!"

"Unfortunate, but executing him will instill fear in those who oppose you, that even a close friend cannot escape your judgment."

"Yousef's father fought beside you in battle. He died fighting the assassin who killed my father. Surely his son deserves better than a traitor's death."

"Your affection for him clouds your judgment, my prince. I warned you about attachments. All favorites eventually betray their lord in their lust for power and wealth. Yousef would be no different."

"No, it is *you* who betray your prince. I will not allow you to do this."

"I am afraid you cannot stop it. Even without you the executions will be carried out—in your name, of course. With you present, however, all doubters will be convinced that you are a ruler to be feared and obeyed, maybe even respected."

Timur took a step forward. "I will kill you where you stand."

"Yes, that you might do—and thus free your friends. But you won't last long afterwards, and your friends will fall with you." The general's gaze softened. "I do not believe that is how you want to be remembered, my prince."

Timur stood alone in the anteroom, his face lifted to the ceiling, fighting the anguish threatening to overwhelm him. Yousef and Sanjar would die, and it was because of him. Tears stung his eyes as he stared at the tapestry. He rushed at it, slamming his fist into the image of his conquering ancestor.

"Not Yousef," he whispered. "Please not Yousef."

He remembered being huddled on the floor of his bedchamber with Yousef the day of his father's assassination six years earlier. Yousef's father too had died, attempting to subdue the attacker. Alternately crying and comforting each other, the boys had forged a bond, and in the aftermath it was only natural that they became inseparable in their common grief. Looking back, he could see how Rodmehr increasingly viewed Yousef's growing influence as a threat to his position and made efforts to weaken their closeness with enforced separations, repeated warnings that eventually all favorites betray their ruler, and even threats to banish Yousef and his family from court. Finally, having failed to undermine their friendship, Timur now realized that Rodmehr had orchestrated its ultimate ending: at his best friend's command, Yousef would die a traitor's death.

A traitor's death. The injustice filled his chest with helpless rage. He recalled the strange woman's question.

Are they Yousef and Sanjar?

That she knew who waited below her window could mean but one thing. She had looked to the stars to determine their fates as well as his.

Today's sun rose upon a prince. It will set upon an emperor bathed in blood.

Calm gradually settled over Timur. Could it be their deaths this day were preordained from the moment of their births? If so, it was not a traitor's death that awaited them. Rather they would die martyrs, their blood sacrificed to preserve a dynasty and make him emperor. Surely continued anguish over their deaths would dishonor the nobility of their fates.

He looked again at the tapestry's triumphant image of Kanishka the Great. *An attack on you is an attack on the realm and must be dealt with quickly, ruthlessly, and without mercy.* Rodmehr's counsel could have come from his ancestor's own mouth. The good of his empire was paramount. Nothing else mattered.

But one last obstacle remained. *Villainy surrounds you,* the strange woman had said.

He took a deep breath and stepped from the alcove.

Only if you survive this day.

Clad in his army officer's dress uniform Timur stood unnoticed in the open doorway of the dungeon's execution chamber. Rodmehr laughed at a comment by one of the four witnesses. Timur recognized each of them, all grown rich and powerful in their service to the general. Shackled to the opposite wall Sanjar softly cried, his head bowed, Yousef stood erect, his eyes closed, his mouth moving, and Nozar hung motionless, beaten and unconscious.

Rodmehr spoke. "It seems the prince is detained, but given we carry out the sentences in his name, there is no reason to delay this unfortunate business." As he motioned to the guards and executioner to proceed, a witness nudged him and pointed at the doorway. If the general was surprised, he did not show it as he stepped before Timur. "It's well you chose to attend, my prince."

"There is no other way?"

With a slight bow of his head Rodmehr answered, "I regret there is none." Then leading Timur toward an empty chair, he said, "If you wish, I can read the charges and sentences for you."

Without responding, Timur moved to the center of the chamber and stretched out his arm. The executioner handed him the axe to the murmured surprise of the witnesses.

Sanjar was first, crying out in terror as the guards laid his neck across the bloodstained block. Without a word, without hesitation, Timur silenced the boy with one fall of the blade.

Once unshackled Yousef shook away the guard's hold and stepped forward. "No mercy, even for me?" Timur shook his head.

Yousef knelt. Eyes focused on Rodmehr he said, "I die loyal and innocent." He placed his neck upon the block.

Timur raised the axe. It wavered before growing still. Then he brought it down. When a second strike was required, he raised the axe again, this time not faltering.

As the guards began to release Nozar's limp body, Timur motioned them to stop.

"Why do you wait?" Rodmehr called out.

"He will know that I do this." To the guards he said, "Revive him."

"Finish this!" Rodmehr shouted.

The confused guards looked first to Rodmehr then at Timur. Finally, the executioner grabbed a bucket and doused Nozar's head with water. As Nozar stirred, choking for air and moaning in pain, the executioner grabbed his hair and pulled his head back. His face was bloodied and swollen, one eye mutilated. Timur stepped before him, and Nozar's good eye opened into a narrow slit.

"Do you know who I am?"

"My prince—"

Expecting a plea for mercy Timur leaned in, his ear close to Nozar's bruised and bloated lips.

"The regent—forced me to—"

Timur spun about as Rodmehr rushed toward him, his sword above his shoulder, its grip in both hands. Timur moved to parry his blow with the axe. The witnesses rushed for the door but did not flee the chamber, spellbound by the struggle. Surprised and uncertain, the guards and executioner stepped back to give the combatants room to maneuver. The general's experience kept Timur on the defensive as they exchanged blows, the sound of their clashing steel echoing in the confined space of the prison chamber. Timur's heel struck a raised stone in the floor, but he managed to keep upright and deflect Rodmehr's next blow with an upward swing that drove Rodmehr backward. The general's boot struck the same stone, and he fell hard, landing on his side, his sword below him. As he struggled to get up, Timur leapt above him, brought the point of the executioner's axe to Rodmehr's throat, and asked in a seething whisper, "Did you not say that an attack on me is an attack on the realm?"

For the first time in his life Timur watched fear fill another man's eyes. He raised the axe above his head.

"Villain!"

PART 1

I NAME HIM CALAF ... I NAME HIM ISHMAEL

231 - 235 CE

CHAPTER 1
231 CE

Minnagara

Shaken awake from a deep sleep to a soldier urgently shouting that the emperor needed him, Demetrius grabbed his physician's bag and rushed after him. But instead of Timur's command tent, the soldier led him into the thick mangrove forest that surrounded the army's encampment. Torchlight drew them to an opening in the trees. Pushing through the soldiers at the grove's edge, Demetrius dropped to a crouch beside a muscular middle-aged man lying upon a wood pallet. One knee was shattered, the leg twisted to an impossible angle, his torso swollen and bruised, blood clotting from lacerations from belly to groin, a shoulder dislocated. Surprisingly his face was untouched, except by agony beyond comprehension, mouth wide open as if in a scream, the only sound ragged gasping.

Timur moved out of the shadows. "Revive him."

Demetrius fought to keep his voice steady. "Such injuries, my lord—surely he would've talked by now."

"Do you defy me, physician?"

"No, my lord."

"Then revive him."

"Yes, my lord." He removed a ceramic vial from his bag.

"No poppy."

"But easing his pain will—" The prisoner began convulsing and coughing up blood. Demetrius shoved him onto his side. The man's choking eased. He inhaled several times in rapid succession then exhaled in a long, slow groan. Demetrius felt his neck for a pulse. "He's dead, my lord."

Timur thundered, "Get him out of here!"

As the soldiers dragged the body away, Demetrius climbed to his feet, struggling to control his trembling. "By your leave, my lord."

"Stay." Then he shouted, "Bring the son!" He grasped Demetrius's shoulder. "Keep this one alive, physician."

The son lived long enough to betray weaknesses in the Minnagara raja's defense of his city. After the bodies of father and son had been dumped in the swiftly flowing Indus, Demetrius remained beside the river retching in rage at Timur and disgust with himself.

Eight years Demetrius had served as Timur's royal physician. Too many times he had witnessed torture administered by Timur's own hand, helping extend a victim's life and therefore his suffering. Demetrius recognized that Timur tested his loyalty by deliberately implicating him—a physician, a healer—in life-destroying atrocities, violating his Hippocratic oath by choosing self-preservation over opposition, however futile, to such savagery.

Demetrius gazed across the dark river's expanse, allowing memories to provide whatever solace they might give.

A prison cell in Baktra, when it all began.

Demetrius sat against the rough-hewn wall of a crowded, dimly lit cell. A small opening near the ceiling provided the only light and ventilation. Surrounded by what remained of the Bactrian king's closest advisors, the former royal physician noticed that, amid cries for mercy and sobs of fear, only he and the fire temple's ousted high priest remained silent. The priest's turban had been taken from him, forcing him to remove his outer cloak so that he could cover his head as he prayed in preparation for his arrival at the Zoroastrian Bridge of Judgment. Recalling the words of the Greek philosopher Epicurus, Demetrius quieted his anxiety with the knowledge that death need not be feared, that it brought an end not only to the body but also to the soul, and that no divine judgment awaited him.

The cell's massive wooden door opened, its hinges creaking as it scraped against the stone floor, the guard kicking a man curled up on the floor in its way. With a grunt of surprise the man crawled aside. Six men had already been taken from the cell. Tortured screams from each passed through the thick cell walls only to end abruptly, setting off panicked babble from those left behind.

"Physician!" yelled the guard. Relief swept through the cell. Demetrius pushed himself up from the floor. As he stepped around the men at his feet, the priest reached out and touched Demetrius's arm and their eyes met. The guard grabbed Demetrius's shoulder, shoved him from the cell, and handed him off to two Kushan soldiers. One took him by the elbow. "This way, physician." The prison guard yelled, "You there. Next." The next victim's cries for mercy faded as Demetrius followed the soldiers up a dark and narrow circular stairway.

When they emerged into the main courtyard of the Bactrian palace, the midday sun blinded Demetrius. He tried to lift his hands in front of his eyes, but the soldiers restrained him. "Be still. General Nozar comes."

Demetrius squinted up at the general's massive height and bulk. He regarded the scarred face and missing eye, glad for a physician's calm detachment where others might struggle to hide revulsion.

"By the gods, physician, you're a skinny one. Didn't that king of yours feed you?" Nozar asked.

"It was a long siege, my lord."

Nozar gave a good-natured laugh. "You're a cautious one, physician, but the emperor soon tires of cautious men."

"The emperor, my lord?" Sudden anxiety filled him, for he had heard tales of Emperor Timur's cruelty.

Nozar nodded. "Better get your wits about you. You're going to need them." He glanced down at Demetrius's bare legs and feet. "That's not your shit, is it?"

"No, my lord, but shit's hard to avoid in a cell full of frightened men."

The general laughed. "Clever, too. What's your name?"

"Demetrius, my lord."

"Macedonian?"

"Athenian."

"The emperor's never had one of you. Not sure what he's going to make of a cautious, clever Athenian." Then turning to the two soldiers, "Clean him up—something to eat, too." He departed, disappearing into the palace.

The soldiers rode Demetrius outside the city to the Kushan camp and led him to the camp's cooking area. Demetrius's stomach cramped at the aroma of roasting meat. He could not remember when he last ate.

"What's that stench?" A man rose from tending a fire below spits of butchered antelopes. Several passing soldiers stopped to stare as the cook pointed at Demetrius and bellowed, "Get him out of here. This is a kitchen, not a pigsty."

"General's orders," the older guard said. "Got to clean him up for the emperor. You have the only hot water."

"Well, no closer," the cook barked. "Water's over there."

"Go get it," the older guard ordered his comrade. Then turning to Demetrius, "Strip."

Demetrius looked about. Soldiers began gathering around them. His survival depended on remaining submissive, but even so he hesitated out of reflex. Traumatic enough in the gymnasium of his youth and avoided once he attained manhood, publicly baring his nakedness often revealed more about his carnal interests than he usually wished known.

"Bashful, are we, Greek?" the guard said with a smirk.

Knowing he had no choice but to get the ordeal over as quickly as possible, he decided an unwelcome erection was the least of his worries at the moment and dropped his soiled clothes.

Jeers and whistles spread through the crowd of soldiers. Demetrius reacted by covering his genitals with his hands.

"Look, she protects her virtue," one mocked.

"No, there's a cock."

"What cock, I saw no cock."

Demetrius dropped his hands in defeat, lifted his shoulders in an exaggerated shrug, and gave a crooked smile.

"You call that a cock, Greek?"

One soldier stepped into the circle and groped his ample crotch through his trousers. "But I hear Greeks don't need cocks except to ride." More laughter and jeers filled the air.

Someone yelled, "You'll kill him with that thing, Torak!"

"But the Greek will die happy," roared another.

"Water coming through," shouted the younger guard as he pushed his way between the soldiers carrying a bucket of hot water.

"Enough!" yelled the older guard. "Unless one of you brutes wants to help him bathe." Even louder laughter followed with much pushing and shoving as the soldiers dispersed.

Demetrius squatted beside the bucket, making quick work of washing himself, the crotch grabber they called Torak awakening an intense desire to survive. *Yes, the Greek would die happy.*

The older guard's voice broke through Demetrius's reverie. "Hey, cook, something to eat for the Greek. Quickly. Also, that boy of yours—he's the Greek's size. Give us one of his tunics."

Bathed, clothed and fed, Demetrius followed his guards to the emperor's tent, which stood at the highest point of the ridge overlooking Baktra from the east. Red and white silk banners, decorated with Kushan royal griffins, hung motionless in the still summer heat. As they approached Demetrius heard a man's cry of prolonged agony. To one side of the tent, tied spread-eagle to the ground, a naked man writhed, exposed to the midday sun. He groaned once again, then became still. The man's torso, legs, and head had been whipped—part of his skull visible where a patch of hair had pulled away—his open wounds exposed. From the burns around his eyes, Demetrius recognized blinding by hot oil.

Time passed slowly, punctuated by buzzing insects and the dying man's diminishing groans. Demetrius almost dozed on his feet when the older guard nudged his shoulder then led him into the royal tent. Dim coolness replaced blinding bright heat, sending a chill through his body. Feeling something soft under his feet, he looked down at a crimson carpet decorated with griffins in each corner.

"On your knees," ordered the older guard, his hand pushing him down.

But even as his knees touched the carpet, another voice boomed, unnecessarily loud for the confined space. "Wait outside."

"Sir!" A momentary shaft of light broke the tent's darkness as the guards stepped out, and Demetrius saw that multiple carpets covered the floor of the tent, casually spread, several layers deep. The rich fragrance of olive oil filled his nostrils. The noise of the camp outside became a soft rumble.

"What did your dead king say about me, physician?"

"A worthy adversary and ruthless in battle and conquest, my lord."

"Ruthless to the point of being feared?" An edge of menace entered his voice. "Is not a ruler to be feared, physician, feared above all else?"

"Yes, my lord, feared above all else."

"You will remember this?"

"Yes, my lord, I will remember."

"Good, because I have need of a physician. Stand and show yourself."

As Demetrius rose he saw only the emperor and his squire before him. Tall, thick, and muscular Timur's naked body gleamed in the dimness, slick with olive oil. His squire, a stocky, dark-skinned young boy wearing a deep blue tunic, knelt and scraped the oil from the emperor's thighs and calves using an ornately carved ivory strigil. A thick scar started below Timur's right shoulder and dimmed near his mid-abdomen. Without thinking, Demetrius allowed his eyes to follow the scar into Timur's groin. At that same moment Timur groped his genitals. Demetrius forced his eyes away, feeling the panic of one who had learned—and just forgotten—to exercise caution in the company of men.

"A ruler's virility is important to his people, is it not, physician?"

"So it is said, my lord."

"Then you need not avert your eyes."

"No, my lord." Demetrius returned his gaze to Timur's groin, attempting to quiet himself for whatever trap awaited him.

"But then you are Greek." Taking his hand from his genitals Timur placed it on his squire's head.

"Not all Greek men prefer boys, my lord."

"Carefully said, physician." With a hint of a smile, Timur paused a moment before adding, "But all Greeks are cunning, are they not?"

"It is true, my lord, that some Greeks are devious. But many are open, frank, and trustworthy."

Again, Timur paused, searching Demetrius's face. "You demonstrate a quick wit, physician. Some say a quick wit is the sword of guile, not sincerity."

"If it please my lord, it may also be the weapon of an educated man who only means to serve one more learned than he."

A sudden scowl crossed Timur's face. Panic invaded Demetrius's gut. Timur had, in fact, trapped him, not into revealing his sexual interest but rather his cleverness. He took a deep breath to steady himself.

Timur turned away as his squire finished scraping most of the remaining oil from his body. While the boy gathered up Timur's clothing, Timur wiped himself down with a towel, finally giving it to the boy so he could clean the excess oil off his back. As the squire helped Timur tie his loincloth and pull on his tunic, Timur continued to talk softly with him, and the boy occasionally responded with a shy smile. Timur sat and the squire began to comb and braid his long jet-black hair.

Why did Timur allow him to witness such domestic intimacy? Perhaps it did not matter because soon he would be dead.

"Go now, Aric, fetch me something to eat, and tell the guards to return." Head down, the squire limped past Demetrius on a shrunken left leg. Demetrius marveled that the boy had survived past childhood with such paralysis. The emperor cleared his throat and jerked Demetrius's attention back.

"You wish to live." A mocking edge entered Timur's voice.

"Yes, my lord."

The guards entered and took positions on each side of Demetrius. Timur stared at Demetrius long and hard, then turned and paced, his fists at his side. Timur stopped a footstep away, his rigid face darkening.

"Physicians are whores!"

Demetrius jerked at the sudden attack but regained himself, fighting to remain composed, fighting to keep his eyes focused calmly on the blazing black eyes before him. Showing any reaction would bring a quick end.

Timur's voice turned low and menacing. "They sell potions, incantations, and promises—promises they do not keep." He leaned closer into Demetrius's face. "A physician could not save my son. My son! My heir! Nor my queen, who died trying to give my son life."

His voice was filled with grief and rage—but grief most of all. Demetrius's mind scrambled for a response. "A tragedy, my lord." Timur's eyes continued blazing. Still Demetrius fought to remain calm, softly repeating once, "A tragedy."

"And now that physician rots outside my tent." Timur spat onto the carpet at Demetrius's feet. He began to pace again, several times pausing to look into Demetrius's face. Finally he stopped.

"The son of my infantry commander was badly injured in the last assault. The guards will take you to him. If he survives, you will live and serve us. If not, you will wish you were the man you replace."

The son of Timur's infantry commander lived.

At first Demetrius spent most of his time tending to the sick and wounded in the Kushan army, only occasionally attending to the emperor himself. That changed the day that the emperor's squire Aric fell ill. Plague had struck the army and over the course of three months two-thirds fell ill and half of those died. Demetrius also fell ill but not severely and continued caring for the sick and dying. Finally, a week passed without a new case, and Demetrius felt confident the disease had run its course. But then he received word to report to Timur's tent. On his arrival, he found Aric feverish with swelling around his groin and under his armpits, the plague's first symptoms.

Timur pulled Demetrius away from the others. His only words were "Save the boy," more of a plea than a command.

"I will do what I can, my lord," Demetrius replied, hoping the emperor would not strike him down on the spot for offering so little reassurance.

He set about applying his usual palliatives, knowing from experience that regardless of his actions, the plague would either take the boy or not.

By the next day, Aric turned delirious, sweating profusely. Demetrius feared for the youth's life—and his own. Timur visited the tent incessantly. Demetrius grew hopeful when the crushed marigold flowers began to reduce Aric's fever. Then on the third day, the squire's fever broke, and his recovery followed. Timur's faint smile of satisfaction and fainter glance of gratitude were Demetrius's only rewards beyond the breath he continued to take. Afterwards, when the lame squire was not assisting the emperor, the ten-year-old Aric attached himself to Demetrius.

One afternoon as Aric helped Demetrius gather medicinal herbs outside the camp, Aric asked, "Do you know about my brother?"

"I'm told he was the martyr Yousef."

Aric nodded vigorously, his smile broad and his eyes alight. "He was a hero. He fought the evil Rodmehr and died to save the emperor."

"Do you remember him?"

Aric shook his head. "I was only two. I want to be a hero just like him, but—" He kicked the dirt with his stunted leg.

"There are many kinds of heroes, Aric. If the Fates put you on a hero's path, I know you will be worthy."

"Do you really believe that?"

"Yes, I do." Demetrius ruffled Aric's hair as an ache of sadness filled his chest. Demetrius had heard various stories about Yousef's death, most of which ended with Timur killing him, and was surprised that Aric was unaware of them. He did not doubt that Timur's inner circle understood that death—or worse—awaited anyone who told him the truth. Still, it could only be a matter of time before Aric would find out one way or another.

On their way back to the camp, they stopped to watch a group of soldiers training with wood swords, battle-hardened veterans matched with new recruits. Demetrius maneuvered to a spot where he could watch one particular soldier.

You'll kill him with that thing, Torak!

But the Greek will die happy.

Aric tugged on Demetrius's tunic. "You stare at him a lot," he yelled over the grunting and shouting of the combatants.

"What?"

Aric pointed. "The big one over there."

Demetrius's face flushed. Aric giggled as Demetrius pulled him in the direction of the camp. When they reached his tent, Demetrius said, "Don't do that again."

"Why? You like him, don't you?"

Demetrius ignored the question. "Why this sudden interest?"

"They say you like men."

"Who?"

"The emperor, General Nozar, everyone."

Demetrius stiffened. "Go." It was barely a whisper. When Aric gave him a confused look, he raised his voice. "Leave me." As Aric rushed from the tent, Demetrius immediately regretted the harshness of his tone, but his usual calm reserve had been shaken.

Born the eldest son in his Athenian aristocratic family and confronted with his father's expectations, he had rebelled. By age seventeen, having been arrested numerous times for public indecency in the alleys surrounding the city's army barracks, he had a final confrontation with his father, who demanded that he fulfill his family obligations by marrying, starting a family, and renouncing his unseemly conduct with men. Demetrius refused, upon which his father disowned him and placed him on the next ship leaving Athens with the demand that he not disgrace his family further by ever returning. Even as Demetrius spat his defiance on the ground between them, he was terrified at what lay ahead and spent the crossing of the Aegean retching at the ship's stern. He disembarked at Ephesus and within a day fell among thieves, who beat him and took the few coins he carried.

An elderly physician named Spyros found him semi-conscious in an alley and took him to his home where he nursed his injuries. Demetrius did not leave that house until Spyros died ten years later, emerging as a physician in his own right. He also emerged a confirmed *kinaidos*, Greek for a man who takes the woman's role in sex. The *kinaidoi* were a target of derision among the larger population, but Demetrius's quiet discretion in addition to his skill as a physician granted him relative acceptance—and willing partners—during his time with the Roman and Persian armies, and then in the Bactrian royal court.

They say you like men. Aric's words echoed in his mind. This Kushan curiosity about the new Greek in their midst did not surprise Demetrius. The resurgence of interest in all things Hellenic that had swept across Rome and Persia during the last hundred years had also reached across the Khyber. Caravans from the west, carrying replicas of Greek statues and copies of philosophical works, sold all that they unloaded. Traveling troupes from Greece performed the plays of Sophocles, Aeschylus, and Euripides to large and appreciative audiences.

"Demetrius?"

Aric's soft voice interrupted his thoughts. The boy stood looking through the parted tent flap. A mischievous grin filled his face as he quickly said, "His name is Torak."

Before Demetrius could respond, Aric disappeared behind the closed flap. A moment later the flap parted and Torak slipped into the tent. While the dust of the training area covered his tunic, arms and legs, he had washed his bearded face and his long hair hung wet to his shoulders. He cocked his head to one side and smiled.

"The boy says you are lonely."

Demetrius came awake at the cries of herons skimming the river's surface, his mind hurled back to the screams of the previous night's torture. He breathed deeply, taking longer than usual to grow calm. He then stretched his arms above his head, wondering how long he had dozed. Too long, his back told him as he shifted his position against the mangrove's exposed roots. He squinted into the first light of dawn at the wide expanse of the Indus delta. Hearing movement, he turned as Aric emerged from the trees.

Now eighteen years old and the emperor's scribe, Aric had remained short and rotund in appearance. To escape Timur's ridicule, he had learned to downplay his limp except when he was agitated or anxious. He dropped beside Demetrius on the riverbank.

"I heard about last night." When he remained silent, Aric said, "The emperor's looking for you."

"Do you know why?"

"Logistics of the march on Minnagara."

Demetrius sighed. Over time he had become one of Timur's closest advisors, even for affairs outside his expertise as a physician. Timur trusted few men, but he had become one of them.

"How much time do I have?"

"Until after we dedicate the campaign to the Martyrs at sunrise. I must go prepare."

Demetrius patted Aric's knee. Aric shrugged and climbed to his feet. Looking down he asked, "How do you do it, Demetrius?"

"The same way you do, one day at a time."

After Aric departed, Demetrius continued to sit a moment. His heart always grew heavy for the youth when the emperor called for the Martyrs ritual. Timur had ordered him to participate when Aric was thirteen years old, soon after he learned the truth about his brother's death.

It was winter and the emperor had taken up residence at his palace in Peshawar. Demetrius approached Timur's work chamber just as the door flew open to Aric's cry, "Murderer!"

Aric almost knocked Demetrius over as he hobbled past, his eyes unseeing and his face a mixture of anguish and pain, and disappeared down the corridor. Demetrius's first instinct was to follow the boy, but the roar of the emperor's rage pulled him back toward the chamber.

Parchments and wine cups had been swept from the work table that dominated the room. The emperor's scribe and attendants crouched against the wall, their eyes fastened on the floor. General Nozar stood before Timur.

"Who told him?" shouted the emperor.

"I do not know, my lord." He answered in a calm, steady voice.

"Find out!"

"Yes, my lord."

"Immediate execution—no mercy."

"Understood, my lord."

Timur spotted Demetrius standing in the doorway. "Deal with the boy." After Demetrius bowed in response, Timur shouted, "Out—all of you—out!"

Moments later Demetrius and Nozar stood alone outside the closed chamber door.

Nozar asked, "Do you know the truth about Yousef and Sanjar?"

"I've heard different stories."

"Then walk with me. He won't listen if it comes from me, but it's important that Aric know the truth of what happened."

After Nozar finished, Demetrius asked, "Why didn't Timur tell him years ago? Surely it would have been easier when Aric was younger."

Nozar shrugged. "I once urged him to, but he refused with such anger that I never approached him again. Now, go find the boy. The emperor will have little patience with further theatrics from him, even if he is Yousef's brother."

Demetrius found Aric at the fire temple adjacent to the palace's main gate. Upon ascending the throne Timur had elevated Yousef and Sanjar to martyrdom and had the temple built over their tombs. Surrounded by a courtyard with stone walls that formed a pentagon, the temple was a small foursquare stone building topped by a shallow dome. Oriented to the four cardinal directions, steps led to tall arched openings in the massive walls that gave access to the central stone altar. The interior darkness bore witness to decades of soot from the eternal fire that blackened the ceiling and upper walls. While the interior's coarse stone was left exposed, three of the outside walls were faced with a smooth plaster wainscot decorated with bas-reliefs of griffins, symbols of the Kushan royal house. Adorning the fourth wall facing the palace were mosaic portraits of Yousef and Sanjar composed of semiprecious stones and colored tiles. Standing, the martyrs faced each other across the arched opening, shields emblazoned with the Kushan griffin at their sides. Demetrius joined Aric kneeling before the mosaic of Yousef, but Aric did not look at him.

"He executed my brother as a traitor." Aric's voice was devoid of emotion, the words softly spoken.

"You've not heard the full truth, Aric."

"He beheaded him. My brother and his best friend. That's correct, isn't it?"

"Yes, but—"

"What more do I need to know?"

"How General Rodmehr is responsible for your brother's death."

As Demetrius told the story that Nozar had told him, Aric did not take his eyes from the mosaic.

"Do you believe it?" Aric asked.

"Nozar was there. Why shouldn't I?"

Finally turning to face Demetrius, Aric replied, "Because my brother was innocent and died, and Nozar wasn't and lived."

"Yes, it is not just, but life is rarely just."

Aric returned his gaze to the mosaic. "I will avenge my brother." His words were spoken without a flicker of emotion behind them.

"Shh. You speak dangerous nonsense. Yousef was no traitor and neither are you. What happened was a tragedy. To this day I believe the emperor torments himself over what he did. You must not allow what happened to your brother to ruin your life, too."

Aric responded by closing his eyes, his lips moving in silent prayer. With a heavy heart Demetrius remained kneeling beside him, offering whatever solace his presence might provide the devastated youth. Finally, Aric rose and without a word returned to the palace.

The next day Aric returned to his duties as apprentice to the emperor's scribe. Neither Timur nor Aric said anything about the previous day's outburst. It was as if it had never happened. Aric refused to reveal to Nozar how he learned about his brother's death, but Timur uncharacteristically dropped the issue. Over the days and weeks that followed Demetrius watched in vain for a return of Aric's innocent good humor and with sadness realized that Aric the boy was gone forever.

When Demetrius returned to the army encampment, the troops were already moving into formation facing the Martyrs altar, which was set up on a rise above the river. He moved through the soldiers to his position beside Nozar just as the Zoroastrian priest lit the fire atop the altar. Then Aric rose and faced the emperor, his voice lifted loud and clear.

Yousef and Sanjar,
Raised to Ahura Mazda as martyrs
To the glory of Lord Timur.
May their courage and deaths
Be celebrated forever in the hearts of all men.

As a stiff-backed, expressionless Aric returned to his place, Demetrius's mind filled with foreboding, as it always did afterward.

CHAPTER 2

WIDE MARBLE STEPS DESCENDED FROM the Buddhist temple and disappeared into the wide Indus, flowing swiftly in late spring. The melting snow of the distant mountains brought the river near flood stage, leaving only the top few steps above the waterline. Downriver the nearby walled city of Minnagara dominated the horizon. Upriver an elderly monk sat on the shore supervising a group of novices in the water. Their orange robes scattered on the bank, their deep brown bodies, naked except for loincloths, the boys tended the temple's fishnets. An eleven-year-old girl, the only daughter of the Minnagaran ruler, sat on the temple steps, cooling her bare feet in the river. She watched the boys, while keeping a close eye on her baby brother, who played on a large rug spread across the steps above her. The boys began shouting and splashing each other. One boy slipped and disappeared under the water, only to reappear, coughing and sputtering, to the teasing of the other boys. As the girl laughed at their antics, the monk called out and the chastened boys returned to the nets.

"Sharina." The girl looked up. Her mother stood in the shade of the temple's roof with the head monk, a man ancient and bent but always showing a smile. Sharina rose from the water, slipped on her sandals, and lifted little Tanay, a month from his first birthday but small for his age and easily carried, except in his increasingly common headstrong moments. The warm late morning sun had made him drowsy, and he offered no resistance.

As Sharina stepped into the shadow of the temple, the head monk said, "Next time you come, a monk will watch your brother so you can join your mother in meditation."

Her mother answered for her. "A kind offer, is it not, Sharina?" Sharina looked into the monk's face, returned his smile and nodded, silently hoping he would forget his offer when next they visited.

Emerging from the front of the temple, they waited as the palace guards readied their covered litter. Loud pounding of horse's hooves filled the air as a Minnagaran soldier appeared over the rise in the road, dust enveloping both rider and mount. As he sped by, his horse near collapse, its mouth frothing, he did not slow or even look their way.

Sharina's mother guided her into the litter. "It's best we return quickly."

As Sharina settled onto the cushioned seat, she held Tanay tightly in her lap, preparing for the jostling ride to come. She asked her mother what was happening.

"Don't worry." Her mother leaned over to give Sharina a hug. "I'm sure it's nothing."

But as the litter moved away from the temple, Sharina watched the head monk moving as quickly as his old legs would carry him toward the monk on the riverbank. He called out, but Sharina could not make out the words.

Later that evening Sharina's father burst unannounced into her mother's chamber, stopping just inside the doorway. Startled, Sharina looked up from the thick carpet where she played with Tanay. Her mother moved across the room to her father.

"The Kushans move against us. Timur breaks our treaty."

Her father's face was twisted in rage, his dark skin flushed, eyes cold and hard, teeth tightly clenched. Never had she seen him that way.

Sharina's sixteen-year-old brother Ashu rushed into the room. Instead of his linen tunic and leather belt, he wore the military uniform from the ceremony marking the completion of his officer's training and coming of age. "My lord, the scouts…"

"Not now." Her brother, surprised at the sharp rebuke, snapped to attention. Her father placed his hand on his son's shoulder. "Tell the council I'll be there shortly."

"Yes, Father."

As Ashu departed, Sharina's mother knelt before her, her calm a marked contrast to her husband's intense agitation. She stroked Sharina's cheek.

"Sharina, dear, please take your little brother into the courtyard to play." Sharina hesitated, uncertain, searching her mother's face for reassurance but finding none. "Please go now. I will come for you in a little while."

As Sharina gathered up little Tanay into her arms, she glanced over at her father. She watched him struggle unsuccessfully to smile down at her. She never saw him again.

"The Kushan siege will fail. Your father is strong and will prevail."

Each day Sharina's mother offered the same reassurance upon returning from the pre-dawn council meeting that, with her husband's permission, she witnessed from behind a screen.

During the month since the siege began Sharina and Tanay were confined to her mother's chamber. One of her father's most trusted men commanded the three-man guard outside the door. Sharina's mother spent most of her time in meditation, doing breathing exercises and reciting the complex Buddhist sutras she loved. When not attending to Tanay, Sharina joined in prayer, both to bring a smile to her mother's face and to ease her fears when the crash of arms reached her ears. Over the years her mother had attempted to share her love of Buddhism, but while Sharina found the breathing exercises practical in bringing calm when she felt upset about something, she could not find a way into deeper religious feeling. Her mother, however, was devout, and Sharina noticed her fervor growing more intense and all-consuming with each passing day.

One afternoon after Tanay settled down for a nap, Sharina's mother motioned her to come sit closer. "Not all Kushans are men of war. In fact, two hundred years ago a Kushan monk wrote a beautiful sutra. Let me teach it to you."

"But, Mother, you know—"

"I know, but it is short, easily learned. It will help you in the days to come." Realizing the moment called for obedience, Sharina nodded as her mother said, "It begins, *Form itself is emptiness, emptiness itself form.*"

Over and over Sharina repeated the Heart Sutra with her mother. *Form itself is emptiness, emptiness itself form. Sensations, perceptions, formations, and consciousness are also like this.* Remembering her mother's earlier teaching, she tried first to tie the rhythm of the words to her breath. *…no eye, ear, nose, tongue, body, or mind; no sights, sounds, smells, tastes, touch, or objects of mind…* But with each recitation, words and breath increasingly defied her efforts to link them. Sharina glanced over at her mother. Trance-like, her mouth now barely moved, the words barely spoken. *Without hindrance, there is no fear. Far beyond all inverted views, one realizes Nirvana.*

As her mother drifted off into deep meditation, Sharina stepped onto the balcony that faced the city's southwest wall. The smoke and dust of battle filled the late afternoon sky, turning the sun into a dark orange ball. *How can something so terrible be so beautiful?* At that moment a catapulted boulder struck the distant wall with a loud thump. Fragments shot into the sky and cries of pain rushed over the rooftops at her. Then from behind, her mother's voice gave counterpoint. *Form itself is emptiness, emptiness itself form.*

As Sharina lowered her head and looked down into the secluded courtyard far below, she found no comforting emptiness, only a dull ache of foreboding embedded deep in her stomach that suffused her mind with unbidden, terrible visions of things to come.

The next day Sharina returned to her mother's chamber from a brief walk in the palace courtyard, accompanied by the youngest of her father's ever-present guards. She flirted with him, and he exchanged a shy smile for hers. Buoyed by this stolen moment, Sharina stepped inside the door.

She found Ashu stretched out on the rug playing with little Tanay, her joy at seeing him tempered by his appearance. He attempted a smile, his handsome, boyish features hidden under layers of sweat and dirt, his eyes red and swollen. His once-pristine uniform, now torn and streaked with mud, lay on the floor just inside the doorway. She dropped to her knees and embraced him.

"It's been over a week, Ashu. I've missed you so much."

"General Narhari just ordered me off the wall. There's a lull in the Kushan assault. Said he needed me rested."

"Then shouldn't you be trying to sleep?" She rose, went to a nearby table, and poured water from a porcelain jug into the basin she used to bathe Tanay.

"I can't—not yet."

Sharina felt his voice break. As she again knelt beside her brothers, she recognized a wooden horse in Tanay's hands. Carved by their father, it was Ashu's favorite toy.

"Well, at least I can clean you up a bit." She pulled a dripping cloth from the basin, gave it a slight squeeze, and began to clean around Ashu's eyes and nose. "You're a mess."

"I look better than most. Water's rationed, so no more lounging around at the baths. Where's Mother?"

"At the temple."

"Father doesn't like it when she goes there. He wants her safe here with you." He winced as Sharina worked the cloth to his left temple.

"You're hurt."

"Nothing really. Damned Kushan catapult—piece of the wall nicked me."

"Looks like more than a nick to me." She got up to change the basin's dirty water.

Ashu leaned over to his baby brother and pointed at the still-raw wound. "What do you think, Tanay? Bet it makes a great scar." Tanay responded with a squeal, then struck Ashu on the cheek with the wooden horse.

Ashu laughed. "Sure glad he's on our side."

Sharina's laughter joined his, but she felt tears fill her eyes. Brushing them aside, she finished preparing a new basin of water.

When Sharina again knelt on the floor, she reached for the tie-string at the neck of Ashu's tunic. He let her untie it and helped her lower his tunic to his waist. She began to bathe his right shoulder and arm.

A long silence passed before Ashu spoke. "How much do you know about what's happening?"

"Very little. Mother tells me nothing."

"I suspected as much." Ashu became silent again. Through her hands she could feel his gathering tension. He continued, "You are strong, Sharina, stronger than anyone knows. That's why you must prepare yourself."

Sharina turned to the basin and rinsed the cloth. "You're scaring me, Ashu."

"I know—I'm sorry."

She touched his shoulder. "Turn so I can get your back." As he shifted around, Sharina asked, "Are you—scared?"

"Yes, I am," Ashu replied without hesitation. "But Father says only a fool boasts he's not scared in battle. He's taught me that being scared is part of courage. When the time comes, you too will find the courage you need. I don't have much time, and there is much you must hear and understand."

Beside them little Tanay had fallen asleep on his stomach, a pudgy arm outstretched, fingers wrapped around Ashu's wooden horse. Ashu took the wet cloth from Sharina's hands and placed it back into the basin. Then he took both of her hands into his and looked into her eyes. "Do you know why the Kushans have come?" Sharina shook her head. "You know we stand along the only part of the Indus that boats can navigate." Sharina nodded. "Anyone who wants to get to the sea and the trade routes to the rest of the world must go past us."

"And they must pay us," Sharina interrupted, remembering something she overheard her father say.

"That's right. For years the Kushans have paid Minnagara for access to the sea. But now they have a powerful army and refuse to pay us anymore. They want to take Minnagara away from us. They want control of the river. They also want to take our wheat and rice and cotton for themselves."

Sharina interrupted, "But Father will stop them, won't he? Mother says he will." The look she saw in his eyes shattered her hope.

Ashu continued, "I overheard Father and General Narhari talking. They expect the Kushans will break through the walls soon, maybe even tomorrow." Sharina bit her lower lip. "But the Kushan emperor has sent an envoy requesting a meeting with Father. There may be a truce."

"What does it mean?"

"I wish I knew, but I don't. What I do know is that the Kushan emperor cannot be trusted. There are stories, bad stories, about his other conquests." Ashu's eyes became dark. "You must be strong, my dear sister. You've seen Mother. She waits for—no, she longs for her Nirvana. If the time comes, only you can protect Tanay."

It took but a moment for the true meaning of her brother's words to hit her. "But can't we?" She stopped, tears filling her eyes as she fought to be as strong as Ashu wanted her to be.

"No, it is too late to escape. The Kushans moved quicker than Father expected. I will stand with Father, as I must—whatever our fate." He reached up and touched the tears on her cheeks. "There is more I must tell you." Tears now glistened in Ashu's eyes. "The Kushans are brutal warriors, known for terrible atrocities, even against women and children. If Timur sacks the city, you and Tanay must not fall into their hands." Ashu's words hung there for a long moment. "Do you understand what I'm saying?"

Sharina tilted her head slightly, only her eyes revealing the struggle to absorb the import of his words. Finally, she said, "I must die and take Tanay with me."

"If I am able, I will return and help you, but if I cannot, you must do it alone."

Silent tears began falling down Sharina's cheeks, and Ashu pulled her into his arms. She buried her face against his chest. Ashu whispered, "Being strong doesn't mean you can't cry."

Once Sharina calmed, she eased herself out of Ashu's arms and sat back. The siblings sat facing each other silently for several long moments. She reached up and took her brother's head in her hands and pillowed it into her lap. His terrible mission to tell her there was no hope completed, Ashu drifted into an exhausted sleep. Sharina sat quietly, protectively, a hand placed on his head. Tanay stirred on the floor beside them, and she lightly stroked his back until he once again calmed. Sharina closed her eyes but did not drift off. Fear, sadness and anger fought for control of her mind. Unbidden the Heart Sutra surfaced, countering her growing despair. *Form itself is emptiness, emptiness itself form. Sensations, perceptions, formations, and consciousness are also like this.* Over and over she whispered the words. Slowly they began to calm her mind, but they did nothing to ease the hot pain that throbbed in her chest with every beat of her heart. All too soon Tanay started to squirm and fuss.

Ashu awakened and lifted his head from Sharina's lap. "I must go." As they rose from the floor, Tanay held up the wooden horse. Sharina reached down, took it and offered it to Ashu. "No, you keep it safe for me."

After he pulled on his tunic, Sharina tied the neck strings and dressed him in his uniform piece by piece, just as their father had done a short few months earlier. She noticed a small gap in the chain mail below his ribs. She stuck her finger in the hole to tickle him. Ashu squirmed and gave her his toothy smile.

"I'll make sure no Kushan arrow finds it," he promised and kissed Sharina on the forehead.

As he shut the chamber door behind him, Tanay began to cry.

The next morning Sharina's mother returned from the council meeting visibly shaken. Sharina rushed into her outstretched arms.

"What's happened, Mother?"

"You must be calm, we all must be calm. We have a new ruler—"

"Timur?" Sharina interrupted.

"Yes, Timur."

"What about Father?" Sharina tried to keep panic from consuming her.

"He has surrendered himself in exchange for the emperor's promise that the city will not be sacked and his family spared."

"Ashu will be spared, too?"

"Yes."

Sharina froze at this news. "Where is he, Mother?"

"He's with your father. He will join us here this afternoon. Then we will be taken—"

"No!" Sharina cried out. "No, no, no."

"Don't be foolish, girl. I just saw the truce. Your father put his mark on it, and so did Timur. No harm will come to us or to Ashu. Now breathe, breathe deeply, just like I taught you."

"No, Mother, it's not true. Ashu came to me yesterday. The Kushans can't be trusted."

A distant rumble filled her ears then loud shouts, punctuated by sword striking sword, then terror-filled wailing. Rushing onto the balcony, she screamed. She rushed to her mother's side, hardly able to breathe through her terror. "They're sacking the city. What do we do?"

But without a word her mother dropped to her knees before the small altar beside her bed. From the alcove Tanay begin to cry. She remembered a storage room where Ashu used to hide as a boy. She knew she could find it again; she knew she must. Grabbing a linen bag, she collected what she could reach, hesitating only a moment before grabbing Ashu's wooden horse. She gathered up Tanay, and then knelt beside her mother.

"Come, Mother, I know a place to hide."

Her mother's eyes were glazed over, mouth moving silently. The panicked cries from the city grew louder, closer. Sharina embraced her unresponsive mother then stood. The chamber door flew open with a loud crash.

"Remember, the emperor wants the girl alive," yelled the first soldier as he rushed into the chamber.

Whatever happens, you and Tanay must not fall into their hands.

Before she could reach the balcony, thick arms closed about her face and neck. Tanay was ripped from her arms screaming. As she struggled against the soldier's hold, he lifted her up. She sunk her teeth into his arm.

"Bitch!"

She fell to the floor. Before she could scramble away the soldier's boot struck her head.

Before darkness enveloped her, she heard another voice shout "Not the girl, fool!" above Tanay's screams.

In a tent halfway between the Kushan line and the city wall Demetrius attended Timur at the meeting with the Minnagaran raja and his council. The Kushan siege had succeeded, and Minnagara would fall the next day. The raja and his council had little choice: surrender or the city would be sacked. Prepared to accept whatever fate the emperor decided, the raja pleaded that his city and its inhabitants be spared. Timur agreed. Encouraged, the raja requested that his family—a wife, two sons and a daughter—be allowed to go into exile. Once again Timur agreed, saying he wished to avoid further bloodshed, then ordered Aric to prepare the surrender agreement.

Timur asked, "Is the prince nearby?" The raja nodded. "Then I must meet him. Demetrius, go fetch him."

When Demetrius led him into the tent, the youth bowed. "My name is Ashu, my lord. It is an honor to meet you."

Timur smiled at the raja. "A well-mannered and handsome youth. You must be proud."

"I am, my lord."

As Ashu moved to his father's side, Aric reentered the room with the surrender agreement. With minimal formality both rulers marked the documents. Timur gave his copy to Aric, who then exited the tent. The raja handed his copy to the head of his council.

Timur signaled his senior officer. "Escort the council to the city and open the gates."

When Ashu held back, his father said, "Go, your mother needs you."

Timur signaled and the tent flaps closed. "He remains here."

"But he must prepare my family's departure."

"He stays."

Ashu reacted first and reached for his sword, but the guards tackled him before it left its scabbard. At a nod from Timur, one thrust his sword into Ashu's chest. With a shout the raja charged, but the guards caught him and threw him at Timur's feet.

Timur smiled down at him. "A brave but foolish boy. Be thankful his death was quick."

"My family?"

"You should have thought of them before you provoked me." Demetrius recognized the surge of anger in Timur's voice and knew the raja faced a terrible death.

Later, Timur ordered Demetrius to the Minnagaran palace to care for the raja's injured daughter. *A royal virgin may prove useful,* he said, which echoed in Demetrius's head as he followed an army detail that guided him through the mayhem of a city at the mercy of uncontrollable, marauding troops. Soldiers were ransacking the palace as Demetrius was led up a heavily guarded marble stairway.

When he entered the chamber, a dozen soldiers were scattered about the large room, impatient about missing the opportunities enjoyed by their comrades in the street. The body of a beheaded woman lay on the floor before a Buddhist shrine, the massive pool of blood around her body obliterating the design of a richly decorated carpet. A soldier pointed to a girl who was crumpled in the corner, but Demetrius rushed to the motionless body of a toddler. The child's head had been flung against the polished marble floor, but except for a small amount of blood near his tiny ear, he looked asleep.

"Animals! Who did this?" He lunged at the nearest soldier but was restrained.

Another approached him, a soldier whose near-fatal wound he tended during the Ganges campaign. Grabbing Demetrius's shoulders, he said, "The girl—she's all that matters now." He brought him a basin of water, and Demetrius cleansed around the girl's head wound through her long, black hair. The girl opened her eyes.

Demetrius whispered, "Stay calm, little one, you're going to be all right." He lifted her into his arms, holding her face against his shoulder. The girl jerked her head back and seeing the bodies of her mother and brother screamed and pounded Demetrius's head and back with her fists. He rushed from the chamber and found his army detail waiting for him at the top of the stairs. By the time they descended, the girl's screams subsided as she slipped again into unconsciousness. A voice from above called out. Demetrius waited as the Ganges soldier approached.

"She had this bag. It may help."

Back in the Kushan camp, Demetrius insisted that Sharina stay with him, as he was the only person qualified to tend to the girl's physical and emotional wounds. Timur agreed, concerned that his valuable captive be well tended. Demetrius slept little over the following weeks, awakened several times a night by Sharina's screams. She only quieted when he placed the carved wooden horse in her hands. Demetrius never saw Sharina cry, even in her nightmare awakenings. During the day she stared with empty eyes at the tent wall. She did not speak until the third week when Demetrius told her that soon they would leave Minnagara and journey to Peshawar.

"My parents, my brothers." He knelt beside her bed. For the first time Sharina focused her deep brown eyes on his. "Were the proper rituals done?"

"Yes, they were—at the temple beside the river."

While Timur could be a cruel tyrant, he had a superstitious fear of the gods, any gods, and took great care to respect the religious rites of the peoples he conquered, particularly the rites of the dead.

"Take me there—please."

Early the next morning, accompanied by a soldier escort, Demetrius took Sharina to the temple upriver from the city. Aric had witnessed the ceremony so he joined them.

Sharina looked about the deserted temple and asked, "Where are the monks?"

Aric touched her arm. "They fled into the countryside."

"Who did the rites?"

"A monk from the city."

Sharina walked through the temple, stopping before the wide, marble steps leading into the river's fast moving water. Slowed somewhat by his boyhood limp, Aric came up beside her. "The monk placed the ashes in painted wooden boats, and while he chanted, he placed each in the river."

As Demetrius joined them, Sharina whispered, "Form itself is emptiness, emptiness itself form."

The soldiers remained in the shade of the temple's roof as the three stepped toward the water, Aric stopping partway down. When Sharina reached the river's edge, she continued into the water, chanting, "Without hindrance, there is no fear. Far beyond all inverted views, one realizes Nirvana."

Demetrius stepped beside her and took her arm.

"Please," she said, her eyes focused downriver.

"I cannot."

"Please."

"Your father would want you to live."

"Only to avenge—" She stopped.

"No, not vengeance, Sharina. Let him live through you and your children."

Quiet moments passed, interrupted only by the lapping water around their knees and the cries of birds skimming the river's surface hunting for food.

Sharina broke the silence. "How did they die?"

"With courage and great nobility. Your brother was very brave."

"You were there?"

"Yes."

She pulled her arm from Demetrius's grasp and ran up the steps pushing Aric aside. As the soldiers moved to block her way, she spun around, fists clenched at her side, eyes ablaze. Demetrius rushed to her, waving the soldiers aside. He reached out his arms.

"Come, little one, all will be well in time."

For several long moments she stared downriver, her lips silently moving. Suddenly her legs buckled, but he caught her before she collapsed. As he brought her face to his shoulder, she whispered, "Remember this day. You will wish you let me die."

"Her virtue will be safer with you than anyone."

With those words and a vulgar laugh, Timur had assigned Demetrius guardianship over Sharina until Timur arranged a suitable marriage. Further he granted Demetrius a larger palace apartment with a separate room for the girl.

Three years passed. Under Demetrius's guidance, Sharina seemed to thrive. She became demure and dutiful, everything one would expect of a royal-born daughter. Timur's queen Adelma took an interest in the young girl, spending time to teach her the manners and customs of the Kushan court. Adelma also arranged for Aric to help Sharina master Bactrian, the language of the Kushans.

Sharina remained a mystery even to Demetrius. Reserved to the point of aloofness, she rarely showed her feelings. Occasionally he heard her laugh at something Aric said, but it revealed nothing approaching joy or pleasure. Only her nightmares, less frequent but just as terrifying as in those terrible first months, revealed the tortured soul she fought to hide. The Kushan court considered her past a distant memory, replaced by a new life, surrounded by people who cared for her. Only Demetrius, a witness to the horror she had experienced, saw something frightfully dark and unpredictable under the mild demeanor she presented to the world. He shared his fears with no one and was determined to thwart any danger she might bring down upon herself—or anyone else.

CHAPTER 3
234 CE

Peshawar

THE MID-DAY HEAT EASED, AWAKENING the palace corridors to frenzied activity, all attending to the emperor, recently returned from his latest military campaign. Court officials in peacock finery paced, seeking resolution to months old disputes. Merchant guild leaders gathered, plotting their arguments against new taxes that exempted caravan merchants. A coterie of gray robed and veiled Zoroastrian priests huddled together, murmuring prayers for the emperor's generosity for their earthquake-damaged fire temple. All competed with officers rushing in and out of Timur's chamber, responding to demands for immediate reports on the fitness of the army for his next campaign.

Aric limped unobserved from the emperor's chamber, dressed simply in white trousers, tunic and cap. Caught up in their own worlds, no one looked his way; no one observed his ashen face, nor the trembling lips that smothered his usual quick smile. He lingered a moment, uncertain, then launched into the corridor's mayhem, like a rudderless boat, carried by an unseen current. A barked curse startled him. He looked toward the retreating source, his eyes registering but not seeing.

Something stopped his forward momentum, jolting him from his inattention. As his agile mind leaped to reengage with the world around him, his muscles tensed, his posture stiffened, as if expecting a physical assault to match the cruel brutality of Timur's words. Demetrius blocked his way.

"Aric, have you seen Nozar? Timur calls for him." Demetrius was breathless and agitated—hardly unusual when carrying out a command of the emperor.

"The general went to—" Aric lost the thought and shook his head. "To the stables. He said the horse master finally has his report."

Demetrius gave a quick nod and began to move on but then hesitated. "Are you all right?"

"Yes, yes. Go ahead. You know how angry the emperor gets when he is forced to wait."

"You're certain?"

Aric nodded then broke for the palace exit. As he escaped outdoors into the chaos of Peshawar's teeming masses, stillness reached for him, like the last ripples fading in a suddenly disturbed pond. He knew the stillness would not last, that more stones would pummel his waters. But he also knew that soon he would be drunk beyond feeling.

The only relief to the tavern's gloom was an oil lamp on each table. Aric did not take his eyes from the flame as a weight dropped onto the bench beside him.

"Leave me alone." He desperately wanted his voice to project firmness but a plaintive whisper was all that he could muster.

A hand moved his empty cup aside and placed a new one before him. "It's unwatered. It'll ease your burden more quickly."

The guttural inflection in his voice said he was not local. Aric drained half the cup and had barely set it down before dizziness sent his head reeling. He began to fall backward off the bench, but the man caught him, holding him upright until he grabbed the table's edge.

"Careful," the man laughed, moving his arm around Aric's shoulder. "That wine is more potent than the swill you've been drinking."

Aric glanced up at the man. He looked only a few years older than Aric's twenty-one years. His broad bearded face was open and friendly, his jet black hair hung in a braid down his back. A modest but well-made robe covered an ample belly and hinted at a prosperous livelihood. The man refilled Aric's cup from a leather flask.

Aric muttered, "You—a wine merchant?"

"Let's just say I'm a merchant who trades many things." He squeezed Aric's shoulder. "So—did she leave you or did she die?"

"Huh?"

"The woman you love. Why else would you be drinking yourself sick in the middle of the day?"

Aric stiffened. "I don't want to talk about it."

"Ah, then she left you."

Aric pushed the man away. "No." It was almost a shout, surprising him with its vehemence. Then more softly he said, "She was never mine to begin with."

The merchant patted Aric's hand. "I'm sorry, my friend, love unreturned is the worst love."

Aric lifted the cup to his lips and took a deep gulp. "No, the worst is that she is forced to marry a monster."

"It's an evil that should not go unpunished, Aric."

"You know my name?" A confused Aric looked again at the man's face. "Do I know you?"

The man shook his head. "But you look like someone who needs a friend." He replenished Aric's cup then rose from the bench. "There's much I can do for you. Ask the tavern owner for The Bear. He'll know how to find me." Then he was gone.

Demetrius found Aric in a squalid corner of a merchant's tavern outside the city wall beyond the gate that opened onto the wide road leading to the Khyber Pass. He sat down at the rough-hewn, knife-scarred table across from the emperor's scribe. "Aric, Timur searches for you." Seven empty tankards, one overturned, littered the table. The one before Aric had just been delivered.

"The bastard can't do this to her!"

"He's the emperor. He can do whatever he wants to whomever he wants. You know that better than anyone."

"But it's Sharina—Sharina!" Aric slammed his fist on the table. An empty tankard near the edge leaped and dropped with a hollow thud on the packed earth floor. Demetrius grasped the full one in front of Aric in time to keep it from falling over. The warm wine sloshed over his hand.

"Shh—you attract attention. What if you're recognized?"

"Here?" Aric jumped up unsteadily, knocking his bench to the floor. "Anyone here know who I am?" he bellowed.

Aric's tirade was cut short when a Kushan soldier seized him. When Aric resisted, shouting curses and showing more strength than his short, rotund body seemed capable of, the soldier wrestled him to the floor and tightened his thick, muscular arm around his neck. "Another sound," growled the soldier. Only when he further tightened his grip did Aric nod vigorously. The soldier pulled Aric to his feet, grabbed him by the shoulder, and pushed him toward the tavern's front exit.

Demetrius moved up behind the soldier. "Torak, there's a back door—this way." The soldier spun Aric about. Demetrius led the way into a dark and deserted alley.

Aric pulled himself out of the soldier's grasp and rubbed his shoulder. "You don't have to be so rough."

"And you don't have to be so stupid," snapped Demetrius, catching Aric as he staggered and almost fell.

"I'm going to—" Demetrius let Aric drop to his knees and stepped away as his friend vomited.

Demetrius said to Torak, "Not the welcome home you expected." Torak lifted his shoulders in his signature lop-sided shrug. *But the Greek will die happy.* Surrounded by jeering soldiers, a filthy, naked Demetrius first encountered Torak ten years earlier in Baktra. Demetrius smiled at the memory and reached for Torak's groin. In the beginning Torak did not allow such intimacy, their encounters strictly limited to Demetrius's upturned ass. Much had changed.

Torak had returned that morning from the campaign along the upper Ganges. He arrived at the room that Demetrius kept for them to the news of Aric's disappearance and the emperor's demand that he be located at once. It was no small miracle that Demetrius and Torak found Aric first.

"He can't go before the emperor like this," Demetrius said to Torak. "We better take him to the room."

Torak nodded, then nudged the still retching scribe with his foot causing Aric to tumble over on his side, fortunately away from his pool of vomit. Torak reached down and pulled Aric to his feet. "Finished?" Aric nodded. Torak then lifted him over his shoulder, Aric's head bobbing down the soldier's back. "If there's more, better tell me," Torak called back, then a bit louder, "You hear?" Aric acknowledged by slapping Torak's ass.

"Do this often?" Demetrius asked as they made their way out of the alley. Torak grunted in reply.

Aric awoke naked on his stomach, his throbbing head turned to one side. He opened his eyes to a bright blue wall. He tried to raise his head and groaned in pain.

"Good. You're awake." Demetrius spoke softly, but to Aric it sounded like a trumpet blast. He groaned again. Kneeling beside him, Demetrius helped Aric ease himself up off his stomach and lean unsteadily against the wall. "Drink this." Demetrius held a deep clay bowl to his lips. As Aric sipped the water, he glanced about. The room was small, clean, and modestly furnished with a balcony overlooking the nearby rooftops.

"This is where you and Torak—?"

Demetrius nodded. "He left before sunrise."

"I—I didn't interrupt—you know—"

"Hardly—it's been six months since I've seen him. It was like you weren't even here. We decided in the off chance you achieved any semblance of awareness, we could just say you were dreaming." Aric smiled a moment then his eyes clouded over. Demetrius continued, "Torak's taken a message to the palace saying you became ill and I'm caring for you. Your servant brought you clean clothes and the message that the emperor requires your presence no later than midday, sick or not." Demetrius paused a moment. "You must go to him soon."

Aric nodded then leaned his head back against the wall. He brought his fists to his eyes, pressing hard. "Have you heard the stories about this raja's cruelty?"

"Yes."

"She's only fourteen. Fourteen!" Aric bent over, giving in to tortured sobs.

Demetrius stood and walked out onto the room's shallow balcony to give his friend some privacy. When Aric quieted, Demetrius turned and found Aric standing in the middle of the room, tying his loincloth. Demetrius said, "Sharina is young, but she is also strong and resourceful. When I told her, she accepted the news well. I even sensed she welcomes it."

"How can you say such a thing?"

"Remember she lives among those who killed her family."

"But after all that she's been through, she deserves better." Aric reached down for his tunic and pulled it over his head.

"One rarely gets what one deserves," Demetrius replied.

Aric glared at him. "Particularly if you are the emperor."

"Careful, my friend."

"Yes, yes, always." Aric pulled on his cloak and began tying his sandals.

"That tavern—" When Aric looked up, Demetrius continued, "It's best no one knows you were there—and you should never go back."

"Why?"

"It's frequented by Persian sympathizers."

"I didn't know."

"It's no secret that you're close to the emperor. Just your presence there could have some question your loyalty. Did you speak to anyone?"

"You saw me," Aric said. "I was too drunk to speak."

"That you certainly were."

Out on the street Aric paused to allow his quickened heartbeat to calm, for Demetrius did not press him about whether he had spoken to anyone. Relieved that he had not faced having to lie to his friend, he now wondered about that strange 'merchant who traded many things' with an even stranger name. Out of the haze of the previous day's stupor the deep, thick voice of the The Bear slipped unbidden into his mind: 'It's an evil that should not go unpunished, Aric.'

As Aric approached the entrance to Timur's chambers, the usually talkative guard opened the door without acknowledgment or any sign of recognition. Aric slipped into the room and the door closed behind him. Timur and General Nozar sat at a table at the far end of the large but sparsely decorated room. Aric waited for Timur to notice his presence.

"Are you certain of this, my lord?" Nozar was asking. Aric's attention heightened. He could not recall the last time Nozar questioned a decision of the emperor's.

Timur waved his hand. "You worry too much. This raja will never rule the Kushan Empire."

"To make him your heir, even for a moment, puts us at risk."

"Baldev's message is clear. It's the only way he will agree to the treaty."

Timur lifted his right arm and motioned to Aric. As Aric approached the table, he glanced down and saw the large map of the Ganges River valley he had procured many months earlier. Embedded in the center of the territory ruled by the raja Baldev was the point of Timur's ruby-encrusted, ornamental dagger, a recent gift from Queen Adelma.

Timur continued, "Anyway, the astrologers foretell that I will have a son and heir by this time next year."

"And you would base a decision of state importance on—?"

"Enough talk!"

"Yes, my lord." Nozar bowed his head.

Timur said, "Scribe."

"Yes, my lord."

"My soldiers searched for you but could not find you."

"It won't happen again, my lord."

Timur rose and walked slowly around the table. The blow came without warning. Timur's fist slammed into the side of Aric's head, below the ear. Aric fell back on his right leg, his good leg, twisting his ankle as he fought to regain his balance. He righted himself, head spinning and stomach reeling.

"Do not fail me again, scribe."

"No, my lord."

Timur patted Aric's shoulder. "This raja arrives within a few days from Srinagar. You will prepare the treaty. Stay here with the general. He will tell you what to write."

After Timur left, Nozar motioned Aric to sit and proceeded to outline the terms of the treaty. *The widowed raja Baldev of Srinagar will be given the Minnagaran princess, Sharina, to wed. The raja will deliver one thousand trained archers to the Kushan army. It is further agreed that should Timur die without an heir, Baldev will ascend the Kushan throne. In return, should Baldev die before his infant son comes of age, Timur will become the son's guardian and regent.*

After Aric clarified several details, he waited to be dismissed. Instead Nozar asked, "Has he struck you before?"

Aric struggled to hide his alarm at the question.

"Truly, I do not ask to trap or harm you." Nozar waited.

Aric replied, "Not recently, sir—and never in front of anyone before."

"You held your ground."

"His boot taught me never to fall."

"You impress me." Nozar gently squeezed his shoulder. "You may go."

Aric rushed from the emperor's chambers, struggling to keep his balance as he favored his twisted ankle.

After the treaty was drafted and delivered to General Nozar for a final review, Aric sat in the courtyard where he had taught Sharina in days past. In the beginning, she had refused to acknowledge his presence, wandering idly along the gravel paths as he followed her, feeling self-conscious about his limp. His attempts to hide it only made it more pronounced. Then one day she stopped and spun about, hands on her hips. Aric stumbled and barely avoided bumping into her.

Sharina shook her head and speaking Greek said, "You are a funny little man."

Aric mimicked her hand-on-hip stance, shook his head and said in Bactrian, "You are a funny little man." Before Sharina could react, he continued in Greek, "Because it evolved from the Greek brought by Alexander, your knowledge of the language is going to make learning Bactrian much easier." Shifting to Bactrian, he repeated, "You are a funny little man."

Suppressing a smile, Sharina said in Greek, "You *are* a funny little man."

"Now try it in Bactrian."

She touched his cheek, met his eyes with a mischievous sparkle in hers, and smiled. "Tomorrow—maybe." And then she rushed away. Aric was in love. He knew she could never love him, an ungainly servant to the emperor who had orphaned her. But from that moment forward he would do anything for her, even it it meant his life.

In the three years that followed, whenever Aric was in Peshawar, he met with Sharina in this courtyard. Often, she was distracted and distant and treated him with impatient disregard. She did apply herself to learning Bactrian, mastering not only the language but the Kushan dialect. One day she surprised him by asking about his brother, saying she had heard conflicting stories about his death. He told her the story Demetrius had told him years earlier with its emphasis on General Rodmehr's treachery. He had been staring at the ground during his telling and was surprised when he looked up and saw tears falling from Sharina's eyes.

"Timur showed no mercy for my brother Ashu either." Without another word she left him.

Footsteps approached to interrupt Aric's thoughts, and Sharina slipped beside him on the bench. "I saw you sitting here. Were you waiting for me?" Before he could answer, she touched his bruised face with her fingertips. "What happened?"

"I fell. You know how clumsy I am."

"The truth. Who struck you?"

"It was my fault."

"Who?" Sharina demanded.

"I can't."

"It was the emperor, wasn't it?"

Aric's face flushed in panic. "No—no."

Sharina took his hands in hers. "Don't be afraid. What happened?"

"I ran away. I was upset and angry. The emperor laughed at how the raja you will marry treats his women. Sharina, he can't do this to you."

"But he can. Come, walk with me." Sharina stepped to one side of the courtyard path, giving Aric space to walk beside her, slowing her pace to match his, instead of rushing ahead as usual. After a long period of silence, she spoke. "Such a marriage has been my fate since he brought me here. I expect that Baldev is no better nor worse than any raja Timur would have chosen. Anyway, who knows what lies ahead? But as I leave, promise me you will remember one thing. You and I are bound by the blood of innocents butchered by the emperor. My family cries for vengeance—as does your brother."

"No, not vengeance." Aric bristled, not ready to rehash this frequent argument, even though he felt his conviction wavering that she was wrong. "The emperor has cared for me."

"Cared for you?" Sharina touched his bruise. "You enable him to live with himself for what he did to Yousef. He deserves nothing from you, except your hatred. Think on this and someday you will realize I speak the truth."

Sharina stood inside the doorway of Queen Adelma's private chamber. Adelma's eunuch Mahesh had fetched her from her room in Demetrius's quarters, telling her that the queen would soon arrive to speak with her. Even though Mahesh encouraged her to make herself comfortable before he rushed off, she hesitated. In the three years since her arrival at the Kushan court, Adelma had never invited her to this room. They had always met in

Adelma's private courtyard to walk or her reception room to embroider or play Twenty Squares, the queen's favorite pastimes. Unlike the rest of the queen's apartment, this chamber had a cluttered appearance that better reflected the queen Sharina had come to know.

In the beginning the queen's friendliness had unsettled Sharina. It seemed genuine, but Adelma was the wife of the emperor who had destroyed her family. Distrust constrained Sharina's feelings whenever they were together. She also recoiled at the thought that the queen, ten years her senior, might try to become her surrogate mother. Adelma never seemed to mind Sharina's reserve, balancing it with her own natural, and at times excessive, gaiety. It amazed Sharina that Adelma flourished in the otherwise restrained Peshawar court. She seemed to thrive on catching staid visitors off guard with a flamboyant reaction to a petition or concern, which she followed with a quick wink and laugh that usually smoothed out the resulting awkwardness. Over time she gently extended her playfulness to Sharina as well, slowly winning Sharina over, one small smile after another. *No, not a surrogate mother, rather an older sister.*

Only once did Adelma invite Sharina to talk about her family. They were walking in the queen's courtyard. It took all the control Sharina could muster not to run away as she answered, "Never."

"Then never will I ask again."

Several days later they sat in the queen's reception chamber embroidering. They had been silent, Sharina lost in her own thoughts, when Adelma spoke up. "We have more in common than you might expect." She hesitated a moment, studying Sharina's upturned eyes as if she were looking for permission to continue. Sharina gave a slight nod.

"I was born the daughter of a nobleman close to Timur's governor who ruled Arachosia. I was nineteen and betrothed to an army officer I had known since I was a child. He was gentle and kind toward me, and I loved him. Timur arrived for a royal visit, and one night after much drink the governor entertained him with a dance of maidens, including me. When Timur saw me, he told the governor he must have me. Informed I was not a servant but of noble birth, Timur decided in that moment he had been too long without a wife and still required an heir, and so would make me his queen. The next day my betrothed was ordered to lead a patrol against a nest of bandits. When news arrived that the patrol had been crushed and my betrothed killed, the governor announced my marriage to Timur, declaring it would deepen the already strong ties between the Kushans and Arachosians. I never saw the body of my betrothed and was forced to hide my grief and rage, both of which continue to live inside me—this is something I've never told anyone until now."

"Why me?"

"Because I see the same grief in you, along with rage as raw as it must have felt those terrible days three years ago."

Sharina's heartbeat quickened. Her embroidery slipped from her lap to the floor as her hands began to tremble. Adelma took them in her own.

"Do not be afraid. You're safe."

Sharina resisted, and then allowed Adelma to pull her into her arms. She shook but did not cry, even as tears fought for release. Adelma's soothing murmurs slowly calmed her, and she slipped from the queen's embrace. Once she retrieved her embroidery, Adelma did not press her, giving her time to gather her thoughts.

Finally Sharina asked, "How am I safe? Don't others see what you see?"

"Perhaps Demetrius because he witnessed what happened to you and is more observant than most. But others? Unlikely, especially the men. Being women we are inconsequential compared to their intrigues, wars, and grasping for riches and power. They are blind to all except what we permit them to see. And you, my dear, are a natural at keeping hidden what you do not want known."

Sharina took a moment to breathe deeply and calm herself. "How do you live with what happened to you?"

"I made the decision to live life to the fullest, bending to its vagaries as I wait for an opportunity to avenge the wrong done to me and to my betrothed."

Shocked at this revelation, Sharina quickly glanced about then whispered, "You seek vengeance?"

Adelma nodded. "As do you. But you, I suspect, would choose death over life this very moment if it meant vengeance for your family." When Sharina did not deny it, she added. "I fear yours is a most perilous path."

"But I know no other."

"Then consider that the danger you face is not the path you walk but how you walk it." Sharina gave her a puzzled look, to which Adelma asked. "Why do I consistently win when we play Twenty Squares?"

"You tell me I rush too fast trying to get my pieces across the board."

"And how do I play?"

"Once your pieces are on the board, you advance patiently, thinking about each move. I rarely send your pieces back to start over. You do it with mine time after time."

"In life, too, I proceed patiently," Adelma said, "watching, waiting, planning. I have vowed to live to see the fruits of my vengeance."

"But you and the emperor—you seem fond of each other."

"That is a perception I have nurtured carefully, though having not produced the son and heir he desperately wants, I am surprised I have managed to hold his interest so long. Another daughter and I fear he will be finished with me, but that is tomorrow's care."

From that moment forward the queen and Sharina became intimate companions.

Sharina's thoughts were interrupted by quick footsteps and the rustling of fabric announcing Adelma's appearance in the corridor.

"Please, please, enter," Adelma said as she pushed Sharina from behind and into chamber. "I hope you like blue silk. On such short notice finding a gown for your wedding has been a challenge. Mahesh's staff has been scouring the fabric merchants. One just returned with something that just might work—if you approve, of course."

"Does it really matter what I want anymore?" Sharina softly asked, giving voice at last to the resignation and helplessness she had been feeling since Demetrius told her that she was to be married to Baldev.

"This is no time to feel sorry for yourself, my dear." Surprised at the hard tone of Adelma's voice, Sharina gave no resistance as the queen drew her to a divan and continued, "Ask yourself, why doesn't Timur attack and conquer Srinagar? That is what he would normally do. Instead he offers you to this raja to seal a treaty. Let us assume this raja is too powerful a foe. Once his wife, you will be in a position to turn his power to your advantage. You have lived in Timur's court for three years. Baldev will expect you to tell him all that you know about the emperor. Would not carefully crafted stories poison Baldev's trust in his new treaty partner? Then how far might winning his heart spur your husband to avenge what Timur did to your family? You must be observant and cunning, at times even ruthless. Do not act or speak rashly. If you push too quickly, Baldev will question your motives. Most importantly, trust no one but yourself."

Staggered by the candor of Adelma's words, Sharina could not speak. The queen waited, studying her face for a reaction. Finally, Sharina asked, "Why are you helping me?"

The queen shrugged. "Maybe helping you is the opportunity I have been waiting for."

Aric stood in the corridor outside Demetrius's palace apartment, breathless from running up three levels. Demetrius opened the door, motioned Aric in, and quickly shut the door behind him. He could hear Sharina's loud weeping coming from her room.

"Then it is true."

Demetrius nodded. "Last night Timur's guards brought her here from Baldev's camp and ordered her not to leave."

"But the rider from Nozar's hunt only arrived this morning."

"He did. I told her the news of Baldev's accident just before you arrived."

This warlord will never rule the Kushan Empire. "Then Nozar had him—"

"Don't say it."

"But—"

"Not here," Demetrius hissed. "She will hear."

"Hear what?" Sharina stood unsteadily, holding onto the door jam of her room, her long dark hair in disarray. "That my husband of only three days has been murdered?"

Demetrius rushed to her, covering her mouth. "Silence! If not for yourself then for those who love you." Sharina bit his hand, and with a cry he yanked it away.

"Why should I care about you or any Kushan?" She spat the words into Demetrius's face. "You butchered my family. And now—and now my last chance—" Sharina struck Demetrius on the chest with both fists and dropped to the floor. "Baldev would have delivered Timur to me, and before he put that monster to the sword, Timur would know that my family is avenged."

Demetrius nodded to Aric. "Check the corridor."

Aric opened the door, quickly shutting it again. "No one."

Demetrius lifted Sharina into his arms. Aric followed as he carried her to her bed. She stared at the ceiling, hardly breathing.

"What does she mean?" Aric whispered.

"Poor girl, it seems she hoped to turn Baldev against the emperor." Demetrius stroked her cheek then said, "Watch her."

Demetrius returned with a small glazed cup. He sat on the edge of the bed, slid his arm under her shoulders, and gently lifted her. "Drink this." She resisted a moment before draining the cup. He kissed her forehead. "Rest now."

Returning to the main room Demetrius took Aric's arm. "She isn't safe here. Go to Mahesh. Tell him we must get her into the Queen's quarters. And, Aric, by your love for her, what she said remains between us."

"I know."

As Timur busied himself preparing for his regency over Baldev's realm, Adelma quietly took Sharina into her household full-time. As the weeks passed the queen and Sharina were rarely apart, often seen walking the gardens and courtyards of the palace, hand-in-hand talking. Demetrius relaxed his vigilant concern for his former charge, seeing her less frequently now that she no longer shared his palace apartment.

Two months after Baldev's death, the queen asked to see Demetrius. Upon arrival at Adelma's private chambers, her maidservant escorted him onto a wide balcony facing the distant Khyber Pass. A cooling breeze brushed across his face as he stepped to the balcony wall and looked down into the queen's private courtyard far below. Workmen repaired the ornate fountain at its center.

Adelma appeared beside him. A large and robust woman, she loved bright, colorful silks. The mix of hues, even when they clashed, matched her lively and at times irreverent personality.

"Last night's festivities to announce your pregnancy were impressive," Demetrius remarked casually.

"I felt paraded around like some prize cow," Adelma responded with a laugh.

"But you carry his child."

"And those horrible astrologers take full credit—as if they, rather than the emperor, bedded me. I almost wish for another daughter so I can watch them grovel at his feet, begging for mercy." Again, she laughed.

Blunt and outspoken, wit often running ahead of decorum, Adelma had more than once joked at Timur's expense, but he was quick to laugh and banter—yet the same jest, coming from someone else, would have resulted in a flash of temper or worse. Still, while her disregard for propriety always delighted Demetrius, he did fear for her should she not present Timur with a son and heir. After five years of marriage and three daughters, Demetrius wondered whether Timur's unusual patience would continue, even though Adelma's hold over him seemed firm.

A servant came onto the balcony with refreshments, placing them on a small table. Adelma sent her away and going to the table poured wine into two glasses. She handed one to Demetrius, who hesitated, momentarily taken aback by her serving him. Before he got the glass to his lips, she spoke.

"Sharina must marry again."

Even Adelma rarely got to the point so quickly without pleasantries or preamble. Demetrius gave the queen a quizzical look. "Has she expressed such an interest?"

"No, but she carries the raja's child. She must marry quickly before the emperor finds out. Otherwise, he will kill her to eliminate the raja's heir."

The news hit Demetrius like a blow to the stomach. "Will the emperor allow her to remarry?"

"She's no longer a virgin, so he has no use for her. Leave it to me."

"You risk much helping her," Demetrius ventured.

"I have grown quite fond of her."

Demetrius suspected the queen's answer was but a small part of the reason. "Do you have a husband in mind?"

"Why, Aric, of course," Adelma answered. "Surely you've seen how he feels about her."

"For quite some time, my lady."

"Then it is decided."

Demetrius paused. "There is one complication."

"Yes, of course. He will know the child is not his. That I leave to you, Demetrius."

"You will marry me?" Sharina asked.

She sat on a large divan in the queen's reception chamber. Aric stood stiffly before her. She did not look at him, her face down, eyes focused on a small pillow in her lap, her agitated fingers pulling at the pillow's frayed embroidery.

"I will," Aric answered.

"The child?"

"I will raise as my own."

She looked up, her dark eyes settling on his face, her voice controlled and tense. "I don't want your pity."

"Pity has nothing to do with it."

"Then what? The emperor's command?"

He jerked at her sudden intensity but calmly replied, "The emperor did not command. He agreed to the queen's suggestion."

She returned her attention to her lap, her fingers not stopping their fevered movement. "I will cause you pain."

"More often happiness."

"Happiness? With me?"

"You knew happiness once," Aric answered. "You will know it again."

"I can never love you."

"Give it time."

"You are a fool."

"So Demetrius has said many times."

Aric looked up as Sharina stepped onto the balcony of their palace apartment carrying a tray with a wine jug and matching cups. He smiled, still amazed at the flurry of events orchestrated by the queen and Demetrius that resulted in their marriage a week earlier. His bride's flowing blue silk gown hid the first signs of her pregnancy. Unlike the thick-bodied Adelma, Sharina's delicate frame would not hide for long that she carried a child. It would be a month or more before a handmaiden would be allowed to attend to her. In the meantime, Aric took the opportunity to dote upon her every need, regardless of how intimate, hoping her coolness around him might in time grow warmer.

"Aren't they beautiful?" she said as she placed the tray on the table where Aric worked. The green-blue glass oinochoe stood three hand-widths tall and rested on a square out-splayed base. A braided strap handle curved from the bowl's widest point and attached inside the trefoil mouth. The cups were of the same glass with matching bases. "I've never seen their like before. They look very expensive." She handed him an ornately inscribed card.

'Congratulations,' it read. But it included no sender's name.

"Shall we?" she asked as she poured.

As Aric brought the cup to his lips, the wine's fragrance transported him to that tavern outside the Khyber Gate, the one Demetrius warned him to never again visit because it was frequented by Persian partisans.

"I wonder who sent it," Sharina said.

There's much I can do for you. Ask the tavern owner for The Bear. He'll know how to find me.

"I recognize the wine from a merchant shop I recently visited," Aric said. "Most likely he hopes I will introduce him to the emperor's steward."

"After a gift like this, it's the least you could do."

"Yes," Aric said, "the least I could do."

CHAPTER 4
235 CE

SHARINA WAS CARING FOR HER three-day old son when the eunuch Mahesh hurried into her chamber, his face etched with fatigue.

As he paused to catch his breath, anxiety gripped her heart. "The queen?" she asked.

"The labor is long and hard. Demetrius has been with her all night."

"The child?"

"Not yet. But we've received word the wet nurse has taken ill. The queen requests you replace her."

"But of course."

"Good." Mahesh spun about to leave then spun back. "I'll send help to move you to the nursery."

The queen's handmaiden burst into the room and bowed to Mahesh. "The physician demands you come quickly."

As the eunuch rushed from the room, the woman winked at Sharina and mouthed the words, 'A boy.'

While Sharina nursed the infant prince, she examined the boy's tiny ankle band, as she had many times in the three days since his birth. The traditional birth gift of a royal father to his first-born son, the band was made of purest gold. An inner ridge, which allowed the band to rest snugly above the boy's foot and ankle, would gradually be filed away as he grew, and eventually be worn on a chain around the prince's neck. It was finely etched with two griffins, symbols of the Kushan royal house, with the words *Son of Timur, Prince, Warrior, Champion of His People* in between. The emperor had ordered his goldsmiths to create the band immediately after the astrologers foretold the birth of a son, and Demetrius had placed the band around the prince's ankle soon after birth on behalf of the absent Timur, who was in Srinagar dealing with the rebellion that erupted in opposition to his regency over Baldev's realm. He had taken Aric with him, denying his scribe's request that he be allowed to remain at Sharina's side until she gave birth.

As the prince suckled her nipple, already painfully raw from nursing her own infant son, Sharina whispered, over and over, the ankle bracelet's inscription: *Son of Timur, Prince, Warrior, Champion of His People—Son of Timur, Prince, Warrior, Champion of His People.* It became a mantra but did not bring the comfort and inner peace taught by her mother. Whenever she spoke the name *Timur*, she let it feed the rage that until recently had been subdued by the contentment that had come to fill her life. *Son of Timur, Prince, Warrior, Champion of His People—Son of Timur, son of Timur—son of Timur, Timur, Timur—*

The prince released her nipple with a soft cry. She jerked, realizing her hold on him had become painfully tight. She relaxed her shoulders and arms and with soothing sounds guided the infant's tiny mouth back to her breast. She stroked the tiny head and despaired over whether she had the courage to do what she must do.

Sharina's son began to cry, stirring the prince into an accompanying wail. Cursing under her breath she arose, having hoped for a few quiet moments. She placed the prince beside her son in the ornate baby bed once used by Timur and his father before him. Initially Mahesh chastised her for presuming to place a servant's son in the bed of a prince, but he relented when he observed the two boys calm when placed together. She too marveled at how the two boys reacted to each other. She could not imagine twins being more connected. The prince stopped crying, but her son continued to fuss. Sharina took the carved wooden horse at her son's feet and placed it on his chest. His tiny, wrinkled hands grasped the horse's tail, and he began to settle down.

Sharina paced the colorful carpet that filled the center of the queen's reception chamber, now a temporary nursery, losing herself in the intricate pattern of intertwining animals and birds. A thin blue vine wound itself around and between fanciful lions, hares, peacocks, dragons, leopards, and hawks. Once she had seen only playfulness in the images at her feet, but recently Demetrius revealed the intense battle for life the carpet portrayed: swift hare fleeing the marauding lion, massive dragons in wait for unwary birds of prey, leopards stealthily moving to catch inattentive monkeys. Her eyes always sought out the two foxes centered in the design—one white, one gold—the only two creatures woven as a pair, neck touching neck, heads turned in opposite directions, eyes attentive to all that swirled about them. Usually the foxes gave comfort but not today. She took a step, pulling her eyes away from the foxes to the hare fleeing the lion. For the first time she noticed the cleverly placed leaves on the hare's back. "Wings," she whispered. "The hare escapes the clutches of the lion."

Another scene invaded her thoughts: a different baby prince in her care, a soldier's hands seizing her brother from her arms, his cries brutally silenced. Fighting to block the memory of Tanay dead on the floor she brought her fists to her eyes.

A hand shook her shoulder. The dark visions retreated, replaced by the colorful, intricate weaving of animals and vines at her feet, and the hare escaping the lion.

"Oh, Tanay, if only I had wings then."

A hand took her elbow, followed by a voice, "Sharina, please come, sit."

As she rose, she leaned heavily against Demetrius's shoulder. He placed his arm around her and guided her to the divan. She took a slow, deep breath as she eased herself out from under Demetrius's arm. "I'm fine." She sat and looked up into his eyes.

Tall and gaunt in face and body, dressed simply in his usual unadorned white tunic and simple gray outer cloak, Demetrius gave Sharina a questioning look. "Are you certain you can continue as wet-nurse?"

"You needn't worry."

"But I do worry. When I came in—that look in your eyes—it's been a long time since—" Demetrius hesitated then frowned. "Let me arrange for another."

"Please don't. The queen chose me. I can't disappoint her."

"Just don't disappoint me by not caring for yourself."

She nodded, gave Demetrius a kiss on the cheek, and then turned away, a painful lump in her throat. *Nothing matters except avenging Tanay.*

"There is a reason for my visit. Timur has returned. Fortunately, the queen's condition has improved, and she is strong enough for the *chakor.*"

"Of course." Sharina bowed her head, hiding a face that she knew revealed the sudden alarm that rushed through her. *The time is now.* She took another slow, deep breath to steady herself before looking back up. "What wonderful, happy news—and my husband?"

"Aric is with the emperor. He prepares the *chakor* documents and"—breaking into a broad smile—"is anxious to greet his son after the ceremony."

"How much time do I have?"

"Not long. The emperor has sent for the head priest. When everyone has arrived and all is ready, Mahesh will come for the child. The queen asked that you be there. You have the prince's *chakor* gown?"

"Yes, Mahesh brought it to me yesterday."

The room filled with crying from first one and then the other awakening infant. Sharina shrugged her shoulders, waved at the departing Demetrius, and went to the boys.

Sharina looked down at the two infants. *I can wait no longer.* The spirits of her parents, of Ashu, and of little Tanay demanded retribution. A large pillow lay at the prince's feet. *It would be quietly and quickly done.* Numbness crept to the edges of her consciousness. For three days she had agonized, overwhelmed by the enormity of what she contemplated. To kill the prince would mean her death, which she long expected and even yearned for, but it would cost the life of her infant son. Demetrius would likely die as an accomplice. Perhaps even the queen for choosing Sharina to replace the original wet nurse.

But had not Adelma told her she must be ruthless.

The prince began to cry. Her son remained quiet but squirming, hand wrapped around the back legs of Ashu's wood horse. Never had Sharina felt so alone. Even the rage that accompanied her from Minnagara and increased upon news of Baldev's death, that had sustained her all these years now deserted her. All feeling, all caring, all emotion drained from her. She wondered if the soldiers who had slaughtered her mother and baby brother felt such numbness. They must have. How else could they have done it?

Sharina moved the pillow toward the prince's face. Her son moved, throwing his arm across the prince's chest, striking Sharina's hand. As if burned by fire, Sharina backed away, pulling the pillow to her chest. Frozen to the spot, tears filled her eyes and flowed down her cheeks. Sharina flung the pillow across the room, her face contorted in agony.

Why the opportunity but not the resolve?

She glanced toward the chamber's balcony then remembered the son that depended on her. She threw herself upon the chamber's carpet, her pounding fists the only sound, tears stinging her eyes. Long moments passed before she calmed. The two foxes—woven as one—captured her gaze. Behind her, the boys began to cry.

As one.

Sharina went to the baby bed. Reaching down she placed one hand on the prince's head, the other on her son's. As she made soothing noises, she stroked them both. The prince reached for her hand, and she gave him a finger. He squeezed it. She gave a finger from her other hand to her son. He grasped it.

Switch them.

Her mind raced. The queen had been barely conscious when she briefly held the prince after his birth and had been too ill to see him since. Neither the emperor nor her husband had seen their sons, returning just today from the emperor's campaign to hold Baldev's territory. Even Mahesh had merely glanced at the boys, concerned more with the queen's care. Only Demetrius would know, having delivered both boys and seen the birthmark on her son's right hip. Would he betray her? *He loathes the emperor. I know he does.*

To take the prince's life would mean certain death, and if anyone knew she switched the boys, the result would be the same. But if it succeeded—Sharina became breathless at the thought—if it succeeded, she would avenge her family without taking a life or causing any deaths. *Will Demetrius betray me?* Over and over the question cried out, demanding an answer she could not give. But the idea took hold and would not let go.

Sharina slipped her fingers from the tiny hands and contemplated the prince's gold ankle band. Looking at her son she felt relief he did not yet have a name—it was the child's father's place to give a name. *Only the spirits of my family will know—but that must be enough—for the moment.*

Sharina removed the prince's ankle band and put it on her son. She placed the wood horse on the prince's chest, and then began dressing her son in the *chakor* gown of a prince.

Sharina placed her son on her lap, his head upon her knees, and stroked his cheeks. She struggled to calm herself, praying to the spirits of her family to give her courage. The child gave a happy squeal. She whispered, "Shh, little one." She pulled him into her arms. "One day you will rule a great empire," she whispered. "You will no longer be mine, but I will always love you." An ache filled her chest and she squeezed her eyes shut against sudden tears.

Given the queen's weak condition, the ceremony, normally held in the throne room, had been moved to her bedchamber, limiting the observers to the emperor's senior advisors and the queen's companions. Sharina had heard that disappointed courtiers were already celebrating in the Great Hall, where Timur would appear to present his heir to the court after the ceremony.

When Mahesh arrived and lifted her son from her lap, Sharina feared he would notice her shaking arms. But Mahesh's eyes focused on the boy. "Look how nicely the *chakor* gown adorns the young prince." Relief flowed through Sharina's now steadier hands as she placed and adjusted the matching cap on the boy's head. Mahesh said, "Come, come, we must hurry. Everyone is waiting."

The emperor, the high priest and the other witnesses stood in place along the perimeter of the queen's bedchamber as Mahesh entered the room with the infant in his arms. Sharina entered behind Mahesh, carrying Timur's son. She moved to the tapestry near the balcony. Aric stood beside Timur, holding the parchment the emperor and high priest would mark after the ceremony. She raised her arms so Aric might see the child in her arms. He acknowledged her with a smile.

Sharina breathed deeply and slowly, trying but unable to remember the sutras her mother taught her. Demetrius caught her eye with the look of concerned uncertainty that she knew too well. *He suspects something.* Panic started to build, but she fought it back, reminding herself that she stood but a few steps from the bedchamber's balcony and its fatal escape. If her plan failed, she would welcome death with the tyrant's heir in her arms.

Mahesh stopped in the center of the chamber, a few paces before the foot of the queen's bed. Adelma sat to one side, wearing a red silk gown. A white bed covering, richly embroidered with griffins, lay across her legs.

The high priest nodded at Mahesh and intoned, "You may take the child to the queen."

As Mahesh moved around the foot of the bed, Timur interrupted. "Stop."

The high priest grimaced. "My lord?"

"Give the child to the physician first. He will confirm the child is mine."

A hush descended over the room. Mahesh hesitated, first glancing at the queen then again at the emperor.

"Why do you wait? Do as I command."

Demetrius stepped forward. Resignation washed through Sharina. She had not counted on Demetrius being asked to confirm the prince's identity. He would have no choice but to reveal her deception. Sharina edged closer to the balcony, preparing to rush through the opening and over the balustrade to join the spirits of her family. *Forgive me,* she whispered silently to the boy in Mahesh's arms.

Demetrius lifted the cap from the boy's head and hesitated. He closed his eyes. Mahesh nudged him. Reopening them he whispered, "Help me lift the gown. The emperor will wish me to be thorough."

After examining the child, Demetrius announced with a firm voice and an unwavering stare into Timur's eyes, "The boy wears the gold band of the prince and has the prince's birthmark on his hip." After smoothing the *chakor* gown back over the boy's legs and replacing his cap, Demetrius stepped back, and Mahesh placed the child into the queen's arms.

Suddenly faint, Sharina leaned against the tapestry. She would have dropped to the floor but for Demetrius slipping beside her and taking her elbow. Softly remarking on the heat, he motioned to someone to bring a stool then remained beside her.

The high priest recited the *chakor* chants, after which the emperor leaned over the bed and Adelma placed the prince into his arms. The ceremony concluded with the high priest anointing the prince, after which the emperor declared with a robust shout, "I name him *Calaf.*"

At that moment the boy in Sharina's arms began to wail, arousing Calaf to cry even louder. Everyone, including the somber high priest, laughed as Sharina moved toward the chamber door, attempting to hush the child. Laughing louder than anyone, Timur called for her to remain.

Timur gazed about the room and extended his arms. "This is a joyous day. I have a handsome, healthy son and heir—and the woman who bore him, my cherished queen, survived the ordeal of childbirth to present him to me." Loud and excited cheers of *Calaf* and *Adelma* greeted his words. Timur raised his hands. "But there is more to our joy this day." Timur paused as a hush descended over the room. "Among our people a permanent family relationship, *rada*, exists between children nursed by the same woman." At this, Timur motioned to Aric and Sharina to approach. When they stood before him, he continued, "Be it known this day: *rada* makes brothers of Prince Calaf and the son of Aric." Timur placed his hand on Aric's shoulder. "Moreover, through my trusted Aric *rada* unites to us the family of our beloved Yousef." Smiling broadly Timur looked down at Adelma, who showed as much surprise as the parents of Calaf's new brother.

Timur nudged the high priest, who began the *chakor* chants for the son of Aric and Sharina. After Sharina presented the child in her arms to her husband, the high priest anointed the boy then nodded to Aric, who proclaimed, "I name him *Ishmael.*"

PART 2

Nothing is More Important than My Empire

249 CE

CHAPTER 5
249 CE

Peshawar

Like a fox alert to imminent threat, Ishmael's eyes snapped wide open then darted to the bed next to his to reassure himself that Calaf lay there. Recurring dreams of searching for Calaf but not finding him had haunted him since he was a young child. Calaf often teased him about his wide-eyed awakening, and one recent morning before daybreak Calaf had brushed a feather under his nose until his eyes flew open. Immediately a sneeze followed. Ishmael had chased the laughing Calaf about their shared quarters and wrestled him to the floor. They were equally matched though built differently, Ishmael lithe and quick, Calaf muscular and strong, neither getting an advantage over the other, until Ishmael began laughing, too, and having lost concentration, gave Calaf the opening to pin him. Afterward they had dozed, Ishmael's head on Calaf's chest, until they were nudged awake by Mahesh, hurrying them to dress as they were late for their lessons with the always punctual and impatient Aric.

But there would be no lessons this day, for it was the fourteenth anniversary of their *chakor*. The emperor had decreed that rather than celebrate their individual births, they would celebrate their name day together. Because Timur had been in the field with his army, their last two *chakor* celebrations had been quiet affairs. But this year he and his army were at home, and the palace had been in an uproar all week preparing for that evening's royal feast.

Ishmael stretched, kicking the tangled sheet free of his legs. The first streaks of dawn filtered through the branches of the white mulberry that reached to their second level window, casting a glow on the opposite wall where his drawings hung in scattered array. From the moment he could hold a piece of charcoal he began to draw. To discourage his artwork appearing on the palace's floors and walls, Aric had given him ample scraps of parchment. Fascinated by the carpet in the queen's reception chamber, he never tired of copying the animals, birds, and flora, his drawings increasingly rivaling the carpet maker's in beauty and intricacy.

Ishmael climbed from his bed and approached the wall, noticing that his latest drawing of the carpet's twin foxes now had arrows surrounding them, some pointing toward them, some pointing outward.

"It's my *chakor* gift to you." When Ishmael turned toward the voice, Calaf sat on the edge of his bed, a wide smile spread across his face. Bounding up beside Ishmael, he lay his arm across his shoulders. "Can you figure it out?"

"It's a message, isn't it?"

Calaf nodded excitedly. A week earlier Aric, frustrated by the prince's inattention to his language lessons, had given him an assignment to create a secret code using words. 'What if you had to get a communication past your enemy?' Aric had asked. 'How would you do it?' Clearly captivated by the task's battle-focused context, Calaf became obsessed. He surprised Ishmael by not demanding his help, his usual practice with all things academic. Even when Aric quickly solved his first effort, switching the first and last letters of words, he did not become frustrated or angry. Instead he questioned Aric about what made codes work. More unsuccessful efforts followed, each time generating further discussions between them. As Ishmael stared at the arrows surrounding the foxes, he recalled hearing Aric tell Calaf, 'An unbreakable code must contain a key known only to you and the receiver.'

They had grown up playing on the carpet in the queen's chamber. While they each had their favorite creatures, the two foxes fascinated them both. When they were quite young, Ishmael said to Calaf, "You be the white one. I'll be the gold."

Overhearing their play Sharina had called out, “No, Ishmael. Gold is the color of a prince so Calaf must be the gold fox.”

That night as they lay in their beds Calaf whispered, “Forget what your mother said. You are the gold fox. It’ll be our secret.”

The key.

Ishmael’s finger touched the arrow pointing outward from the white fox’s head. It was thicker than the others.

“You’re calling out—”

Then he touched the one pointing inward toward the gold one’s head, the only one with a shaft feather.

“—to me—”

Then he traced a bent arrow whose tip touched the white fox’s hind quarters.

“—for help because you’ve hurt—your leg?”

Calaf beamed with satisfaction.

“Wait’ll you show this to my father,” Ishmael said.

“No, it must be our secret. You will teach me to draw the foxes as well as you do. Then we’ll agree on what the different arrows mean. If we’re ever separated, our enemies will search our words for coded messages but not a drawing they see every time.”

Ishmael laughed. “‘Such silly boys’ they’ll say.” Then concern filled his voice. “But we’ll never be separated, will we?”

“Of course, we won’t,” Calaf answered.

Ishmael rushed for his bed and from beneath it pulled out a black silk-covered package. “Your *chakor* gift.” When Ishmael tossed it, the silk fell away as Calaf caught it. “A new chainmail shirt,” Ishmael called out excitedly.

Calaf examined it closely. “It’s lighter than my old one.”

“And the Persian merchant said it’s much stronger with smaller and tighter rings. Do you like it?”

“I do.” Calaf pulled it on. “It fits perfect.”

“I got a matching one for myself.” Ishmael pulled another package from underneath his bed and donned it.

"A secret code and new chainmail," Calaf said, "we're invincible."

"Invincible!" Ishmael shouted and threw his arms around his *rada* brother.

The doors to the palace hall opened to a fanfare of horns followed by the banquet master's solemn declaration, "Calaf, son of Timur, prince and heir to the throne of the Kushan Empire."

Dressed in Calaf's army cadet uniform, Ishmael marched stiff-legged down the row of tables, battle shield extended arm's length before him, sword pointing toward the ceiling, shouting, "One—two—three—five—no, four—five—seven—damn! lost count—one—two—three—"

Gasps of surprise and suppressed laughter followed Ishmael as he moved past the gathered court, his eyes focused on the emperor, sitting on his throne behind a massive raised table. *Laugh, please laugh.* To his relief Timur's open mouth of initial shock turned into a smile and he began to clap.

At that moment the banquet master intoned, "Ishmael, son of Aric, *rada* brother to Calaf, son of Timur."

Calaf skipped into the hall wearing Ishmael's familiar tunic and cap, a lute raised above his head, his voice lifted in an off-key screech. "My love awaits me / crying herself to sleep / her heart broken / as I roam the world / searching for—searching for—hey, prince, I forgot what we're searching for?"

"Six—seven—*a camel—a camel, stupid*—eight—eleven—damn—"

Calaf rushed forward. Lute, shield, and sword clattered to the floor. Arms around each other's shoulders the boys sang, "My love awaits me / crying herself to sleep / her heart broken / as I roam the world / searching for a stupid camel to love."

To laughter and cheers, by then the loudest from the emperor, the boys bowed then raced for the emperor's dais. Ishmael reached the prince's throne first but stepped back to allow Calaf to take his place beside his father. But Calaf shoved Ishmael onto his throne and took the other chair.

Amid more cheering someone shouted, "All hail Prince Ishmael!"

Ishmael visibly cringed. Calaf laughed and slapped him on the back. "They love you."

Timur leaned toward them. "And whose idea was this?"

In unison, they pointed at each other and said, "His."

Timur stared at them through narrowed eyes, lines tightening across his brow. Ishmael recognized the expression from his years as the emperor's squire and grew anxious for it often preceded an angry outburst. But then Timur's face relaxed into a wide smile. "I doubt the banquet master will ever forgive you for ruining the solemnity of the entrance ritual."

Calaf grinned. "His face said he was appalled, but his eyes said he loved it."

As the commotion from the boys' entrance began to subside, Timur whispered past Ishmael to Calaf, "It's time to take your place."

As Ishmael began to rise, Calaf stopped him. "Father, today I honor my friend and *rada* brother."

Ishmael felt tension leap between father and son. "Please, Calaf, allow me to switch," he whispered.

But before Calaf could respond Timur answered. "No, Ishmael, as my son honors you, so must I."

Sensing the emperor's irritation, Ishmael tried to ignore his discomfort by gazing over the hall as it began to settle in anticipation of the arrival of the feast. He spotted his mother at the royal household's table. He tried to catch her eye, but she was distracted by the talkative Mahesh. Ishmael smiled to himself. The *chakor* anniversary was the only time he sat at the emperor's table for a royal banquet. Otherwise he joined his mother, and she always placed him between her and Mahesh so that he was the focus of the eunuch's incessant chatter.

Timur placed his hand on Ishmael's forearm. "Your father tells me that your mastery of the Persian language is improving. That will be an important skill as the prince's future scribe."

"His scribe, sir?" While not a complete surprise, Ishmael fought to hide his disappointment. He did not want to be a scribe. His sights were set on a physician's life. Aric was vocal in his disapproval while Demetrius remained diplomatically neutral. Calaf's only reaction was, "Everyone knows being a scribe is better." But Ishmael had always hoped that the choice would be his.

Timur responded, "You will continue to follow in your father's footsteps. You served me well as my squire, as did he, and now you shall become the scribe to my son and heir."

"A great honor, sire. My father will be most pleased." Ishmael hid the deep ache that filled his chest and gave a quick look at the table assigned to the emperor's advisors and found Demetrius, who glanced up at him. His sad expression told Ishmael that he knew what had happened. Timur waved the ancient scholar Darvash to approach. Bent but refusing a walking stick, the white-haired man hobbled quickly forward until he stood before the emperor and twisted his head at an awkward angle so his eyes met Timur's.

"Aric is too occupied to provide the instruction you now need, so Darvash will become your teacher."

Darvash pulled a small package from his robes and lifted it toward Ishmael. Ishmael leaned across the table and took it from the scholar's ink-stained fingers. "I understand you enjoy drawing," Darvash said.

"Colored chalks." Ishmael showed them to Calaf then retook the scholar's hand. "They're beautiful. Thank you."

Darvash stepped back from the table, bowed to the emperor, and as he hobbled back to his seat, Timur shouted, "Nozar—now."

Nozar motioned Calaf to join him in front of the dais. He then clapped his hands several times, and the palace hall doors opened to soldiers in full battle armor carrying a low table. By the time the table sat before Nozar and Calaf, the emperor stood proudly beside them. Arrayed upon the table was a set of the battle gear worn by the soldiers.

Timur's voice boomed, "Armor fit for my heir."

"Even a new shield," cried Calaf lifting it high above his head. Glancing toward Ishmael, he called out, "Come see."

But as Ishmael stepped off the dais, Timur glared at him and shook his head. Ishmael went to a side door and left the hall. Leaning against the corridor wall, his mind reeled as banquet attendants rushed around him. Never had he felt so unsettled around the emperor. Adding to Ishmael's confusion was its happening now, the one time a year when Timur treated Calaf and him as *rada* brothers, not as prince and servant. The emperor had even dramatically emphasized that difference by calling Darvash forward to announce that Ishmael was to become Calaf's scribe. Why would he do such a thing at their *chakor* celebration? Had their entrance prank gone too far? Had he drawn Timur's anger by making sport of the prince before the entire court?

The door to the hall opened and Sharina slipped into the hall. Ishmael forced a smile as she approached. "Mother."

"You will be missed if you're away too long," she said, placing a hand on his shoulder.

"But the emperor dismissed me."

"I saw," Sharina said, "but it's only because he wanted that moment with Calaf alone."

"No, there's more. I've offended him somehow."

"Haven't you learned yet that rulers are easily offended?" She grinned and patted his cheek. "Careful you don't offend him even more by walking out of your *chakor* celebration in front of his court. Come."

Ishmael pulled back. "I can't walk back in *with* you."

"Of course. I forgot that you're a young man now and can't be seen doing your mother's bidding."

They both smiled and he gave her a slight bow. "Mother."

She returned to the banquet hall, disappearing with a small wave of the hand. He took a deep breath to steady himself.

He and Calaf were seven years old, a year after the queen had died. The emperor had charged Sharina with managing the royal household, including raising the child prince. They were playing on the floor as Sharina embroidered nearby. He went to her and stood. He remembered waiting a long while before she looked up. When she did, it was to scold him.

"Oh, Ishmael, look what you made me do. I missed a stitch."

"I'm sorry."

"So, what is it?"

He blurted out, "Are you really my mother?"

She carefully set her embroidery aside before speaking. "Why ask such a terrible question?"

"I heard—" He froze. Her lips had turned into a thin line, always a sign that she was about to yell at him. Instead she lifted him onto her lap. He kept as still as he could, feeling his heart beating fast. He looked toward Calaf, who now stood staring at them.

"What did you hear, Ishmael?"

Something in her voice scared him and he tried to climb down, but her grip tightened. "You can tell me. I won't be angry."

When he began to cry, Calaf rushed forward. "Your handmaidens—they said you are more like a mother to me than to him."

She let Ishmael squirm off her lap then pulled both boys into her arms. "Oh, Ishmael, I am now mother to you both. You know why, don't you?"

Through his sniffling, he said, "Because Calaf's mother died."

"That's right. And I must pay more attention to him because the emperor expects me to. Don't forget he is the prince and someday must wisely rule his father's empire. You understand, don't you?"

He nodded vigorously.

"Good," she said and kissed his head. "Now go play and forget this nonsense."

Even though Sharina began to pay more attention to him—at least publicly—Ishmael never felt certain from one day to the next which mother he would find. Most days she was distant, and because she grew impatient in his presence, he learned to steer clear of her unless it was necessary. But then without warning she would change. She would greet him warmly. He would stiffen when she embraced him and she would say, 'That's no way to hug your mother,' then playfully tickle his sides. Then she would invite him to join her for a meal, just the two of them, and encourage him to talk about whatever interested him. He might relate something funny and she would laugh. She would stroke his cheek after the meal and say they should share a meal more often. He would always feel a moment's exhilaration, hoping her affection might last. But by the next day her usual distance would return. He did not observe such mood swings when she was with Calaf and decided she must feel compelled to control them around the prince to avoid being reported to the emperor.

Over time he grew reconciled to his mother's devotion to Calaf. In fact, his initial jealousy became relief, particularly as they grew older and he watched his friend's frustration turn to concealed hostility at her increased supervision, demands and restrictions. Rarely did they apply to him, unless they involved Calaf as well, and typically it was Calaf's transgressions that found the two of them facing her wrath together, such as one time when he and Calaf were ten years old.

Demetrius often took them to play in the cooling waters of the stream that flowed outside Peshawar's walls. On the hottest days, men and boys crowded the pools and banks. Most were naked, pulling on loincloths only as they neared the city gate on their return. No women or girls were allowed into this area—they bathed further downstream in a secluded area surrounded by thick brush and trees.

Late one afternoon they were playing chase along the top of the city wall when Calaf abruptly stopped. Ishmael careened into him, sending them falling into a jumble of arms and legs. Calaf signaled him to stay down and be quiet, and standing on his toes he peered over the wall.

"They're going to the trees to bathe."

"Who?"

Calaf slapped him on the head. "Women, stupid."

"So?"

"Let's spy on them."

"They'll catch us."

"No, they won't." Calaf pulled him to his feet. "Look."

A little taller than Calaf, he did not need to stand on his toes to see over the wall. "At what?"

"The bushes—see how they go from the wall to the trees. We can crawl between them."

"Now?"

"Yes, now." Calaf grabbed Ishmael's arm and pulled him toward the spiral stairs that descended into the street. Emerging from the city gate he said, "We go slow and act like we're looking for lizards."

Ishmael never resisted Calaf's enthusiasm for long. But after navigating the bushes and rushing to the first tree, a stout elderly woman caught them. Scolding them as two other women stripped them of their clothes, she sent them running naked back the way they came. The whistles and shouts of guards atop the wall betrayed an audience to their misadventure. When they reached the wall, Calaf stood defiantly while a chagrined Ishmael crouched, trying to disappear. A guard saved them from further embarrassment by tossing down a cotton sack that they ripped into strips for makeshift loincloths.

They navigated the city's back alleys, managing to avoid anyone who might recognize them. It was dark by the time they climbed the palace wall and dropped into the courtyard that fronted the royal quarters. As they crept toward the white mulberry whose branches gave them access to their shared quarters on the second level, Calaf whispered, "We made it."

Relief washed through Ishmael. But at the base of the tree they found Mahesh waiting.

"My prince, Master Ishmael, Lady Sharina awaits you. Come."

When the eunuch ushered them before Sharina, she sat erect on a couch, her hands clasped tightly in her lap. Ishmael remembered her eyes blazing while her face remained like a stone statue. Their clothes were folded on a table before her. Sharina did not speak. She focused a long stare at the prince but only glanced briefly at Ishmael.

Finally Calaf broke the silence. "It was all my idea. Ishmael didn't want—"

She interrupted him with a raised hand. "There are those who would laugh at what you did and call it a boyish prank. If you were not the prince, I might agree. But you are the prince and have a responsibility to behave like one."

Calaf muttered under his breath, "My father would laugh."

"What did you say?" she snapped.

"My father would laugh." Loud and insolent this time. Ishmael resisted kicking him, fearing Calaf just made their punishment worse but also knowing Calaf did not care.

Sharina did not react to the prince's defiance, remaining calm as she said, "But he is not here, and my word is his—at his command. For one month you are confined to your quarters. Guards will be posted at the door—and below the window. Defy this punishment in any way, and I will extend it." She paused a moment but Calaf held his tongue. Then she turned her gaze on Ishmael. "You are also confined but will not share the prince's quarters." Even though there could be no punishment worse than separation from Calaf, Ishmael knew he dared not react.

Afterward Calaf schemed to make another attempt to spy on the women. For the first time, Ishmael sensed this difference between them, for he had no interest in those trees, preferring to remain around the men. A year later they were at the stream when Calaf disappeared. Soon afterward shouts arose from the distant trees. Several men grew attentive but the clamor immediately ceased and they resumed bathing. Not wanting to attract attention, Ishmael waited before slipping away downstream, arriving in time to see his mother storm into the trees, obviously summoned by the bathing women. Moments later she reemerged with a naked Calaf in tow. Ishmael dropped to the ground behind a bush, but not before Calaf spotted him and gave an exaggerated wink. Later he regaled Ishmael with the story of a successful mission that only ended because he leaned out on a branch to get a better look and it snapped, sending him splashing into the stream to the screams of the women.

As Ishmael followed, scrambling low to the ground between bushes, Calaf did not resist Sharina's pulling him until they neared the city gate. When he did balk, she slowly turned to face him.

He dropped his free hand to cover his crotch. "Give me something to cover myself."

"No," she said. "You will proceed to the palace as you are." When he tried to break her hold on his arm, she called out and two guards approached from the gate. "Walk before them or they will drag you. Choose."

Calaf chose to cavort. Playing to loud cheers and laughter, the prince frolicked and danced, greeting all who stopped to watch. He did not go far before one of the guards handed him a loincloth. After the prince tied it, the guards took his elbows and following Sharina, guided him toward the palace. Afterward, an unspoken—and uneasy—truce developed between them, only occasionally erupting into open confrontation and then never publicly.

When Ishmael slipped back into the banquet hall, Calaf rushed up to him, now fully outfitted in his new battle armor. "What do you think?"

"The enemy will take one look and run."

Calaf jabbed at Ishmael's stomach with a quick fist. "No, they must fight me first. Then they can run."

Seeing the emperor approach, Ishmael absorbed the punch, resisting the temptation to grab Calaf's arm and try to wrestle him to the floor. He bowed deeply. "My lord, it is a fine and princely gift."

Timur acknowledged Ishmael with a distracted nod before guiding Calaf back onto the dais where he directed him to the prince's throne. Ishmael was about to follow when Aric called out, "A moment, son." When Ishmael turned, his parents stood before him. "While not as grand a gift," Aric said, "it is one we believe you will enjoy." Sharina stepped out from behind her husband and presented Ishmael with a short, almond-shaped lute.

"A barbat," Ishmael whispered in amazement. He recognized it from a year earlier when a troupe of Bactrian musicians entertained at court. Having only seen long-necked lutes, he had begged and been allowed to play it, and it was all he talked about for weeks afterward.

After thanking and embracing Aric then Sharina, he turned to find Calaf before him. "Ah, your barbat."

"You knew?"

Calaf nodded. "You must play something."

"Here?"

"But of course."

By then Demetrius and General Nozar had joined them, along with a growing number of others, all encouraging Ishmael to show them what the unusual instrument sounded like. Calaf pulled a bench behind Ishmael. "Play."

Ishmael sat and held the instrument high on his chest, angling the neck while keeping the soundboard turned slightly toward the ceiling. He placed curved fingers on the animal gut strings, glanced up at Calaf, and played a subdued melancholy tune. The banquet hall quieted around them.

When Ishmael finished and rested the barbat in his lap, Sharina said, "Such a somber melody for a festive moment."

"It's the lament of Orpheus after he fails to rescue Eurydice from the underworld."

"I recognize it from my youth in Athens," Demetrius said. "How did you learn it?"

"A Greek I met at last year's *Holi* festival taught it to me."

Demetrius said, "You did justice to a difficult piece."

Calaf nudged Ishmael's shoulder with his hip. "Enough of sorrow—now play something we can dance to."

A quick, spritely tune quickly returned the banquet hall to its earlier boisterousness. Ishmael caught his mother's eye and smiled, but she seemed not to notice.

Aric waited in the courtyard below the royal apartments. From the shadows he watched three soldiers emerge with an excited Calaf, who was pestering his escort with questions. Soon afterward an agitated Ishmael appeared and crossed the courtyard. Aric knew his son went in search of Demetrius. He could not recall the last time Ishmael came to him when troubled. The emperor had surprised everyone at that morning's council meeting with his decision to separate Calaf and Ishmael. When Demetrius ventured to ask why, Timur answered, "The prince must move beyond boyhood attachments—and favorites."

Head down, hands behind his back, Aric walked around the courtyard garden before climbing the stairway to Sharina's quarters. For several years after their marriage they had shared the apartment, but upon his return from one of his long absences with the emperor she suggested he take a nearby apartment *for his comfort.* Seeing his distress Demetrius had urged him to insist they continue to share an apartment. But Aric said, "I will not force her," and let the moment pass.

As Aric entered her quarters, Sharina emerged from her bedchamber. Without a word or glance, she walked across the reception room onto the balcony. Aric waited a moment, took a deep breath and followed, stopping at the balcony opening.

Sharina kept her back to him but turned her head in profile. "How many years ago did the queen die?"

"The boys were six, I believe."

"So it's eight years since the emperor ordered that I oversee the royal household and raise his son."

"Yes, eight."

"And he's satisfied, is he not?"

"I have heard him compliment your efficiency."

"And yet, he did not see fit to inform me of the decision to remove the prince from my care. I only learn of it as he is being escorted from the palace by armed soldiers."

"He forbade anyone tell you beforehand."

She spun about and glared at him in silence.

Aric stepped across the balcony and placed a hand on her shoulder. "Please do not take offense. It is actually good news. You are no longer burdened with the prince." He stroked her face with his fingertips. "Think now of Ishmael. With Calaf gone, he will need you more than ever."

Sharina pushed his hand away. Without a word she left the balcony and returned to her bedchamber.

Sharina sat on the edge of her bed. Beside her, red silk flowed out of an open black enamel box. In her lap lay a small wooden horse, battered by childhood play. Beside it rested its tail, separated from the body.

When the boys were toddlers, she had watched in anguish as Ishmael—son of that monster—played with Ashu's gift from his father. The boys sometimes fought over the horse. One day when they were three years old, Calaf took the horse from Ishmael's hands. When Ishmael tried to take it back, he grabbed the horse's tail and broke it off. Sharina's scream startled both boys. Calaf scrambled away leaving the horse behind. Ishmael started to cry. Sharina took Ishmael by the shoulders, shaking him and wailing into his face, as he howled in terror and dropped the tail. Afterward neither boy asked for the wooden horse or ever saw it again.

Carefully Sharina rewrapped the horse and its tail in the red silk and returned them to their box. Tears began to slide down her cheeks, and she covered her face with her hands.

"Calaf, my Calaf," she murmured.

She should have had another year to prepare herself. An ache rose from her chest and a constrained cry escaped her mouth. She pulled her knees to her chin and rocked. A noise. Her eyes flew open. Aric stood inside the closed door.

"Go away!" she screamed.

He approached, his steps cautious, his face etched in concern. "Not while you are in such despair."

She hid her face. "Please, leave," her voice now a whisper.

He sat beside her. When she tried to move away, he reached his arms around her. She resisted, but his embrace was firm and surprisingly gentle.

"Allow me. It has been a long time since I held you."

He eased her head to his shoulder and as he stroked her hair, she relaxed and began to softly cry.

Torak was dying, and nothing Demetrius did could change that. Soon after Timur's army had returned to Peshawar for the winter, the abdominal pains had begun. Torak insisted it was something he ate, but his nighttime sweats raised Demetrius's fears. Within weeks the swelling began and the pain, increasingly unbearable, sent him to the garrison infirmary.

It wasn't long before Torak asked, "Am I dying?"

At first Demetrius could not answer, and his eyes became moist. Torak squeezed his hand and smiled. "You're always so calm and strong with your other patients."

"You're not my other patients."

Torak lifted his arm. "You thought I'd lose it after the battle at Mathura."

"You were fortunate the infection didn't reach the bone."

"Maybe I'll be fortunate again," Torak said.

"Maybe."

Torak sighed. "But not likely."

As much as Demetrius wanted to offer hope to his lover, he knew Torak demanded nothing but truth from him. He shook his head.

"Will it be bad?"

"I'm afraid so," Demetrius answered. "The tumor grows quickly. The poppy might not be enough."

"I always thought I'd die in battle."

"As did I," Demetrius said as he stroked Torak's face.

Demetrius had risen before dawn to tend to Torak, fretting over the late arrival of the woman who cared for his dying friend during the day. Then he endured Timur's public reprimand when, out of breath, he appeared only moments after the emperor's council meeting began. Now as long shadows from the late afternoon sun stretched across Peshawar's central square, he walked slowly on the uneven pavement, favoring his left leg, bruised several days earlier in a fall while navigating the palace's marble steps. He gave wide berth to a group of boys kicking a hemp-covered ball, which rebounded off the low wall of the central fountain and rolled into his path. He moved aside moments before the boys descended, oblivious to his presence, arms and legs flailing, while driving the ball toward an imaginary goal across the square. At one boy's excited shout he smiled, remembering playing a similar game on the streets of Athens. Too long ago, he thought, feeling all his fifty-four years. Stopping to rest on the stone edge of the fountain, he looked toward the smell of roasted meat. A small queue waited outside a tavern he and Torak often frequented. A pottery merchant stood before his shop and yelled at the boys to take their game elsewhere. A young mother rushed along the shaded perimeter, scolding the child beside her to keep up.

A loud voice calling his name startled him. Ishmael weaved through the group of boys, kicking their ball toward a side street, sending them scurrying after it. As their shouts faded away, the gangly youth, out of breath, his face tight with distress, dropped onto the fountain wall. "Soldiers came. They took Calaf away."

Demetrius placed his hand on Ishmael's knee. "The emperor announced it this afternoon. Calaf begins his military training."

"But that's not until next year. We will train together—next year—when we're fifteen."

"The emperor wants the prince to begin now."

"Then I'm going, too, right?"

Demetrius shook his head and watched disbelief wash across Ishmael's face.

"Why not?"

"You're only fourteen."

"But—"

"The emperor decreed Calaf must have no distractions."

"That can't mean me." Ishmael was incredulous.

"I'm sorry it does."

"But can't you—?"

"Your father and I both tried. The emperor was most emphatic." Demetrius watched tears wet Ishmael's eyes and gave his knee a gentle squeeze. "Your time apart will pass quickly."

Ishmael jumped to his feet. "You don't understand!" The shout attracted the attention of those waiting in front of the tavern.

Demetrius grasped Ishmael's hand. "I do, believe me I do."

Ishmael yanked away from the physician and ran from the square. As Demetrius watched him go, his eyes came to rest on Torak's caregiver rushing toward him.

Torak had been raised Buddhist. His mother had taught him the Heart Sutra, just as Sharina's had taught her. So despite Demetrius's aversion to religion, when Sharina appeared with two monks at the door of their room, Demetrius stepped aside, motioning them to enter. She covered her mouth to contain a cough. The burning sulfur did little to mask the smell of impending death. After the monks bowed and offered quiet words of solace, Demetrius led them to the low bed where Torak lay on his side, one arm holding his swollen abdomen, the other extended between his bent legs, unconscious but moaning with each labored breath. The monks knelt and began to chant.

Sharina touched Demetrius's arm. "They may bring him comfort the poppy does not."

Demetrius led her to the room's shallow balcony where several pillows lay. They knelt facing each other and Demetrius turned his face to the evening sky. "It won't be long now."

Sharina placed her hand on his leg. "It was kind of Nozar to allow you to move him here from the infirmary."

"Yes, it was." Demetrius rested his hand on hers. They sat in silence, listening to the steady rhythm of the monks' voices. "My mind is at peace with his passing." He paused a moment before reciting, "Therefore understanding that death brings both body and soul to an end makes every moment of life enjoyable."

"Your Epicurus?"

"You remember." He squeezed her hand, then added, "There is nothing after death to be feared."

"But it's not your mind that seeks consolation."

Demetrius returned his face to the sky. “For myself I have no difficulty accepting that what I have here and now is all there is.” He lowered his face and looked into the darkened room. “But how do I accept losing him?”

Torak took his last breath as dawn brightened the eastern sky.

CHAPTER 6

Captain Barzin looked up as the flap of his tent parted and General Nozar entered. Barzin rose and the two men grasped each other's forearms.

"You could have sent for me, Father."

"I needed the air, and your tent is on the way."

"On the way where?"

Nozar gave his son a gentle cuff to the head. "She won't be pleased you forgot."

Barzin hesitated then remembered. "Mother's party."

"Looking forward to it, are we?"

"I'd rather fight the Persians."

Nozar gave a hearty laugh. "Your mother says Governor Zubair's niece is quite lovely." Barzin groaned, and Nozar punched his shoulder. "It's just one evening, and next week we leave for Srinagar. Speaking of which—"

As Nozar moved to his son's cot, Barzin sat on a log stool and began his report on the supply caravan that would accompany the army's three-month march to Srinagar, concluding with, "We still don't have enough spare wagon wheels."

Barzin watched his father struggle to hide his anger at the news that a close associate of Governor Zubair had failed to deliver as contracted. Nozar barked, "Get a message to the garrison commander at Guirat to have what we need ready when we get there next month. I'll deal with Zubair's wheelwright." He took a deep breath before asking, "Anything more?"

"That Roman mercenary you ordered transferred from the garrison at Rajanpur arrived this morning." Hoping to ease the tension, Barzin gave a laugh and said, "And the stories are true. He *is* bigger than you."

Nozar grunted. "Talked to him yet?"

"I tried. He speaks just enough Bactrian to take and give orders. His Greek's not much better, but then neither is mine. Why bring him here?"

"His commander reported he had an unusual mercenary, an escaped Roman gladiator. It seems this Flavus took command when his patrol officer was injured in a rebel skirmish and saved them all at great risk to his own life. Afterward he declined extra gold for his bravery. After a story like that, I had to see him for myself."

"Where do you want him assigned?"

"To my guard detail. And how's the prince?"

"Exhausted but thriving. Happier than any recruit should be. But he wants to say goodbye to Ishmael."

"You've told him what the emperor ordered?"

"Yes, but he doesn't understand why being the prince denies him the contacts with family and friends the other recruits are allowed."

"Then deny the other recruits."

"Sir?"

"You know I have no choice in this." Nozar rose and patted his son's shoulder.

Barzin said, "I heard that Torak died."

"A horrible death. Aric asked me to approach the emperor about allowing Demetrius to stay in Peshawar for a few months so Sharina can watch over him, but the emperor will never agree. He demands his physician's presence wherever he goes."

"There's always the spare wagon wheels." A puzzled look crossed Nozar's face. "Listen, even after we reach Srinagar, we'll need extras. Even more so in the mountainous terrain. Who better than one of the emperor's most trusted advisors to make certain that the wheelwright completes the job and the wheels are safely delivered?" A broad grin spread across Nozar's scarred face. Barzin returned the smile, followed by a conspiratorial wink. "This earns me a pass for Mother's party, doesn't it?"

Nozar returned the wink and moved to leave but hesitated. "The Roman—he's really bigger than me?"

Barzin nodded.

"But not as handsome, right?"

Both laughed as Nozar pushed aside the tent flap and departed.

Flavus pulled his cloak tighter around his thick neck and stretched his long legs before the fire's glowing embers. The steady rumble of camp life was easing early that night. At dawn the emperor's army would depart Peshawar to begin a three-month winter procession through the southern provinces on its way to its spring and summer encampment in Srinagar's mountain valley. Except for those on watch, most soldiers were already asleep in their tents or rolled up in blankets on the ground against the chill of winds from the Khyber Pass's snow-covered slopes.

Earlier that evening he had reported to the general and was still bristling at his orders.

Nozar had sat at a folding table and glanced up from a parchment as a guard parted the tent flaps and Flavus entered.

The general smiled. "You *are* as big as they said."

Flavus returned a quizzical expression. "Sir?"

"Don't you speak Bactrian?"

"A little."

"Greek?"

"A little more."

"Learn more Bactrian," the general ordered.

"Yes, sir."

Shifting to Greek, Nozar said, "I understand you were a gladiator."

"Yes, sir."

"Then you will teach the emperor's son to fight."

Flavus struggled to hide his surprise. "Sir?"

"The boy is younger than the other recruits. You will ready him to train with them once we reach Srinagar. Do you understand?"

"Yes, sir."

"Then report to Captain Barzin. Dismissed."

Two years he had labored as a Roman gladiator-turned-mercenary, noted as much for living hard and fighting harder as by his size and otherness. Disciplined, good-natured, and well-liked by his comrades, he had earned the attention of his commanders but resisted their entreaties to leave the mercenary ranks. One even offered to place him over his own company if he would simply learn the Bactrian language. But Flavus insisted—in broken Greek—that he wished nothing more than what he had, leading many to speculate that the gladiator had taken too many blows to the head in the arena. But it had all been a ruse that had finally brought him, one of the Roman Emperor's personal network of spies, within reach of his objective to imbed himself in the highest levels of the Kushan army to determine its strengths and weaknesses. The Emperor wanted to know if the Kushans might be a possible ally in Rome's ongoing conflict with Persia. But instead of an assignment that would allow him to begin ingratiating himself to leadership, he was playing nursemaid to a boy prince. Not only that, until they reached Srinagar he was assigned to the first watch over the prince and his fellow recruits.

Flavus tossed more wood on the fire. As sparks leapt from the embers, he spotted a recruit slipping out of his tent and disappearing into the darkness.

Flavus groaned and climbed to his feet.

The two boys huddled together in a hollow between two boulders outside the perimeter of the army encampment. No moon lit the night, only the stars cast a faint light.

"It's not fair." Anger caused Ishmael's voice to rise above a whisper.

Calaf covered his friend's mouth. "Shh. We'll be discovered."

"Your father can't do this—I'll run away, follow you."

"That's dumb."

"What? You don't want me around?"

"That's even dumber."

"Then it's her." When Calaf did not respond, Ishmael's voice rose again. "I hate her."

"Shh. You must not—she's your mother."

"But she drives you away from me."

"It's Timur's decision not hers. Anyway, the time will pass quickly."

"Maybe for you it will."

A snapped branch cracked nearby.

"Go now—quietly," Calaf said, leaping to his feet and disappearing into the darkness.

Ishmael did not move, silent tears wetting his cheeks. Why did he care whether or not he was discovered?

Flavus stepped into the straying recruit's path and knocking him to the ground, he placed his boot on the boy's chest. "If I enemy, you dead," he said in broken Bactrian.

The boy pounded Flavus's calf with his fists. "Let me up."

Flavus dropped down, replacing his boot with his knee, and grasped the boy's jaw and squeezed. "Hit me again, I break you." When the boy went limp, Flavus said, "I hear voices."

"A friend. I was saying good-bye to a friend."

"In dark?" Flavus growled.

The boy remained silent.

"I on watch. You make me look bad. Not again." Flavus released the boy's jaw and stood. "Go!" As the boy scrambled to his feet and bolted toward the camp, Flavus grinned, satisfied that once word of this encounter spread among the recruits he would have no further problems with them.

As the army prepared to depart at dawn, Captain Barzin marched up to Flavus with the prince, a fresh bruise clearly visible along the boy's jaw. Flavus cursed under his breath.

Pointing at Calaf's jaw, Barzin said to Flavus, "I understand this incident happened on your watch."

"It did, sir." Flavus braced himself to accept the consequences for assaulting the emperor's son.

"You will not allow fighting among the recruits again, soldier."

"Sir?"

"And while I respect the prince's desire not to implicate the other recruit, he now understands—king's son or not—we do not tolerate fighting in the ranks. Your training better exhaust him so much he's not tempted to do it again."

Confused but relieved, Flavus saluted. "It will, sir."

Barzin gave Calaf a stern look. "No more trouble, recruit."

"Understood, sir," the prince said.

When Barzin departed, Calaf whispered, "Last night was best kept between us, don't you agree?" Without waiting for an answer, he rushed off to join the other recruits.

"Brazen whelp," Flavus muttered under his breath.

CHAPTER 7

Srinagar

Ishmael stood apart as Calaf convinced his three bodyguards to remain on the road at the foot of the hill. Then taking him by the hand, Calaf led him up the steep incline to the edge of a forest of chir pines. Calaf's baggy cotton trousers were tied loosely at the waist, his shirt open, revealing a muscular chest. The gold ankle band he wore as an infant hung from a chain around his neck. Ishmael—taller and slimmer—had arrived that morning from Peshawar with Demetrius, and in his eagerness to reunite with his friend still wore the dust-covered trousers and flowing tunic of his journey. A shout from below stopped them, the officer responsible for the prince's protection waving for them to stop.

Calaf groaned. "Naveen worries too much."

"And what, you've never given him any reason to?"

Calaf delivered a sharp jab into Ishmael's ribs. Before he could pull his hand back Ishmael grabbed his wrists, twisting them and bringing Calaf to his knees. He pushed him onto his back and planted his knee on Calaf's chest.

Calaf laughed. "Show respect to your prince."

"Always your humble servant." With a flourish of his arms Ishmael moved to rise, but Calaf grabbed his leg and pushed, throwing him off-balance and sending him onto his back. Calaf scrambled on top of him, planting his knees on either side of Ishmael's waist and sitting back on his thighs. Ishmael put his hands behind his head and looked up at his friend. “I’ve missed you.”

Calaf grinned, then grabbed and tweaked Ishmael’s nose. “It’s only been three months.”

Ishmael laughed and batted Calaf’s hand away. “But we’ve never been apart this long.”

“You’re right—I hadn’t thought of that.” Calaf glanced about. “We forgot the food. Wait here. I’ll get it.”

When Calaf returned, Ishmael was looking toward the city. On their journey from Peshawar, Demetrius had told him Srinagar was ancient—over a thousand years old—and that it sat on an island in the middle of the Jhelum River, which flowed through the fertile Kashmiri Valley on its journey from the distant Himalayas to the Indus, a twenty-day caravan journey to the southwest. Ishmael could see only three of the city’s five bridges. The closest and largest—named after Ashoka the Great, who ruled all of India after Alexander—was the one he and Demetrius had used that morning.

Ishmael said, “Everything is so green.”

“And wet.” Calaf dropped to the ground at Ishmael’s feet and started opening pouches of dried fruit and nuts. Calaf handed him a leather flask. “Watered down compliments of Naveen—you may actually taste the wine.”

After Ishmael drank and handed the flask back to Calaf, he scanned the panorama before them. “Where do you live?”

“See the tents to the south of the city, on the far side of the river? That’s where the army is. The small ones closest to the river—mine’s there with the other recruits. Father insists I eat, sleep, train and live just like everyone else. I love it.” Calaf lay back and yawned. “But it’s nice being out of uniform.” Putting both hands behind his head, he focused his gaze on the cloudless sky beyond the pine canopy. After a few moments he said, “I still can’t believe Father agreed to your becoming a physician.”

“Demetrius can be convincing.” Ishmael stretched out on his side with one hand propping up his head. He traced circles on Calaf’s chest and stomach with a pine needle.

"But Father ordered you to be a scribe." Calaf brushed Ishmael's hand away. "And Aric says you're the best student he's ever had."

"Now I'll be the best apprentice Demetrius ever had."

Ishmael grabbed Calaf's thigh and gave it a hard squeeze. Calaf yelped and threw himself on top of Ishmael, grabbing his wrists and planting them against the ground. Ishmael howled and tried to kick free, but Calaf locked his feet around Ishmael's legs. Face to face, they laughed and cursed each other between quick, excited breaths. Finally Ishmael nodded in submission. Calaf sat back on Ishmael's thighs, arms raised in triumph.

Ishmael massaged his wrists. "You're stronger and quicker."

"It's because of Flavus. He's teaching me to fight. A real Roman gladiator. Wait'll you see him. He's bigger than Nozar."

"Nobody's that big." Ishmael touched Calaf's stomach with his index finger and moved it down to the waist of Calaf's trousers and began playing with the drawstring, which had loosened in their wrestling.

"No, he is. He's fought in the Colosseum at Rome—you have to be big to fight there." Calaf climbed off Ishmael and lay back down on the ground next to him and retied the drawstring. "He's from some place called Germania and has white skin and yellow hair."

"Now I know you're making it up."

"You'll see. Tomorrow you'll come watch me train." Calaf waited until Ishmael nodded. "Good. He's a *retiarius*, you know."

"A what?"

"He fights with a net."

"Sounds stupid."

"It's not. Just wait."

The boys became quiet. The silence was interrupted only by an occasional shout of a herder or merchant on the road that rounded the foot of the hill before making a straight line toward the bridge and gate of Ashoka.

Calaf asked, "Is your mother still angry?"

"I believe so. The emperor's taking you away was a surprise—for all of us."

"It was only a year early—anyway, I was ready."

"To get away from her?"

"That too. How's Demetrius?"

"Better. After you left, Mother finally roused him from his room. They took Torak's ashes to Minnagara where the monks chanted over them, and then placed them in a small boat to float to the sea."

"But Demetrius doesn't believe in all that."

"No, but she said it helped him. He said it was a beautiful ceremony." Ishmael paused then added, "So sad about Torak—a soldier all his life and to die like that."

"Remember when we surprised them having sex in the woods—"

"—and Torak chased us with Demetrius running after him screaming, *Stop, your clothes!"* Laughter consumed both boys.

Struggling to catch his breath, Ishmael gasped, "Have you ever seen a bigger cock?"

"Never." Then Calaf turned serious. "I will miss him."

Ishmael traced Calaf's jaw line with his finger. "You're growing a beard."

"You got hair on your legs first."

"I'd rather have a beard."

"Will you stay with Aric?"

"No, I'll be with Demetrius. Remember I'm his apprentice now." Calaf's jaw became rigid, his mouth tensing as his lips formed a tight line. "What's wrong?"

Calaf brushed away Ishmael's hand. "You were supposed to follow your father. One day you were going to be my scribe, just as your father is to mine."

"Now I shall be your physician."

"You know it's not the same." *Not the same at all.* In the hierarchy of royal servants, scribes were near the top, physicians near the bottom. And scribes were rarely removed for an error in their work while physicians rarely survived theirs—Demetrius's longevity was far from usual.

"But doing what my father does—you know it would drive me crazy." Ishmael hesitated before asking, "Are you angry at me?"

"I should be."

Ishmael remained silent and lifted the gold band from Calaf's chest, turning it around on its chain, whispering its inscription, "Son of Timur, Prince, Warrior, Champion of His People." Releasing the band, he said, "I'm glad it's you and not me." Once again, he made circles on Calaf's chest, this time with his finger. He circled a nipple. It became hard and a bulge grew in Calaf's trousers.

Calaf swatted Ishmael's hand away, "Now look what you've done." Ishmael laughed and tried to scramble away, but Calaf jumped on his back, sending them tumbling down the hillside. Their howls ended in groans as they careened into a large boulder. As they sat up, Ishmael quickly looked about and seeing they were hidden from view, reached between Calaf's legs, but Calaf took Ishmael's hand and lifted it away.

"Don't you want to?" Ishmael asked.

"Something better." Calaf's face filled with a broad grin. He stood, pulling Ishmael with him. "Come."

"Where?"

"A surprise. You're going to love it!"

Calaf bounded down to the road. He waved back at Ishmael, shouting, "Come on—hurry!" and began a fast walk toward the city. Caught unaware, his bodyguards scrambled to follow him. Ishmael stood motionless for a few moments. He took a slow, deep breath before loping down the hill and running to catch up with his friend.

Demetrius and Aric sat outside a tavern fronting on a small square near the Ashoka Gate. A green and white awning provided shade from the intensity of the late afternoon summer sun. Demetrius removed his cap and took a long draft of watered wine from the red clay tankard. His once curly dark hair was gray and receding, leaving most of his head bald. He rubbed his scalp before resting his hand on the small wooden table. Aric, still boyish in his late thirties, reached over and patted Demetrius's hand.

"The journey has exhausted you, my friend."

"I'm getting too old for all this. You can't believe how relieved I am that Ishmael's officially my apprentice."

"You're fortunate Timur is distracted by the Persians. I doubt he would have agreed otherwise—at least not so quickly."

They sat quietly, drinking their wine and watching the flow of people passing through the square. Demetrius traced the tankard's rim with his finger several times before breaking their silence. "My petition couldn't have been a surprise. Surely Timur has noticed Ishmael's hanging around me."

"Yes, he mentioned it several times. First it was, 'He better not be turning the boy Greek,' but later he spotted him gathering roots and herbs."

"First time I ever saw Timur truly angry with him," Demetrius said.

"He applied himself to his language studies after that. But then—" Aric's voice trailed off. He stared into his wine.

"I'm sorry. I know how much it meant to you that he follow in your footsteps."

"Now he's following in yours," his voice almost a whisper. Aric shook his head and laughed. "What do you think these Srinagarans would do if they knew you just wandered into town," he lowered his voice with a complicit wink, "with the son of their dead raja?"

Stunned, Demetrius grabbed Aric's wrist and whispered, "Have you lost your mind?" He scanned those seated around them, relieved that they were engaged in their own conversations.

Aric pulled his wrist free. "I was just—"

"Out of here," he drained his tankard. "Now."

Aric limped after Demetrius and grabbed the sleeve of his tunic. "Forgive me, the wine loosened my tongue."

Demetrius pulled him into a deserted alley. "You put us all at risk." Demetrius took hold of Aric's tunic. "Have you said anything before—anything?"

"Nothing." Aric's voice shook. "Nothing—never."

Demetrius loosened his grip, fear still coursed through his veins. "Forget you and me, we both know what he'd do to Sharina, and he'd do it himself before our eyes—before he ripped them out. And Ishmael, you heard what he did to—" His voice caught. He released Aric and stepped back, dropping his arms to his side. Aric did not move. Long moments passed, neither man speaking.

Aric straightened and placed his hand on Demetrius's shoulder. "You're exhausted."

Demetrius looked up. "I am." He reached out his arms. As the two men embraced, Demetrius felt not only the physical exhaustion of the long journey from Peshawar but also the weariness of his long years surviving in the shadow of Timur.

They emerged from the alley, and Demetrius nudged Aric's shoulder. "I believe you mentioned a bath."

Ishmael jogged around the soldiers following Calaf. He came up beside his friend and matched his quick pace through the late afternoon crowd of shepherds and their flocks, farm workers returning from the fields, and merchants rushing to enter the gates hoping to secure the city's still scarce lodgings.

Calaf punched Ishmael's arm. "To the gate!"

"To the gate!" Ishmael repeated.

Ishmael barely took two steps before tangling with Calaf's outstretched leg and finding himself on his face. As he looked up—coughing in the dirt—he spotted Calaf dodging around a merchant's cart. With the laughter of Calaf's guards burning his ears, he leapt to his feet and gave chase. While he could not match Calaf in strength, he could easily defeat his friend on foot—particularly over a long distance—unless Calaf resorted to trickery, which he often did when faced with defeat. Ishmael maneuvered around the merchant's cart and spotted Calaf charging through a herd of panicked, bleating sheep. By the time Ishmael reached the sheep they were scattered in the fields on both sides of the road, their shepherd cursing and his dog barking. Ishmael gained ground.

Through the thick kicked-up dust he spotted Calaf disappear in the midst of a caravan's wagons, laden camels and mounted guards. While Calaf zigzagged between and around the caravan's obstacles, Ishmael dropped into the dry irrigation ditch that ran parallel to the road. By the time the boys emerged at the front of the caravan, Calaf ran but a few paces ahead, close enough for Ishmael to tackle, a tactic Ishmael often used to teach his friend—to no avail—that cheating did not pay.

The Ashoka Bridge drew close. Predictably Calaf grew tired. Realizing that he could not only win the race to the gate but also take the lead before the bridge, Ishmael pushed his long legs harder. But just as Ishmael pulled up behind his shoulder, Calaf swerved to the right and leapt over the irrigation ditch.

"Unfair!" screamed Ishmael as he watched Calaf redefine the race by taking off toward the river. Calaf ripped off his shirt, flung it behind him without breaking stride, and plunged into the thick reeds bordering the shore.

Ishmael rushed onto the bridge, crossing a quarter of the way before looking down. Calaf emerged from the reeds and began to swim. Pulling off his tunic, Ishmael released a loud cry and dropped feet first into the river. A stronger swimmer, Calaf quickly reached him, grabbing his foot and spinning him about. With a laugh Calaf pushed Ishmael's head underwater. Resurfacing and gasping for breath Ishmael grabbed the fleeing Calaf's ankle. They grappled to excited cheering from the now clogged bridge. When Ishmael broke free, a breathless, sputtering Calaf cried, "Current's getting us!"

As the cries from the bridge drowned out their labored breathing, the boys overcame the slow but steady current and made it to the shore. Ishmael lunged into the reeds, brushing a hand across his face to clear his eyes. Calaf was ahead but slowed by the mud. But Ishmael found firmer ground and emerged first. As he raced through the excited crowd for the Ashoka Gate—encouraging hands slapping his back—he felt Calaf at his heels. He slammed his palm against the gate's rough stone portal and collapsed to the ground, eyes closed, lungs struggling for air, stomach heaving, head throbbing to the cheers around him. He opened his eyes expecting to see a defeated Calaf standing before him. Instead he found the crowd pointing upwards.

Calaf was climbing the city wall.

The noise from the crowd around the Ashoka Gate diverted Aric and Demetrius from their path toward the public bath. A caravan had stalled as it entered the city, its mounted guards distracted by something happening outside the gate. As Aric and Demetrius pushed their way through the commotion, loud cries erupted, followed moments later by cheers.

A distant voice shouted, "The skinny one almost fell off the wall."

Demetrius looked at Aric. "You don't think—?"

Aric pointed at the open gate. The young officer responsible for Calaf's bodyguard was looking up. "Either Naveen allowed this mayhem or couldn't stop it. Either way it's likely we'll see him bruised and digging ditches tomorrow."

Demetrius groaned. "And Ishmael's here less than a day."

"Shall we see what they're up to?"

"I think I'd rather plead ignorance."

Aric hid his disappointment and guided his friend toward a side alley.

Two soldiers waited as Calaf pulled Ishmael over the wall, both collapsing in a heap on the wood deck.

"You cheated." Ishmael's voice broke in fatigue.

"I always cheat. Don't forget, you almost fell, and I saved you."

"After you kicked my head!"

Loud cursing interrupted their squabble. Naveen rushed toward them, his dark face flushed, his eyes blazing. "Do you have any idea what you have done?"

Calaf stood, stretching to his full height to face the taller officer. "I won, sir."

The officer faltered then recovered. "Prince or not, I am your superior officer. Again, I ask, do you have any idea—?"

"Sir, I won."

Naveen looked toward the two soldiers and pointed at Ishmael. "Take him to Demetrius." Then turning to Calaf, "You will return to the garrison with me." The officer turned away.

"Sir, I promised my friend—"

Naveen spun about and glared. "I gave you a direct order."

"My pass—signed by General Nozar—says I am to report to my unit at sunrise. That's an order, too, is it not?" When Naveen said nothing, Calaf added, "Just say we ran a little race, sir."

Neither moved nor spoke for several long moments. Finally, Naveen took a step back. Calaf reached down and pulled an open-mouthed Ishmael to his feet. A soldier handed Calaf his shirt. "We couldn't find your friend's." Calaf nodded his appreciation and led Ishmael off the wall.

Aric and Demetrius emerged from the public bath to darkness, the only light coming from the torch-carrying city guards and scattered oil lamp-lit windows. Even though the nightly curfew had been lifted several months earlier, few walked the narrow streets.

Aric caught Demetrius's elbow as the physician's foot missed the bottom step. "You're certain you don't want a litter?"

"No, no, walking is fine," Demetrius replied. Moments later they moved aside as an ox-pulled cart lumbered by. "That smells good."

"Farhad is delivering his bread." Aric jogged ahead, spoke to the driver, and returned with a round flatbread, which he tore apart. "It's still warm." He handed Demetrius the larger portion. "Best na'an you'll ever taste. Not sure when the old man sleeps—bakes all day, delivers all night."

Demetrius nodded his appreciation. "I hope he has sons to help him."

"Five. Nozar recruited one for the garrison kitchen."

The two men crossed an open square. Two city guards were loudly talking in the shadows at the far end. Demetrius picked up the word *wager* and smiled. Torak loved to gamble. Demetrius placed his arm around Aric's shoulders. "The bath attendant—it was thoughtful of you." Demetrius had not enjoyed the attentions of a man since Torak's passing.

"I wasn't sure but figured you could say no."

"I'm glad I didn't. He was very kind."

They walked in silence to the end of a row of houses. Across the street two soldiers—Calaf's bodyguards—were sitting on the ground reclining against the side of a building with windows ablaze with candles.

Demetrius looked at Aric. "Those soldiers—are they waiting for—?"

"Yes."

"And that building—isn't it a house of—?"

"The candles give it away, don't they?"

"So Calaf has taken Ishmael to a brothel?"

"I'm surprised he took him the first night."

Demetrius groaned. "We'll be picking up the pieces tomorrow."

"What are you talking about?"

"Sharina wasn't the only one distressed at Calaf's sudden departure."

"I know Ishmael was upset, but Calaf missed him, too. He told me so."

Demetrius placed his hand on Aric's shoulder. "Believe me, it's not the same."

Understanding washed across Aric's face. "You've talked to Ishmael?"

"I had to," Demetrius answered. "After Calaf left, he became so withdrawn I was afraid for him."

Aric persisted, "And you're certain?"

"I've seen such feelings pass in others—but right now, it's real to him."

Aric nodded in the direction of the brothel. "Maybe his being with a woman?"

Demetrius replied, "Not likely—but who knows?"

"You urged Ishmael to be careful revealing his feelings, didn't you?"

"Of course—but he's only fourteen."

"And Sharina—what's she think?"

"I've said nothing."

"Surely she suspects it."

"Ishmael could grow three heads and she wouldn't notice." Knowing Aric's exasperation over Sharina's indifference to Ishmael, Demetrius wished he could pull the words back. Instead he shifted the subject. "So, what's Calaf doing in a brothel? Does Timur know?"

Aric laughed. "He told Nozar to take him there about three weeks ago after Calaf walked in on him."

"Female or male?"

"Both—he was fucking a man who was fucking a woman."

Realizing that Aric wanted to launch into the salacious particulars, Demetrius held up his hand. On too many occasions Demetrius was forced to witness Timur's sexual depravity. "Spare me the details."

Aric shrugged. "Timur spotted Calaf. He climbed off the man, and invited Calaf to take his place. Calaf bolted."

"Smart boy."

"The next day I overheard Timur and Nozar having a laugh over it. Nozar thought Calaf might still be a virgin. That's when he got the order to make a man out of him. Calaf's making his father proud every chance he gets."

Demetrius sighed.

"Don't worry about Ishmael," Aric said. "He's a strong boy."

"You misunderstand. I worry for them both."

CHAPTER 8

THE PHYSICIAN LEFT THE CAMP infirmary at midmorning and began the long walk to the city only to be interrupted by a shout.

"Demetrius!"

Calaf ran from between two tents. He leapt over a ditch, almost falling as his foot slipped in the mud on the other side. Calaf laughed as he recovered his balance and then almost careened into Demetrius. "Where's Ishmael? I thought he'd be with you."

"He stayed in the city to study."

"But he promised to come see me train with Flavus. It's been two days. He thinks fighting with a net is dumb, but wait'll he sees it! He must have told you about Flavus. Come on, Demetrius, it won't take long—you know he'll make it up."

He held up his hand to Calaf's rush of words. "I do not keep him away. It's his choice."

"Not one of his spells, is it?"

"It seems so."

Calaf turned and kicked a stone toward the ditch. "But why now?"

"Did something happen when you two were together?"

"We had a great time. He told you, didn't he? And the race over the city wall—can you believe Father didn't get angry about it? I kept changing the race to make it better. Ishmael says he hates when I do that, but I know he loves it."

"Ishmael told me nothing."

"Nothing? But why?"

"Perhaps because of the brothel?"

"You know about that?"

Demetrius smiled at Calaf's shocked expression. "Aric and I saw your bodyguards outside. Can you walk with me for a while?"

Calaf fell into step beside him saying, "Flavus doesn't expect me back until midday." After a few moments of silence Calaf spoke. "But Ishmael loved the brothel."

"I'm sure he seemed to."

"You mean he didn't?"

"I really don't know. What I do know is that he's missed you terribly and was very excited when we arrived."

"But I missed him, too."

"I know you did."

Calaf helped him cross an irrigation channel.

"Is it because—?" Calaf hesitated then remained silent.

"What?"

"Is he like you?"

"If you mean, does he prefer men," he waited for Calaf to nod, "I don't know for certain. What I can say is your friendship is the most important thing in his life. You will never know anyone more loyal, but I believe you know that."

"If he is, it doesn't matter."

"Ishmael may think it does. I expect you will want to reassure him."

"Now?"

"Maybe—maybe not—you will know if and when the time is right."

As they resumed their walk toward the city, Calaf said, "I'm sorry about Torak. He was a good man."

"That is very kind."

"It must be hard."

"It is, but Sharina has helped me so much." After a moment's pause, he added, "I understand you quarreled with her before you left Peshawar."

Calaf snapped, "She would turn me against my father."

"Because she praises the virtues of the last raja of Minnagara?"

"More than that—she would make me like him."

"He was her father, Calaf. Of course she wants to commend him to you."

"But he fell to my father, he could not defend his country or his family, he died weak and defeated at my father's feet. And she wants me to be like him!" When Demetrius did not respond to the outburst, Calaf added, "I do not want to be either of them."

"Then you must be yourself. I can finish the walk alone. It's almost midday, and you don't want to keep your Roman waiting."

The spring afternoon was unseasonably hot and humid, the ground muddy after the previous night's torrential rain, the low clouds heavy and dark. Even with his sturdy walking stick—a gift from Sharina, delicately carved with animals and birds—Demetrius slipped several times as he navigated the fallow, rocky field toward the Kushan garrison. Ishmael trailed several paces behind him, eyes focused down, his feet kicking the ground.

Demetrius stopped. "Give me your arm." He struggled to keep the annoyance out of his voice. Ishmael caught up and extended his arm. "It's unattractive."

"What?" Ishmael asked.

"Your pouting."

"You tricked me."

"No, we're going to the camp infirmary afterward."

"Then you go watch him," Ishmael said. "I'll wait at the infirmary for you."

"Calaf wants to see you."

"I don't want to see him."

"Of course, you do."

"No, I hate him."

"Yes, so you've said over and over. Now help me over to the arena. I've been hearing a lot about this golden-haired Roman giant."

Ishmael stepped in front of Demetrius and mouthed the words, "I hate you, too."

Tears appeared in Ishmael's eyes. He dropped onto the muddy ground, burying his head between his knees. As his shoulders began to shake, Demetrius placed his hand on top of his unruly, thick black hair and waited. For the past three days Ishmael had refused to talk about his time with Calaf—except to say that he hated his friend and never wanted to see him again. On the second day when Demetrius ventured to mention that he knew Calaf took him to the brothel, Ishmael's face turned pale, but he remained closed, retreating further into himself.

Ishmael leaned against his leg and Demetrius stroked his hair. "It was so—" Ishmael's voice cracked. He stared across the field at the garrison tents.

"I know it was. Come, stand up. Forget the arena. We'll go to the infirmary then back to the city."

Ishmael pushed himself up with one hand and gave a small smile. "I guess I could go see what he's so excited about."

"Are you sure?" Not for the first time, Demetrius marveled at the quick emotional swings of the young.

Ishmael nodded.

An overflowing irrigation ditch bordered one side of the makeshift arena, a wood fence stretched along the remaining three sides, enclosing a space large enough for twelve pairs of soldiers to wrestle, parry and fight. At the far corner near where the fence and ditch met Calaf trained with his Roman gladiator. Ishmael smiled, his eyes bright. "Calaf's right. He is bigger than Nozar."

Demetrius gave him a shove. "Go ahead. I'll catch up."

Ishmael ran along the fence then climbed the cross beams, leaning over the top one.

Calaf spotted him. "Flavus, it's Ishmael!" Flavus took advantage of Calaf's distraction to whip his net around Calaf's ankles. Calaf hit the ground on his side and spun about, struggling to free his legs. The Roman planted a sandaled foot on Calaf's chest and thrust a short sword at his throat.

"Focus! No focus—you die!" Flavus roared in simple Greek.

"No focus—you die!" Ishmael yelled from the sidelines, mimicking the gladiator. Flavus gave a hearty laugh and hurled the trident from his other hand in Ishmael's direction. Ishmael dodged and the trident flew past him, landing with its three prongs in the ground beyond the fence.

"Focus!" Flavus shouted, pointing at Ishmael. "He lives!"

"I live!" Ishmael laughed and dropped back to the ground and retrieved the spear. By the time Ishmael climbed back up, Calaf had untangled himself from the net. He rushed the fence, climbed up and embraced Ishmael.

"You came!" Calaf took the trident, handed it to Flavus, who stood almost as tall as the fence, and helped Ishmael over. Demetrius arrived and peered between the cross beams, relieved to see Ishmael laughing.

Calaf showed Ishmael his net. "It's called a *rete*, that's Latin for net. See, it's weighted here and here, just like fishermen use. Aiming it is the hardest part." Calaf pointed at the trident Flavus had set against the fence. "That's the *tridens*. In the arena you use it to spear men instead of fish. The short sword is called a *pugio*." Calaf took the net and began showing Ishmael how to throw it.

Flavus looked over the fence at Demetrius and struggling with his Greek said, "Prince learn quick. Great warrior someday."

Demetrius replied in Latin, "Yes, but he is a strong and willful youth, who needs a firm, steady hand. Yours, perhaps?"

Flavus brightened. "You speak Latin?"

"Yes, I grew up among Romans. I'm Demetrius."

"I know—the emperor's physician."

A loud curse rang across the arena. With long strides the Kushan officer in charge of the exercises moved toward them. Calaf gave Ishmael a shove in the direction of the fence while Flavus gave Demetrius a long-suffering smile, shrugged his shoulders, and grabbed the trident.

"Focus!" Flavus shouted. Calaf moved into position with the net and short sword. As Ishmael scrambled over the fence, the officer slowed his pace, then stopped. Calaf spun the net over his shoulder in a wide arc. With a snapping sound the weighted end wrapped itself around Flavus's knees. Satisfied, the officer cursed and pivoted in the direction of some new infraction.

On their walk back to the city, Demetrius did not mind Ishmael's incessant chatter about the things he and Calaf would do one day, grateful that his apprentice was once again content.

Demetrius and Ishmael sat alone in a tent beside the garrison infirmary. Each cradled a cup of warm wine in his hands. Bandits had ambushed a small group of soldiers patrolling a mountainous area east of the city. The bandits were routed, but four soldiers perished and seven lay injured in the infirmary, two unlikely to survive the night. Broken limbs set, wounds cleaned and dressed, the poppy given for their pain, they had done all they could for the men—nothing left to do but wait.

"Did Torak like women?" Ishmael's question jolted Demetrius out of an exhaustion-fueled numbness.

"What?" Demetrius heard Ishmael's question but needed a moment to gather his thoughts. It had been two weeks since Calaf had taken Ishmael to the brothel. Soon he would have another leave, and over the past few days Demetrius again observed Ishmael become quiet and withdrawn.

"I'm sorry—I shouldn't."

Demetrius placed a hand on Ishmael's knee. "It's all right. I don't mind talking about him—and yes, Torak had sex with women. In fact, he loved sex with women."

"Were you jealous?"

"Yes, I was, especially at first. But then I understood he loved being with me, too. That made it easier." A long silence followed, interrupted by a lone dog barking in the distance. Demetrius ventured the same question, "Were you jealous?"

"Huh?"

"At the brothel."

He nodded. "Calaf told me she was the emperor's favorite. He wanted us to have her together. I loved watching him. But I hated it, too. Then my turn came." Another long silence followed. "I couldn't." Demetrius did not expect him to continue, but he did. "After she left he tried to help me"—his hand made a jerking motion over his lap—"but his guard was there—" Demetrius squeezed Ishmael's knee, trying to let him know he understood. After a long moment of silence Ishmael asked, "Did Torak hurt women?"

"I can't imagine it."

"But once I overheard him with you—sorry, I didn't mean to—"

Demetrius patted Ishmael's leg. "It is all right. Go on."

"It sounded like he was hurting you."

Demetrius chuckled, "Let's just say Torak humored my baser proclivities."

Another moment of silence passed before Ishmael said, "Calaf—he twisted her arm—she cried out. I told him to stop, but he said she liked it."

"I'm sorry to hear that."

"But why'd he do it?"

"Maybe he wants to be like his father."

"But he's not like that."

"No, he's not."

A cry of pain came from the infirmary. Demetrius began to rise, but Ishmael placed his hand on Demetrius's shoulder.

"No, I'll go. You rest."

As the tent flap closed behind the youth, Demetrius sipped his wine, his thoughts turning—as they often did—to Torak. Memories of his last painful hours were fading, replaced with memories of his lover's easy laugh and wry humor. He brushed a tear from his eye and smiled.

CHAPTER 9

The sun reached into the narrow opening between the distant eastern mountains and a heavy cloud layer that had settled over the Kashmiri Valley. A beam of light burst across the dark valley floor, highlighting tiny huts and rain-soaked fields. As the sun again moved behind the clouds, the valley faded into an overcast darkness that would soon give way to the bright sky and unseasonable warmth that had dominated the spring.

Calaf tugged on Ishmael's sleeve and nodded toward the open doorway behind them. Demetrius stood shivering in his sleeping tunic, hand raised in a wave. Ishmael returned his wave then rushed ahead. Calaf gave a more energetic wave to the old physician before running after his friend.

Calaf caught up and grabbed Ishmael's shoulder. "Slow down."

Ishmael shook off his grip. "You said it's a half-day climb."

"Yes, a half-day climb—not a half-day run. What's wrong?"

"Nothing."

Calaf laughed. "What? I have to beat it out of you?" He grabbed Ishmael's waist and then let Ishmael slip free. He looked into the overcast sky and gave a loud sigh.

Ishmael looked up. "What?"

"Hope the sun comes out soon."

"Why?"

"Sun always helps."

"Helps what?"

"You—when you're like this."

Ishmael swallowed his retort as an officer and two soldiers approached, the same ones who accompanied them on Calaf's last leave.

Calaf brightened as he nodded in their direction. "At least I have them to entertain me."

"I doubt they'll be entertained."

"Caught you!"

"What?"

"Smiling!"

At that moment Naveen stepped in front of them. His two soldiers stopped a few paces behind.

"The general—"

"Yes, I know," Calaf interrupted. "Utmost obedience and respect, right?"

The officer gave a stiff nod.

"Good—that's settled. Come on—" he motioned to Ishmael "—let's go." As Ishmael drew alongside, Calaf threw his arm around him. "I hear there's a fox den below the falls."

Demetrius led the Roman giant into the tavern. The room's clamor hushed and eyes followed the two men as they made their way to an empty table in the back. As the chattering around them resumed, Demetrius sat and looked up. "I assume you always attract attention."

Flavus ducked under a ceiling beam and sat across from the physician. "Yes, even in Rome they stared—some frightened—" he paused but a moment "—some hungry."

Surprise filled Demetrius's eyes. "Is the gladiator always so direct?"

"The arena teaches that the swift win."

"I'm that obvious?"

"Not really." Flavus smiled. "But the interests of the emperor's trusted physician are well-known."

"Yes, I guess I've been around too long to have many secrets."

"Except how you survive under such a tyrant." Demetrius tensed. Flavus placed his hand over Demetrius's. "We speak Latin, remember."

"You can never be too cautious."

Demetrius slid his hand out from under Flavus's and called out to a nearby serving girl. The two men remained silent until their pitchers of wine and water arrived. Demetrius filled each cup with wine before adding water to both.

Flavus took a long draught, then scratched his chin with the edge of his cup. "But seen with me, don't you show a disregard for caution?"

Demetrius became thoughtful and lowered his voice. "Ah, yes, the crafty Roman gladiator turned mercenary who is a Persian spy scouting out Kushan defenses and vulnerabilities in advance of Shapur's march across the Khyber to push the great Timur and his Kushan hoards into the sea." Demetrius took a moment to catch his breath. "So, are you?"

"You'd believe me if I said no?"

"Of course not, but you must admit I needed to ask. Anyway, I figure I can protect myself from suspicions of impropriety by spreading the more reasonable rumor that you're a hapless, thick-skulled barbarian who's drunk too much wine and fucked too many camels to do more than teach boys to fight by flinging nets about."

"And they'd believe you?"

"Only about the camels."

With a roar Flavus slapped his massive palm on the table, sending the pitcher of water crashing to the straw-covered floor. The tavern went silent, all eyes turning in their direction.

Flavus raised the wine pitcher into the air. "Not the wine!" he shouted in broken Greek. The crowd erupted in cheers before resuming its previous din. Flavus looked into his cup. "Never did care for the watered stuff." He emptied what remained into Demetrius's cup and refilled his—without water. "That's better. Now what were we talking about?"

"Hapless and thick-skulled." Demetrius paused. "But you're not, are you?" Flavus lifted his shoulders and gave a grin. "I suspect that a German who speaks fluent, high-born Latin has a story to tell."

"A peasant youth defending his homeland against the Roman onslaught is captured into slavery and survives the arena?"

Demetrius shook his head. "You don't speak peasant Latin."

"A German king's youngest son—eight years old and his mother's favorite—becomes the guarantor of his father's treaty with Rome and grows up as the ward of a prosperous Roman merchant's family, educated alongside the family's own sons."

"Much better."

"The boy's father dies. A usurper becomes king. He ignores the treaty and attacks Roman military supply lines."

"I suspect this wasn't good news for the boy. How old was he?"

"Eighteen and no longer useful to Rome except as an example to other barbarian tribes contemplating their own betrayal of Rome. The youth is ordered executed in a public and gruesome manner. Fortunately, his Roman family intervenes, and he is sold to the owner of a gladiator school, where he is renamed Flavus."

"Ah, yes, Latin for yellow-haired. I must assume you did well."

Flavus nodded. "I survived four years in Rome's Colosseum and at various games throughout Italy. I was part of a group of champions taken to Antioch to compete. Afterward we sailed for Alexandria. The ship sank in a storm. I made it to shore, saw my chance for freedom, and took it."

"You didn't return to Germania?"

"Nothing for me there. I'd become Roman. My ancestral language and ways were foreign to me."

"So a mercenary's life became your freedom?"

"Could be worse."

"Agreed. You could have become a hapless, thick-skulled barbarian who's drunk too much wine and fucked too many—"

"Enough of camels." Flavus reached across the table and clamped his hand over Demetrius's mouth. "Didn't you say your apprentice is away for the day?"

Demetrius pushed Flavus's hand away and grinned. "And unlikely to return until dawn if the prince has anything to say about it."

Calaf was relieved. By the time they left the valley and began their ascent of the wide mountain canyon, Ishmael's mood improved. Calaf wanted

Ishmael to enjoy the day. Taking Ishmael to the brothel that first night had been a bad idea. After being apart for three months he should have planned something for just the two of them. It did not help that Naveen kept guard inside the room at the brothel, even though the officer stood out of sight behind a curtain. Calaf knew that as a future emperor he could expect no privacy—even when having sex—but it was too much to expect of Ishmael.

Calaf had spoken with Nozar. In exchange for Calaf's promise to exercise *utmost obedience and respect*—that is, no mischief—the general agreed that after Naveen secured the room he would station himself *outside* the door. Calaf had not yet mentioned a return visit to the brothel to Ishmael, deciding to wait until the hike back, figuring a day's fun in the mountains would smooth away any unpleasant memories. Calaf even planned to tell Ishmael he could have the woman first—*I owe him that much at least.* He felt himself harden in anticipation of the evening and wondered if he and Ishmael could escape the soldiers for a few moments to relieve his sexual tension behind some bushes. But his promise to Nozar and what obedience meant for the coming night held him in check. Anyway, he was a man now and had outgrown that sort of thing.

Naveen had stationed Javid, the younger of his two soldiers, farther up the trail while Sudesh followed behind them at a similar distance. Naveen himself walked about twenty paces back, far enough to give the boys privacy but close enough to respond to any threat.

The beginning of the trail was wide enough for the two friends to walk side by side. Ishmael remained pensive, on occasion noting the beauty of the canyon. At one point they stopped and marveled at a herd of mountain goats that picked their way up what appeared to be a sheer rock face. As they resumed walking, Calaf mentioned that he was teaching the gladiator to speak Bactrian. "He struggles with it even though our language is close enough to the little bit of Greek he already knows." After a pause, Calaf added, "And he's teaching me Latin."

Ishmael stifled a laugh. "You—learning Latin?"

"It could come in handy someday. Maybe I'll go to Rome. Flavus says he'll take me."

"Your father's going to let you wander off with a barbarian?" Ishmael laughed outright. "He won't even let you go on a hike without bodyguards."

Calaf ran ahead a few paces and kicked a rock up the trail—then another. They emerged into a broad meadow. Calaf looked at Ishmael. "*You* could do it though."

"Do what?"

"Leave if you wanted."

"It's different with me. I'll never be emperor, but you will."

"As if your mother will ever let me forget." Calaf kicked another rock, this time into the river, which now ran alongside the trail.

"But you'll be a great ruler."

Calaf swung about. "I don't want—" Seeing Naveen draw closer he cut his words short then whispered, "Forget it." He picked up several stones and handed some to Ishmael. He pointed across the water. "The yellow boulder on the other bank." Hidden by water but for a small outcropping, it was at least thirty paces distant. Calaf hit the target with his first throw. It took Ishmael three to hit the mark.

Calaf slapped Ishmael on the back. "Not bad."

"Didn't want to embarrass you."

Before Calaf could counter the jest, Naveen jogged up. "Listen." The falls roared in the distance.

The trail narrowed as they climbed into the pine forest at the upper end of the meadow. Pushing on, they were surrounded by a jumble of massive boulders that created treacherous cascades and deep pools. Above the cascades another long, wide meadow opened before them, rising toward a bend in the mist-shrouded canyon wall. Naveen called for a rest and sent Ishmael up ahead to alert Javid. Calaf sat down with Naveen and watched them come back down the trail. Javid smiled at something Ishmael said. Ishmael gave him a gentle shove, which Javid returned. Ishmael lost his balance but Javid caught him before he fell. Both laughed as they reached Calaf and Naveen. Naveen got their attention and waved them to the ground.

"Down. Quiet. The foxes. Up there to the left." Naveen pointed. "You can just see them in the rocks below the canyon wall."

Ishmael yanked Calaf's arm. "See the white one."

Calaf's eyes did not leave the foxes. "There's a gold one, too."

Sudesh came up from behind and knelt behind them. He had been to the falls a month earlier and told Calaf about the fox den. "The mother should be nearby, maybe hunting for food. The pups have grown. I'll bet they're starting to hunt, too."

Javid cried out, "Look, the white one jumped the gold."

The two pups tumbled about, a blur of gold and white against the meadow's deep green.

Ishmael jumped up. "They're rolling toward the water. We've got to—"

Sudesh grabbed Ishmael and pulled him down. "Just watch. See—the mother."

A mottled gray fox appeared above her bickering pups. She nipped the white one, who scampered away and charged up the sloping meadow.

"He doesn't look happy about that," Calaf said.

Naveen laughed. "Maybe he doesn't like being told what to do." He ducked Calaf 's playful swing.

"Watch," Sudesh said.

The mother poked the gold one's belly with her muzzle. He pawed his mother's nose then leapt up to race after his brother. The mother loped after her pups.

"They're heading to the den," Sudesh said.

Ishmael stood. "Let's get closer."

"We must head back soon," Naveen said.

"Please, a little longer," Ishmael pleaded.

"Let him go," said Calaf.

Naveen gave in. "Only a few moments. Javid, stay with him."

Ishmael and Javid were creeping low to the muddy ground below the fox den when Ishmael lost his footing and then his balance. Javid shouted and reached for him in vain. Ishmael slid down the embankment feet first. Finding nothing to grab to stop his rapid descent, he dug his heels into the soft earth, which spun him about, throwing him over the edge. He somersaulted before splashing into the icy flow, his cry absorbed into the current's roar. The river swallowed him without a trace before spitting him headfirst, facedown, arms flailing into the boulder-strewn cascades.

"Ishmael!" Calaf shouted as Ishmael's foot got caught between the rocks, stopping his progress. Churning water buried and thrashed him. His head bobbed up, his open mouth gasped for air but took water. Calaf pushed past Sudesh.

"No!" Naveen grabbed Calaf, bringing him to his knees, but Calaf broke free, scrambling down the slope and plunging into the water above his struggling friend. Calaf grabbed and twisted the trapped foot, freeing it. Both boys were now captured in the torrent, their arms yoking them until a boulder ripped them apart, sending each on a separate course.

Aric stifled a yawn. Since before dawn he had sat at the table in Timur's tent, situated on a small hill outside the city and surrounded by the Kushan garrison. In Peshawar Timur conducted military affairs in the comfort of the palace, but away from the capital he insisted on attending the empire's business in the midst of his troops. A long day grew longer when Timur called for the evening meal to be delivered, dashing any hope Aric had that he might return to the city before dark.

Aric had not written on the parchment lying before him for some time. He cast his eyes upward as Timur and Nozar once again began debating how to respond to the first item in Shapur's non-aggression treaty proposal: the Kushans must give Persians unrestricted access to Baktra to worship at the birthplace of Zoroaster. Aric stretched his legs and mouthed Nozar's words as the general once again said, "This is nothing but a pretext for a Persian takeover—lose Baktra and Persia will control the Khyber Pass within months."

This time Timur did not wave away Nozar's counsel, clearly giving up on finding a diplomatic resolution to the impasse. He jumped up and slammed his fist on the table upsetting Aric's ink repository, ruining his parchment and obliterating most of the day's notes.

"No more talk—more troops at Baktra—make a big show of it—that'll be our answer to that Persian bastard."

Nozar lowered his head.

"Arachosia is quiet," Timur continued. "The regiment there grows soft. Give it to Barzin to take to Baktra." Timur glanced at Aric, who was distracted trying to clean up the spilled ink and save as many of his notes as possible. "Did you get that?"

"Yes—yes—Arachosia—quiet—regiment soft—Barzin—Barzin—to—"

Aric looked at Nozar, who stared at a sudden commotion inside the tent's opening then leapt off his bench, knocking it over and rushed toward a young soldier being held upright by two of Timur's bodyguards. The soldier leaned over, his chest heaving as he gasped for breath, his uniform wet, soiled and torn, his right arm bleeding from a deep wound. Nozar grasped the soldier's head and lifted it. In spite of the exhaustion and mud that covered the soldier's face, Aric recognized Javid, the youngest of the prince's guards, and jumped up, sending his bench tumbling over behind him.

Timur bellowed, "What's going on?"

The injured soldier's mouth moved.

Nozar's back stiffened before he turned to face the emperor. Aric had never seen the general's composure shaken. "My lord, there's been an accident."

Demetrius woke with a start; anxiety gripped his heart. *A dream?* No, too piercing. *A premonition?* No, only fools believed in such things—but the pain in his chest was sharp and severe. His left temple began to throb. He closed his eyes and breathed deeply. The anxiety eased, the pain in his temple dulled. He opened his eyes once again. His head rested on Flavus's chest, his hand between his muscular thighs. Flavus's arm held him. Demetrius stretched and eased himself out of his embrace. Flavus pulled him back.

"Where are you going?"

"The gates must be closing soon. Don't you have to get back to the garrison?"

"A guard at Jammu Gate is a friend."

"What kind of friend?"

"Jealous already?"

"No, interested—just interested."

"I doubt he'd be."

"Pity."

Flavus climbed on top of Demetrius. "You Greeks are incorrigible."

"So they say." Demetrius gave Flavus a push. "You're crushing me."

Flavus rolled onto his back, stretched and moaned. "A real bed—do you know what a luxury this is?"

Demetrius sat up and stared down at the Roman.

"What?" Flavus asked.

"Are you?"

"Am I what?"

"A Persian spy?"

"No."

"Good," Demetrius said with a smile.

"Now you believe me?"

"Does it matter?"

"It does."

"Then, yes, I believe you," Demetrius said.

"You just want my cock."

"That, too."

Flavus laughed. "Like I said—incorrigible."

Demetrius slipped off the bed. "I've got some of Farhad's na'an and yesterday's caravan brought in dates and a passable wine. Want some?"

Loud pounding at Demetrius's door interrupted Flavus's response.

A hundred torches flickered along the trail paralleling the river's track through the canyon's wide meadow. Clouds blocked the night sky. The silence of the searchers was as complete as the darkness that surrounded them. Carefully, slowly, each stepped within the tight circle of light cast by his torch, straining to hear the slightest cry for help over the flow of the nearby water. Timur and Nozar were on horseback at the front of the column leading ten mounted officers. Behind them Aric helped Demetrius navigate the twisting, rocky trail. Flavus came next, marshaling a small group of soldiers burdened with packs and pulling litters piled with blankets and other supplies. Nozar had nodded in recognition when Flavus appeared in the doorway of Demetrius's lodging, then ordered him to tend to whatever the physician required for the rescue effort.

As they left the city, Demetrius listened as Aric told him what little he knew. "It seems that Ishmael fell into the river. Naveen and the other soldier failed to stop Calaf from going in to save him. Then Naveen ordered Javid to go for help."

"Nothing else?"

"We were fortunate to get even that." Aric lowered his voice to a whisper. "Timur flew into a rage at the news and before Nozar could stop him, he struck and killed Javid—poor fellow. Then he nearly killed one of his own bodyguards, but Nozar got between them and calmed him."

"The torches won't last."

"That's what Nozar told him, but Timur won't listen."

Most of the searchers made it into the canyon's wide entrance before the extinguishing torches plunged them into total darkness. At the front Timur demanded they continue but Nozar's steady coaxing got Timur to dismount and await first light.

Dawn's first indistinct shadows began to appear when Flavus crept over to Demetrius and Aric, followed by Nozar. Flavus carried a blanket and one of Demetrius's supply packs. He nudged Aric and pointed upriver. Aric rose, folding his blanket over his arm. Nozar took Aric's arm, his voice a whisper. "If you find him, bring me word first. I must be the one to tell the emperor."

"I understand."

As Aric followed Flavus into the darkness, Nozar sat beside Demetrius. The physician placed his hand on Nozar's knee and leaned into his ear. "Should Calaf perish and Ishmael survive, you know I will be unable to contain the emperor's wrath. Therefore, you must. Timur cannot be allowed to take Ishmael's life."

"I will do whatever I can to protect the boy, but you of all people know—"

Demetrius interrupted him by squeezing his knee. Nozar said, "What?"

Demetrius hesitated, knowing that once he spoke there would be no going back. He had never considered the possibility that he would be forced to choose between saving Ishmael's life and betraying not only Sharina's treason but his own. For a moment he considered the senselessness of revealing the truth if Ishmael was already dead. Ultimately Ishmael's innocence in the face of the guilt he shared with Sharina forced him to lean toward Nozar's ear and say, "Ishmael is Timur's son."

Nozar jerked away, and in the light of the emerging dawn Demetrius saw that his words had staggered the normally composed general. Quickly, Demetrius added, "Sharina switched the boys before the *chakor* ceremony."

Nozar looked away. When he returned his gaze, Demetrius saw that he had regained control. His voice low and threatening, Nozar asked, "You choose to tell me this now?"

"But should Ishmael live—"

Nozar snapped, "It will be best for everyone if he doesn't."

At that moment, a shout rose above the roar of the stream. Nozar leapt to his feet and shouted for everyone to remain where they were. As Timur and several officers rushed past, Nozar glanced down at Demetrius. "With us." The physician pushed himself up with his walking stick and followed.

The body rested face down half buried in a sandbar where the river's flow made a sharp detour around a massive boulder. After testing the depth with a branch Nozar stepped into the shallow eddy. "One of the soldiers," he called out. He knelt and freed the dead man's shoulders from the sand before lifting the head. "It's Sudesh."

In the dim light Timur paced back and forth, his head down, his hands locked behind his back. He kicked a large stone into the water. Demetrius offered his thin arm to help Nozar return to the bank. Nozar pulled himself up and brought his face close to Demetrius's ear.

"When we find the prince, I may not be able to control him."

"Will the officers support you?"

"My son Barzin will, but the others—their loyalty is to the emperor. No matter what happens, don't get involved, and stay close to Barzin."

Another shout seized their attention. Nearby a soldier pointed at a cluster of bushes that overhung the far bank. Trapped in the tangle of branches floated another battered body, most of the clothing torn away. Because the water flowed too deep and swift to traverse, Nozar ordered two men downriver to find a way across. A short time later they appeared and waded into the overhanging branches. When they reached the body, they waved and shook their heads.

Nozar called to Timur, "It's Naveen." Then turning to Demetrius he whispered, "The boys can't be far away."

As Nozar began ordering his officers to form search parties, Barzin appeared running from upriver. "Barzin!" Nozar shouted. "I want you to organize—" He must have seen the look on Barzin's face at the same moment Demetrius did. Nozar jerked around and called out, "My lord!"

When Nozar swung back, a breathless Barzin stood in front of him. "The Roman—he's got—"

Nozar did not let him finish. He bolted around him and ran toward the swell of murmuring that rose to drown out the rush of water. Men scattered off the trail as Nozar and Barzin rushed by, followed by the emperor and Demetrius. When they reached the encampment, an uneasy quiet descended over the meadow. In the middle of a wide circle of soldiers the Roman cradled a body wrapped in a blanket. He knelt and let the blanket fall away revealing Ishmael.

Flavus looked up at the emperor. "He lives."

Demetrius let his walking stick fall to the ground, dropped down beside Flavus, and placed his fingers on Ishmael's neck. The pulse was weak but steady. Demetrius stroked the youth's forehead.

Excitement began to spread among the soldiers. But their celebration ended abruptly when the emperor roared, "You bring me *him*?"

Demetrius rose. "You would wish him dead, my lord?"

Nozar stepped between them, facing the emperor. "All of us are overwrought, my lord." He kept his eyes focused on Timur's. "Tend to the boy, physician."

As Demetrius knelt, Timur glared at Nozar, then pushed him aside and advanced toward the nearest soldiers. As they stumbled backwards, the emperor spun about, his arm outstretched at the circle of men. "The prince!" Timur raised his fist into the air. "Bring me the prince!" As his voice echoed up the canyon, another, weaker but clear, answered.

"I am here."

Thirty paces away at the meadow's edge, where the horses were tethered, Calaf stood, wrapped in a blanket, Aric beside him. Calaf stepped forward. He lost his balance and the blanket fell away, exposing his scraped and bruised torso, torn trousers, and an open gash down his right calf. Aric took Calaf's elbow to steady him. The soldiers parted, allowing them to pass. Calaf patted Aric's arm and motioned him to wait. Calaf approached, eyes focused downward, grimacing when he placed weight on his injured leg. He stopped before his father and lifted his face.

"I saved him, Father."

Timur's fist caught Calaf on the side of his head and sent him to the ground.

"You fool! You risk your life—you risk my empire—for *him*?" Stepping around his son Timur shouted, "Squire!" The soldiers backed away, shocked into silence.

Calaf pushed himself up on one arm. Demetrius caught his eye, shook his head, and mouthed *Don't.*

The squire led the emperor's horse into the circle and turned it so that Timur could mount. Releasing the bridle the squire jumped back. When Timur reined the horse about, Calaf struggled to his feet and stood before him. He swayed and shifted his good leg outward, his eyes never leaving his father's face.

Timur reached for the hilt of the sword, buried in the saddle's scabbard. Flavus released Ishmael into Demetrius's arms and rose behind Calaf. Several paces back, Nozar—head still, eyes shifting about the scene—rocked forward on his toes then eased back onto his heels. He placed his hand atop the short sword at his waist. Several paces to Nozar's right, Barzin did not move, his eyes shifting from the emperor to his father and back. Long moments passed, father and son locked in invisible combat.

Calaf's voice broke the standoff, ringing clear and strong across the meadow. "I *saved* him!"

Timur grasped the sword hilt and began to pull the sword free. He hesitated and then looked at the surrounding men as if emerging from a trance. He released the sword, allowing it to slip back into its sheath, and with a hearty laugh shouted, "Get the prince a horse!"

A roar of cheers erupted, and the emperor propelled his mount forward, scattering the men. In the excitement and relief that followed, few noticed Calaf collapse, caught by the giant Roman before his knees hit the ground.

CHAPTER 10

UPON THEIR RETURN TO THE city with the injured boys, the emperor ordered Calaf taken to the royal quarters. When he made no mention of Ishmael, Nozar pulled Demetrius aside.

"Your quarters will be best for Ishmael."

"Understood." Then Demetrius nodded toward Flavus. "I request you assign him to me." At Nozar's questioning look, he said, "A gladiator knows something about wounds, does he not?"

Several days later Flavus stood in the doorway of Calaf's room, watching Demetrius bathe the feverish and unconscious prince with cold water. Flavus caught the scent of the herbs he had purchased the day before and glanced at a nearby table. The mortar laid on its side, the pestle and a clay bowl beside it. He dipped his finger in the bowl and brought the ointment to his nose. "I couldn't have blended it better."

Demetrius gave a tired smile. "He's due."

Flavus took the bowl and knelt beside the physician. He lifted the soiled gauze, cleaned the seepage in and around the wound, and began applying the salve. "We may not be able to save the leg."

"Then he will die." Demetrius motioned to a boy sitting inside the doorway. The boy circled the bed, stooped to pick up the basin of used water and the soiled bandages, and withdrew.

"The emperor will not change his mind?"

Demetrius shook his head. "He'd rather a dead heir than a one-legged one." He handed Flavus a clean dressing.

Once he applied it, Flavus touched the physician's cheek. "When did you last sleep?"

Demetrius shook his head. "I can't leave him."

Flavus rose and pulled Demetrius to his feet. "I will watch him while you rest." He guided Demetrius to the room's second bed. Flavus shifted him onto his stomach and began rubbing his shoulders and back.

Demetrius lifted his head. "If anything—?"

"Of course." Flavus felt Demetrius begin to relax under his touch.

Flavus had wondered how much Demetrius would trust him. But when Demetrius went to his residence to care for Ishmael, Flavus remained at the side of the more seriously injured prince. When Flavus remarked on this trust, Demetrius gave Flavus's arm a gentle squeeze. "I trust a good man."

Since his days as a gladiator, Flavus heard himself described many ways. Courageous. Ruthless. Smart. Deceitful. Cunning. But never *good*—not since the day the gladiator master came to the home of his Roman family to take him away. As his Roman mother hugged him, both of them fighting tears, she said, "You are a good boy. Don't let your new destiny change that." Overhearing this, the gladiator master laughed. "Don't tell him that, my lady. In the arena, the good boys die first."

As Ishmael's condition improved, Demetrius spent more time with Flavus caring for Calaf, only sleeping when Flavus drew him to the second bed and pulled him into his arms. In those quiet moments, Flavus listened as the old physician reminisced about watching the boys grow up: their mischievousness, their fights, their differences, their tenacity when Calaf's headstrong impulsiveness confronted Ishmael's gentle but unyielding resistance, but most of all, their intense attachment, beyond any bond he had ever witnessed. He also spoke of Sharina, his raising her after the emperor executed her family, his struggle to help her find a life beyond the horror she had witnessed, and his ultimate failure to do so.

At one point, his head resting on Flavus's chest, Demetrius had asked about his life in Germania.

"I was very young when the Romans took me, but I do remember my father teaching me to hunt with a bow and my mother giving me a taste as she cooked." Flavus stopped speaking and gave a forced laugh. Demetrius lifted his head. Flavus moved to slip from the bed, but Demetrius pulled him back. "Words are not needed." Flavus tried to pull away, but Demetrius held tight until he relented and allowed the physician to pull his face into his arms. His eyes stung with tears, but he stiffened against their demand for release, finally letting sleep take him as Demetrius stroked his head. Many days—and many conversations—had passed since then, filling Flavus with growing admiration and unexpected affection for Demetrius, leaving him conflicted over his deceit in using the physician to achieve his mission among the Kushans. *I cannot afford to love him* dominated Flavus's thoughts.

One evening he massaged Demetrius's shoulders and back, hoping the exhausted physician would succumb to sleep, if but for a short time. He felt Demetrius grow tense.

"Relax, my friend."

"My heart is heavy."

"What do you mean?"

"I fear for them."

"Who?"

"The boys—and Sharina." Demetrius turned onto his side, glanced up at Flavus, then closed his eyes. "After so many years, I no longer have the strength." Flavus stroked Demetrius's forehead and remained silent. "To protect them. So many dangers."

"We all face dangers."

"Not like theirs—not like theirs." Demetrius pulled Flavus's hand to his lips and kissed it. "When I am no longer able, I can think of no one else. Promise me."

"I don't understand."

"Promise me you will protect them."

Flavus felt himself standing at a precipice. Nothing prevented his stepping back, nothing except the urgent plea in the eyes of one he held dear. Flavus stepped over the edge. "Yes, my friend, for you I vow to protect them."

Calaf stirred and Demetrius rose from his chair. He went to a basin and dampened a cloth before sitting on the edge of the bed. He wiped the perspiration from Calaf's forehead. For the first time the boy's eyes opened then blinked several times. He shifted his head, moaned and closed his eyes again.

Demetrius placed his hand on Calaf's shoulder. "Easy."

Calaf's eyes reopened. He whispered, "Ishmael."

"Alive—thanks to you." Demetrius patted the cloth around Calaf's neck. "But we almost lost you."

"Ishmael." Stronger, louder.

"Rest, Calaf—I need you to rest."

The prince tried to rise. "Ishmael." He groaned in pain but continued to push himself up.

"Easy." Demetrius took Calaf's shoulders and guided him down to the pillow. "Easy. Ishmael is all right." Demetrius felt Calaf's body relax, but his eyes still darted about.

"Where am I?"

"The emperor's lodgings. Your father ordered you brought here."

"How long?"

"Eight days."

"Eight?" Calaf grimaced in pain, reaching for his right leg.

Demetrius rose then returned with a flask. He held the opening to Calaf's lips. "Take this—just the poppy."

Calaf shook his head. "Ishmael." Again, he groaned, this time louder.

"Please, he wouldn't want you in such pain."

"I will see him now. Poppy after."

The pain forced him to cry out. Demetrius held the flask opening to Calaf's lips and stroked his cheek. "Ishmael will be here when you awaken."

Calaf's lips parted.

Demetrius knew he could not keep his promise.

Demetrius stood outside Calaf's room and watched Nozar approach, led by Calaf's guard. Nozar motioned the physician into an adjoining chamber as the guard resumed his post before the prince's door.

After closing the room's door, Nozar asked, "So the news is good?"

Demetrius nodded. "Thanks to Flavus the infection subsides. I have much to learn from this Roman."

"Yes, I heard him say that in the arena surviving wounds is more important than surviving swords. The emperor will know of the Roman's role in saving his son's—" Nozar paused, only continuing after several moments, choosing his words carefully. "That story about the boys—tell me you only wished to protect Ishmael, nothing more."

"I wish it were—then it still would be a story known only to Sharina and me."

Nozar roughly grasped Demetrius's arm. "Known until when? What do you conspire at?"

"It was nothing but a moment of madness by a young girl. Once she did it, she was trapped—discovery not only meant her death but also her son's." Demetrius eased his arm from the general's grasp and searched his face for any sign of understanding. "I witnessed what she did and remained silent. That is all."

Nozar laughed. "*That is all?* You justify yourself with *that is all*?"

"Nozar, look at me. I justify nothing but compassion. There is no conspiracy—not then, not now. She and I—we've never even spoken about it."

"You expect me to believe that?"

"Believe what you will, but by our friendship I speak the truth."

"And Aric?"

"He knows nothing about Sharina's switching the boys." Demetrius steadied himself with a deep breath.

After a long moment of silence Nozar said, "You will not speak of this again—ever. If you do, I will personally see you and Sharina die traitors' deaths."

"Understood. What will you do?"

"I tell you what I will not do." Demetrius felt Nozar struggling to control his anger as he continued. "With the Persians threatening our borders, I will not throw my emperor into turmoil and his empire into chaos. Calaf has been raised the prince. He demonstrates the courage and strength of a prince. By the gods, he is the prince—nothing changes that."

"And Ishmael?"

"Ishmael is the son of a scribe and a physician's apprentice—nothing more, ever—but I realize now that Timur must not take his life or the judgment of the gods will fall on us all."

Demetrius waited a moment for a sign that Nozar's flash of anger had abetted then said, "I've heard that Timur plans Calaf's marriage."

"Yes, to the daughter of the king of Tur, a kingdom across the Khyber and east of Persia. Timur has summoned envoys from Tur proposing that our two realms unite to defeat the Persians. The union of Calaf and the princess Turandot would seal the treaty and hopefully the empire's future."

"Not to mention separating Calaf and Ishmael," Demetrius ventured.

"An added benefit," Nozar said and turned to leave.

Demetrius took his arm. "The prince asks for Ishmael. We must find a way."

"Are you crazy? You know the emperor flies into a rage at even the mention of his name."

"What do I tell Calaf?"

"Whatever you like. Tell him the truth."

"That the emperor has ordered Ishmael's death if they are seen together?"

"If you must. He'll know it soon enough."

Ishmael swung about and faced Demetrius, his face flushed with incomprehension. "I can't see him?"

Demetrius still marveled at Ishmael's recovery. Two weeks since his ordeal and except for some bruises it appeared as if nothing happened to him.

For days Demetrius had kept from Ishmael the news of Calaf's recovery but he could not hold it back any longer.

"The emperor will not allow it."

Ishmael laughed. "So sneak me in—the emperor doesn't allow many things but—"

Demetrius cut Ishmael off and delivered the words he had dreaded for days. "He's ordered your death if you are seen with him."

"My death? What are you talking about?"

Demetrius hesitated then plunged ahead. "You'd already be dead but for Nozar's intervention." Demetrius hated the brutality of the words but Ishmael needed to understand the seriousness of his situation. "The emperor has commanded that you and the prince are never to see each other again."

"He can't do that."

Demetrius took hold of his shoulders. "You know he can. Now listen—and listen carefully. In time the emperor is certain to relent, but only in his own way and for his own purpose." Demetrius took a deep breath. "In the meantime, you must go away."

Ishmael's eyes opened wide. "What do you mean go away?"

"The emperor has ordered you to accompany Captain Barzin to Baktra. There you will become the scribe to the emperor's governor."

"Baktra? I can't go to Baktra. I'm your apprentice."

Demetrius sat on the edge of his bed and nodded toward a chair. "Sadly, no longer." Ishmael sat and Demetrius continued, "I know this is much to absorb, but you must trust me and do all that is asked." Demetrius dropped his head, weariness overtaking him.

"I'm being sent away because of my uncle, aren't I?"

Demetrius looked up in surprise. "You know the truth about Yousef?" Ishmael nodded. "How? Few know."

"The queen's old eunuch. He told me before he died last year."

Demetrius sighed. *Ah, Mahesh, ears everywhere, holder of many secrets.* "What did he tell you?"

"That Timur killed Yousef to become emperor."

"Mahesh told you about the treachery of General Rodmehr, didn't he?"

Ishmael nodded. "Regardless, Timur chose his empire over his best friend, and now he wants Calaf to do the same."

Demetrius stood and placed his hand on Ishmael's head. "That decision haunts him to this day—and now it haunts you and Calaf."

"And my father?" When Demetrius returned a quizzical look, Ishmael added, "He often prays before the mosaic of Yousef at the fire temple."

Demetrius nodded. "Aric is tormented by how he benefited from his brother's death. I've told him many times he profits because of Timur's guilt not by anything he's done—but to little avail."

"Just as the emperor's guilt torments us."

"I'm afraid so."

"I wish him dead."

"Words best kept to yourself, especially if you ever hope to see Calaf again."

CHAPTER 11

CALAF STOOD BEFORE HIS FATHER, back straight, eyes focused on the far wall, his right calf uncovered, the swelling almost gone, the wound now a pale scar against his dark skin. Graying but still robust, Timur ignored his son as he worked at a table covered with maps and parchments. Calaf's cane, which Timur ordered taken from him when he entered, leaned against the corner of the table. Aric sat beside the emperor taking occasional notes while Nozar paced the room. While a year older than the emperor, the more animated Nozar appeared younger.

During a lull in the discussion Nozar nodded in Calaf's direction. "Do you wish us to continue this later?"

"No, we will finish." Timur drained his cup, refilled it from the pitcher, and called to his squire to bring more.

Calaf's leg throbbed. The poppy Demetrius gave him no longer dulled the pain. He swayed.

Timur barked, "Attention!"

"Sir!" Calaf steadied himself.

At last Timur stood, dismissed Nozar and told Aric to wait in the corridor. As the two men departed, Timur called out, "Guard, tell my squire more wine and station yourself outside." Moments later the squire returned, filled both the pitcher and the emperor's cup, and then withdrew.

Timur returned to his place behind the table and drained his cup. As the emperor busied himself with the parchments, Calaf noticed a tremor in his father's right hand, the one with the pale scar from a long ago battle. Calaf's eyes traveled to Timur's face. Timur stared at him. Calaf's senses heightened; all pain and fatigue vanished.

"Three soldiers dead."

Calaf held himself steady, eyes straight ahead.

"Three soldiers dead!"

"Sir!"

"Heir to my empire near death."

"Sir!"

"For what?"

"To save my friend—sir."

"To save my friend," Timur repeated, his tone mocking. Calaf stiffened. "The prince risks his life, risks my empire, for what? A servant?"

"No, sir, a friend."

The emperor swept his hand across the table and leapt to his feet. The wine pitcher overturned, and red wine spread across the scattered maps and parchments. The empty wine cup struck Calaf's cane, which fell to the floor. Timur stared at his son before he said in a controlled voice, "Nothing—do you understand—nothing, no one, neither friend nor servant is more important than my empire."

"Ishmael is."

"You would defy me?"

"No—but I would not let my friend die."

Timur's faced reddened. His fists tightened at his sides. He stormed around the table but stopped short, the fallen cane between him and his son. Calaf's eyes remained focused forward. Long, silent moments passed before Timur stooped, picked up the cane, and stepped before Calaf. He took his son's hand and placed the cane into it.

"Nothing is more important than my empire." It was a simple, dispassionate statement, and Calaf felt a chill run through him.

Timur strode to the chamber door and threw it open. He shoved aside the surprised guard. The emperor's heavy footsteps echoed down the corridor.

Calaf rushed to the chamber doorway and shouted to the guard, "The general—find Nozar!" Then turning to a startled Aric. "Ishmael—warn him—hurry!"

Breathless, his knee bloodied from a fall, Aric reached Demetrius's lodging first. He threw his body against the door, breaking the inside latch and tumbling face first into the entryway.

Staggering up he shouted, "Ishmael—flee!"

Demetrius appeared at the end of the hall, leaning on his walking stick, followed by Ishmael.

Through hacking coughs Aric cried, "The emperor—he's coming—"

"Ishmael, out the back—find Barzin—"

"What's happened?"

Demetrius shoved him. "Go, now!"

Ishmael spun about, but soldiers—several with torches—appeared from the rear of the house, blocking his way. When he looked back, the emperor's silhouette, framed by torchlight from the street, filled the doorway. He held a sword at his side.

Demetrius stepped past Aric, glad his walking stick gave him a reason to move slowly, anything to buy time. "You appear at my door armed, my lord?"

"The boy comes with me." Pitched low and menacing and slurred by drink, Demetrius knew this tone of voice well and fought the fear rising deep inside him.

"Ishmael leaves at dawn for Baktra—as you commanded, my lord." Demetrius looked past the emperor into the street. A handful of soldiers stood silent and still. He did not see Nozar.

"He comes with me—now."

"May I inquire for what reason, my lord?"

"He is a threat to the empire. Now step aside, physician."

Demetrius caught sight of Nozar pushing through the soldiers. Behind him he spotted Calaf and Barzin. The words leapt unbidden from the physician's mouth. "I will not, my lord."

Timur's face darkened. Seeing the flash of steel, Demetrius raised his walking stick above his head.

"Villain!" screamed Timur.

"No!" Ishmael's cry reverberated down the hall as Timur's blade fell, splitting the walking stick and striking Demetrius between his neck and shoulder, driving him downward. As Timur pulled the blade free, Demetrius groaned and slumped onto his side. Ishmael pushed past Aric to the fallen physician, dropping to his knees and pulling Demetrius into his arms. Timur again lifted the sword above his head. Ishmael raised his face to meet the blind savagery that consumed Timur's. The muscles in Timur's arms tensed. As the sword began to fall, hands grabbed Timur's wrists from behind, stopping the blade's descent. Surprise swept across the emperor's face. He spun about, the sword still raised. Nozar stood before him.

"The wine, my lord, the wine. You're not yourself—tomorrow's best, don't you think?"

Nozar searched Timur's eyes. Ferocity became uncertainty, then recognition. "Nozar?" Timur lowered the sword. "Tomorrow—you think?"

"Yes, my lord, tomorrow's better." Nozar eased the sword from Timur's grasp and handed it to Barzin. Nozar took the emperor's arm. "Come, my lord."

Barzin pushed Calaf back and whispered, "Down—he must not see you."

As Nozar guided the emperor away, he nodded at Barzin. He mouthed *Quick* and motioned for the soldiers gathered outside to follow him. Barzin looked about and gestured for silence. Nozar and the emperor disappeared around a corner. Barzin gave a nod and Flavus rushed forward. Aric pulled Ishmael off the physician.

"Light!" Flavus called out and leaned over the fallen Demetrius. A soldier from the back of the hallway moved forward with a torch.

Flavus looked up. “He breathes.” Flavus lifted the groaning Demetrius into his arms. Ishmael rushed ahead of Flavus toward Demetrius’s room.

Barzin ordered a soldier to assist Flavus. He sent another to the garrison to have his regiment readied for immediate departure. The other soldiers were placed as guards at the dwelling’s front and rear entrances. At last he looked at Calaf, kneeling over the bloodstained entry.

“My prince, we have little time.” When Calaf looked up, Barzin added, “We must act.”

Aric stepped between them. “What’s happening?”

Barzin answered, “Ishmael’s life depends on his leaving Srinagar immediately. We must get distance between him and the emperor. Unless my father calms the emperor, it may already be too late.”

Calaf rose and laid his hand on Aric’s shoulder. Looking at Barzin he asked, “The plan?”

“We must get Ishmael on his way to Baktra. I’ll ride with him as fast and hard as we can before dawn. My regiment will follow. If the gods are with us, the emperor will let us go.”

Ishmael stepped into the hall and motioned toward Aric. “Father, he asks for you—alone.”

As Aric rushed past Ishmael into the room, Flavus emerged.

Calaf looked from Flavus to Ishmael and back. Flavus shook his head before slipping back into Demetrius’s bedroom.

A soldier called from outside the front entrance. “The horses are here.”

Barzin took Ishmael’s arm. “Come, we must leave now.”

Ishmael pulled away. “But Demetrius—I can’t leave him.” He looked at Calaf, his eyes pleading, tears down his cheeks.

Calaf whispered to Barzin, “Give us a few moments. I’ll bring him.” Barzin headed outside.

Ishmael threw his arms around Calaf, burying his face in his friend’s shoulder. “I never thought I’d see you again.” Ishmael’s body shook as he fought to stifle his sobs.

“When I saw you drowning—” Calaf’s voice broke as he fought to keep control.

Ishmael whispered, "Demetrius, he—"

"I know, I saw—" Calaf eased himself from Ishmael's embrace and cupped Ishmael's face in his hands. "His last act saved you. Go now or he will die in vain."

"I cannot leave you."

"You must—you must live."

Barzin appeared in the doorway. "Ishmael—now."

"I'm coming," Ishmael called out then noticed an angry, deep wound around Calaf's neck. He touched it.

Calaf winced. "In the water the chain cut into my neck, but I didn't lose it." He reached into his pocket. When he opened his fingers, the circle of gold—his infant ankle band—lay in his palm. He took Ishmael's hand and gave the band to him.

"I can't. It's yours," Ishmael said.

"Please keep it safe for me."

Ishmael pulled Calaf back into his arms, holding him tightly, and whispered, "I love you." He released Calaf and rushed outside.

When Calaf reached the doorway, Ishmael sat astride his horse, following Barzin toward the end of the street. As Calaf waved at their backs, he heard Aric cry out from inside the house. Flavus appeared and placed a hand on his shoulder.

Calaf said, "Ishmael's gone."

Flavus squeezed Calaf's shoulder. "And so too departs our dear friend Demetrius. But, my prince, there is no time for grief." He spoke in highborn Greek catching Calaf by surprise. "You must remain strong."

As Aric's lamentation filled the air, Flavus drew Calaf into Demetrius's dwelling.

General Nozar entered Calaf's darkened room without knocking. A guard accompanied him. "Light that candle," he ordered, pointing at the room's only table, "then leave us." As the guard began to shut the door Nozar called out, "No one is to disturb us—no one."

Calaf sat on the bed, hands on his knees, his uniform stained with Demetrius's blood. He and Aric had sat with the physician's lifeless body, one moment crying, the next muttering prayers to gods Demetrius never honored in life.

Calaf reached for his cane and pushed himself to his feet.

"Remove your uniform. It must be burned. There can be no evidence you were there." As Calaf undressed, Nozar found a robe and handed it to him. Nozar tossed the bloodstained clothing toward the door, and Calaf returned to the bed.

Nozar pulled a chair from the table, moved it before Calaf, and sat.

Calaf spoke first. "Ishmael?"

"Out of the city and on the road to Peshawar. The emperor sleeps, so there is no pursuit at the moment."

"Later?"

"I will do what I can. But if he orders Ishmael taken, I will have to obey."

"But he can't! Not Ishmael."

"Your decision to defy the emperor tonight had consequences, my prince, and you must live with them."

"Yet you defy him by allowing Ishmael to escape."

"I only protect the emperor from an unwise action."

"Protect him? He murders one of his most loyal servants while trying to kill my closest friend—and you speak of protecting him?"

"I regret what happened to Demetrius. If I had arrived in time, I would have prevented his death."

Calaf pushed himself to his feet and stared down at Nozar. "How do you live with yourself?"

"Because I have to. Sit down. In your grief you forget yourself, my prince."

Calaf sat. "Where is Aric?"

"I ordered him to make arrangements for the body as quickly and discreetly as possible to conceal the circumstances of his death. But I am more concerned about the witnesses."

"You would stand by—?"

"Ishmael has already left the city, and Flavus will soon. As for Aric and the soldiers, I will do what I can."

"And if it's not enough?"

"He is the emperor."

"Then I'll talk to him."

Nozar shook his head. "I'm afraid that will guarantee their deaths. This night you had your chance with the emperor and failed. No one doubts your courage—least of all me—but you are reckless. You may think yourself safe, but you are in as much jeopardy as the others, maybe more, so I am forced to protect you—as I would the emperor—from actions that would bring you harm." Calaf started to interrupt but Nozar held up his hand. "What were you thinking tonight? That you were simply a son rebelling against his father? No, you were a dangerous and disloyal subject."

"What are you talking about?"

"The troops talk of little but your rescue of Ishmael and your standing up to the emperor shouting *I saved him*. The emperor fears your defiance. You would not be the first prince raised up to overthrow his father."

"But I don't even want to be emperor."

"So I have heard, and those who believe you think you a fool. Those that don't, think you're shrewd beyond your years. But your birth, my prince, gives you no choice. Even if you don't act, others who oppose the emperor might do so in your name."

Calaf got to his feet and walked to the table. The candle's wick sputtered in the melted wax. Calaf used a knife to channel away the wax, and the flame burst forth, once again casting a bright light around the room. Resigned and calm Calaf turned to face the general.

"We must separate you from the emperor and the army," Nozar said. "Once you're away, it won't be difficult to replace memories of your heroics with fear of the Persians and their need for the emperor's battle-hardened leadership."

"Where will I go?"

"Minnagara. An escort waits outside. I have assigned Flavus to you. He earned Demetrius's trust, so he has mine." Nozar removed a folded parchment from his cloak. Calaf recognized the general's seal. "Present this to the Minnagara commander. It identifies you and Flavus and orders him to continue your military training. There you will await the time when your father will again test your obedience and loyalty."

"I *am* obedient and loyal. What he demands is unjust."

"Justice means nothing if you are dead—ask Demetrius." Nozar stood. "Use your time in Minnagara to consider how you will respond when he calls, but do not deceive yourself into thinking he won't strike you down should you defy him again, and Ishmael will join you should he still live." The general gathered up Calaf's bloodstained uniform and opened the door. "Collect your things quickly." Then to the guard, "Stay with him until he passes the city gate. Then report his departure to me."

The general then disappeared down the dark corridor.

The soldiers returned to their barracks outside the king's quarters. They were quiet—even the unit's buffoon, for whom silence was an invitation to jest and cajole. Still in uniform, their swords sheathed at their sides, they stretched out on their beds, faces fastened to the ceiling. They stripped to their tunics and collapsed into the corners, their eyes unblinking but unseeing. They sat in chairs, their swords across their thighs, fingers polishing the blades, intent on the smallest blemish. The buffoon stood facing the wall, his weight against a planted fist.

They all knew Demetrius. The physician marched with them, nursed their illnesses, tended to their wounds, comforted them in pain, and brought life from the edge of death. They were soldiers hardened to the life of war. Men die. Friends die. But to die as Demetrius just died, taking the edge of a drunken king's sword—

The buffoon straightened, turned about, and sat on the packed earth floor. They joined him, rising from their beds, their corners, and their chairs to take places around him, none observing rank. Knees touched, arms reached around shoulders, eyes glanced about. A single cough broke the tomb-like silence.

"He took the blow intended for the boy."

"You saw it?" There was no reply.

"We must flee." It was the newest recruit. The oldest placed his hand on the young man's knee. "A deserter's fate is worse, my son."

Another voice, the buffoon's voice. "The old fool." His fists were clenched in his lap, the muscles of his naked forearms bulged. He raised his eyes to old faces of calm resignation, mature ones harboring impotence in the face of approaching injustice, and young ones aching with disbelief and crushed dreams. "The old fool made us witnesses to the king's atrocity."

Aric sat at a table in the empty tavern, his head in his hands, the urn containing Demetrius's still-warm ashes before him. The message he had received while waiting for the priests to complete the rushed cremation rites lay unfolded beside him on the bench. The tavern owner had returned to his bed after Aric declined his offer of wine while he waited. Still reeling at the horror of the evening and at Nozar's fears for his safety once Timur sobered, he must keep a clear head as he fought the panic that threatened to engulf him.

Demetrius's dying plea echoed through his mind. "I beg you, Aric, cleanse your heart of the hatred that threatens to destroy you and those you love." But how could he forsake the vengeance that had consumed him since learning that Timur had murdered his brother—and then destroyed the life of the woman he loved? Especially now, after helplessly witnessing Timur brutally kill his closest friend? Then, as if the Fates had not given him enough to deal with, there was the surprise of The Bear's message. In the midst of crippling grief and fear, he tried to weigh what he would say to him—and more importantly do—in response to The Bear's likely entreaty. It had been fifteen years since Aric had first encountered the Persian agent, drunk and out of his mind with grief at Sharina's forced marriage to the Srinagar warlord. They had rarely met since, and although Aric had long anticipated his reason in seeking him out, it was only five years ago that The Bear made that reason known.

"There is much we can do for each other," he had said.

"You once told me you are a merchant who trades in many things," Aric had replied.

The Bear had smiled. "And I have a Persian client."

"What's this client want?"

"Whatever you're comfortable giving him."

"When?" Aric had asked.

"Whenever you're ready. He knows that such trades can take time. For the right items, he can be very generous."

"You know I care about only one thing," Aric had said.

"Sharina."

Aric had nodded. "It's a big decision. I need more time to consider your offer."

"Of course."

No mention of this conversation had taken place since. A seed had been planted, and The Bear—and his client—seemed content to wait for him to make the next move.

A door opened, and then closed. Aric rose and waited as The Bear maneuvered among the tables with an agility belied by his massive bulk. After a quick embrace they sat facing each other.

The Bear glanced at the urn. "I'm truly sorry."

"You know what's happened?"

The Bear nodded. "A soldier who witnessed the atrocity came to me." When Aric gave him a questioning look, he added, "My business requires many contacts. Anyway, he escapes the city as we speak—as you must do if you are in as much danger as he believes you are."

"And risk Sharina being seized in my place. I cannot."

"I can assure her safety," The Bear insisted.

"Only I can do that."

"By dying?"

"If I must," Aric answered.

"If you change your mind—"

"I won't."

"If you do, the tavern owner will hide you until I can be summoned."

Aric stood and cradled Demetrius's urn in his arm, but before he turned to depart, he asked, "It's odd, you being here. What brought you to Srinagar?"

"You, of course."

"But I've promised you nothing."

"A time might yet come."

"If I survive."

The Bear took and squeezed Aric's free hand. "Survive, my friend."

While life had long ago taught Flavus that the gods took as suddenly as they gave, the death of Demetrius staggered him. He prided himself on the cold calculation he brought to every mission. The arena taught him detachment, for today's friend became tomorrow's fallen comrade, or worse, opponent. One learned to display emotion, but never feel it. Many friends died at his side or by his hand—first in the arena, later on assignment—but he mourned none of them. No fleeting memories of a face disturbed those moments between wakefulness and sleep. Until now. Until Demetrius. Standing in Demetrius's bedroom, unable to do anything to save his life, Flavus's eyes had welled up with tears—eyes that had been dry since the day his gladiator school master pulled him from the arms of his Roman stepmother and bound him in chains.

But there was not time for Flavus to absorb the shock of unfamiliar grief or to grasp any meaning it held. General Nozar had appeared before him, ashen faced but resolute. In this moment of crisis and given the general's faith in the advice of the dead physician, Flavus the foreigner had been entrusted with the future of the Kushan throne. While Nozar's decision making him responsible for Calaf during his exile to Minnagara puzzled him and removed him from his long-sought proximity to the emperor, he had learned that if seized, changing fortunes might lead to even greater opportunities, particularly when enhanced with secret knowledge. For the dying Demetrius had told Flavus the truth of the prince's birth, and then reminded him of his pledge to do whatever was necessary to protect and save all three of them: Calaf, Ishmael, and Sharina. Afterward Flavus stood close as Demetrius begged Aric to cleanse his heart of the vengeful hatred for Timur that could only destroy him and those he loved.

PART 3

Ishmael Can Bear No More, His Heart is Breaking

249 - 251 CE

CHAPTER 12

Jhelum River Crossing

Barzin and Ishmael stood above the muddy torrent of the Jhelum where the Neelum joins it from the north, squinting at the sun as it dropped below the clouds and reached for the horizon. After fleeing Srinagar, they had ridden night and day without stopping, except to exchange horses at two army encampments, but the flooded river blocked their way to Peshawar. The barges that normally crossed the Jhelum were beached, their oarsmen refusing to venture upon the treacherous waters. When Barzin pulled a gold coin from his purse, hungry eyes looked but heads shook. Only a fool would tempt the angry flow, and Barzin found no fools.

Barzin covered his ears against the deafening roar, but Ishmael's arms hung at his sides, his eyes watching but unseeing. While responsive to Barzin's direction, the youth had not spoken since mounting his horse outside Demetrius's dwelling. During brief rests when exchanging horses, Barzin tried to engage him but gave up the effort when he received only a shoulder shrug or head nod. If Ishmael wanted to talk, Barzin would listen, but his priority was his father's order to get the boy to safety.

Barzin nudged Ishmael's arm and yelled, "Look!"

An uprooted tree appeared in the river's flow, its roots heavy with debris. With a crack it struck the dock, reducing it to tinder before the surging water carried both away.

"Unbelievable! Did you see that?" Barzin shouted with amazement.

When Ishmael did not respond, Barzin shook his head and led him to higher ground. "We dare not go to the garrison downriver. If the emperor sends orders to seize us, they'll go there first."

"You needn't worry," Ishmael responded, touching his arm. No longer distant and dazed, his eyes were bright, certainty filled his voice. "Demetrius will find a way to help us."

Dread washed through Barzin. On several occasions, he had observed such denial after battle and once watched it turn to madness when the truth could no longer be denied. Taking Ishmael's hand, he said, "Demetrius can no longer help us." He held his breath.

Ishmael laughed. "Of course, he can. The emperor listens to him."

"Don't you remember?"

Ishmael cocked his head. "Remember what?"

"The emperor striking Demetrius."

Again, he laughed. "Not Demetrius. He has struck my father Aric many times, but the emperor's never struck Demetrius—never."

"Please listen to me. Demetrius is dead."

For several long moments, they faced each other like statues, eyes locked, neither moving. Barzin searched for some reaction—tears, rage, anything. Instead Ishmael's arms collapsed to his sides and his eyes resumed their earlier lifeless gaze.

With a sigh Barzin said, "Come, it'll be dark soon."

The oarsmen invited them to join their camp. Around the fire one played a lyre as the others sang. Ishmael began tapping his fingers on his knee.

"Sing with us," Barzin whispered.

A slight smile broke Ishmael's blank expression. At first he hummed.

"That's it," Barzin said, humming along.

Softly Ishmael began to sing, his voice rising with the songs he knew. Relief filled Barzin, certain that Ishmael's animation meant recovery from the shock of his mentor's death.

The lyre player asked Ishmael, "Do you play?"

Ishmael nodded and took the instrument. He practiced a melody, stopping to replay some segments several times to get them correct.

Barzin did not recognize the song. "What is it?"

"A Greek merchant taught it to me."

"Sing it for us," an oarsman called out.

Ishmael played the melody through then blended the Greek lyrics with the lyre's strings.

Oh soul, torn by unbearable concerns,
stand up, defend yourself from your enemies,
outsmart them moving cautiously
through their ambushes.
But do not triumph when you win,
nor lay down crying when defeated,
nor get overjoyed in your joys,
or overwhelmed in your sorrows.
Just learn what rhythm governs human affairs.

An oarsman asked, "What's it mean?"

After explaining the song lyrics in Bactrian, he turned to Barzin, "It's a surprise for Demetrius when he returns."

Peshawar

Sharina maintained her composure, only a slight stiffening in her shoulders revealing any reaction, as the emperor's courier delivered the message that Demetrius had died after a sudden illness. "I passed Captain Barzin and your son on the road," he added. "They should arrive soon." Without a word, she dismissed him.

"No one disturbs me," she said to her maidservant. "No one."

After the chamber door closed she walked to the balcony. The heat of midday rose in waves above the city's rooftops obscuring the Khyber's distant mountains.

Demetrius is dead.

It was but four months since she returned with him from Minnagara, having helped him with the funeral rites for Torak, and bid him farewell on his departure for Srinagar with Ishmael.

Demetrius is dead.

She raised her face to the sky and took a deep breath as tears began to slide down her cheeks. Even though he aged noticeably after Torak's death, she never considered a life without his presence.

Demetrius is dead.

An ache grew in her chest. Slowly she sank to her knees, bringing her hand to her mouth, biting into it, squeezing her eyes shut, and rocked.

Demetrius is dead.

She awoke with a chill in the half-light of dusk, lying on her side, her knees pulled tight against her body. Sudden anxiety gripped her as the face of Timur filled her mind's eye, but Demetrius's voice shattered the loathsome image with the words, 'The boy wears the gold band of the prince and has the prince's birthmark on his hip."

Her son's birthmark used as the proof of her deception.

She had never acknowledged what Demetrius did, never asked why he helped her, at first terrified to give voice to the enormity of what she had done, but later fearful he would demand that she forsake her vengeance in repayment. For the son of Timur still lived, and she knew that the spirits of her family would not give her rest until Ishmael lay dead at the feet of his true father. Often, she agonized over whether Demetrius suspected that she had not absolved Ishmael of being born of a monster. But when he died, he took her secret with him. A complicated grief consumed her: tears of anguish at the loss of a devoted friend fought with relief that he no longer threatened to thwart her mission.

The next day, her face pale, her hair disheveled, Sharina did not rise from her couch when Captain Barzin entered her chamber and bowed. She scowled, "You're told I'm in mourning, yet you insist on seeing me?"

"I apologize, my lady, but General Nozar ordered I speak to you immediately upon my arrival." With a listless wave Sharina motioned for him to continue. "Contrary to what's reported, Demetrius did not die of a sudden illness." After a pause he added, "The emperor killed him."

Shock swept across her face as she sat up. "But Demetrius is most loyal."

"An accident, my lady. He took a blow intended for your son."

"Why would the emperor wish to kill Ishmael?"

"He became enraged when the prince said he'd choose Ishmael over the empire. My father arrived too late to calm the emperor. He ordered me to flee with Ishmael while he negotiated a course of action. Fortunately, there's no longer an immediate threat to Ishmael's life. I received this message at the Jhelum River crossing." He retrieved a folded parchment from his belt and handed it to Sharina. "The emperor orders Ishmael banished to Baktra, but if he and the prince are ever found together again, Ishmael will be executed for treason."

"Where is Ishmael?"

"He waits at Demetrius's apartment."

"For what?"

"Demetrius. He does not accept his death."

"But you said he witnessed it."

"Yes, but it can take time for someone so young."

"And the prince?"

"I've heard nothing."

"When you do?"

"Of course."

After Barzin departed, Sharina's earlier tears of grief for a beloved friend became cries of impotent rage at Timur for once again slaughtering someone close to her. As exhaustion eased her rage, the realization that Timur had almost killed Ishmael filled her mind. Would her vengeance have been pure had he not known he killed his own son? Would the spirits of her family have released her if he lived in ignorance of the life he had taken? But these were questions with no answers, for Demetrius was dead and Ishmael lived.

Inconsolable, she poured words onto parchment.

Never to experience pure grief,
untainted by cruel outrage.
Never memory's healing tears
rather those that lay waste.

Words written only to be consumed in a candle's flame. More words rushed forth, targeting an innocent, unknowing but complicit.

Oh, that Timur's sword had found
his true son's mark,
Ishmael's broken body,
entwined with the bones of Minnagara.

They, too, were consigned to the fire. Another parchment, the pen, a life of its own.

Draw not close to innocence,
to Ashu, to Tanay,
to Calaf, to—

Sharina snuffed out the candle, wrapped her arms around herself and rocked, softly keening.

Morning's light reached across the small table. Sharina opened her eyes and lifted her head, her eyes coming to rest on the parchment, and she read the words aloud.

Draw not close to innocence,
to Ashu, to Tanay,
to Calaf, to—

She hesitated then whispered, "To Ishmael."

No, she must not falter.

Once she had allowed an infant's innocence to distract her. But she was no longer a young girl. She would not succumb to such emotions. While innocent of his father's crime against her family, Ishmael's lifeless body would seal her vengeance.

Draw not close to Ishmael's innocence.

Sharina went to the chamber door and opened it. Her bodyguard bowed. "My lady."

"The governor's son—" Sharina paused.

"Gar, my lady."

"Yes, Gar. Send for him."

Two days later Sharina stood on the balcony, one hand resting on the balcony wall, eyes focused on the Khyber's distant mountains. A stocky youth of seventeen stepped onto the balcony. Sharina turned and smiled at Gar. "Has there been any change?"

"No, my lady. He still goes to the East Gate at mid-morning and watches for Demetrius's arrival until the last caravan arrives. Otherwise he sits in the physician's quarters copying pages from bound parchments."

"Yes, that's how Demetrius taught him. Does he mind your being around him?"

"No—mostly he ignores me."

"Have you convinced him to eat?"

"A little bread, a few olives and dates, nothing more."

"And sleep?"

"He dozes sometimes at the table. But not for long. Early this morning he woke crying out for the prince."

"Has he said anything else?"

"Nothing, my lady."

"Where is he now?"

"The apartment. We've just returned from the gate."

Sharina studied the composed youth for several moments and then approached him. She took his hand and placed a gold piece in his palm.

"I've always been able to trust your father's discretion." Sharina closed Gar's fingers over the coin but did not release his hand.

"As you will mine, my lady." His voice steady, his gaze confident. *So like his father.*

Still holding his hand, she stared into his eyes. "What would you do to protect the emperor and his prince?"

"Anything asked of me, my lady," he did not blink, "without hesitation."

Sharina drew Gar's hand to her face and guided his fingertips to her parted lips. She watched the boy smile as she sunk her teeth into them. When she released his hand, it slipped to her silk-covered breast, his fingers digging into her. She opened her mouth and gasped. Her hand went to the front of his trousers. Gar kept his eyes focused on Sharina's but blinked several times as Sharina caressed him. *Endowed and easily aroused. So like his father.* She squeezed. His turn to gasp. She smiled, and then he laughed.

From her bed Sharina heard her apartment's heavy door open then close behind Gar. She stretched then groaned. She massaged her soreness. *What the boy lacks in finesse, he makes up for in enthusiasm.* She smiled. *Next time he learns finesse—and I begin to prepare him for his role in avenging my family.*

She relished her sexual urges and knowing she could easily be tempted to excess, each new encounter evoked Adelma's warning to exercise extreme caution around men. For soon after the birth of her son, Sharina had begun flirting with one of the palace guards. Within a few days Mahesh escorted her into the queen's private chamber.

"Secure the door, Mahesh," Adelma said. "Under no circumstances are we to be disturbed."

As the eunuch slipped from the room, Adelma motioned Sharina to join her on the divan. "I will be blunt, my dear. Your dalliance with a certain palace guard has been noticed, and to avoid scandal I have arranged for his reassignment."

Sharina's face flushed in embarrassment at this invasion of her privacy, but she held herself in check, keeping her expression alert but wary.

"Let me be clear," Adelma continued, "your sexual interests do not concern me, but what you do about them does. You are a beautiful woman. Men will seek to possess you. It will be flattering, but I assure you that succumbing to passion will be your undoing. You have not forgotten your family, have you?"

"Of course not," Sharina snapped.

"Then you must do nothing, sexual or otherwise, that does not bring you closer to the vengeance for which you long above all else. For the present I urge you to wait, watch, and focus on what lies ahead. You are recently married and have a new son. You must let others see you as the dutiful wife and mother."

"But Aric is so—" Sharina hesitated.

"Ardent but awkward?"

Sharina nodded.

Adelma returned an understanding smile. "I am not surprised. But do not underestimate him. You may find in him an unexpected ally, just as I found in Mahesh. I realize it might be difficult, but you must nurture his passion for you. Give him no reason to turn away from you. You do not want him to become an adversary."

"You mean use him," Sharina said.

"Why of course. Start with him. Perfect how to manipulate passion to your advantage. I once knew an old courtesan from whom I learned the art of ensnaring men. I will teach you her secrets. The men you pursue will not even realize the power you exercise over them. But you must select your targets sparingly and carefully. You cannot afford to be seen as wanton in your affections. Each assignation must advance you closer to Timur's destruction."

Sharina understood that the queen aimed to achieve her own vengeance through her. It had begun with Adelma's deception of Timur by orchestrating Sharina's marriage to Aric, thereby saving her and the Srinagaran raja's son, someone Adelma was certain would one day prove useful. Afterward she mentored Sharina on the ways of deceit and conspiracy—*so that you, like me, might live to see the fruits of your vengeance.* The queen began to appear in her dreams, sometimes standing beside her father, their voices joined in the cry for Sharina to act. But sometimes Adelma replaced him, crying out alone, her face contorted in fury. Sharina awoke from these dreams uncertain about what her father truly expected of her and confused by shifting feelings toward Ishmael, her eyes seeing a boy hungering for a mother's love not the child of the monster who killed her family. And in those moments she reached out to him—holding him, playing with him, listening to him—until the shadow of his father again clouded her vision, driving her to distance herself until the next time the dream recurred.

When the boys were six years old, the queen lay dying of a sudden and mysterious illness of the stomach. Sharina had persuaded Mahesh to allow her a few moments alone with her. Taking Adelma's hand and leaning close to her ear, she revealed that she had switched their boys before the *chakor* ceremony, that Ishmael not Calaf was the queen's true son. The queen's eyes had opened wide, and her mouth lifted in a slight smile as she murmured, "Ah, Timur's heir does not carry his seed." Squeezing Sharina's hand she continued, "You have done well, my dear. But the emperor must know you have done this."

"When the time is right, he will." Sharina kissed Adelma's forehead. That night Sharina joined the death vigil at the queen's bedside. While Mahesh and the others loudly mourned as Adelma breathed her last, Sharina stood quietly, her attention captured by the serenity of the queen's face.

These memories faded with the soft knock at Sharina's bedchamber door. She called out, and her maidservant slipped into the room.

"An officer to see you, my lady. He says it's urgent."

"He has a name?"

"Captain Barzin, my lady."

"Tell him to wait, then return to dress me."

Barzin stood at the opening to the balcony, holding an urn. "Demetrius's ashes," he said. As she took it and placed it on a nearby table, he continued.

"My father's most trusted lieutenant arrived overnight. There's a message for my ears only—and yours. Is it safe to speak here?" She nodded. "To eliminate witnesses the emperor is executing all who were at Demetrius's lodgings that night."

"Calaf?"

"I kept him out of sight, so the emperor did not see him. For the moment the prince is safe, but his rescue of Ishmael did not go unnoticed by the troops. More than that, his public defiance of his father only increased his popularity—a fact not lost on the emperor. Timur's spies brought stories of loose tongues speaking of a time when the prince becomes emperor. Those tongues no longer speak—but, real or imagined, the emperor now sees the prince as a threat to his rule."

"But Timur would not act against Calaf, his only son and heir."

"My father fears that he might. The threat of Persian invasion weighs heavy on the emperor. He rightly demands utmost loyalty and unquestioned obedience, so the prince's defiance cannot be allowed, lest it encourage others. The emperor may feel he has no choice. My father has removed the prince from Srinagar to separate him from the troops. Intensified training and battle exercises have the army thinking more about surviving a Persian onslaught than the heroic exploits of a boy. It also gives Calaf time to come to his senses and prepare for his marriage."

"Marriage?"

"Yes, to a princess of the kingdom of Tur. Timur seeks a military accord with her father against the Persians. The marriage of Calaf to the Princess Turandot will seal the alliance."

"Where is the prince?"

"He goes to Minnagara."

My homeland?

"My father requests that you take Demetrius's ashes to the temple there, like you did with his friend Torak's. Go quietly, and while there, meet with the prince. My father is concerned that unless you help dissuade him of it, Calaf will continue to defy the emperor over Ishmael. You must convince him to pledge his loyalty and obedience to the emperor in all things."

"And if I cannot?"

"Most likely the emperor will complete what he set out to do when he killed Demetrius. He will rescind Ishmael's banishment to Baktra and order his immediate death. I will arrange your escort to Minnagara."

"I will need tomorrow to prepare. The day after?"

He nodded. "I am afraid there is also news of your husband. Timur imprisoned him. He may already be dead."

"But Aric is Yousef's brother. The emperor would never harm him."

"Except that he witnessed Demetrius's death. Beyond that I only report what I have been told." When Sharina did not respond, Barzin shrugged. "My regiment has arrived from Srinagar and the reinforcements from Arachosia are due in two days. In three days, at the most four, I will leave for Baktra. Ishmael must be ready to depart."

"I will inform him."

"How is he?"

"Little has changed. If you have no objection, I have arranged for the governor's son Gar to accompany him."

"A good idea. He should not be alone—it will ease things for him when we get there." He began to leave then hesitated.

"There is something more?"

Barzin looked uncharacteristically ill at ease. "Actually, a question, my lady. I asked my father why we were going to such great lengths to protect Ishmael. He answered because he is the prince's friend. When I pressed him that friend or not, Ishmael is a mere servant, he became angry, forbidding me to speak of it again. My father puts himself at terrible risk, as do I. Some of the soldiers the emperor executed were my men, friends and good, loyal men—" He stopped, unable to continue.

Sharina raised her hand. "I believe General Nozar's order is clear, is it not?"

He regained his composure. "Yes, my lady. I shouldn't have troubled you."

At his departure Sharina collapsed onto a couch, Barzin's words screaming inside her head: *going to such great lengths to protect Ishmael.* She covered her face with her hands.

Nozar knows.

Oh, Demetrius, what have you done?

The next afternoon Sharina waited in Demetrius's palace apartment when Ishmael and Gar returned from their day at the East Gate. Gar acknowledged her with a nod, stepped back into the corridor, and closed the door. Ishmael stood motionless. His eyes scanned the apartment, coming to rest upon the bronze urn she placed on the desk. He disappeared into his bedroom. When he did not reemerge, she went to the open doorway. He sat on the foot of his bed, his head down.

"May I enter?"

Ishmael raised his head then leapt to his feet and bolted past her. Throwing open the apartment door, he pushed Gar aside and ran down the corridor.

"Follow him," she called out to Gar. "Report to me where he goes."

Ishmael ran through the palace, his eyes registering but not seeing. Broad, crowded stairways; long, empty corridors; dark, quiet passages. Then he slowed, stopped, and looked back. A door he recognized. He played with Calaf here when they were very young. He pushed the door. It offered little resistance as it creaked open, revealing a musty, dimly lit chamber, unused, he remembered, since the day Calaf's mother the queen died. Streaks of light peeked under the drapes that covered the balcony opening. He pulled them aside, flooding the room with late afternoon light, filtered through the fronds of palm trees. The trees had not reached the balcony then. Calaf and he would hang over the wall, their arms and legs extended, pretending to be eagles flying over treetops below. Sharina would pull them back and scold them, but the queen would laugh. He smiled recalling her hearty laugh.

Ishmael spun about, fearful it would be gone, but the carpet still covered the floor. Even under the dust of neglect its bright reds and blues, freed from the gloom of a darkened room, hurtled at his senses. He dropped to his knees on the carpet's edge. Several swipes of his hand sent dust motes into the still air, ricocheting particles animating the light from behind. Ishmael squeezed his eyes shut and sneezed twice. Upon opening them again, he smiled at the feast of intertwining animals, birds and vines arrayed before him. His finger went to the lion—always the lion first, its head turned and teeth bared at the fleeing hare. He remembered his mother pointing out that the weaver placed two falling leaves above the hare's back. *See, they look like wings, so the hare escapes.* Ishmael stroked the hare's back. "Fly," he whispered. He reached across to the nearby tiger—Calaf's favorite—crouched, front paw raised, ready to pounce on two unsuspecting parrots. Unlike the hare, the weaver gave no hint of escape for the birds. Ishmael stroked them. "Fly," he whispered even though he knew nothing would save them from the tiger's claws.

Ishmael took a deep breath and closed his eyes against a sudden sting. When he reopened them, he looked again at the hare, tried to hold his focus on the wings of leaves. But he could no longer ignore the image that rested between lion and tiger, between escaping hare and doomed parrots. Finally he rested his gaze on the two foxes—one white, one gold—woven as a pair, neck touching neck, heads turned in opposite directions, eyes attentive to all that swirled about them. Ishmael covered his face with his hands, his shoulders shaking.

A voice called out, "Ishmael." Then louder, "Ishmael."

Ishmael dropped his hands and looked toward the voice. Sharina stood in the chamber's open doorway, Gar behind her. She entered, and Gar closed the door.

Ishmael glanced back down at the two foxes. Tears began to fill his eyes. He looked up again.

"Mama."

Ishmael cried himself to sleep in Sharina's arms. She eased his head into her lap and stroked his tear-stained cheek and thick, curly hair. She could not remember when she last held him, last held anyone in pain and distress. A memory intruded—*holding Ashu the night before he died, the night before they all died*—then an ache filled her chest, an ache that demanded her own tears. She looked down at the son of the man who butchered her family. A cold, steely calm replaced the ache and aborted the tears.

Sharina was stunned when Gar, after following Ishmael's flight, led her to the queen's abandoned reception chamber. Fourteen years earlier in this very room she nearly ended the life of the boy she now held. Fourteen years later she struggled with the same decision. But this time it would not be by her own hand. Should it become necessary, she would instruct Gar, and he would see to it.

She had never expected Ishmael to become a threat to her plans. That Timur's true son would answer to her own—not even as his future scribe but as a lowly physician—added to the vengeance she longed to see consummated. But now Calaf's attachment to Ishmael threatened everything. Who could have predicted that Calaf would defy the emperor, would risk everything for a servant? And Calaf could only save his friend by denying him. As she smiled at the irony, she felt Ishmael stir. He opened his eyes and stared at the ceiling. She waited, looking down at him. Finally, he glanced at her then returned his gaze to the ceiling.

"It's all my fault."

"I don't understand."

"I wanted to see the foxes—tried to get closer. The others wanted to start back—but I insisted. My foot slipped then I fell into the water. My foot got caught in the rocks. I couldn't free it. I couldn't breathe." He stopped. His eyes darted about before returning to rest on hers. "Calaf freed my foot. We held on to each other but got pulled apart. I don't remember anything after that—until I awoke with Demetrius—Demetrius—" Ishmael covered his eyes with his fists.

"It was an accident."

"If I hadn't—he would still—"

She took his wrists and pulled his hands from his face. "Listen to me." Her tone hardened. "You did not kill Demetrius. The emperor did."

"But—"

"No!" Her voice was sharper than she intended and his eyes widened. More softly she added, "Stand up."

He scrambled to his feet and extended his hand to help her rise. She walked to the balcony opening. After several moments, she turned around. Ishmael stood on the carpet, his feet, she noticed, planted on either side of the two foxes embroidered into the carpet.

"Your guilt dishonors the friend who saved you. Even more it dishonors the man who died to protect you. The only guilt rests with Timur." She watched Ishmael's face, watched him grapple with her words. "Do you believe you grieve alone? He took Demetrius from all of us: from Calaf, from Aric, and from me." She stepped up to him, lifted her eyes to his, and placed her hand on his cheek. "He takes Calaf from you now, threatening your death if you are seen together. And for such disobedience, Calaf also would certainly die. The emperor would kill your closest friend." Slipping her free arm about his back, she embraced him and brought his ear to her lips. "Make him the target of your rage." She kissed his forehead then swept around him and left.

Gar waited in the corridor. "Return him to the apartment. Afterward—" She placed a fingertip on his chest and traced a line to the top of his trousers. He reached for her, but with a laugh she rushed away. Descending a broad staircase, she emerged into the courtyard garden, now totally in shadow. She looked up into the late afternoon sky, satisfaction filling her face at the thought she may have begun turning Ishmael against Timur. Carefully nurtured, might not his fears for Calaf's life, if not his own, derange him enough to kill the emperor? And it mattered not whether he succeeded or failed: be it patricide or filicide, her vengeance would be complete without her having to act. She would only have to remain alert, so that she had the opportunity to reveal the truth of Ishmael's birth to Timur at the right moment.

CHAPTER 13

Between Srinagar and Rajanpur

The sun reached its height on their second day from Srinagar. Calaf sat beneath a pine tree while Flavus knelt beside him rummaging through his leather pack for the areca nuts he purchased from a passing caravan the previous day. Their army escort rested with the horses nearer the river.

Calaf asked, "The night Demetrius died—why did you reveal yourself to me by speaking fluent Greek?"

Flavus answered in the same highborn Greek tongue. "So that by trusting you with my fluency in return you would place your trust in me. Ah, here they are." He pulled two of the betel-leaf wrapped nuts from the pack and handed one to Calaf.

"But I already rely upon you."

"Yes, I know you *rely* on me and my experience. However, I seek more than that. I seek your trust."

"So you would have me put my faith in you?"

"Perhaps in time, just as I will put my faith in you."

When Calaf did not respond, Flavus joined him under the tree. He spat his wad of chewed fibers beyond his feet. Feeling a surge of euphoria, he laughed and gave his head a shake. "This one's potent. They're rare in Rome. I didn't have my first until I came here."

Calaf sent his wad beyond Flavus's. "Ishmael can spit farther than that."

"You've finally said his name."

Calaf shrugged then asked, "Did Demetrius know you speak fluent Greek?"

"He never asked. We only spoke Latin."

"Does anyone else know?"

"Only you."

The escort officer Mubashar called out, "Time to move on."

Before standing Flavus winked. "Oh, and no one knows I speak fluent Bactrian either."

Flavus was impressed by Calaf. His play on the two Greek verbs for trust—'rely' versus 'faith'—spoke to a comprehension of his situation and its dangers that revealed a maturity that Flavus did not expect. He would have to take it into account as he mapped his next moves. Flavus knew he risked much. Would Calaf choose to use an outsider's knowledge and experience to gain an advantage in his struggle with his father? Or might he expose an outsider's potential treachery to regain his father's approval? But given the circumstances surrounding Demetrius's death and Timur's threats against Ishmael, Flavus felt confident the prince would use him.

Calaf had vanished. One moment he sat beside the fire, the next he was gone. Flavus made a quick circuit of the camp and spoke with the posted guards. None had seen the prince. Suppressing the anxiety in his gut he reported the prince's absence to Mubashar.

"Taking a piss?" the escort officer asked.

"Too long."

"His weapon?"

"Here."

Flavus waited while Mubashar moved among his men, motioning them to silence and directing several to guard the clearing, sending others into the darkness upriver, downriver and inland. He nodded in Flavus's direction, and Flavus moved toward the river.

Flavus returned first. "He sits by the river."

Mubashar ordered, "Bring him back."

"No. I watch him."

Before the officer could protest, Flavus headed toward the tent he shared with Calaf. He retrieved a blanket and disappeared into the trees.

A half-moon had risen above the pine forest and cast a soft glow over the river's smooth but rapid flow.

No moon shone the last time Calaf sat beside a river at night. The sound of rushing water had been louder then, drowning out all but the intense cold. After freeing Ishmael's foot, he had remained face up and feet first in the torrent, realizing later that this twist of fate saved both their lives. Grabbing a branch of a pine tree that had fallen across the stream, he had pulled himself onto the trunk. Ishmael floated on his back in a nearby eddy, unconscious but breathing, his head bloodied from striking the rocks.

A short distance from the stream he found a tree with low hanging branches. Underneath, within the thick bed of dry pine needles and dry earth, he dug a hollow into which he pulled Ishmael. He wrapped himself around Ishmael's body—chest-to-chest, his face buried in Ishmael's neck—and slipped into unconsciousness. He awakened later to intense throbbing in his right calf and fought the pain by concentrating on matching each breath Ishmael took. *As he breathes—I breathe.* Several times Ishmael's breath slowed, almost stopping. He refused to panic, held Ishmael more tightly, and kissed his neck. *You will not, you cannot leave me—breathe, live, live.* Each time, Ishmael's breath resumed, and his heartbeat sent reassurance into Calaf's chest.

Awakened to their names being shouted, he had crawled from the shelter to excitement that turned to dismay when Calaf insisted that Ishmael be carried to Demetrius first, cutting off Aric's "The emperor will expect" with "Your prince expects." Flavus growled something in a language he did not understand, wrapped Ishmael in a blanket, lifted him into his arms, and rushed off.

His father's reaction had stunned him. But it was not the blow. 'You fool! You risk your life—you risk my empire—for him?' Those words propelled him to rise in defiance and shout, 'I saved him!'

Later, as he recovered from his injured leg, Demetrius attempted to explain the emperor's actions, telling him that his father did not want him to confront the same decision he had faced.

"But I am not my father, and Ishmael is not Yousef."

"That is true," Demetrius had said, "but you must understand that your father cannot free himself from his past."

"I only understand that he would have let Ishmael die—for *his* cursed empire."

"For *your* cursed empire someday."

"Not at the price of my friend."

"And therein lies your father's greatest concern."

A few days later Demetrius stood between Ishmael and the emperor's sword.

Calaf's chest convulsed in pain as his face lifted to the sky.

His eyes squeezed shut as his mouth opened.

His cry ripped through the silence of the night.

Nearby water birds took flight.

Calaf's cry brought Flavus to his feet. He approached. Calaf leapt up and began striking Flavus's chest with his fists. Flavus offered no resistance and backed away when Calaf ceased his blows. Calaf curled up on the ground exhausted. Flavus placed the blanket over the sleeping prince and watched through the night.

On the eighth day, they left the pine forests near midday and began their descent into the wide Indus River valley. Tall pines gradually gave way to the great expanse of mangrove forest. Their party encountered a caravan coming from the south and stopped with them for the night, bathing themselves and the horses in a creek that flowed into Jhelum. The sun had set, leaving the subdued light and shadows of dusk. Calaf and Flavus sat before their tent, a fire at hand. The night's watch posted, the remaining soldiers lounged nearby absorbed with dice, bringing with it the shouts of triumph and groans of defeat that marked every evening since departing Srinagar.

Calaf added a branch to the fire. "You watch me but do not probe."

"What would probing get me, my prince?"

Calaf smiled. "Not much."

"And I would have missed that smile."

"What?"

"You just smiled. First I've seen since—since before that night." Flavus hesitated a moment, then ventured, "You avoid saying their names."

"What good would that do? What good? Men die. Friends die."

"Yes, Demetrius is dead, but Ishmael—he may still live."

"Alive or dead Ishmael is lost to me."

Flavus remained silent for several moments before responding. "We cannot know what lies ahead, my prince. The Fates subject gods and men alike to their whims. We can choose to persevere in the face of whatever they bring or crawl into a hole in fear and defeat. Do you know of Aeneas?" Calaf shook his head. "A hero of Troy who founded the city that later became Rome. The Fates and the gods themselves threw obstacle after obstacle into his path, but he endured. A poet called Virgil wrote his story.

I sing of arms and the man, he who, exiled by fate,
first came from the coast of Troy to Italy, and to
Lavinian shores – hurled about endlessly by land and sea,
by the will of the gods, by cruel Juno's remorseless anger,
long suffering also in war, until he founded a city
and brought his gods to Latium: from that the Latin people
came, the lords of Alba Longa, the walls of noble Rome.

Flavus smiled. "As a boy I lived with a Roman merchant's family and went to school with their three sons. We were forced to memorize large parts of this story, first in Latin to satisfy the merchant, then in Greek to satisfy our Athenian teacher." Flavus nudged Calaf's knee. "I'll teach it to you. You still want to learn Latin, don't you?" Calaf did not respond. Flavus shrugged and stood. "I'll get more firewood."

When Flavus returned, he found Calaf drawing in the dirt with a twig. As Flavus stacked the branches, he recognized two animals, neck touching neck, heads turned in opposite directions. Calaf added arrows, pointing at them in a circular array.

Flavus touched Calaf's foot with his. "What are they?"

"Foxes," Calaf answered then rubbed out the drawing with his hand and pulled his knees close. Flavus added wood to the fire.

Calaf took a stick and stirred the embers. "When you spoke of him, the night he died, you said *our dear friend*."

"Yes, a friend as no other."

"And lover?" Flavus nodded. "Did he tell you about Torak?"

"Yes. I've heard of few men so devoted to each other."

"And you and he?"

"I hope I brought him some pleasure, my prince."

"I hope so, too." Calaf again stirred the embers. "Flavus."

"Yes."

"You may call me Calaf—that is, when we are alone."

Calaf and Flavus rode far enough behind the escort to avoid the dust kicked up by their horses.

Calaf said, "Mubashar no longer comes back to talk to us."

"He must now agree with General Nozar that this foreigner isn't a threat to you."

"Ah, but you could be," Calaf said. Flavus's face turned quizzical and Calaf broke into a broad grin. "After all, you are a spy."

"Somewhat farfetched, don't you think?"

"Then why is it so important that no one knows you speak fluent Greek and Bactrian? So they don't know you understand what they're saying, right? And you don't talk much—you watch and listen. You keep quiet—unless you're acting like a big, dumb gladiator—and when you speak, you ask questions."

"So, it's decided?"

"It's the only thing that makes sense. The only question is who you're spying for." Calaf paused and a serious look crossed his face. "It better not be the Persians."

Flavus reined his horse to a stop. Calaf brought his mount about and moved to Flavus's side.

"Romans," Flavus said.

"What?"

"I'm a *frumentarius.*"

"A *frumen-* what?"

"A covert unit of the Roman army, the *frumentarii.* We report only to Emperor Philip. We're his eyes and ears throughout the Empire, and we do whatever he demands of us."

"So you are a spy."

"The *frumentarii* play many roles."

"But my father's empire is not part of the Roman Empire."

"The Kushans, like Rome, hate the Persians, and an enemy of Rome's enemy is Rome's friend. My emperor has sent me to determine whether your father will keep Shapur's army occupied in the east. That would create an opportunity for Rome in the west—to the advantage of both Kushans and Romans. If I decide Timur can meet our needs, I am charged to reveal myself to him and offer to coordinate the delivery of Roman weapons and supplies to the Kushan cause."

"And if my father can't?"

Flavus patted Calaf's thigh. "Demetrius told me you are quick." Mubashar signaled their stop for their midday rest. "Listen, your father is strong and likely to prevail, but as you've seen, the winds of fate can bring the unexpected. Come, for now we must join the others."

CHAPTER 14

PESHAWAR

BARZIN STRODE THROUGH THE KHYBER Gate, heading toward his regiment's encampment. With a shout, Ishmael ran up to him, surprising Barzin with his transformation. He was no longer a boy paralyzed with grief, rather a poised young man showing no hesitation in step or stance. Sadness still dominated his face, but his eyes showed determination.

Ishmael asked, "Has my mother departed?"

"Yes—she seemed eager to be on her way."

"And why not? She goes to the prince."

Barzin sensed intense emotion, tightly controlled, and noticed Ishmael did not, perhaps could not, speak Calaf's name. "We leave for Baktra beginning the day after tomorrow at dawn."

"Mother told me. That is why I need to speak to you."

"Walk with me then. I must meet with the Arachosian commander. Something about a brawl last night between some of his men and mine. Not surprising. Those Arachosians are a hot-tempered lot."

"Demetrius said they go crazy when they're drunk."

Barzin smiled in relief at Ishmael's casual mention of the dead physician's name. "Smart fathers hide their daughters when the Arachosians come to town."

"Sons, too, Demetrius said," Ishmael added with an easy laugh.

"So I've heard. But you should see them on the field of battle. None braver."

They continued to chat on the path, but Barzin could tell Ishmael had something on his mind. Finally, he blurted out, "My banishment order, does it still require that I be the governor's scribe?"

"No, it only requires that you remain in Baktra until the emperor orders otherwise."

Barzin felt Ishmael visibly relax.

"Then I request you accept me into your regiment as both recruit and physician. I have Demetrius's library. I will bring it with me and continue my studies when I'm not on duty. Demetrius told me the army needs physicians as much as it needs soldiers. I can be both." Barzin raised his hands to stop Ishmael's rush of words but Ishmael ignored him. "There has been a terrible mistake. I must prove to the emperor that I serve only him. I can begin by serving you. Please, sir."

Barzin tried unsuccessfully to hide the broad smile filling his face. "So you wish to step into Demetrius's sandals?" Ishmael nodded once, his expression serious. "And you wish to defend your emperor as a soldier in his army?" Again, Ishmael nodded once. "You needn't do both. Choose one."

"I choose both, sir." Barzin smiled. "Do you agree, sir?"

Barzin slapped Ishmael's arm, almost knocking him over. "Of course, I agree." As Ishmael regained his balance, Barzin stepped around him, calling back, "With me, soldier. I have some Arachosians to deal with."

As sundown neared, Ishmael rose from the knee-deep stream that meandered through the desert valley outside the city wall. A father sat in the water nearby watching his two young sons play. Enveloped in oppressive late summer heat, Ishmael fought the urge to drop back into the stream. He stepped onto the bank, groaning as he flexed his arms and legs. Never had he been this sore. He reached down and recovered his loincloth from the spread of once sweaty and dust-stained garments that he washed before collapsing in the water.

After a tense meeting with the Arachosian commander, in which it was decided that the soldiers involved in the brawl, both Kushan and Arachosian, would be denied their wine allotments for five days, Barzin left Ishmael with the officer responsible for the army's new recruits. Drilled beyond endurance that afternoon, Ishmael barely could lift his arms to tie the loincloth around his slim waist. His only consolation were the words of another recruit, already a week into training, assuring him that if he could get out of bed the next morning, it would get easier.

Loincloth in place, Ishmael knelt and tied the rest of his clothing into a bundle, the suffocating heat precluding any thought of donning them. Sweat already covered his dark skin, and he sighed as the gentlest of breezes passed around him. He looked about, once again surprised he did not see Gar, his shadow for the last week. Gar had been sneaking out of the apartment the past few nights, making him wonder if his mother had decided he no longer required someone to watch over him. Surely now that Barzin had agreed to his enlistment, a companion was no longer necessary. If Gar showed up that night, he would tell him so. Anyway, given Gar's nocturnal absences, he likely would welcome the opportunity to remain in Peshawar, rather than follow him to Baktra.

He spotted a group of Arachosians bathing. Their distinctive braided hair and beards made them hard to miss. One of them began walking upstream. At that moment an older man stood. From the back he looked like Demetrius. An ache rose from Ishmael's chest to his eyes. As he wiped his cheeks with the back of his hand, the father called his sons out of the water. Ishmael smiled remembering how Demetrius had to physically pull Calaf and him from the stream when they were boys—except, that is, when Demetrius's friend Torak bathed with them. After a single swat on their bare behinds, he never questioned Torak's orders. Surprisingly, neither did Calaf. He watched the father put one foot into the stream then laughed as the two boys leapt from the water and rushed to gather their clothing.

He resumed walking, his mind jumping from one memory of Demetrius to another. Demetrius enjoyed retelling the age-old stories of Alexander. Calaf loved the one about the thirteen-year-old Alexander winning and taming his horse Bucephalus. Alexander's heroic exploits in battle upon his great black steed held both boys enthralled, but as he grew older Ishmael preferred that Demetrius retell the story of Alexander and his friend Hephaistion. He learned the story word for word from its opening lines, *Hephaistion was by far the dearest of all Alexander's friends. He had been brought up with Alexander and shared all his secrets,* and surprised Demetrius by reciting the story in its entirety one afternoon as they bathed alone. Afterward he blurted out a long-unspoken desire, 'I will be Calaf's Hephaistion,' to which Demetrius responded, 'I have little doubt it is meant to be.'

The path forked ahead. To the right it widened and led to the Khyber Gate. Most of those around him walked in that direction. To the left the path followed the stream, passing near the entrance to an abandoned tunnel before joining the caravan road to the Khyber Pass. No one bathed there, the banks being rocky and the pools shallow, and few men walked the path. Occasionally Demetrius would send them directly to the city while he took the longer way. The evening meal awaited them so they would rush off without question. Later, as Ishmael realized that, like Demetrius, his sexual interests focused on men, he began wondering what Demetrius did down the path.

Ishmael stood long moments at the fork, excitement stirring in both his chest and groin, before he started down the leftward path. After a short distance, he stepped aside for several men to pass him. One caught his eye and smiled. Ishmael returned the smile and watched the man look back at him after he passed.

When Ishmael resumed walking, he saw the Arachosian drop off the path into a dense copse that concealed the abandoned tunnel. As Ishmael drew closer, another man emerged from the same copse tying his loincloth. Ishmael hesitated only a moment before walking past the man to disappear into the bushes.

The next day Ishmael awoke to Gar shaking his bed.

"Go away," Ishmael groaned and pulled the blanket over his head. His aching body reminded him of the previous day's exertions. Gar grabbed the blanket and flung it to the floor. Ishmael opened his eyes. Gar looked down at him, hand on one hip, the other scratching his head.

"By the gods, you stink. What've you been rolling in?"

"Go away!"

"I guess you've looked worse." With a laugh Gar grabbed Ishmael's foot and pulled him off the bed to join the blanket. Gar left the room to Ishmael's curses.

When Ishmael emerged from his room fumbling with his loincloth, he found Gar lying on the couch. "There's a pack animal in the courtyard. The soldier delivering it says it's yours."

"It's for Demetrius's library. I'm taking it with me to Baktra."

"He said you joined the army. That should surprise your mother."

"Good news for you though. No need for you to come with me."

"Sorry, you're not getting rid of me that easily," Gar said. "I have other business in Baktra."

"What business?"

"I go to represent the interests of my father Governor Zubair."

"And my mother's interests?"

"Of course, should they overlap." Then swiftly shifting the subject, Gar said, "Those Arachosians. I hear they can be vigorous—and demanding."

"Care to be introduced?"

Gar protested his lack of interest, and Ishmael smiled, realizing he responded just as Demetrius would have.

CHAPTER 15

RAJANPUR

CALAF AND FLAVUS WALKED DOWN the wide stone steps that descended into the river. Rajanpur dominated the junction of the Jhelum and the Indus, a major meeting place for caravans from the interior and the merchant boats that plied the Indus River to Minnagara, where sea-going ships exchanged the spices and silk of the East for Rome's gold. The steps and river shallows were crowded with men stripped to the waist, most bathing but many exercising the rituals of their gods. Naked boys frolicked and swam under the watchful gaze of their fathers and grandfathers. Several men greeted Flavus by name.

Calaf pulled off his tunic. "They know you?"

"I was assigned to the garrison here before getting transferred to the northern army."

As they stepped into the water, the boys descended upon a delighted Flavus. Some reached out to stroke his white skin, and he leaned over so they could touch his long yellow hair. Flavus began playing with the boys, heaving some into the air and allowing others to climb onto his shoulders to dive shouting into the muddy river—much to the entertainment of all but those attempting to pray.

Calaf moved away to a quieter spot near a group of old men. As he soaked, his mind wandered to the stream that flowed outside the walls of Peshawar where he and Ishmael often played as boys under Demetrius's watchful gaze. *Demetrius.* A jab of pain penetrated his chest. He hoped someday such memories would bring comfort. *Ishmael.* A stronger jab, this one rising to his eyes. Calaf looked up into the sky and squeezed his eyes shut, fighting the onrush of memories: a darkened, blood-stained corridor, a prince's gold band exchanged, a friend's embrace and hurried profession of love. The memories were swallowed by his father's words: *Nothing is more important than my empire.* Calaf felt heat flush his face and imagined his hands tighten around the throat of his father, the man who would take the life of his friend.

Jerked back to the present by a boy's elated cry, Calaf found Flavus untangling himself from several persistent boys and pointing toward the city wall. Spotting an unexpected figure, Calaf leapt up and rushed into Aric's open arms. Joining them, Flavus enveloped the smaller man and lifted him off his feet.

Returned to the ground, Aric pulled Calaf close, his voice low. "The emperor imprisoned me with the others who witnessed Demetrius's death. But for Nozar's intervention I would have died with them."

"All of them?" Calaf asked. Aric's anguished eyes answered him. "But you're the brother of the martyred Yousef. Surely Timur wouldn't—"

"Even that would not have saved me this time. Nozar still fears for my safety. That is why he sent me here, to put distance between the emperor and me until he is too occupied with other things to care—or remember."

"And Ishmael?"

"He's safe, still on his way to Baktra. Dress and let's find a place to talk. I must return to Srinagar at first light, and we have much to discuss."

Flavus pulled on his trousers. "I know a tavern."

Aric gave Flavus a puzzled look. "You understood what I was saying?"

Calaf stepped between them. "I'm trying to teach him Bactrian. He's teaching me Latin."

Aric chuckled. "You? Learn Latin?"

"Maybe I wasn't your best student but—"

Aric cuffed Calaf on the side of his head. "You keep surprising me."

Flavus pointed at the city gate. "Come—tavern."

Returning from the latrine, Aric reentered the dark tavern from the back and worked his way around the scattered tables and benches, crowded with boatmen and soldiers, boisterous with drink. Aric pushed away several hands intent on his trouser pockets—looking for the coins he kept safely in a leather pouch about his neck—then to his surprise a hand groped his genitals. Grasping the hand, he twisted it until he heard its owner cry out, then felt another hand buried deep in his pocket. He grabbed the other wrist and swinging about found himself holding two boys, neither older than ten. They flashed winsome grins, causing Aric to relax his grip. The boys wrenched themselves free and disappeared into the crowd. Aric shrugged and continued pushing through the crowd.

Upon their arrival at the tavern, Flavus had spoken to the owner, who cleared a secluded alcove of its besotted occupants, their protests met with two pitchers of wine. When Aric returned to the alcove after using the latrine, he found that Flavus had moved to a nearby table and was talking with the tavern owner. Calaf picked at the remnants of their meal of lamb kabobs, rice, grilled vegetables and na'an. The earthy, dusty scent of saffron still hung over the meal, as did its bitter taste in Aric's mouth. He grabbed the arm of a serving girl and mouthed *More wine.*

As Aric sat, he squeezed his nostrils shut. "Latrine's three alleys away but no missing it. Worse than the ones in Srinagar, but at least they have the excuse they're still rebuilding after your father demolished the place."

Calaf grinned. "The price you pay for that sensitive nose of yours."

"Now don't *you* go repeating Demetrius to me."

Both became quiet at the mention of the physician. Calaf studied the tabletop as Aric's eyes wandered about the tavern. Flavus's head almost touched the tavern owner's. He talked while the tavern owner nodded in close attention.

Aric touched Calaf's hand. "What's Flavus doing?"

"He says we can go by boat now, so he's making arrangements for a merchant to take us to Minnagara."

"You're certain that's all?"

Calaf shifted on his bench so he could see Flavus. Another man now sat at the table and joined the tavern owner in listening to Flavus. "What do you mean?"

"I know Nozar likes the Roman and believes he's an able bodyguard, but—"

Calaf interrupted Aric with a raised hand. "Just because he's a foreigner—"

"Listen to me. You must be cautious. These are dangerous times. And as the emperor's heir, the danger is greatest for you. Many will attempt to use you to achieve their own ends. Some may even seek your death—or the deaths of those close to you."

Calaf's jaw tightened as his face darkened. "You tell me nothing I do not already know. There are two people I trust with my life: one is dead, the other banished. The one who is dead trusted Flavus enough to commend him to Nozar. That's good enough for me."

The serving girl arrived with a pitcher of wine. Aric slipped her a coin, and after a slight smile of acknowledgement, she tucked it into the belt about her waist. Calaf took the pitcher and poured wine into their cups.

"Calaf, understand I mean no disrespect to Demetrius, but in his grief over Torak he allowed passion to be rekindled by this Roman gladiator. I beg you to consider that his judgment may have been blinded by lust and Flavus may have taken advantage of him for his own purposes—and will take advantage of you."

"Oh, Aric, *blinded by lust?* Not the Demetrius I knew. Anyway, it's more likely that—even as he enjoyed a little lust along the way—Demetrius took advantage of Flavus for *his* own purposes." Calaf took Aric's hands in his. "Still, you have observed and learned much at the emperor's side, even before I was born. I would be a fool to ignore your wisdom. You give me good counsel—as you would to your own son. I value it and will consider it carefully. Now, tell me about this princess of Tur my father's decided I am to marry."

Surprised by Calaf's adeptness at changing the subject, Aric hesitated a moment before replying. "Turandot is said to be a virgin and beautiful. There is some question about her age, but I understand she is at least twenty."

"Twenty? Then she must be ugly."

"Not necessarily. It seems she has refused all of her father's choices."

"Refused? What kind of country is this Tur?"

Aric shrugged his shoulders. "The king is said to be a great warrior with a large, well-disciplined army. It seems that his only weakness is a tolerance for his daughter's whims."

"And she will accept me because—?"

"Her father fears Persian might—even more than we do. A Kushan-Tur alliance will put a stop to Persian expansion. To ensure that Tur honors the treaty your father demands that it be sealed by the marriage. She will have no choice."

"Unless I refuse."

Aric's eyes opened wide. "How can you talk such nonsense after all that has happened?"

"It is *because* of what happened that I speak as I do."

"By the gods, the emperor will crush you."

"But you yourself have told me why he won't. He needs me to seal his alliance, to marry this princess, to save his damned empire. In exchange, he will give me what I want."

"And that is?"

"Ishmael restored to me."

"You play a fool's game. It can only end in disaster."

A crash of pottery and angry shouts interrupted Calaf's response. The tavern owner leapt from his table, his voice booming curses before he even reached the kitchen opening. Flavus embraced the other man before rising and returning to the alcove. He grabbed the pitcher, refilled his cup, and downed it in a single swallow.

"Come. We have a boat. We go tomorrow."

They passed through the town gate and headed toward their camp. Flavus walked ahead, Calaf and Aric several paces behind. Aric slowed. "There is one other thing you should know." Calaf matched Aric's stride. "Sharina is bringing Demetrius's ashes to Minnagara."

Indus River

At thirty-five paces, the boat Flavus hired was longer than most that navigated the Indus River delta, attesting to the spice merchant's prosperity. Raised and covered in thatch, the rear third of the boat provided protection for the cargo. In the front of this thatched deck, a man's height lower, twelve oarsmen maneuvered the boat in the slow and steady river current. On the journey downriver the oarsmen talked, joked and sang to pass the time. Only burning muscles, loud groans, and unending sweat would be their companions on the return upriver.

It was the third day of the journey from Rajanpur to Minnagara. Flavus and Mubashar rested with the merchant Kabir under the shade of the thatched deck. The soldiers were scattered about the boat. If the gnarled and weathered merchant felt any resentment at having his boat commandeered, he kept it to himself. Calaf sat at the stern on the thatched deck, his dark legs hanging over the side, gazing at the thick forests of mangrove that covered the shore on both sides of the river. Since leaving Rajanpur his thoughts had hovered around Sharina. How long had he wanted freedom from her oppression? He could not imagine anything worse than to be thrust back into her presence, to hear her soft voice cajoling him to bend to her will, to be left confused by her words and wondering at her motives.

After Aric departed, Calaf had unburdened himself to Flavus, all caution cast aside. He erupted with a lifetime of memories about this woman who would live his life for him—this woman, his best friend's mother, who long ignored her own son to torment him. He told Flavus of their fights, including when she forced him to parade naked through the streets of Peshawar for spying on women bathing. They erupted over issues large and small, her anger in equal measure to his defiance. Afterward he would storm to Demetrius's apartment to find Ishmael, for only Ishmael could calm him. Ishmael listened as Calaf raged at her tyranny until exhaustion extinguished the flame of his anger. He would awaken lying in Ishmael's arms, the only place he found solace. Emerging from Ishmael's room they would often find Demetrius, who would counsel the impossible task of Epicurus's *moderation in all things*—impossible for everyone but Demetrius. Ishmael and he grew up hearing rumors of Sharina's bedding other men when Ishmael's father accompanied the emperor on his campaigns, men who often sought out Calaf to give advice, always with words that reflected Sharina's own. Rumor became fact when Ishmael walked in on her and the Peshawar governor Zubair. Afterward the governor called

Ishmael to the palace and terrified him with threats of the dungeon should he speak a word of what he saw. Calaf still seethed at this injustice to his friend. Later Sharina told Calaf he must expand his friendships. The next day Calaf found himself on a hunting trip with the governor and his son Gar. Calaf remembered the older Gar being as uncomfortable as he was, but without a word spoken both understood the roles they must play. Their act satisfied Sharina, while the governor only cared that Sharina was satisfied.

When Calaf stopped speaking, Flavus offered his counsel. "Sharina ruled you when you were a boy. That is what adults do to children. But you are no longer a child, whose only recourse is the impotence of a tantrum. You are the prince. She is your subject. It is time that you rule her."

Calaf reflected upon these words as a pod of dolphins appeared behind the bow with their loud whistles and clicks. He counted eight approaching the boat's stern, their tails moving up and down faster as they gained speed. Two breached, side-by-side, sending a spray of water into the air. The oarsmen were shouting. Calaf scrambled across the thatched deck shouting, "Dolphins! Dolphins!"

Pointing and laughing Calaf dropped to the main deck and rushed among the oarsmen, joining in their excitement as the needle-nosed creatures passed the boat, swam about and returned. Four breached this time as several swept within arm's length of the boat's hull. Calaf reached out, almost fell from the boat, and then looked back with a face of unrestrained happiness. As the dolphins circled for another pass, Calaf shouted, "They're coming back."

Kabir called out, "Hold the boy over the side. It brings good fortune if they let him touch them."

As the dolphins moved toward the bow, Flavus took hold of Calaf's hips, allowing him to lean over the water, his hands outstretched above the surface. The dolphins swam past without drawing near.

Gahdi, the lead oarsman, shouted, "Slap the water."

Again the dolphins circled about and approached the stern.

Over and over Calaf slapped his hands against the water, getting the attention of one that breached then slowed and moved alongside the boat. As Calaf touched the dolphin's head behind its blowhole, the dolphin lifted its tail out of the water. With a crack the tail came down, splashing all within reach. The dolphin sped away to the cheers of the crew. Three more times a dolphin came to the boat's side to accept Calaf's hand in greeting—the same dolphin, Calaf insisted, *my dolphin*—before the school dropped back to resume feeding.

As Flavus pulled Calaf back into the boat, Calaf's face glowed. "Wait until Ishmael hears about this!"

The next afternoon the boat reached Minnagara. Calaf, Flavus and the soldiers stood in front of the thatched cargo hold as the oarsmen fought the current to keep the boat just downriver of the jetty. With a precision honed over many years, a dockworker swung a rope in ever-widening circles before releasing it over the water. At the bow Gahdi extended his arm and the knotted end of the rope slapped into his out-stretched hand. Two oarsmen joined him and together they hauled the boat to the dock among the other vessels. Flavus led Calaf and the soldiers down the center of the boat's deck, dodging the rowers, who were shipping their oars. When they stepped off the boat, Kabir stood on the dock in an animated argument with the port's toll collector.

"That's twice what I paid before!" The merchant pulled on a chain around his neck and an engraved disc appeared from under his tunic. He thrust the medallion in the toll collector's face. "See, a spice trader—a *Kushan* spice trader—like my father and his father before him. Don't treat me like some thick-skulled Persian you can gouge at will."

The toll collector took hold of the medallion and studied it before giving a pronounced nod in the direction of several soldiers near Minnagara's River Gate. One advanced half the distance, then stopped.

Kabir studied the toll collector's face. "You threaten me?"

"I collect what I'm told to collect. Those who pay may unload and load their cargo." He fingered the medallion then pulled it, bringing Kabir's face up to his. "I trust there is no need to tell you what happens to those who refuse to pay." He released the medallion, and Kabir rocked back on his heels, took a step backwards, and bumped into Calaf. When he swung about, Calaf dropped a leather pouch into his hand.

"Something extra for the dolphins."

CHAPTER 16

Minnagara

SHARINA TOOK HER TIME JOURNEYING from Peshawar to Minnagara. While her desire to see Calaf was strong, the painful memories of traveling through the lush Indus River delta were stronger. The last time she traveled this road—a mere six months earlier—Demetrius sat beside her, diverting her thoughts while bearing his own grief at the death of Torak. Now she rode alone, her mind a prisoner to events twenty years past. Her mother beheaded, little Tanay's head crushed, lying silent and still on the marble floor. Demetrius telling her that her father and Ashu were dead, and then preventing her from following their ashes into the Indus to the sea. She had told him, 'Remember this day! You will wish you let me die.' Not for the first time she wondered if he ever regretted pulling her from the river's flow. If not before, he would now if he were alive. *It is good you are not here to see what is to come.*

Her horse-drawn wagon slowed to a stop. She parted the curtain as the escort officer rode up. "We approach the temple, my lady."

"And the prince?"

"I'm told he waits with the monks."

"I will walk now."

The officer placed a footstool below the wagon gate, helped Sharina descend, and then unloaded and opened a large chest. Composed, her tears for Demetrius long ago shed, Sharina lifted the bronze urn containing his ashes.

"Are you sure you don't wish me to accompany you?"

"Thank you, but no. Once I have entered the temple, you may follow and wait."

Sharina stood alone at the top of the rise, looking down upon the unassuming temple that clung to the banks of the Indus and beyond to the distant walls of Minnagara. She took the first step down the road, feeling all her twenty-nine years and too many more.

Inside the cool shade of the temple a young monk approached Calaf and bowed, hands together, fingers pointed. Calaf bowed in return, his hands together in the same manner. Calaf responded to Flavus's quizzical look. "Sharina taught me. Seemed the right thing to do—especially today. She's here. Come."

Calaf followed the young monk to the entrance of the temple and joined an elderly monk. Flavus took his place behind Calaf. Sharina approached, looked up, and shaded her eyes from the sun's glare.

"You didn't tell me how beautiful she is," Flavus whispered.

"Be wary—she hides her claws."

Calaf descended the steps to greet her. After handing him the urn, she placed her hand on his cheek. He did not meet her eyes.

"You look well, my prince."

Calaf stepped beside her. "As do you, my lady." He took her arm and escorted her into the temple.

Sharina and Calaf stood together as the monks transferred Demetrius's ashes from the urn into a painted wooden boat, their chants reverberating within the ancient wood walls. Sharina noticed Calaf fighting to control his grief, eyes straight ahead, teeth biting into his lower lip. She wanted to reach for his hand but knew he would refuse. A history of too many words—his of defiance, hers of anger. Several times she noticed Calaf glance toward his giant bodyguard, whose return nod seemed to calm him. Sharina studied him. She caught his eye and gave him a slight smile, which he returned with a formal bow.

The ceremony completed, the community of monks led Sharina and Calaf out the temple's rear porch. They placed the boat a step above the flowing Indus then dispersed into the surrounding fields to work. Flavus waited in the shadow of the temple's roof. Sharina and Calaf sat with the boat between them. The final act remained, left to those closest to the departed one to do in their own time, after their final good-byes.

Calaf spoke first. "Ishmael should be here."

"Yes, he should."

"It is not right."

In the quiet strength of his words, Sharina felt General Nozar's fears confirmed. Convincing him to pledge obedience to the emperor could prove difficult. She might need Gar to eliminate Ishmael sooner than expected.

Long moments passed. Finally, Sharina asked, "Shall we?"

"It's hard to let him go."

Sharina did not respond. After a few moments he continued, "Remember how he called himself an Epicurean? When I asked him about it, he had me memorize what Epicurus taught about death. He said it was all I needed to know." He lifted the boat and stepped to his waist in the flowing river. Sharina followed and ventured to place her hand on his shoulder.

Calaf's clear, strong voice reached out across the water. "Therefore, understanding that death brings both body and soul to an end makes every moment of life enjoyable by removing the yearning for immortality. For there is no fear while we live if we thoroughly grasp there is nothing after death to be feared, be it divine judgment or an unknowable afterlife."

He held onto the boat for several long moments, feeling the river's current pulling to capture it. "Rest with Torak, dear Demetrius. Regardless of what Epicurus says, I know he waits for you."

He released the boat.

Sharina and Calaf departed the temple and headed toward Sharina's waiting escort. Flavus followed a few paces behind. Sharina glanced at Calaf several times, but he kept his eyes focused ahead. She placed her hand on Calaf's arm. "May we have a word?"

"As you wish, my lady."

Sharina drew him out of the sun to a small grove of trees. She nodded at Flavus, who followed them. "Must he?"

"Certainly you understand it is his duty to protect me. But you need not concern yourself, my lady. He speaks Latin, a bit of Greek and only enough Bactrian to give and take orders."

"Must you be so formal?"

"Is it not proper?"

"Among those who are not family—of course."

"My family is the emperor and his army, my lady."

Sharina turned away. She took several breaths before facing Calaf again. "We parted with angry words. I said things I now regret and wish to make amends. I ask you to allow me this."

"I leave on patrol for three days. We can meet upon my return. The governor's arranged lodging for you in the palace. Flavus will assign your guard and show your escort where to garrison. I must now join my company." With an abrupt turn he strode toward his horse.

CHAPTER 17

MINNAGARA

SHARINA AWOKE AT FIRST LIGHT to the cries of a peacock in the courtyard below her balcony. Her mother kept peacocks and taught Sharina their calls, some to warn of danger, others to attract a mate. But these were cries for the sheer joy of making noise, cries that always provoked Tanay's squeals of delight. *Tanay.* He would be seventeen now, a year older than Ashu was then, but she would not lie in bed stewing in memories—not today.

She rose, pushing her long, black hair over her shoulder, and walked onto the balcony, rubbing her eyes. She approached the low wall and looked down on the courtyard one floor below. The peacock strutted, its massive tail spread wide. Five peahens moved around him, pecking among the low-lying plants that bordered the intersecting packed-earth paths. *There used to be a fountain.*

A door on the far side opened and Flavus entered the courtyard. He wore a sleeveless, knee-length tunic of white cotton, his short sword sheathed in a scabbard secured to a wide leather belt. The peacock shrieked—his danger cry. She watched the peacock advance as his harem scurried behind him. Flavus whirled at the bird, threw up his arms, and pushed out his chest. The tunic's thin fabric stretched across his knotted muscles; its hem lifted baring Flavus's thick thighs. Flavus emitted a low, guttural growl. The peacock maintained its defiance—tail spread, head thrust forward, repeated cries—but stepped backwards. The Roman erupted with a hearty laugh.

Vain as the peacock. Her mouth lifted in a slight smile. *He would be easy.*

Damp from the night's humidity, Sharina's diaphanous sleeping gown clung to her curved midriff, slender hips and small rounded breasts. Flavus looked up. Sharina observed no surprise.

"I relieve the guard," he said in imperfect Greek.

"If I were queen, you'd be executed for seeing me like this." She had not spoken Latin in years but knew it was still nearly perfect.

At her use of his tongue Sharina saw no change in Flavus's expression. He gave her a slight nod and replied in Latin. "Then I'm greatly relieved you aren't the queen, my lady." The Roman disappeared below her balcony.

His quick, confident retort was unexpected. Warmth flushed Sharina's face. She spun about and retreated into her apartment. The peacock resumed its shrill cries of exaltation.

She pushed her gown off her shoulders into a pool at her feet.

A breath of air wafted over her sweat-damp nakedness. A shiver.

Her hand descended, the lightest of strokes. A sigh.

Again, the peacock shrieked.

Flavus stood near the closed door to Sharina's apartment. Her maidservant delivered her morning meal soon after Flavus relieved the night guard. Now he waited for her next move, recalling how her eyes lingered on him at the temple. But unlike the predictable matrons of Rome whose desires were limited to what he could do between their legs, he knew Sharina was clever, seeking gain first, then pleasure—that much was clear from Calaf's rant about her infidelities.

He had been involved with such opportunistic women before. In Rome, a daughter of a wealthy patrician family, married to a Roman senator old enough to be her father, had appraised him with such boldness. *Lucia.* She had taken a lover and wished her husband out of the way. When she discovered that the senator liked to dress up as a soldier and have Flavus subdue and fuck him, she began her own affair with Flavus, hoping to convince him to kill her husband. She became enraged at his refusal to cooperate with her plan. *Only in the arena do I kill.* A well-placed word in the senator's ear and a divorced wife was sent back to her family in disgrace and remarried to an aged uncle in Gaul. The grateful senator recommended Flavus to the head of the *frumentarii* and soon afterward Flavus entered the Emperor's service under the continued guise of a champion gladiator.

Certain his bond with the prince interested Sharina, Flavus decided to personally guard her to present her with an opportunity to approach him. Given her position in the Kushan court, perhaps he would learn something important to his mission. Flavus suspected she played the long game, just as he did himself. Like Lucia, did Sharina have a lover that made her marriage to Aric inconvenient? Or was it the emperor she wanted dead? While she had every reason to hate Timur, she must have had opportunities to kill him over the years, opportunities that she had not taken.

Flavus cleared his mind. He had learned that while speculation might entertain, it could distort judgment and blind him to the truth. His only certainty was that when the time came, he would act based on furthering his mission. Nothing else mattered, including the removal of a woman in his path. Lucia had only been the first.

The apartment door opened, and Sharina stepped into the corridor. She kept her eyes averted—demure as a young girl before her beloved—exchanging the harlot brazenness of the balcony for a virgin's modesty. Her sari of indigo silk wrapped about her narrow waist and draped her left shoulder. In the Minnagaran style a short blouse of the same silk fell from her neck, leaving her midriff and back bare. The sari's border was brocaded with gold and silver threads into an intricate design of vines and flowers. Her braided black hair hung to her waist. She looked up, her face at ease, her eyes in silent inquiry. For several moments their eyes locked. Then Sharina's gaze moved down. Flavus's genuine interest now tented his tunic. Her eyes hovered then snapped up, struggling to recapture their earlier modesty.

Finally, she approached. "I will walk in the market."

"My lady." Flavus stepped behind her—while tall for a woman, the top of her head did not reach his chin—and followed the scent of jasmine.

As they passed through the courtyard the peacock and his harem were settled in a far corner out of the sun. The peacock lifted its head and seeing no threat settled back into his slumber. Flavus opened and held the door to the street. The dead-end street was quiet, deserted except for three men squatting nearby and a young girl sitting in a doorway. One of the men wore a battered red cap and glanced in his direction. The sound of thrown dice ricocheted about the narrow two-story alley.

Even though the courtyard door opened wide enough to pass without touching, she brushed against his arm. "You were not surprised by my speaking Latin?"

"No, my lady."

"Are you not curious?"

"You grew up here and Roman trade is important to Minnagara, my lady."

A quick look of exasperation, almost a pout, crossed Sharina's face. "No more *my lady.* Sharina from now on, if you please."

"Then Flavus from now on—if you please." A broad smile accompanied his mimicry.

Sharina laughed and stepped into the street. While Flavus's sexual engagements were often counterfeit, either to play a part in another's fantasy or to achieve some purpose of his own, there were occasional encounters ripe with abandon. Whatever her goal in pulling him into her orbit, Sharina's laugh signaled that passion would not be taking second place. Flavus secured the courtyard door and hoped that their walk would be a short one.

The blow to his head came from behind. A second brought him to his knees. If a third struck, he did not feel it.

Awareness returned. Flavus did not move, did not open his eyes, kept his breathing steady. He lay face up. His head rested on something soft. *A pillow.* Pain burst from the back of his head into his temples. Faint light penetrated his eyelids. The smell of burning wax. *A candle. On the right, near my shoulder.* Another scent. *Jasmine. Nearby, on my left.* A slight breeze disturbed the humid stillness. A momentary chill. *I am naked.* A sound, another's breath, a step, from the left. *The jasmine draws closer.* He tried to flex his arms. They're outstretched. *I am bound.* Flavus opened his eyes. Sharina stood above him. *Naked—of course.*

She sat and leaned across his chest, her kiss moist and leisurely. Flavus broke it by turning away his face. Resting her head on his chest she circled his nipple with her index finger.

"Don't be angry with me. I didn't know they were going to hit you so hard."

"Who are *they?*"

She sat back. "Friends." She slipped her hand between his legs. He hardened under her touch.

"One blow would have been enough."

"They didn't think so."

Sharina climbed over his hips. As she eased herself down, he thrust up. She cried out. His head convulsed in pain.

What friends?

Sharina slept beside him, her breathing shallow, her arm thrown across his chest, her scent of jasmine now lost to the musky aroma of spent lust. Flavus lifted his head. A dull throb, a reminder. The candle had burned out. Dim light from the balcony cast dark shadows about the room. He flexed his thighs to the pleasant ache of a demanding lover. Distant shouts of carousing slipped into the room, signaling the dead of night had not yet arrived. He was no longer bound, having promised her unimaginable pleasures taught him by the matrons of Rome. Breaking through her fears took time, but when she finally acquiesced he did not disappoint, and she soon fell into an exhausted sleep beside him.

Flavus lifted Sharina's arm and eased himself to the edge of the bed. Her breathing remained steady as he moved his pillow and placed her arm upon it. He sat up to dizziness and grasped the side of the bed with one hand. The other reached for the back of his head. His hair was matted with blood. As he probed the tenderness with his fingers he looked about the room and spotted his clothing. He rose on unsteady legs, pulling his tunic over his head and reached for the leather belt. His short sword still rested in its scabbard. After securing the belt about his waist, Flavus approached the bed. He stared down at Sharina. She stirred and moved onto her back. Flavus removed the sword and thrust it into the bed between her thighs.

When Flavus emerged from Sharina's chamber, the guard jumped to his feet, almost upsetting the heavy wood bench and bumping the spear that rested against the wall. Flavus caught the spear and motioned the guard to silence. He was but a boy, at most a year older than Calaf.

Flavus leaned the spear against the wall then brought his lips to the guard's ear. "Asleep on duty. I should execute you straight away."

"Sir." His whisper quavered. Flavus smelled his fear.

"But I wasn't here, was I?"

A pause. "No, sir." Relief entered the boy's voice.

Flavus stepped back and stared into his face. "If it ever be said I was—?"

"I would deny it, sir."

"Even to your mother?"

The boy hesitated a moment. His eyes told Flavus he understood the threat. "Even to my mother."

"I require your sword."

"But I need it."

"Your spear's sufficient."

Flavus took the sword and slipped it into his empty scabbard, swung about, and disappeared down the corridor.

When Flavus entered the sitting room of Callista's brothel, an old woman reclined on the worn silk brocade couch near the entrance. Incense did little to hide the odor of sex that permeated the two-story structure; the music of lutes did nothing to hide ecstasy's outbursts behind thin walls. The brothel catered to the region's local officials and merchants and Minnagara's small but thriving Roman community. The arrival of a Roman trading ship always boosted Callista's business with sailors too long at sea and local customers tantalized by the exotics she regularly procured. Yesterday's ship brought Nubian twins. News of their arrival spread fast.

"Looks like a busy night, Agatha."

The attendant rose. "All rooms are taken and six wait their turn in the baths. But from the looks of you, you don't seek pleasure this night." Flavus shook his head. Agatha went to the second-floor stairway and called, "Callista!"

The Emperor's *frumentarii* never operated alone. Flavus knew of four others in the Kushan Empire, which meant there were likely double that. Caution was critical, for in their duplicitous world the reward for revealing the treachery—real, suspected or fabricated—of a fellow *frumentarius* was as great as uncovering an imperial assassination plot. A change in Emperors was always a dangerous time for those strongly aligned with the deceased, and often disgraced, ruler. Three Emperor assassinations preceded Philip's ascension to the purple five years earlier. Flavus was recruited afterwards, so was only subjected to horrific accounts of Philip's *frumentarii* purge. It helped that Flavus was far from the center of power, but every *frumentarius* learned to watch his back and trust no one, even if that person had put her life at risk to save his, as this transplanted Roman madam had. While Callista was not *frumentarii* herself, Flavus had more than once taken advantage of the services she provided to the Emperor's operatives.

A robust, black-haired woman draped in flowing blue and green silk swept into the entryway and threw her arms around Flavus. "Jupiter be praised, I was about to storm the palace to rescue you." Flavus long ago learned there was no containing Callista's exuberance; like a flame it only ceased when there was nothing more to burn. "Let me see your head." Flavus leaned down and she pulled his head against her ample breasts. He winced as she probed the wound. "May Jupiter himself strike down those ruffians." She looked over at Agatha. "A tub and hot water to my quarters." As Agatha left the sitting room, Callista called out, "Clean tunic, too." Then to Flavus, "Go—I'll join you." Callista disappeared into the street.

When Flavus entered Callista's chamber, her personal servant, Kawtara, a Minnagaran girl of twelve, was waiting. After securing the door he asked, "You followed them?"

Kawtara nodded. "I told my mistress everything, just as you instructed."

Flavus patted the side of her face. "Thank you. You're a good watcher."

A shy smile crossed Kawtara's face. "Did it hurt?"

Flavus reached for the back of his head. "A little." He undressed and eased himself into the tub's warm water. Jasmine blossoms floated on the surface, rekindling thoughts of Sharina. He tensed as Kawtara poured water over his head, then appreciated her gentleness as she washed the dried blood from his hair and cleaned around the wound. He was standing beside the tub when Callista returned, the girl on her knees drying the back of his legs.

Callista gave an exaggerated nod at his crotch. "I assume Sharina wasn't disappointed." He shrugged, to which Callista laughed. "Men! Flaunt it but never talk about it."

She glanced at Kawtara. "You may go now."

Callista handed Flavus the clean tunic. "You're getting old. It took those ruffians only two blows to bring you down. Maybe it's time to change your line of work." Callista ran a finger up his inner thigh. "Always a place for you here." The tunic caught on her arm as it dropped.

"What? Work for you?" Flavus wrapped his arms around her and kissed the top of her head. "And ruin a wonderful partnership?"

Callista guided Flavus to a table. "A bit more wonderful would be nice."

Flavus laughed as they sat. "And here I thought those Nubian beauties were more to your liking."

"I thought you learned never to presume what a woman wants?"

"You'll never let me forget, will you?"

"And lose the chance to watch you squirm? Never. Rescuing you from certain death is the highlight of my life." Flavus watched the twinkle in her eyes fade and her expression turn serious. "It was the three dice throwers."

"Yes, I saw them—and their clubs lying beside them."

"Of course, you did, and played the dumb gladiator as you walked into their trap."

"But using Kawtara as a watcher was inspired. Who'd pay attention to a child?"

Callista shrugged away the compliment. "After they clubbed you, they carried you into the palace."

"And with no guard until I was relieved at nightfall, Sharina was free to go where she wished."

"She came out with two of the men, in cotton instead of her silks. The third stayed with you—most likely with club at hand should you awaken. Kawtara followed them to a house near River Gate. Fifteen men, one or two at a time, entered the house after she arrived. She and her two cohorts left first and returned to the palace near sunset. Sharina did not come out of the palace again, but the three men left. Your guard passed them in the street outside the courtyard."

"And the house?" Flavus asked.

"A known gathering place for the Friends of Ashu."

"Ashu?"

"The name of Sharina's older brother and heir to the Minnagaran throne before Timur murdered him along with his father, the raja. The Friends of Ashu were formed in his memory. They have organized the town's festivals for years. They also help the poor and run a home for orphans. It's where I found Kawtara. Ten years ago, their festival turned into a riot and several Kushan soldiers were killed. Leaders of the Friends of Ashu were arrested and executed, more as warning than anything else. The Kushan governor dared not crush the group entirely without risking a full-scale Minnagaran uprising. After that they went about their work quietly, doing nothing to raise suspicion. They risk much should this meeting with the deposed raja's daughter become known. I've just returned from visiting one of their leaders, a man who owes me favors. When I asked about yesterday's meeting, he turned pale and would not talk, except to swear me to secrecy."

"Will he betray you?"

"Not likely. That would reveal his close ties to me, a foreigner, and raise questions about his loyalty. Last year he was more fearful than outraged when one of their inner circle turned up in the river, stabbed in the chest. Seems the dead man's business dealings with the Kushan governor became suspect."

"Do these Friends of Ashu plan insurrection?"

"Unclear, but if that's their intent, they'll distract and weaken the Kushans, just when you're trying to strengthen them for a fight against Persia. Sharina's dangerous. Best to remove her. Her death will mean little to the Kushans, but living she could galvanize a Minnagaran revolt. Listen, one of your brethren has been called to Alexandria. He's in Minnagara waiting for the next ship. He could do it, quiet and quick, and be gone."

"Drusus?" Callista nodded and Flavus shook his head. "He's already doing something for me." Flavus ignored the rise of Callista's left eyebrow, always a sign of aroused curiosity, and pressed on, "Anyway, dangerous or not, my instincts tell me I need her."

"Your instincts have led you astray before. But for me you'd be dead, and we wouldn't be having this conversation."

"Trust me, it's different this time." He cocked his head and winked.

"And the Fates abandon fools, my friend, much to the delight of the gods."

Sharina awoke with a start. Eyes wide open. On her back. *Sounds?* She strained to listen. *All is quiet.* She moved her legs and felt something between her thighs. She looked down her body, and in the predawn light from the balcony she confronted the sword's silhouette, its hilt pointing toward the ceiling. Hot blood rose to her face. *Not a time for anger.* She took a deep breath and counted slowly as she let the air escape. *Move with calm intent.*

Another deep inhale, then slow exhale. Followed by another. And another. Her blood cooled. Her mind cleared, and she sat up and knelt before the blade.

She grasped the sword's hilt in both hands, ripped the blade from the mattress, and raised it above her head. No sound escaped her mouth as over and over she thrashed the bedding, only stopping when she collapsed in exhaustion across the ruined bed, the sword lying beneath her outstretched arm.

Dawn and the peacock's first cry found Sharina pacing her chamber. She approached the ravaged bed, seized the sword, and studied it. Etched in the blade at the hilt were Latin characters that spelled *Flavus*. His personal sword. She turned it over. *Eberulf.* The word felt strange on her tongue. She repeated it several times.

Sharina dismissed her maidservant. "Tell the guard I wish to see him."

Stepping to the balcony entrance, a warm breeze flowed about her, shifting the folds of her blue sari. The chamber door closed, then silence. Flavus stood inside the door, his posture relaxed, his head cocked, his eyes intent. The belt about his waist held an empty scabbard.

"My lady." He held her gaze.

"Eberulf?" His eyes darted to his sword where she had reburied the blade in the ruined bed. For a moment he seemed discomfited. She stifled a smile.

"The name I carried as a boy."

"A barbarian name?"

"A Germanic name—after my grandfather."

"You may recover your sword."

Flavus ran his hand over the ripped bedding. "Your sleep wasn't pleasant? Did I not please you?"

"The sword did not please me."

"Your friends did not please me."

"Your size alarmed them."

"Will the Friends of Ashu be alarmed to discover they attacked someone in the personal service of the Kushan emperor? Are not many of them merchants and dependent upon Timur's largess?"

She blinked in surprise then dropped her eyes to the floor. Only a moment passed before she lifted an icy stare at him. "The Friends of Ashu?"

"You met with them."

"That is no concern of yours."

"Anything that might place the prince in danger is my concern."

"You dare accuse me—?"

"I do not accuse, but you attacked his chief bodyguard. Of course, if you'd rather speak with the Kushan governor about your meeting, I will take you there now."

"And you'll look the fool, disturbing him about such an innocent matter."

"Innocent? Then tell me."

"Trust me."

When he laughed, she rushed for the door, but he seized her before she reached it. She struggled in vain against his hold then spat in his face. She shot her knee toward his groin but lost her balance. He swept her into his arms and fell onto the bed. She grabbed his hair in both hands and pulled his lips to hers. When the frenetic sparring of their tongues slowed, he entered her. She matched his thrusts with her own, forcing him to relinquish control. When he lifted his hips in climax, he stifled his cry with his face buried in her neck.

Sharina did not fall asleep after Flavus collapsed beside her, his arm draped across her stomach. The air was heavy, making it hard to breathe. Their bodies were drenched in sweat, the air still in the stifling humidity. Flavus's breathing became deep and slow. Sharina smiled, realizing how easy it would be to take his sword and kill him in his sleep. She took his wrist and eased his arm up off her stomach, then cried out in surprise as Flavus flung himself on top of her.

"Going somewhere?"

She pushed against his shoulders. "Get off me." He rolled on his back, and put his hands behind his head. She climbed onto his chest. "You're a brute."

"No, a boar."

"There's a difference?"

"Boars aren't brutes. They're strong, intelligent, and brave." He placed a fingertip between her breasts and traced a slow line downwards. "That's why my father named me Eberulf."

"The boar?"

He nodded. His fingertip continued down past her stomach.

"Suits you." She batted his hand away and sat on the edge of the bed.

"Are others aware of my visit to the Friends yesterday?" she asked.

"Just one, who will only make it known should something unfortunate happen to me."

He climbed from the bed and after he dressed, she took his hand. "We should be friends, you and I."

"Friends who help each other?"

"I only seek news of the prince, his comings and goings." She reached under his tunic. "When will I see you again?"

"Calaf returns from patrol at dusk. We should be discreet."

"But of course."

She withdrew her hand. After he left, she curled up on the bed and smiled.

Flavus collapsed on the couch beside Callista and stared at the ceiling. "Your message said to come at once."

"I encouraged that client of mine to be more forthcoming about Sharina's meeting with the Friends of Ashu." When Flavus turned his head, Callista winked. "Catering to a man's baser motives often loosens his tongue against his better judgment."

"How loose?"

"Should what I tell you go beyond this room, I would think he's a dead man." After Flavus nodded, Callista continued. "The Friends indeed plan insurrection against the Kushans."

"When?"

"When the Persians reach the Khyber Pass."

"Makes sense. Minnagara will be lightly garrisoned when Timur amasses his armies at Peshawar to face Shapur. But that's at least two years from now. Shapur must first take Baktra and the western approach to the Khyber. Given his army's strength that will most likely be next year. Then he would move against Peshawar the year after. And where does Sharina fit into their plans?"

"Given that she's the sister of their namesake and the last descendant of the old raja's family, the Friends have a long history with her, going back to their formation. However, they never involved her in their political plans. That changed six months ago."

"When she and Demetrius were here with Torak's ashes," Flavus interjected.

Callista nodded. "She agreed to deliver her son to lead Minnagara's rebellion, giving the Friends of Ashu immediate legitimacy by having the former raja's grandson lead their revolt." Flavus rubbed his eyes with his knuckles and groaned. Callista touched his arm and said, "What?"

"Did your contact mention the name of her son?"

Callista hesitated, looking confused. "No, he didn't. Why?"

"I suspect she intends to kill Ishmael."

"But Ishmael's her son."

Flavus shook his head. "Soon after their births she switched her infant son for the emperor's."

"You must be joking." He shook his head. "So the Kushan prince is her son?" He nodded. "So who will she deliver to the Friends?"

"I expect Calaf," Flavus said. "If she succeeds, it's a brilliant plan."

"But you said Calaf hates her."

"He does, but I'm learning not to underestimate her."

"Who else knows about the boys' true identities?"

Flavus replied, "Demetrius told me before he died. I know of no one else."

"And Sharina, does she suspect you know?"

"Unlikely."

"What will you do now?"

"The Nubian twins?"

Callista laughed and slapped his leg. "An amazing woman, this Sharina of yours. And she seriously believes she can convince the Minnagarans that Calaf is their raja's grandson?"

"So it seems."

"And take her revenge on the emperor by killing his real son?" Flavus nodded. "But didn't Demetrius pledge you to protect her and him—along with Calaf, who the emperor thinks is his son but isn't?" Flavus nodded again. "You're certain Demetrius was your friend?"

"Don't jest."

"Believe me, I don't. But surely you don't think your job includes safeguarding two boys from the crazed obsessions of this woman and, beyond that, protecting her, too."

"It does now."

"Because of a pledge to a dead Greek?"

Flavus rarely heard Callista's voice so hard. He swallowed an angry retort, not answering for a few moments. When he did, he whispered, "Yes."

"You've always said a warmhearted *frumentarius* is a dead *frumentarius*. Jupiter be damned, you loved him, didn't you?"

Flavus did not reply.

CHAPTER 18

East of the Indus River

On the patrol's final morning Calaf awakened before first light and stared through the mangrove canopy. He had fallen asleep to the stars, but fog now obscured the sky. He pulled the mist-dampened blanket over his head, curled into a ball, and shivered. He stood watch the first two nights—in fact, volunteered, knowing that memories and the decisions facing him would keep him awake. But the patrol leader refused to allow him to stand watch a third night, insisting he sleep. To his surprise, he was able to.

Finally giving in to the demand of his bladder, Calaf pushed aside his blanket. The bedding next to him lay empty. Sami drew the second watch along with the patrol leader. At seventeen Sami was the closest to Calaf in age among the patrol's other eight soldiers and the youngest of the bodyguards that Flavus assembled upon their arrival in Minnagara. Calaf looked about, but darkness and the thick fog hid both watchmen. A nearby soldier stirred under his blanket. Another coughed. Then it was still, except for the fog's moisture dripping from the mangrove branches. Calaf stepped off the warm bedding, and shuddered as his bare feet touched the damp ground. He glanced toward his sword, hesitating a moment before hurrying to the closest tree.

As Calaf relieved himself, he heard the patrol leader call out, "Who goes there?" The shout was followed by a muffled cry then silence.

"We're under attack!" Calaf shouted as he rushed for his sword, but a thick arm encircled his neck. A large belly pushed him against a blade at his stomach. Lips touched his ear. "Don't move." The man's breath smelled of rancid fish.

Men with torches crowded the clearing. Calaf struggled against his attacker's greater strength and leverage. The man tightened his grip. Calaf gagged and fought to remain conscious. Shouts and clashing swords filled his ears until there was only the sound of one terrified voice pleading for mercy, then a slap, hard and loud.

"Silence or you will join the others." The man's voice was deep and gravelly, and he spoke Bactrian with an accent Calaf did not recognize.

Someone kicked his legs from under him. As he fell forward on his palms, a sharp pain shot from his wrists to his elbows. He smelled blood. Someone grabbed his hair and pulled him up. A terrified soldier stared wide-eyed at him. Sami knelt nearby, a captor holding a knife at his throat. Beyond him lay a dead soldier tangled in his blood-soaked blanket.

The man standing above the terrified soldier barked, "Which one is the prince?"

The soldier thrust his arm in Calaf's direction.

After the terrified soldier and Sami were executed, the big-bellied man yanked Calaf to his feet and covered his nakedness with a tunic. He dropped a hood over his head and lifted him onto a horse, tying his hands to the reins and his bare feet to looped leather straps that hung from the saddle. He strained to make sense of the mumbled talking around him but could not make out the words. Men mounted their horses. The torches were extinguished. Hooves faded into the distance. All became still.

The horse snorted, shook his head then remained still. Calaf held his breath and listened, but only the pounding of his heart and dewdrops falling from the mangrove branches reached his ears. He shook his head to one side several times until the hood slipped off. He struggled against the leather strips that dug into his wrists. A branch broke and the dim shape of a large man on horseback emerged from the shadows. The man dismounted and retrieved the hood. Calaf tried to kick him but could not free his foot. Without a word the man struck Calaf's knee with his fist. Calaf cried out in pain. The man remounted and placed the hood on Calaf's head.

"They only ask that you are alive." It was the deep voice with the strange accent. "How you fare beyond that is my choice—and yours."

"Who are you?"

The man did not answer, only tightened the leather strips binding his wrists.

"Who are—?"

The man gripped Calaf's shoulder and struck Calaf in the stomach. Calaf grunted as he fell against the horse's neck. He refused to cry out.

The man yanked Calaf up by the hair. "Do we have an understanding?" Calaf nodded.

As they rode, Calaf's heartbeat finally slowed along with the frantic pace of his thoughts. He remembered Sami's eyes meeting his, the moment the blade sliced his neck. Bile rose from his stomach and stung his throat. He gagged.

"Tace," hissed the man. *Be silent.* Calaf perked up to the Latin. Flavus often used that word to get his attention when training him.

Calaf banished the memory of Sami's face. *Mourn later, not now.* A surprising calm enveloped him. Only once before had he truly faced death, but when he had leapt into the river to save Ishmael, his only thought was saving his friend. That he risked his own life never entered his mind. But now there was no avoiding he was at the mercy of someone who killed to get what he wanted. Calaf took a deep breath. While anxiety hovered at the edges of his mind, heightened awareness trumped disabling fear. A moment of elation filled him, and he longed to ask Flavus if this is what he felt in the arena. Shifting in the saddle he lost his balance, his fall halted by a hand grabbing his neck and righting him.

"Imbecillus," the man barked.

The chill of the forest gave way to the warmth of open land, the sun on his back. *His back.* They headed west—toward the river. Soon he heard the roar of water in the distance. The sun neared its zenith when the man pulled him from the horse, shoved him to the ground, tied him to a tree, and yanked the hood from his head. Calaf squinted against the sudden brightness as the man tore the cloth of the hood apart, tying one piece across Calaf's mouth, the other over his eyes. In those brief moments, he saw the man for the first time. Muscular, his wide face scarred from disease and battle, he had a dark complexion, but he was not Kushan or Persian or any ethnicity Calaf had seen before.

The man grasped Calaf's chin. "I don't go far, so don't even think of escape." Calaf felt the point of a blade on his inner thigh, moving up to touch his genitals, and nodded.

When the sound of the horses faded, Calaf struggled against his restraints without success. In frustration he cried out, but the gag swallowed his curse. He struck his heel against the ground, his head against the tree. As he calmed, he realized his mouth was parched. Pangs of hunger awakened his stomach. In the distance, he heard the bellow of an ox and the approaching wheels of a cart.

Minnagara

"What do you mean the patrol did not return last night?"

Flavus stood before the garrison's second in command, who was in charge while the commander toured fortifications upriver. The officer squinted his eyes against the first light of day. Holding an untied loincloth over his groin, he dropped backwards, almost losing his balance. Behind him a curly-haired youth rose from the bed and began to dress. Flavus recognized him as one of Callista's boys.

The officer straightened and glared at Flavus. "Who do you think you are to—?"

"You know very well who I am."

The officer held his ground. "It's not unusual—"

Flavus leaned into the officer's face. "What's unusual is that your emperor's son is on that patrol. Search parties should be out there as we speak. Need I tell you your fate should the prince come to harm?"

"But—but they patrolled friendly territory."

"And that's what you will tell the emperor?"

Now dressed, Callista's boy slid along the wall toward the door. Flavus stopped him and whispered, "Tell your mistress what's happened." He slipped the boy a coin. "Quickly." Then to the officer, "If anything happens to the prince, know that you will answer to me first." Flavus stormed away, but once out of sight, he slowed and smiled.

The plan begins perfectly.

East of the Indus River

The mid-day sun baked the clearing as Flavus dismounted and stepped around the bodies. Behind him a voice called out from the surrounding mangroves, "The patrol captain's dead, too." Flavus grimaced and rubbed his forehead with the back of his hand. *This is not the plan.*

Flavus knelt beside Sami's body and traced the youth's jaw with his finger. His throat had been cut. The garrison commander did not want his youngest son to join the prince's bodyguard, but Flavus wanted someone close to Calaf's age who might become a friend. So he convinced the commander that the opportunity to forge a relationship with the future emperor would secure Sami's future. Flavus recognized Calaf's blanket lying nearby. He retrieved it, and as he covered Sami's body, a soldier came up behind him.

"Eight bodies but no sign of the prince. We've recovered only three of our mounts. Fresh tracks head east, at least ten horses, likely more." *He was supposed to act alone.*

More soldiers entered the clearing. One approached and pointed west. "Two horses head toward the river." *So he still takes Calaf where we agreed.*

Flavus waved to the oldest of his party. "Gather the other search parties and pursue the band to the east. I will follow the tracks going west." He called out to three soldiers standing apart, "You're with me. Wait here." He led his mount into the trees where Callista's boy waited on horseback.

"Tell her he's taking the prince to the river. Bring back anything she's learned. You'll find me heading upriver."

Without a word, the youth pulled himself atop his horse. Flavus grabbed his ankle. "What's your name, boy?"

"Taj."

"Like the wind, Taj."

"Like the wind."

Flavus watched him disappear into the mangrove forest.

Drusus, what are you doing?

Flavus reached the Indus when the afternoon sun was halfway to the horizon. He came upon a man and his young son bathing two horses. Ordering his men to stay back, he dismounted and walked toward the river. The man sent his boy running into the trees. Flavus reached the water's edge. The man held ropes that looped about the horses' necks. Face impassive but eyes alert, he gave a slight nod.

Flavus smiled. "Fine horses. They look familiar." The man's knuckles whitened about the ropes.

"They're mine."

"The emperor may disagree."

"It was a fair trade."

"For what?"

"A cart filled with harvested cotton and my ox."

"Did he go upriver or down?"

The man dropped to his knees in the water. "He said he'd kill me if—"

The man looked past Flavus. His eyes opened wide. A soldier held the man's frightened son. The man pointed upriver. Flavus waved, and the soldier released the boy.

"I will return your cart and ox, so treat the emperor's horses well. Also, should a curly-haired youth on horseback ask for me, tell him where I've gone."

The sun had just set when Callista's boy caught up with them. Taj dropped from the froth-covered horse into Flavus's arms. Laying the youth against a nearby tree, Flavus gave him water to drink. A soldier brought more water and poured it over the boy's sweat- and dust-covered head.

"Rajanpur—he goes to Rajanpur—made a deal with—" Taj began to cough.

Flavus waited but knew the rest. The *frumentarii* had assigned Drusus to infiltrate Persian partisans inside Kushan territory.

Taj's coughing subsided. "He's made a deal with the Persians for the prince."

"If he goes to Rajanpur, then he's got a boat."

"Callista said a boat without cargo left this morning for Makli."

"Makli. Riding through the night we might catch him. Anything else?"

"The garrison commander's returned. He wants your head in exchange for the death of his son."

Makli

The fishing village of Makli sat on a hill surrounded on the other three sides by open marshland, its wood structures built atop mangrove trunk stilts against the river's monsoon flooding. The scattered remains of fallen structures were a testament to the river's destructive power. A single causeway accessed the village along a ridge of high ground that bisected the marsh. When the people of Makli were not fishing, they were fortifying the causeway against the erosion of wind and water.

As the first rays of the morning sun reached across the wide expanse of marshland, the bellowing of an ox interrupted its usual tranquility. The cart left the causeway and headed away from the village and the fishermen beaching their boats after their morning catch. Waterfowl took flight, and the sound of their wings and cries awakened Calaf from the restless stupor of the night. Buried under the harvested cotton that filled the cart, Calaf tried to stretch his bound legs. His right calf knotted but he swallowed the pain. His captor's blows had taught him the value of silence.

As he attempted to move his legs into a position that would allow his calf muscle to relax, the cart stopped. The man climbed from the cart. Footsteps crunched on the ground—then stillness. Only the cries of the marsh birds reached Calaf's ears. The man paced again, then stopped, then paced again. The man climbed back onto the cart, and it began to move.

When the cart stopped again, Calaf heard a distant voice call out. The man responded with a loud, "There—beach the boat there."

The man's hands grabbed his feet, yanking him from the cart. Landing on the ground, Calaf shut his eyes against the sudden light. When the man pulled him up, his cramped leg collapsed under him. The man cursed, propped him against the cart, and tested the leather strips that secured his wrists. Calaf now saw that the man was a head taller than him. Except for muscular arms out of proportion to a thin, wiry body, there was little to distinguish him. Calaf tried to look about, but the man grabbed his jaw in his thick hands.

"To these men you are nothing but cargo to be delivered before they receive a season's wage for this single run. Remember that before you think of escape." As he sliced the bindings around Calaf's ankles with his short sword, Calaf glanced about. The bow of a merchant boat rested on the sandy shore. Eight crewmen were in the water straining with ropes to keep the boat in place against the current. Two men approached them. Calaf figured the older to be the merchant.

"Drusus." The merchant walked up and clasped both of his captor's arms. *A Roman name?* "News of his abduction spreads fast. We must leave quickly." Then turning to the younger man, "Gahdi, take the prisoner to the boat."

Drusus laughed. "Chain him to an oar. The Fates may be kind to one who rows himself to his doom."

Gahdi approached, seized Calaf's arm, and whispered, "Trust me, my prince." Before Calaf could react Gahdi pulled him away from the cart and shoved him in the direction of the river. "Get moving, boy." Calaf stumbled but regained his balance just as Gahdi grabbed his arm and began dragging him toward the shore.

Drusus said, "This Gahdi—he's new."

Calaf strained his ears for the merchant's reply. "Just stole him from that old swindler Kabir."

"Isn't Kabir the gladiator's—?" Before Drusus could finish, the merchant yelled, "The current—it's got the boat," and ran past Gahdi and Calaf.

Drusus paused beside them and gripped Gahdi's arm. "You're dead if he escapes." Then he rushed to join the crewmen at the ropes.

Gahdi's dagger went to Calaf's face. "The dolphin favored you." One slice and the gag dropped.

"I remember you," Calaf said, recognizing the boatman who had told him to slap the water to get the dolphins' attention. "You were there when I touched the dolphin."

The leather binding around Calaf's wrists fought the blade but finally gave way. Gahdi slipped the dagger's grip into Calaf's hand. Their eyes locked for a moment before Drusus realized what Gahdi was doing. His scream of rage filled their ears.

Gahdi yelled "Go!" and turned to face Drusus. Calaf ran past the cart and glanced back just as Gahdi charged headfirst into Drusus's stomach, sending both crashing to the ground. Calaf looked up the causeway then toward the village then back to Drusus, who, sword in hand, had regained his feet. Calaf ran toward the village.

Even as he tried to ignore it, the lingering leg cramp slowed Calaf. Drusus's pursuing footfalls grew louder. Calaf dropped to the river's edge. *Can Drusus swim?* Even if he escaped Drusus, the Indus rarely released one caught in its clutches. Unless—*the dolphin favored you.* Just as he turned to plunge into the river, he spotted the fishermen, who had stopped spreading their nets to watch the chase approaching them, and rushed toward them. They scattered as he grabbed what little he could use as a weapon.

Drusus slowed to a walk. Calaf stood silent and still, Gahdi's dagger in his right hand, a fishing net hanging from his left. Drusus stopped and scratched his head. He looked at the fishermen, who had retreated into the shadows of their stilted homes, their women and children watching from doorways and windows above them.

Drusus threw his arms into the air, his sword held high, and laughed. "An arena to match the grandeur of Rome's great Colosseum." He began to circle. Calaf swung the fishing net in a low arc to keep it away from his feet. "How pretty you move, boy. Flavus would be pleased." Drusus lunged. "Oh, yes, Flavus and I work together." Calaf swept the fishing net outwards, trying to snare Drusus's legs, but Drusus leapt into the air and stumbled to his knees, leaning against his sword. A cheer of young voices greeted his fall. As Drusus stood, he glared up at the children. A woman's voice silenced them.

Again Drusus circled, drawing closer but keeping out of range of the net. "Flavus wasn't a true gladiator. He didn't tell you that, did he? The *retiarii* are too weak for armor, heads exposed so all can see their fear, evasive trickery instead of real man-to-man combat. He's taught you to fight like a woman, my prince."

Calaf remained calm, his ears closed to Drusus's voice. Rather he heard Flavus's: *Words are the weapon of the weak.* Calaf focused on how Drusus moved, how he shifted his feet, how he leaned, how he balanced his weight, how he carried the anger hiding below the surface of his words. And how he only stared at Calaf's face.

Drusus eased closer. Calaf saw an opening but waited. *The first is rarely successful.* Then Drusus stopped circling. "You know it's just a matter of time before they secure the boat. Remember a season's wage awaits them. Make it easy on yourself. Drop the knife and that ridiculous net and come with me." Drusus lowered his sword to his side, reached out his other arm, and smiled.

Drusus favored his right leg, which threw him off-balance when Calaf released the net. It wrapped around both of his legs below the knees—a perfect throw. With a loud grunt, Calaf yanked the net with all his strength. Drusus, arms flailing, fell to his face. The crack of bone told Calaf that Drusus's wrist took the force of the fall. Calaf threw himself onto Drusus's back.

"Die!" Calaf plunged the dagger into his neck. Drusus screamed as blood pumped from the wound then began to gag. Several times he pushed up with his uninjured arm, fighting to dislodge Calaf, but to no avail. Calaf twisted the dagger deeper as Drusus writhed beneath him. "Die, die, die!" Drusus began to weaken and finally grew still. Calaf leaned into his ear and whispered, "Die."

Moments later, hands grabbed Calaf's shoulders and pulled him off the lifeless body. Calaf scrambled to protect himself from another assailant.

It was Gahdi. "They've secured the boat, my prince."

Shouts reached Calaf's ears, growing louder. But abruptly their voices fell to murmurs. Brandishing spears and hooks the fishermen now stood in a line facing the boat's crew. The boatmen, led by the merchant, were outnumbered and lightly armed, and seeing Drusus's lifeless body began shouting amongst themselves. Several raised their fists.

A woman rushed toward Calaf and Gahdi, pointing at the closest fishing boat—a small dugout fashioned from mangrove. The morning's catch had been unloaded, its nets stretched out on the sand. Gahdi reached it first and pushed it into the shallows. Throwing themselves into the boat, they paddled away from the beach. Several crewmen plunged into the river to intercept the escaping boat, but the strong current carried it out of reach.

Only then did Gahdi collapse into the bottom of the boat, his hand pressed to his side. Blood escaped between his fingers.

MINNAGARA

At midmorning, after the last of the previous night's customers had departed, Callista found Flavus stretched out in the cool waters of the brothel's *frigidarium*. She unclasped her sleeping gown, letting it drop to the red tile floor, and slipped into the pool beside him.

"Agatha says you and Taj arrived before dawn."

"An abandoned fishing boat was found a half-day downriver. We searched the surrounding area through the night. Nothing." Two days had passed since Flavus had arrived at Makli to find that Calaf had killed Drusus and escaped down the Indus.

"Have you slept?"

"No, but I worry Taj may never awaken."

"He'd better. No more playing soldier. Two Roman ships are docking today."

"You should give him the night off."

"Telling me how to run my business?" Her hand slapped the water, sending a spray into his face.

He ducked away then stood, hands on his hips. "If it's business you demand, he's mine for tonight—no, make that the next two nights."

"You can't afford him."

"Heartless." He slipped below the surface and came up spitting a mouthful of water in her direction.

She mimicked being wounded. "You injure me!"

They shared an easy laugh. He poked her calf with his toe.

"No."

"If not for him, do it to make me happy."

"You forget you're the one who owes me."

"You know you'll give in."

He floated on his back. Her quick kick to his ribs pushed him against the other side of the pool. He went under and came up sputtering.

"You still pay for one night, but I'll give Taj two."

Arms outstretched, massive grin across his face, he launched himself across the pool, only to be stopped by her hand on his chest. "But he can't stay here. I need his room."

"Understood."

He wrapped his arms around her, pulling her against his chest.

She squirmed free and squealed, "Stop poking me with that thing."

"But I get excited when I get my way."

"Not with me, you don't."

He released her and laughing they both fell back into the pool. Then in silence they floated around each other, not touching. Finally, Callista came to rest with her shoulders against the side.

Flavus stopped across from her. "Last week I received approval of my recommendation that we provide arms and supplies to the Kushans for their fight against Persia."

"That's good news, isn't it?" Callista asked.

"Not totally. In my last report to Felix, I was with Timur in Srinagar. That's where he believes I am."

"You work for Felix now?" When Flavus nodded, Callista uttered a sympathetic groan.

"He won't accept that my being stuck in Minnagara is out of my control, so I had to come up with a plan to return to Srinagar as quickly as possible." Flavus slammed a fist onto the red tile bordering the pool. "So simple—it was so simple. I tell Drusus where to find the prince. He abducts him. When I come to the rescue, he takes flight. Then out of concern for his heir's safety, Timur orders Calaf's immediate return, accompanied, of course, by his faithful bodyguard. Instead, a patrol is slaughtered, and the prince is captured to be traded to the Persians. And what happens? Calaf doesn't need rescuing. He single-handedly dispatches a battle-hardened *frumentarius* twice his age. Then add his disappearance. It couldn't be a worse disaster."

Callista's voice, now soft, reached across to him. "There's no way you could have known Drusus had turned."

"And that makes a difference?"

"Only if your arrangement with him is uncovered, and it seems he didn't implicate you. My contacts know nothing of your involvement."

"But if he said something to Calaf?"

"Then it's the word of his loyal bodyguard against a man whose treachery has been laid bare."

Flavus disappeared under the water. When he rose, he smoothed his long, blond hair back over his shoulders. "It's been two days and still no sign of him. We continue to search both sides of the river, but I fear he may have gone past the city and entered the delta. Without water and food—"

"But I heard he's not alone."

"Yes, he is with one of the boatmen. The Makli fishermen said he helped the prince escape, but he might have seized Calaf to finish what Drusus started. The Persians would handsomely pay anyone who brings them the prince."

Callista took his hand. “Cecilia didn’t work last night. If you’d like—”

Flavus kissed the top of her head. “Thank you, but the garrison commander expects my report on his son’s death.” Flavus climbed out of the pool and began to dress. “When Taj awakens, send him to the barracks. I’ll arrange a place for him.”

“No recruiting him. He’s one of my best.”

“Now that you mention it.”

“Don’t you dare.”

Giving Callista an exhausted smile, he headed for the brothel’s entrance and the street.

A morning breeze swept about Sharina as she ascended the steps of the Buddhist temple. Eight days earlier she mounted these same steps with the ashes of the slain Demetrius. Now each passing day increased the likelihood the river had taken Calaf to join the physician. That is, unless he had been delivered to the Persians. Did she dare hope that Timur would fight or bargain for his heir’s release? Or would the emperor allow Calaf to rot in Shapur’s dungeon out of fear that the prince’s defiance threatened his rule? Sharina squeezed her eyes shut. *Better the river take him.*

Inside several monks were on hands and knees scrubbing the dark wood floor before the Buddha statue that dominated the temple’s interior. Sharina knelt before the wall of a hundred Buddhas, behind which stood the monastery’s dormitory. Her mind would not calm. She recalled Flavus’s visit the previous day: his recounting the fishermen’s tale of Calaf overpowering and killing his captor, his flight in a fishing boat with one of the captor’s boatmen, and her rage at Flavus for his failure to protect the prince. Her stomach churned. Without Calaf her vengeance was defiled. She would be forced to embrace Ishmael as the tool of her revenge, allowing him to live and raising him up as Minnagara’s raja. *The son of the loathed Timur on my father’s throne? But no one would know, only I and the spirits of my family.* Unable to find the peace she hoped to find, she decided to leave.

At that moment one of the monks began to chant. "Form itself is emptiness, emptiness itself form." Another monk continued, "Sensations, perceptions, formations, and consciousness are also like this."

The words transported Sharina. She was a young girl kneeling before her mother learning the Heart Sutra. The monks voices became her mother's as Sharina joined their chant: "…no eye, ear, nose, tongue, body, or mind; no sights, sounds, smells, tastes, touch, or objects of mind…" She did not remember all the words, but it did not matter. She allowed the monks' voices to carry her. "Without hindrance, there is no fear. Far beyond all inverted views, one realizes Nirvana." Her eyes closed, her breathing deepened.

"Sharina."

The voice was soft. The chanting ceased. She kept her eyes closed and whispered, "Mother, don't go."

"Sharina." Still soft but closer.

She opened her eyes. Calaf stood before her, his hand extended. He helped her to her feet then embraced her. When he stepped back, his hands remained on her shoulders. "I'm pleased to find you here." The corners of his mouth lifted into a slight smile, his brow furrowed.

Sharina stared, unable to find her voice for a few moments. "We thought you were lost."

Calaf gently squeezed her shoulders then took her hand and led her through the doorway into the dormitory. In the nearest bed lay an injured man. A monk knelt beside him wiping his face and chest with a damp cloth. Blood stained the bandage around the man's lower torso. Kneeling beside the monk, Calaf took the man's hand. The man's eyes fluttered but did not open.

"I think he knows I'm here," Calaf said.

Sharina knelt on the other side and extended her hand. The monk handed the cloth to her. As she bathed away heat and sweat, she knew the man would be gone soon.

Calaf's dark eyes, calm and intent, rested on the man's face. "His name is Gahdi. The dolphin sent him."

"The dolphin?"

"On the river, when we came to Minnagara, a dolphin swam beside the boat so I could touch him. Gahdi was there."

Sharina nodded, recalling her mother's words. *A dolphin's blessing brings good fortune.*

"When he saw me in trouble, he remembered the dolphin."

"But his wound—you should have taken him to the city."

"He begged me not to. He feared what they'd do to him."

"They?"

"Those who recruited him." Calaf paused before continuing, "He was dying. I knew the monks would care for him."

The monk refreshed the cloth. Sharina laid it around Gahdi's neck. "You didn't let anyone know you were here?"

"I didn't know whom to trust."

She glanced at him. "And now?"

Calaf lifted his shoulders in a shrug. "Will you sit with me?" Sharina answered by taking Gahdi's other hand in hers.

When Gahdi breathed his last, Calaf leaned over and kissed his forehead. Then taking Sharina's hand he helped her to her feet. "I have arranged for the monks to perform the necessary rites. Come, I will return to the city with you."

No breeze cooled them that afternoon as they descended the temple steps. Calaf nodded at the surprised soldiers standing beside Sharina's horse-drawn wagon. As he helped Sharina into the wagon, one spoke. "Good to see you." Calaf thanked him and climbed beside Sharina.

As the wagon moved, Calaf placed his hand on Sharina's. "Is Ishmael well?"

"He joined the army and goes to Baktra with the reinforcements the emperor sent there." Then after a pause, "You remember Gar, the Peshawar governor's son?" Calaf nodded. "He's gone to Baktra, too, and tells me that Ishmael still studies to be a physician."

"You will let me know if Ishmael needs anything—anything at all?"

"Of course."

Neither spoke until the carriage neared the River Gate. Then Sharina asked, "Did Gahdi say who recruited him?"

Calaf was lost in thought, staring at the docked Roman ships. "What?"

Sharina repeated the question.

"Oh, he said friends of someone called Ashu." Then after a pause, "That was your brother's name, wasn't it?"

"Yes, but it's a common name." Sharina turned her face away to hide her dismay.

Calaf climbed from the wagon at River Gate. Sharina bowed her head. Calaf returned a bow from the waist before jogging toward the garrison's quarters. Soldiers called out. Calaf waved in response, and some drew near to embrace him. As more soldiers approached, he disappeared into the crowd.

After a day of fruitless searching, Flavus returned at nightfall to the news of Calaf's reappearance. His initial relief became surprise when the garrison commander told him that Calaf had spent the days since his escape at the Buddhist temple upriver of Minnagara.

"I've whipped soldiers for much less," the commander shouted from his map-strewn table.

"He must have a reason, sir," Flavus said.

"He feared for the life of that boatman." The commander jumped from his chair. "Gahdi? Can you believe it? He defends Gahdi. In and out of our prison for years for smuggling, theft, and even assault. Only a sword thrust in his gut prevented him from turning the prince over to the Persians for their gold. And now my troops look upon Calaf as some kind of hero." His eyes darkened. "A *hero*. But for him, my son would still be alive. He can't be back with his father soon enough."

"Back with his father?"

"The pup asked to return to Srinagar. I approved it. Two days. You have two days to be on your way. I've removed him from the barracks. The governor's given him a room." When the commander turned away saying nothing more, Flavus slipped out with a quick, "Sir."

On his way to the palace Flavus walked past Callista's and resisted the urge to seek her counsel. Delay would not resolve the questions that filled his mind. Flavus noted that the soldier at Calaf's door was not one of the bodyguards he recruited. The soldier nodded as Flavus approached. "The prince is expecting you."

Calaf rose from the bed and clasped Flavus's forearms. Flavus returned Calaf's grip with a wide smile. "You amazed those fishermen."

"Without them I wouldn't be here." Returning to the bed he stared at the ceiling. "Are you angry I didn't tell you where I was?"

"When I first heard, yes. Not now."

Calaf did not speak for several long moments. "Do you remember the first man you killed?"

"It's something you never forget."

"Tell me."

"It was at the gladiator school. At the end of the training I had to prove I would fight to the death. Rarely did the test mean death to either combatant. We were too valuable for that. Because of my size, I expected to be faced with the strongest in my class, but when I entered the training circle, a new arrival stood before me. A short sword dangled from one hand, a shield hung from the other. I looked up into the shaded platform where the school's owner sat, knowing he had uncovered my weakness. I had but moments to decide. Indecision itself meant failure. I approached the terrified man, told him to close his eyes, and then plunged my sword into his heart. When I looked up, the owner stood and slowly clapped his hands."

"Who did you kill?"

Flavus understood the question. "In my mind, I killed the owner. And afterward, it's his face I see, his flesh I strike, whenever I must take a life." Flavus wanted to ask the same question, certain the answer would be Timur. But he waited instead.

Calaf did not speak for several long moments. Finally, he said, "Drusus didn't have to kill Sami and the others."

"No, he didn't."

"Then why did he?"

"To shock the search parties," Flavus answered, "and direct their immediate retaliation at the bandits he employed."

"To buy himself time?"

"Most likely."

"A strategy you would have followed?"

"I would not do what he did," Flavus said.

"He said you worked together."

"Just because we're both *frumentarii* doesn't mean we work together," Flavus said. "He was assigned to gather intelligence about Persian groups in the Kushan Empire. He turned traitor. It sometimes happens."

"Few knew the patrol's route."

"A *frumentarius* develops many contacts, Calaf."

"You answer carefully."

"I answer truthfully. Do you not trust me?"

"I rely on you. I trust no one. He said you taught me to fight like a woman."

"Yet you prevailed."

"You will teach me to fight like a man," Calaf said.

"Of course."

"I return to Srinagar."

"But Nozar ordered you to remain here until called."

"Delay fuels my father's suspicions. I must remove all doubts of my loyalty. Leave me now. Tomorrow you will show me your plans for the journey. And, Flavus, *Calaf* seems too familiar, don't you think?"

"Yes, my prince."

CHAPTER 19

Srinagar

Three weeks after they left Minnagara, the morning sun broke through an overcast sky as Calaf dismounted and entered the Kushan garrison, Flavus trailing by a short distance. Word of his arrival quickly spread, and a growing number of soldiers joined the procession, while many others stopped their activities to watch, the rumble of their murmuring replacing the usual din of the camp, excitement and anxiety filling the air. One shouted the prince's name, only to be silenced by the others.

When Calaf reached the emperor's command tent, a hush swept through the soldiers. He knelt and placed his sword on the ground. Flavus stopped behind him and remained standing. Only the cries of birds disturbed the silence. The tent flap parted then closed, but Calaf did not see who peered out. As time passed and nothing happened, soldiers moved away to resume their duties, and the hubbub of garrison life resumed, officers entering and leaving the command tent, the changing of the emperor's guards, the delivering of food and wine. All ignored Calaf's presence. His only movements were shifts from kneeling to sitting as he waited. When the sun slipped behind the mountains, sending pre-dusk shadows over the garrison, the emperor's squire rushed from the tent then returned with horses. Timur and Nozar emerged and without a pause or glance mounted and rode toward the city. Soon afterward Aric stepped out, a bundle of parchments under one arm, secured the tent flaps, then nervously scanned the area before approaching Calaf.

"You take a great risk by surprising him."

"He still intends that I marry the daughter of Tur, doesn't he?" Calaf asked.

"Yes."

"Then there is little risk. He needs me alive."

"You risk everything," Aric said.

"You worry too much."

"And you too little."

"I've missed you, too." When Aric hid a smile behind a groan, Calaf continued, "How did the emperor react?"

"Besides saying 'Let him rot' he didn't."

"A good sign."

"If you say so."

"Listen, there's a boy who came with us," Calaf said. "A hard worker. You'll find him useful."

"What's this about?"

"Just helping him—lost his family, nothing left for him in Minnagara—good-natured, did everything we asked him."

"Where is he?" Aric asked.

"With the horses."

"And if he doesn't work out?"

"Send him on his way."

"You're up to something."

"Then forget I asked," Calaf said with a shrug.

Aric grumbled, "All right. His name?"

"Taj."

As Aric headed in the direction of the horse enclosure, Flavus said, "Thank you, my prince."

Calaf replied, "Don't forget your promise."

"I won't. You will know all that Taj hears."

As the sky turned from dusk to night, a soldier approached Flavus. "The general's ordered me to relieve you."

"Thank him, but I will remain."

After the soldier left, Calaf said, "It's not necessary that you stay with me."

"But it is, my prince."

The sun had set on the third day when the emperor's guard called out, "The emperor will see you."

Flavus moved to Calaf's side to steady him as he climbed to his feet and took the first few steps. Soldiers passing nearby stopped to watch. Calaf gave a nod and Flavus backed away.

Entering the command tent, Calaf knelt, keeping his head bowed in humility. "My lord and emperor, I kneel before you, your obedient—"

"Enough!"

Calaf looked up. "Sir?"

With a hearty laugh Timur waved at the stool across from him. "You must be hungry. Sit." Then to his squire, "Serve us," followed by a shout to his guards, "Dismiss his bodyguard." Timur raised his wine cup. "To your return." As Calaf lifted his, Timur grabbed his wrist, spilling wine over both their hands. Their eyes locked. Calaf held the stare a few moments then lowered his face.

"My lord."

Only their breathing filled the quiet that followed. Then Timur whispered. "If ever I so much as doubt your loyalty, I will strike you down with my own sword."

"You will never have cause, my lord."

Timur slapped Calaf's shoulder then said, "Then let us eat."

The next day Calaf entered Nozar's tent. When the general looked up from a portable table spread with parchments, Calaf saluted. "You asked to see me, sir."

"This morning the emperor spoke well of your audacity in arriving without orders. Was that your idea or the Roman's?"

"Mine, sir."

"Did he counsel against it?"

"Yes, but I thought it best. The emperor said he liked my boldness."

"And you'd best not forget he distrusts it, too. Did you speak of Ishmael?"

"I chose to wait."

"A wise decision. All you gained will be lost with one mention of his name."

"Do you have news of him?"

"Barzin reports he's adapted to army life better than expected."

"Hard to imagine him with a sword."

"Not what I expected either." Nozar motioned him to sit. "Flavus waits for a meeting with me. He also wants you present. Do you know what this is about?"

"I suspect that Rome will offer to support us in our fight against the Persians."

Always restrained in his reactions, the general's face showed no surprise, but Calaf knew the news had to catch him off guard. "You know this for certain?"

"No, but he told me the Romans sent him here to assess our military strength—and our needs."

"So there is more to this unusual man than we expected," Nozar said.

"Much more, sir."

"Anything I should know before we meet?"

"He speaks fluent Greek—and Bactrian."

Nozar sighed. "Of course, he does." Then he called out, "Send him in."

Calaf took a position beside Nozar as the general's guard lifted the tent's entry flaps and Flavus entered. Calaf blinked in surprise. While imposing as usual, Flavus now carried himself with a gravity that Calaf had not seen before.

Nozar said, "Calaf tells me that you work for the Romans."

Flavus gave a formal bow. "Emperor Philip asks me to extend to the Kushan Empire the hand of friendship of the Senate and people of Rome.

While he apologizes for the deception of my presence in your midst, he trusts you and Emperor Timur will set such concerns aside in the name of our mutual interests."

"What interest does a faraway Rome have in the Kushan Empire?"

"A common foe."

Nozar leaned back from his writing table. "I'm listening."

"By coordinating our efforts, we stand a better chance of curtailing Shapur's ambitions. If he faces strong enemies at both ends of his empire, he'll be forced to spread his own, allowing both Romans and Kushans to contain him, and hopefully make advances into his territory."

"And your emperor proposes?"

"Rome will provide the Kushan army with military weapons and supplies, including our most advanced siege engine. In exchange, we require that our engagements with the Persians be aligned. We also request that Roman officers who have recently engaged Shapur in battle be allowed to assist in your military planning."

"Spies like yourself?"

Flavus shook his head. "Rather, advisors. Of course, they would report to Rome any changes they observe in Persian tactics that could prove useful."

"Spies, advisors. An unnecessary matter of semantics among friends, don't you agree?" Nozar said.

A smile broke Flavus's serious countenance. "I've always appreciated your bluntness, general." He retrieved a folded parchment from the leather pouch at his waist and handed it to Nozar. "This is the Imperial communication authorizing me to offer Rome's assistance. If the emperor agrees, the flow of supplies and arms through Minnagara can begin in six months with spring's favorable trade winds."

Nozar studied the parchment then said, "I shall discuss Rome's offer with Emperor Timur. He won't be pleased to discover that a foreign spy penetrated so close to the throne, so you can expect he'll have many questions for you."

"I will answer them to the best of my knowledge." Flavus bowed and departed.

The next evening Calaf sat talking with soldiers around a fire when Nozar called him away.

"The emperor accepted Rome's offer," the general said. "He also agreed to Flavus's request that he remain assigned to you."

"His job is done. Why doesn't he go back to Rome?"

"An ongoing liaison, he says, but he seems to have a particular interest in you." Nozar paused a moment. "Do you trust him?"

"No."

"Then report any suspicions to me, however insignificant they may seem."

CHAPTER 20
251 CE

Khyber Pass

Fumes of burning sulfur filled the tent amidst the moans of injured soldiers. There were no cots, so the men found space on the ground wherever they could. Ishmael knelt beside an unconscious youth no older than his own sixteen years and examined a calf wound, relieved to see that the tissue remained healthy. The leg stirred. The poppy had worn off and soon his moans would join the others. Ishmael signaled and called for wine.

A boy laid a basin beside Ishmael and handed him a small cup. "Not water this time?"

Ishmael began irrigating the wound. "I get better results when I alternate wine with the boiling water."

The boy slipped another bowl below the leg to catch the excess. "The Arachosian just died."

Ishmael steadied his hands on his thighs.

"Do you know where their camp is?" The boy nodded. "Go tell them. Their rites must begin before nightfall." The boy stood and began to find his way around and over the wounded. "And hurry back."

Ishmael closed his eyes. From the day he met him in the tunnel outside Peshawar's Khyber Gate, the Arachosian had been a good friend and vigorous lover.

A hand touched his shoulder. The chief physician leaned over him. "Finish with this one and go rest."

"But—"

"That's an order, son," the physician said. "You're no good to me, or them, without sleep." Ishmael nodded. He had not left the tent since the Arachosian was brought in three days before. As he returned to the young soldier's wound, the chief physician patted his shoulder and said, "I'm sorry about your friend."

As Ishmael stepped from the infirmary tent, the sun disappeared behind the barren ridge to the west. If he climbed it, he would be able to see Peshawar, only an army's two-day march to the east. Their camp was below the Khyber Pass's highest point, where the Persian army had encamped for the winter. Few dared speak of the late-summer loss of Baktra and the disastrous retreat to the Khyber's eastern slopes. Only the approaching winter stopped Shapur from pushing Timur's army to the gates of Peshawar.

Ishmael rubbed his sulfur-irritated eyes with his knuckles and allowed fatigue to wash through him. Quiet enveloped the camp, the night patrols already departed, the day patrols still not returned. Several days earlier, a skirmish between a patrol and a larger Persian scouting party had filled the infirmary tent. The Arachosian was the third, and likely the last, to die. He considered going to the Arachosian camp but knew he would not be welcome. Their death rituals were private affairs.

Once in his tent, Ishmael undressed and slipped under a blanket. He reached for the chain about his neck, brought Calaf's infant ankle band to his lips, and closed his eyes. When he opened them again, it seemed only moments later, but streaks of sunlight invaded his tent and he lay atop his blankets, his body bathed in sweat from the captured heat. He crawled out and sat, his legs crossed, shielding his eyes from the midday sun. He stretched his arms then shivered as a cold breeze enveloped him. *Soon there will be snow.*

A camp errand boy ran up to him. "Commander wants you."

The boy fetched a bucket of water as Ishmael reached into his tent for the most presentable of his three tunics. Water still dripped from his hair and face as he jogged with eyes downcast toward the headquarters tent. As he drew near, he stopped, surprised at seeing a familiar but unexpected face. Ishmael rushed into his father's outstretched arms. Aric broke their embrace and held Ishmael at arm's length. A wide smile filled his face. "Come." Aric led Ishmael through the open flaps.

The commander leaned over a map at the back of the tent. The oldest officer in the emperor's army, he was one of the few who had served under the disgraced General Rodmehr. Because he was Nozar's uncle he survived Timur's purge upon ascending the throne, but his connection to Rodmehr limited his advancement, even as his nephew rose to a position second only to the emperor.

Ishmael stood stiff at attention, eyes focused straight ahead.

"At ease, soldier," the commander said and stepped forward. "Because of your actions when the Persians attacked the infirmary at Baktra, fifteen soldiers owe you their lives. In recognition of your bravery in his service, the emperor has awarded you an honor for valor." The commander lifted the bronze armband from the table. "I understand that General Nozar personally requested your name be engraved on the band." He closed the armband around Ishmael's right bicep. "You're a fine soldier and, if the chief physician is to be believed, a better healer. May the gods go with you as you depart."

Ishmael blinked in surprise. "Depart, sir?"

"Yes, the emperor orders you to return to Peshawar with your father."

Once they were outside the tent, Ishmael grasped the shoulders of a broadly smiling Aric. "Peshawar—does it mean—?"

"Yes, I brought the order lifting your banishment, signed by the emperor himself."

"Is Calaf still in Srinagar?"

"No, he has returned to Peshawar with the emperor."

"Does this mean I can see him?"

"I don't know for certain, but hopefully so. But first you must appear before the emperor. Come, I have horses—if we hurry, we'll be in Peshawar by nightfall."

CHAPTER 21

PESHAWAR

FOUNDED ONE HUNDRED FIFTY YEARS earlier by Vima Kadphises, the first great Kushan ruler, the cemetery dominated the rolling hills beyond the city's north wall. During summer its gulmohar trees displayed splashes of crimson, orange and yellow flowers, but this day only their feathery leaves provided cover from the early morning mist. Barzin threaded his way among narrow stone monuments as tall as he, pausing several times to study an inscription before resting his palm along the marker's pointed top. When he spotted his father sitting on a stone bench under one of the gulmohars, he quickened his pace.

Nozar patted the bench. "You received my message?"

Barzin nodded and looked at his mother's newly placed stone. "She would have been fifty today."

"It is good she's not here to witness what is to come," Nozar said.

"You're exhausted, Father."

"Exhaustion is my life, you know that. Saving the emperor from himself and preserving his empire dominate my life." Nozar's eyes took on a faraway look. "I will rest soon enough with your mother."

"You can't believe that."

"I do."

"Our situation is that bad?" Barzin asked.

"Considering what happened at Baktra, likely worse. I am forced to consider how we might salvage the Kushan Empire without Timur—and without my guidance in his name. As difficult as it is to spare any forces, the Minnagaran revolt gives me a reason to send your detachment away from the Persian front. You will also take the prince as your second in command." Barzin started to interrupt but Nozar held up his hand. "Once you deal with Minnagara you will remain in the south. Under no circumstance will you return to Peshawar. We will fall with or without you. And you will protect the prince with your life, as I have his father."

"But I belong at your side."

"As your father, I agree. But it is not your father who gives you this charge."

Nozar knelt before the many funeral gifts that decorated the ground before his wife's marker. He picked up Timur's gift, an oval bronze disc engraved with her likeness, and placed it in the leather pouch at his waist. He embraced his son then began walking toward the city.

Nozar's face flushed with anger as the emperor's astrologer emerged from the royal quarters and swept past. Approaching the guards at Timur's door, he demanded, "Has anyone other than the astrologer been with the emperor this morning?"

"Only the prince, sir. He's still inside," one guard answered as the other opened the chamber door. Since the day Timur ascended the throne thirty-six years earlier, Nozar was the only person allowed immediate and unannounced access to the emperor.

"Nozar!" Timur's voice boomed across the room from the table that dominated the room. Noting the jovial greeting, Nozar scanned the table and saw no wine. He glanced at the attendant, who sat nearby. The attendant was a new boy named Taj, who had arrived with Calaf and Flavus from Minnagara and soon afterward joined the emperor's service. Full pitchers of fresh wine and the emperor's empty cup sat on a low table beside Taj. Nozar restrained a smile. Aric once again must have paid the astrologer to find something in the emperor's chart about no wine before midday.

Nozar bowed. "My lord." He nodded at Calaf, who stood at the table's far end. "My prince."

"Come, come." Timur waved Nozar to the table. "Calaf, give Nozar the report."

The general stepped beside the prince and looked down at a large map of the city. He recognized Aric's meticulous hand.

Calaf began, "The tunnel beneath the eastern wall is now cleared and new supports are in place. Outside the wall it's been rerouted and will emerge here, a better-protected location, nearer to the river, and farther away from the expected enemy position to the west. Should we suffer a long siege, our water supply will be secure."

Nozar pointed to a tangle of marks on the map. "And this is Flavus's maze?"

"Yes. These false tunnels will branch off the old one outside the wall. All will be made to look like they collapsed. If discovered by enemy scouts, they'll conclude we aborted our tunnel efforts."

"Just as likely they'll keep searching, my prince."

"Even so, it buys us valuable time."

Nozar looked at Timur. "The maze is a waste of time. The walls—all efforts must be there. You saw what the Persian siege engines did at Baktra."

Timur's face darkened.

Calaf rushed in. "But Flavus says his people in Germania fooled the Romans for an entire campaign season with such a tunnel maze and kept water and supplies flowing."

Timur's dark eyes did not leave Nozar's face as he motioned to Taj, who leapt to his feet, grabbed a wine pitcher and the emperor's cup, and rushed to the table. Timur ripped the pitcher from Taj's grasp, brought it to his mouth, and drained it halfway. He thrust the pitcher back at Taj, who managed to catch it without spilling the wine or dropping the cup. Timur pushed himself up from the table. "The tunnel will decide our success with the Persians."

Nozar recognized the voice of the astrologer in Timur's words, and for the second time that morning fought to contain his anger. He bowed deeply. "It is as you say, my lord."

Timur dropped back into his chair and started to raise his fist. Instead he let it fall into his lap. "Out—both of you. Boy, more wine."

As Taj set the emperor's cup on the table and filled it, Calaf tucked the rolled tunnel map under his arm and followed Nozar from the chamber.

"A word, my prince." Nozar led him into an anteroom off the corridor. A massive tapestry celebrating Kanishka, Timur's great-grandfather, dominated one wall. Across from it hung a newer and larger one depicting Timur's victory over Minnagara, a victory that gave the Kushan Empire control over the lower Indus River and access to the sea. The figure of Timur dominated the center, but to his right, only slightly lower, stood his one-eyed general.

Nozar spoke. "My words were harsh. The tunnels are important, and you've done an excellent job overseeing their restoration."

"It's the men who did the work, sir."

"They will always work hard for someone they respect." Nozar sensed Calaf's discomfort and wondered when he would begin accepting such compliments as his due. "But I'm afraid I must reassign you."

"Sir?"

"The Minnagarans are in revolt. We expect that it's a minor affair, but we must respond quickly and with force. Otherwise we risk emboldening other provinces. Barzin's detachment leaves in two days to crush this disturbance. His second in command will remain here to complete the tunnel work. You will replace him at Barzin's side."

"But, sir, I am only sixteen."

"The same age as your father when he became emperor."

Calaf stared up at the heroic image of Timur in the tapestry. "Does he know?"

"Not yet. I'll tell him after you've gone and convince him that you must prove yourself battle-worthy before the spring campaign against Shapur. He'll understand."

"He won't like it."

Nozar shrugged his shoulders then asked, "Did the astrologer predict anything else?"

"No, but he was emphatic about the tunnels."

"Damn fool."

Calaf flashed a smile. "You *are* speaking of the astrologer, aren't you?"

Nozar acknowledged the jest with a wink then said, "There is news from the Khyber Pass. Our scouts report that the banners of Tur have joined those of Shapur's Persian lords."

"Ah, final proof that upon my return from Minnagara you should have sent me straightaway to Tur. Had I won the heart of the princess, Baktra and the Khyber Pass would still be ours."

"You forget that Turandot beheads her suitors."

"Not me," Calaf grinned, "according to my father's astrologer."

Nozar held up his hand. "Please, no more astrologers." Then he asked, "Has Aric left to bring back Ishmael?"

"Before sunrise."

"You will not forget your pledge."

"Yes."

"I know the temptation is great, but—"

"Sir, I understand. My father must be the one to decide when we meet again."

An officer appeared outside the anteroom. "Sir, another informer is at the palace gate."

Nozar sighed. "At least ten this week alone. People are suspicious of anything out of the ordinary—trouble is there's nothing ordinary in Peshawar anymore. Then you have the feuds. I expect last week's public execution of that merchant lying about his rival will stem that tide. Go now, Barzin expects you."

As Calaf left the anteroom, Nozar stepped up to the Minnagara tapestry and touched the white-cloaked figure tending to the injured and dying soldiers of Timur's army.

CHAPTER 22

THE NEXT MORNING'S FIRST LIGHT struck the wall surrounding the Zoroastrian fire temple beside the main gate of Timur's palace. Passersby slowed to watch the frantic efforts of the priests scrubbing the wall, attempting with little success to remove a crude drawing of Timur on his hands and knees being sexually assaulted by the Persian Emperor Shapur. Above it the name *Baktra* was drawn in flames. For months, few nights passed without the discovery of such vulgar expressions of the growing unrest of Peshawar's population. The graffiti was usually scrawled on outlying buildings, but now the vandals were so bold as to despoil the temple dedicated to the martyrs Yousef and Sanjar.

A cloaked youth paused to watch the priests before proceeding through the palace gate, slipping past the guards with a nod. Sharina's handmaiden waited at the stairs leading to the royal living quarters. Gar shed his hood as he approached.

"My mistress awaits you," the handmaiden said.

Gar stroked her cheek then cupped her chin and brought his lips to hers. She pulled away with a giggle. "Not here. Someone might see." She started up the stairs.

Gar stepped beside her. "She rises early."

"My mistress has not slept."

Gar laughed. "Then she should have called me sooner."

"Even you would have not calmed her last night."

"What's happened?"

The handmaiden quickened her pace. “I dare not say.” She reached the top of the stairs and ran down the corridor toward Sharina’s chambers. Gar began to rush after her but then stopped. Sharina’s usual bodyguard did not stand at her door. Instead, an army officer waited, an unsheathed sword at his side. Gar spun about. Two soldiers with spears blocked his escape. He backed up against the corridor wall and watched the officer hand a coin to the handmaiden.

“Sorry,” she whispered as she dashed past and disappeared down the stairway.

“This way.”

Gar looked toward the voice. The officer held open the door to Sharina’s chamber. Gar looked back at the two soldiers. Their spears now pointed toward him. He straightened and walked to the open door, hesitated a moment, then stepped across the threshold. The heavy door slammed shut behind him.

“When did you last see Governor Zubair’s son?”

After a morning of interrogation by two different officers, Ishmael sat on a couch in General Nozar’s private quarters. He looked up into Nozar’s scarred face and tried to contain his frustration and hide his fear. “I’ve already told—”

“Yes, I know, and now you’re telling me.” Nozar sat down beside Ishmael and rested his hand on the youth’s leg. “When was the last time you saw him?”

“In Baktra before the Persian siege. Gar left with the last Kushan civilians and asked if I had a message for my mother.”

“And did you?”

Ishmael nodded. “I told her good-bye. That I would die loyal to the emperor. That I hoped she would—” He hesitated.

Nozar squeezed Ishmael’s leg. “Mourn and honor you. Yes, we found the letter in her chambers. There was nothing else?”

"What else would there be? My mother and I had little in common."

"And Gar? You've had no contact with him since Baktra?"

"No, sir."

"You did not see him when you returned to Peshawar last night?"

"No, sir."

"And your mother?"

"No. I planned to visit her today after my audience with the emperor."

After a pause, Nozar asked, "Do you know why Gar was in Baktra?"

"He said he was working for his father."

"Did you see him doing this work?"

"Not unless it involved whoring and gambling."

"I understand he spent time with you when you were off duty."

"I believe my mother asked him to spy on me."

"I see." Nozar stood, circled the room, and then stopped, staring at the floor.

"Sir, please tell me what's happened."

"Yesterday an informer gave me documents proving that Governor Zubair, his son Gar, and your mother conspired with the Persians to overthrow the emperor. The heads of Zubair and Gar now rest on spikes above the Khyber Gate."

"My mother?"

Nozar sighed. "She fled to Minnagara, apparently to join her homeland's insurrection against the emperor."

"And my father?"

"Not implicated." Nozar scratched his ear. "You take the news calmly. Are you not surprised?"

"I know she hated the emperor for what he did to her family. After Demetrius died, she tried to turn me against him."

"And—"

"I am loyal to the emperor, sir. I was horrified by Demetrius's death, but he would be the first to tell me not to grieve him with vengeance—that such actions would devour then destroy me."

"As will I if I even suspect you wish the emperor harm."

"Sir?"

Nozar again sat beside Ishmael. "The emperor intends to make you his personal physician."

"His physician? But I'm too young and inexperienced."

"I agree. While I admire your fortitude during your banishment, and your heroism at Baktra demonstrates resourcefulness and courage, I would not place you so close to the emperor. Later maybe, but not yet. I would see your loyalty more fully tested."

"Because of my mother's betrayal?"

"That doesn't concern me as much as your devotion to the prince. To be frank, I'm uncertain of your loyalty to the emperor should you have to choose between them. You've not faced that decision."

"Sir, I have pledged my life to the emperor and his service."

"Yes, and I know you expect me to hold you to that vow."

"Given what my mother has done, I don't understand why the emperor would trust me."

"The words of his astrologer transcend even her treachery."

"Not *the young healer saving the life of the emperor* story?"

"The very same. The astrologer recast the emperor's chart, this time with yours, and is most emphatic."

"And heavier in the purse compliments of my father?"

"I see you share Demetrius's skepticism of the mystical. Around the emperor you'll be wise to choose your words with care."

"Of course." He paused a moment before asking, "When can I see Calaf?"

Nozar shook his head. "The emperor still mistrusts the prince's attachment to you. Calaf leaves tomorrow with Barzin's detachment to pursue your mother and put down the Minnagaran insurrection. For the moment, serve the emperor well and await Calaf's return. It may be different then. But there's more." Nozar hesitated several long moments before adding, "Before he died, Gar revealed a plot against you."

"What kind of plot?"

"Gar was to deliver your head to the emperor with a message from your mother."

Ishmael stood and crossed the room, not speaking for several long moments. Finally he turned. "You're telling me that she wanted me dead?"

"So it seems."

"Why?"

"She told Gar you were a threat to the empire."

"Me, a threat? That makes no sense. What was the message?"

"She had not given it to him yet." Ishmael lifted his eyes to the ceiling as Nozar added, "I know it's a terrible burden to bear, but you must know the treachery of this woman you call mother. If I'm to trust you close to the emperor, your loyalty to him, not her, must be unquestioned."

Ishmael lowered his gaze to Nozar's face. "It is, sir."

"Good, then we'll have no reason to speak of this again." Nozar moved to the chamber door. "Remain here. Your father will come when the emperor is ready for you."

Alone for the first time since he had awakened the previous morning at the Kushan camp on the Khyber, Ishmael gave in to his exhaustion. As he wrapped his arms around his body to control the shaking, his mind rushed from the elation of the king's lifting his banishment, to the dashed hope that he and Calaf would be reunited, to the shock that his mother planned to kill him. He wanted to deny the truth of Nozar's words, but he could not, not after the years of neglect and indifference he had experienced with her. *A threat to the empire?* No, he knew it was more personal. She hated him. Enough to want him dead. *But why?* It was a question that would never be answered, for she would likely be captured at Minnagara and face a traitor's death, and he would never see her again.

As they walked from the emperor's chambers, Ishmael noticed his father's limp was pronounced. "Are you in pain?"

Aric waved off the question with a forced laugh. "Stiffness comes and goes. Nothing more."

After a few moments of silence, Ishmael ventured, "Nozar said my mother betrayed us to the Persians. Is it true?"

Aric pulled him into a deserted alcove. He shook with emotion as he whispered, "Do not believe the accusations. Someone framed her."

"But she hates the emperor."

"Not enough to help the Persians," Aric insisted. "Stay true to her as I do."

Ishmael fought the urge to lash out with, *What, stay true to the woman who plotted my death?* But knowing that his distraught father did not know this, he simply embraced him and said, "I will."

When they arrived at Demetrius's former quarters, Aric made a show of opening the door and motioned Ishmael to enter. "Just think, two nights ago you slept under a tent on the ground." He pointed at the battered but unopened crates piled around the walls. "I'm glad you got your medical books and papers out of Baktra before the siege." But Ishmael's eyes were trained on the floor's carpet. Aric placed his hand on Ishmael's shoulder. "After I reminded the emperor how much the queen loved seeing you play on it when you were small, he ordered it moved here." Ishmael dropped to his knees and traced his finger around the two foxes—one white, one gold. When he looked back at Aric, his eyes were damp. Aric knelt beside him. "It is yours now."

"Why is he being kind to me?"

Aric scratched his head. "Who knows? He often says you were his favorite squire. And you proved yourself loyal at Baktra. My advice, enjoy it while it lasts. He was kind to me when he first became emperor after my brother died."

"How long do I have?"

"I had a year, but he didn't drink so much wine back then." Aric laughed. "I give you a few weeks."

"But he never struck Demetrius, did he?"

"Not until—" Aric stood and was silent.

Ishmael rose and wrapped his arms around him. "There's not a day that I don't think about him, too."

Aric stiffened, broke Ishmael's embrace, and headed for the door. "I'll go now so you can get settled."

"Father." Aric turned. Ishmael smiled. "Thank you."

Ishmael wandered into the small room that had been his and his mother's before him. Two years earlier, grief-stricken by Demetrius's death and his separation from Calaf, she had comforted him. Now? *Gar was to deliver your head to the emperor with a message from your mother.* Out loud he cursed Nozar. *Why was it necessary to tell me?* From childhood he had accepted that she did not love him. But to be told that she planned his death? How could he understand, much less accept, such evil?

There was a soft knock at the apartment door. For a moment, with fatigue and despair enveloping him, Ishmael considered not answering. Then he remembered. Like Demetrius before him, his every hour now belonged to the emperor. He walked to the door and opened it.

Calaf stood before him.

Taj waited at the bottom of the stairway leading to the palace apartments and glanced at the hooded figure standing in the shadows of a nearby alcove. Turning back, he saw Flavus on the stairs, descending two steps at a time.

"Where's Kabir?" As they stepped into the alcove, the gnarled and weathered face of the Indus river merchant appeared from under a hooded cloak. Flavus grasped Kabir's shoulders. "No one could have played a better informer, my friend."

Kabir reached up with a soft jab to Flavus's chin. "What if Nozar had discovered the documents were forgeries?"

"Fortunate for us he didn't."

"That governor was a corrupt bastard, but I feel badly about the son."

"As do I, but Sharina's plan to use him to kill Ishmael gave me no choice."

"You got her away?"

Flavus nodded. "She had an escape plan already, just used it sooner than expected." He turned to Taj. "Anything new with the emperor?"

"He still meets with his astrologer every day. Drinks his wine and rages at everyone. Except this afternoon when he met with Ishmael. He seems quite fond of him."

Flavus took Kabir's arm. "Your boat?"

"Docked at the river, waiting my next voyage to Minnagara."

"Then go tonight and make your preparations, but do not leave until you've heard from Taj." He pulled a sealed parchment from his cloak. "And take this to Callista. It directs her to pay you as we agreed. Tell her all that you know. If she has further instructions—"

Kabir held up his palm. "As always, my friend."

Flavus embraced Kabir. "These are dangerous times. May the gods keep you safe." As Kabir departed, Flavus turned to Taj. "You're certain the emperor will sleep until morning?"

"The potion is strong. And I'm assigned to attend him, so if he stirs, you will know it. Will I ride at dawn?"

"Uncertain. But I confirmed the horses wait at the East Gate. Now go—and quickly. The royal guards must not question your absence."

Flavus waited until Taj disappeared down the corridor to the emperor's quarters before climbing the stairway to guard Ishmael's new quarters.

They neither moved nor spoke, just stared. At last Calaf's face broke into a lop-sided grin. "Maybe invite me in?"

"Yes—yes—of course." Ishmael stumbled as he stepped back and closed the door. They embraced. "You—here?"

Calaf did not reply, just held his friend, an arm around his back, a hand pulling his face into his neck. Ishmael dug his fingers into Calaf's back, repeating his name. Calaf tried to loosen his hold, but Ishmael gripped him tighter.

"Ishmael, I'm here—I'm here."

Finally they eased apart, and Ishmael touched Calaf's face. "But how? If the emperor—"

"Flavus has made sure he sleeps soundly and now stands guard at your door. We won't be discovered or disturbed."

"You're bigger," Ishmael said.

"You're taller."

Both laughed. Ishmael pulled Calaf's forehead to his, their noses touched. He kissed Calaf's cheek then stepped back.

Calaf's eyes dropped to the carpet. "It can't be."

"It is. The emperor gave it to me." Ishmael went to his knees at the carpet's edge.

"You've done well regaining his favor."

"And you?"

Calaf shrugged. "Maybe never. He accepts me. Nozar says that is enough." He knelt facing Ishmael. "You did well at Baktra."

"I killed."

"I know."

"So have you," Ishmael said.

"Yes, but not in battle, not heroically like you. I only saved myself."

"Escaping that kidnapping is heroic to me." Ishmael stroked Calaf's face. "I could have lost you." After a pause he added, "You've heard that my mother is a traitor?"

Calaf nodded. "A bit of a shock. She certainly had no love for the emperor, but it's unbelievable she'd go so far as to conspire with the Persians."

"And plot my death."

"What do you mean?" Calaf asked.

"Gar was to kill me and deliver my head to Timur with a message from her." Ishmael turned his face away.

"But why?"

"I don't know."

"Are you all right?"

Ishmael leapt to his feet. "Besides finding out that my own mother wants me dead?"

Calaf rose behind him, his hands first on his shoulders then around his chest. A wooden Ishmael resisted the embrace, a rapid heartbeat the only sign of his feelings. Calaf kissed his neck. "We have each other." Ishmael's body relaxed. Calaf drew him to the carpet and lay down behind him. Ishmael placed a finger on the head of the carpet's lion, its teeth bared at the fleeing hare. Calaf moved it to the wing-like leaves on the hare's back.

"Fly," Ishmael whispered and turned his hand over.

Calaf clasped it and pressed himself closer to his back. "Fly." He closed his eyes.

When he opened them again, he was on his back, Ishmael's finger lightly tracing his forehead. Calaf sat up, crossed his legs, and stretched. "I slept?"

"Not long. When must you go?"

"Barzin expects me at first light. Flavus will fetch me. But first, you must leave."

"Leave?" Ishmael rose and knelt before him. "To go with you?"

"No, I will join you later. Flavus has it arranged. A day's ride from here, on the Indus, a boat waits for you. I know the merchant. His name is Kabir. Irascible, but a good man and trustworthy. He will take you to Makli, a village above Minnagara, where I escaped the kidnapper. The fishermen know me and will hide you until—"

"But my place is here. The emperor—"

"The emperor who wanted you dead and killed Demetrius? Who keeps us separated to this day?"

"Do you forget I am bound to a life where obedience and loyalty are everything? I am a servant like my father and like Demetrius. Since the emperor banished me, it is their example I have followed. Now that I am restored to the emperor, am I to betray him?"

"So that you are safe, so that we can be together? Yes."

"And who would I be then? The son of a traitor, who also turned traitor? Would anyone believe I didn't follow her?"

Shock turned Calaf silent for a moment. The last thing he had anticipated was Ishmael balking at his escape plan. Incredulous, he asked, "You choose him over me?"

"No. I choose to stand at your side honorably, Hephaistion to your Alexander."

"Oh, Ishmael, those are heroic tales told to impressionable boys. The real world is vicious and cruel. Your mother proves that. Listen to me carefully. Timur will fall. After our defeat at Baktra everyone knows it. Even Nozar. Why do you think he sends me to Minnagara to quell a bit of provincial rioting? To gain battle experience? That's what he'll tell my father. But that's not the real reason. Nozar would keep me out of harm's way, so I can lead the Kushan resistance and retake our empire. I will be emperor then. Whether or not you honor my father's newfound trust, it will mean nothing once he's gone."

"No, Calaf, it will mean more, because no one can ever accuse me of disloyalty to your father. And later no one, even you, will ever doubt my loyalty."

"But if you die?"

"Then I die, but I will not have brought dishonor on myself or on you."

"Is there no way I can convince you?" Calaf asked.

"Only if I ride out of Peshawar at your side will my loyalty to you be unquestioned."

"But my father will order your death if we're seen together."

"Then we have no choice."

Calaf jumped to his feet and stared down at Ishmael. "I will not allow it. I order you to leave."

Ishmael stood. "You are not my lord."

Calaf's face darkened then he threw himself at Ishmael, sending them to the carpet. Ishmael tried to scramble out of reach, but Calaf grabbed and twisted his leg, flipping him onto his back. What Ishmael lacked in strength he compensated with quickness, frustrating Calaf's repeated attempts to pin him. Ishmael began to laugh with each escape, turning Calaf's initial fury first into exasperation then into his own laughter. Finally managing to wrestle Ishmael onto his back, Calaf subdued him by sitting on his stomach with arms held down by the wrists, their faces almost touching.

Calaf spoke through labored breaths. "I *am* your lord."

Ishmael lifted his lips to Calaf's. Calaf hesitated a moment then eased Ishmael's mouth open with his tongue. Ishmael pulled his hands free to caress Calaf's head as they kissed. When Calaf sat back up, Ishmael placed his hand on his chest. "Your heart beats fast."

Calaf did the same. "Yours, too."

Ishmael's hand slipped between Calaf's legs and touched his erection. Their eyes locked, neither moving. Calaf pulled his tunic over his head. Ishmael did likewise and began to turn onto his stomach. Calaf stopped him.

"I would see your face."

Ishmael's head rested on Calaf's chest, his arm lay between his legs. Calaf ran his fingers through Ishmael's curly hair.

"You won't change your mind?"

"I can't."

"And Demetrius always said I was the stubborn one." Calaf kissed Ishmael's head. "You better not die."

"You neither."

Calaf grinned. "You're hard again."

"Can't help it."

"Never could." He laughed then gave Ishmael's hair a firm tug.

"Ow!" Ishmael batted Calaf's hand away, scrambled up and sat on his thighs, his knees hugging Calaf's hips. His expression turned serious. "Do my desires trouble you?"

"No more than Demetrius's troubled Torak."

"So you think about them, too?"

"Of course."

"I hoped you would."

"But like Demetrius, I know you yearn for more."

"What you give will always be enough."

Calaf pulled him into his arms.

Three soft knocks.

"It's Flavus." Calaf eased himself from Ishmael's embrace, went to the door, and cracked it open.

"Dawn is near, my prince. If he goes, it must be now."

Calaf shook his head. "Give us a few moments more." When he turned back, Ishmael was standing and pulling a chain over his head. "No, keep it."

Ishmael extended the gold infant ankle band. "But it's yours."

Calaf took the chain and returned it to Ishmael's neck. "Yes, and it belongs with you."

Ishmael drew Calaf to a nearby table and lifted the bronze armband given to him by the emperor. He closed it around Calaf's bicep. "Then this is yours."

Calaf ran his finger over Ishmael's engraved name. "The emperor won't miss it?"

"No. I'm no longer a soldier, so it would be pretentious to wear it."

"You will see it again soon. Minnagara will not keep me away long." Calaf laid his palm on Ishmael's cheek and then dressed.

Their final embrace was cut short by three quick knocks and Flavus's voice. "The palace stirs, my prince."

They held each other's eyes for several long moments before Calaf slipped out the door.

The eastern darkness reached across the sky to extinguish the sunset over the distant Khyber, where the smoke of Persian army campfires stretched across the distant mountains. To the south, the horizon's rippling heat swallowed the cloud of dust trailing Barzin's forces. Ishmael stood atop the Peshawar wall and searched for a final glimpse of his departing friend. His fingers touched the infant ankle band hanging about his neck.

A plaintive melody reached Ishmael's ears. He looked down into the bustle of the street. Merchants were packing their wares, soldiers milled about, mothers shepherded their children. Sitting on a pile of grain sacks, a gray-bearded blind man played random notes on his flute. No one paid attention to him until two men emerged from the crowd, one carrying a long-neck lute, the other a large drum. They climbed onto the grain sacks and embraced the blind man. When he resumed playing his flute, the lute player eased into the melodic line like a lover into his love. In response the drummer answered with a slow, deep pulse. Movement in the street began to slow. The flute went quiet, followed by the lute. The drummer then erupted, filling the evening air with unbridled tumult. No one in the street now moved, no sound but the drum echoing against the city wall and the street's buildings—until Ishmael launched his voice into the drum's turbulence.

My lord, hear me!
Oh, hear, my lord!
Ishmael can bear no more,
his heart is breaking!

The drum ceased. A child cried out. A dog barked. A drunken shout was silenced. Then stillness filled the street. The blind man's face lifted toward Ishmael. He brought the flute to his lips and played. The lute joined. The drum resumed its slow, deep throbbing. Ishmael stared into the flute player's unseeing eyes, felt their permission, and continued.

Alas, how far have I walked
with your name in my heart,
with your name on my lips?
But if your fate
tomorrow be decided,
I shall die on the path of exile,
Ishmael will lose his lord,
The remembrance of his arms, his lips,
Ishmael can bear no more!

As the instruments continued to lift his sorrowful melody into the evening air, Ishmael once again looked toward the distant south.

PART 4

I'M A BIRD … I'M A CAMEL

251 - 260 CE

CHAPTER 23
251 CE

Indus River

The Kushan Empire stood on the brink of collapse. Peshawar had fallen. To the south, Minnagara was lost to the rebels. To the west, Arachosia overthrew its Kushan governor and negotiated a truce with the Persians.

Calaf stood before the command tent at the center of the Kushan camp on the west bank of the Indus, a day's march upriver of Minnagara. Three months earlier three thousand Kushan soldiers cleared the mangrove forest, using the trees for the barricade that surrounded the clearing. Now, the thousand who remained alive were breaking camp, evacuating across the river using a flotilla of small boats seized from local fishermen. Barzin waited on the other side, organizing the detachment's march north to join the last stronghold of the Kushan army at Rajanpur, its next battle—and likely annihilation—with the Persian army but days away.

Calaf coughed and rubbed his eyes against the dust and asked Flavus, "How many do you think will desert?"

"You'll be fortunate if half march into Rajanpur."

"And you? Will you head back to Rome?"

"One job remains."

"Admit it, you're avoiding your emperor. He can't be pleased that my father wasted his weapons and supplies."

"Win or lose, Timur was going to help us. I grant we had hoped for a better result last summer, but I'm confident the Romans were pleased with my Baktra report."

"Ah, yes, all those Persian tactics, strengths, and weaknesses you couldn't stop talking about." A small group of soldiers passed below them, burdened with packs and headed toward the river. "Do you believe yesterday's report about Timur escaping to Rajanpur?"

"Anything's possible, my prince, but Taj saw the Persians storm the palace, and he's certain Timur was inside with—" Flavus did not finish.

After a lengthy silence Calaf said, "I should have forced Ishmael to leave."

"How? Bound and screaming vulgarities all the way to Makli?"

"If it meant him safe and alive."

"And who says he's not, my prince? Who can doubt his resourcefulness after his bravery at Baktra?"

Taj's approach interrupted Calaf's response.

"My prince." Taj bowed then turned to Flavus. "Kabir's arrived. His boat is at the river, and his men are at the barricade."

"Go wait with them. We'll join you soon."

As Taj left Calaf asked, "Kabir's here?"

"We'll use his boat to cross the river. His men will escort us."

"But my guards."

"They'll pack the tent and follow us."

Shouting erupted over the din of breaking camp. Soldiers dragged a Buddhist monk toward them, the monk's bare feet, shaved head and face covered in caked mud. Calaf recognized the tattered remains of the Minnagaran temple's yellow robe. The soldiers threw their prisoner at Calaf's feet.

"Explain this," Calaf snapped. "Your orders are to grant safe passage to refugees."

The senior soldier spoke. "Pardon, my prince, but this is no refugee."

Flavus knelt and turned the monk's shoulders. The monk spat at him, and he grabbed the monk's chin. "Sharina?"

Calaf fought to hide his surprise as he addressed the soldiers. "Well done, men. Captain Barzin will know of your vigilance. You may go." Then to Flavus, "Bring her."

Inside the tent Flavus held Sharina by the elbow.

Calaf said, "Leave us."

"But, my prince."

"Leave us." Flavus backed out. "Close the flaps."

Calaf circled her twice, coming to a stop behind her. He leaned into her ear. "I never expected to see you again. It must be a surprise for you as well." She stiffened but did not answer. He touched her shaved head, and she shook his hand away. "It was such beautiful hair. What have you done to displease your friends so much? Is it true that Minnagara's new raja is an aged uncle of yours? Did you know him? But, of course not. Your father had no living brothers, did he? What a puzzle it must be for you. Though, his taking the name Ashu was a nice gesture."

He moved to stand before her, but she refused to meet his gaze, focusing on a spot beyond his shoulder. He clapped his hands and her eyes jerked to his. "Much better." He stroked one cheek, then the other, freeing flakes of dried mud. "We really must bathe you before taking you to my father." She blinked in surprise. "Oh, you haven't heard. We've received word that he escaped Peshawar and gathers his forces at Rajanpur. We go there now. I should send a message informing him of your capture, so he can expect your arrival. You'd be a nice diversion for him. But then, maybe not."

Calaf's fingertips traveled to Sharina's neck. "Gar was a poor choice of executioner." Her eyes grew wide. "You would kill Ishmael, your own son, and deliver his head to Timur?" Calaf's thumbs closed around her throat as he pushed her to her knees. She struggled, digging her fingernails into his forearms, drawing blood. Her mouth was open, but the only sound was choked breathing.

Flavus appeared and grabbed Calaf's wrists. Calaf tightened his grip around her neck, and she went limp. Flavus seized Calaf's jaw. They locked eyes. "Release her."

"No!" Calaf shouted.

Flavus broke Calaf's hold on Sharina's throat and struck him across the face, hurling him across the tent.

As Sharina, choking for breath, crawled beside Flavus's legs, Calaf climbed to his knees. "For that you will die with her." Then leaping to his feet, he shouted. "Guards!"

"No one's close enough to hear you."

Calaf rushed for the tent flaps, but Flavus seized his arm, stopping him.

Calaf fought his hold and raged, "You protect the woman who would kill Ishmael?"

"No, Calaf, I save you from killing your mother."

Flavus eased his hold and Calaf wrested his arm from Flavus's grasp. Calaf's mind went blank at Flavus's words, and he staggered backwards, collapsing to his knees.

Sharina gasped, "You knew?"

Flavus nodded, his eyes never leaving Calaf. "Demetrius told me as he lay dying."

"You lie!" Calaf shouted.

Flavus looked down at Sharina. "Tell him."

"I switched you with the prince before the *chakor* ceremony."

Shock and disbelief battled for control as Calaf stared open-mouthed at Sharina then Flavus. "What game do you two play?"

"No games, Calaf," Flavus answered.

"Then Ishmael's the true prince?" Calaf asked.

"Yes," Flavus answered.

"So everything I am and have lived for is a lie?"

"Call it what you will," Sharina snapped, "but because of me you are heir to the Kushan throne."

"And that wasn't enough? You would kill Ishmael, too?"

"Yes."

"You raised us both. Played with us. Taught us. What evil consumes you?"

"Ishmael is the son of the monster who butchered my family—our family."

"And for that Ishmael must die?"

"So Timur knows we are avenged? Yes!"

Calaf lunged but Flavus blocked him. "It grows late, my prince. Kabir's men wait to escort us to the boat. Let her come with us to face your father's judgment."

Calaf backed away. "To Rajanpur then," he spat. Then looking down at Sharina he added, "After Timur's through with you, we both know you will wish you had died with my hands around your throat."

Outside the tent Calaf seethed as Flavus bound Sharina's wrists and signaled Taj and Kabir's men at the barricade to join them. Mother or not, he would see Sharina dead. And but for Flavus's intervention she would have known it was her own son that brought her miserable life to an end. Any sympathy he once felt for what she suffered at the hands of Timur had vanished with the news that she plotted Ishmael's death. Her total lack of remorse only condemned her further in his mind.

Spotting a spear leaning against the tent, he glanced at Sharina. Her back was to him. It would take only a moment and no longer matter whether or not Timur lived and waited at Rajanpur. But before he could act Flavus stepped between him and the tent and took the spear.

"You really must learn to hide your intentions, my prince." Flavus passed the spear to Taj.

"Then you had better keep her close," Calaf said.

"Do I need to remind you that the gods do not look kindly upon killing your mother?"

"You and your gods be damned," Calaf snarled.

The path through the mangrove forest to the Indus was wide and well worn. Taj led the way with two of Kabir's men. Flavus followed with Sharina, her hands bound behind her. Calaf and Kabir's remaining men came behind. Within sight of the river Taj moved off the path.

Flavus called out, "Kabir's boat is beached downriver."

Calaf called back, "Not with the others?"

"Taj said it was too crowded. It's not far."

The trail was narrow, forcing the group to move singly through the brush and around the trees. Calaf called out for the men ahead of him to move faster. Once out of Calaf's sight, Flavus shoved Sharina to the ground and cut her restraints.

"Thank Demetrius, not me." Flavus thrust the dagger's grip into her hands. "Now, go." Sharina leapt to her feet and disappeared into the trees.

When Flavus looked back, Kabir's men held an angry, shouting Calaf. Flavus pushed through the men, pulled his sword from its scabbard, and raised the tip of the blade to Calaf's throat. Calaf became silent.

Flavus lifted Calaf's chin with the flat of the blade. "Will you come quietly?"

"You're a dead man!"

"A *no* it is." Flavus swung his sword in a wide loop and brought the hilt down on Calaf's head then shouted, "Taj!"

By the time Taj ran back, Kabir's men were lifting the senseless Calaf from the ground. Flavus pulled Taj aside. "Head to Rajanpur. Spread word that the prince is dead. After that, go to Peshawar to discover Ishmael's fate. If he lives, find out where he goes but make no contact with him. Then return to me."

"Like the wind?"

Flavus smiled and cupped Taj's chin. "Like the wind."

Thank Demetrius, not me.

Flavus's words pounded in Sharina's mind, drowning out the roar of the rushing Indus as she squatted in a copse of thick brush at the river's edge. Even though her breathing had calmed as she rested and she heard no one in pursuit, her heartbeat had not slowed and her eyes darted about frantically. Her hand gripped the dagger Flavus gave her, ready to plunge it into her chest at the first sign of imminent recapture and the horror she knew would follow.

Thank Demetrius.

For what? That she could now live with the memory of her son's hands around her throat as he howled his condemnation for whatever remained of her wretched life? That she lost the opportunity to confront Timur with her vengeance, to shout into his face that Ishmael not Calaf was his true son, and then pray that her family's open arms awaited her after she endured whatever brutality he would inflict on her?

Her family.

She had failed repeatedly to avenge their brutal deaths. After fleeing Peshawar mere moments ahead of arrest for the false accusation of conspiring with the Persians, she sought the protection of the Friends of Ashu in Minnagara. When they demanded assurance that her son would soon appear to lead their insurrection, she confessed she was forced to abort that plan and offered to lead them herself. However, word arrived that the Kushan army advanced to put down their revolt. Fearing that she had betrayed them, they turned on her, and she only escaped death because they could not bring themselves to kill the daughter of their former raja and sister of their namesake.

She reached for her family's presence. Always at the edge of her consciousness they gathered. Comforting, cajoling, waiting. But now there was emptiness. Confusion gripped her. Then panic.

Don't leave me.

She crawled through the brush then stopped as her hands and knees sank into the river's muddy edge. A bit farther and the water's rapid flow would take her to her family. It would take but a moment. She hesitated.

What if they did not wait for me?

Calaf awoke on his back, the floor rocking beneath him. *A boat.* He tried to sit up, but dizziness stopped him. He grimaced as he touched the lump on his head. Out of the darkness came Flavus's voice.

"You gave me little choice."

Calaf scrambled to his knees before dropping onto his hands, his head reeling, his stomach nauseous. "Bastard!"

"Don't make me do it again."

Calaf lunged, fists connecting with flesh until Flavus grabbed his arms, flung him onto his back, and straddled his legs. "Calm yourself."

"Fuck you!" Calaf began to retch, and Flavus flipped him on his side, slapping his back until he finished. "Fuck you." Now a weak whisper.

"Get up."

On unsteady legs Calaf followed Flavus out from under the thatch-covered cargo hold onto the open deck of Kabir's boat. Memories of the dolphins gave him a moment's exhilaration. *So long ago, yet still so vivid.* High in the sky a half moon cast a soft glow across the river. The bow was secured to mangroves on the shore where Kabir's men slept or kept watch. Kabir rose from the shadows, pitched a wine flask to Calaf, then climbed from the boat to join his men. Calaf moved to the bow and stared into the trees.

"You could try but don't expect to get far," Flavus said.

Calaf lifted the flask to his lips, drank, and tossed it to Flavus. "You won't get away with this."

"I already have. No one's coming to your rescue. Everyone believes you're dead."

"Why let Sharina escape?"

"Because Demetrius swore me to protect you and Ishmael—and her." When Calaf remained silent, he continued, "I was also the one who thwarted her plot to kill Ishmael."

"And now you save me from certain death when the Persians attack Rajanpur."

Flavus nodded.

"Then why hold me? You've fulfilled your oath to Demetrius. Go back to Rome."

"I *am* returning to Rome, but I'm taking you with me."

"Why? I'm the son of a lowly scribe," Calaf said.

"You are not the son of a scribe. Aric is not your father."

"You go too far!" Calaf shouted. Confused frustration consumed him. *Sharina's my mother, and now Aric's not my father. What game does Flavus play?* He turned away, grabbed the bow, digging his fingernails into the wood. *Leap, flee, find Ishmael.* But he stood rooted to the deck. The river lapped against the side of the boat, the cries of distant birds reached across the water, the muffled words of Kabir's men came from the trees.

Flavus stepped behind him. "The truth of your birth is more than your mother's switching you with Timur's son. She was married to the raja of Srinagar, was she not?"

"Yes, he died soon after the wedding. Some say Timur had him killed."

"She carried his child when she married Aric. She carried you. If the emperor had known, he would've killed her—and you before you were born. Demetrius conspired with the queen, who convinced Timur to allow Aric to marry her. Aric agreed to claim the raja's child as his own, but he knows nothing about her switching you with the prince."

"So Aric believes Ishmael is the raja's son."

"Yes. Only Sharina and I know the full story, and now you. You see what this means, don't you?"

"What? Even as a pretender to the Kushan throne, I'm still useful to Rome?"

"You're not a pretender," Flavus replied. "You may not be Timur's son, but the royal bloodlines of Srinagar and Minnagara flow through your veins."

"The blood of the dynasty of Kanishka the Great flows through Ishmael's veins."

"Believe me, it won't matter. Do you still want Timur's throne?"

"You know I do."

"Then let Rome help you."

"Why should I trust Rome? Or you?"

"You shouldn't. Timur trusted no one and built an empire. Follow his example. Use Rome, use me, but never trust us—never trust anyone."

"I trust Ishmael."

"He's your rival."

"He doesn't want to be emperor."

"Easy to say when he believes he's the son of a lowly scribe."

"You will not turn me against him."

"But you must be cautious."

"No, I must be free to search for him. Release me."

"I can't. You're too valuable."

"You would use me?"

Flavus laughed. "Of course, I use you, and you will use me. I've already sent Taj to Peshawar to look for Ishmael. Taj is resourceful, knows the city, has contacts, and won't attract attention. If Ishmael's alive, he'll find him. If not, he'll learn his fate. As for you, the Persians won't rest until you're found, dead or alive, so it's best you disappear for a time. We will go to Alexandria. There we'll await word from Taj, and you will learn how Rome can help you."

"And if I say no?"

"It will be a long voyage made longer in chains." Flavus gave Calaf a gentle cuff to the chin and handed him a rag, nodding at the cargo hold. "Might want to clean up your mess before Kabir comes back."

CHAPTER 24

Rajanpur

Battered soldier's sandals covered Ishmael's feet. His trousers and tunic were torn and soiled, a faded cap sat upon his head. He rubbed a bandage on his forearm, grimaced, then reached for the gold band hanging beneath his tunic. First in Baktra then Peshawar he witnessed the savagery of the Persian army. Now he sat in the midst of the devastation of the Indus River port of Rajanpur and fought the fear he would never see Calaf again.

He took a deep breath and stared at the pack beside him. It was all that remained of his former life. Clothing, a thin blanket, a dagger, a clutch of parchments in Demetrius's meticulous hand. Escaping the inferno that engulfed the emperor's chambers using the kitchen servants' passageway, he had wandered the horror of Peshawar's ravaged streets, the stench of rotting bodies, the cries of the living and near dead, the sight of heads decorating the ramparts. In a darkened alley, he found himself holding a blood-stained sword, standing over a dead Persian soldier, with no memory of what happened.

He had sought refuge outside the city walls in the abandoned tunnel where he first encountered his Arachosian lover. There he found wounds to treat, a crying child to comfort, and stories of the treachery of the emperor's scribe. Fortunately, no one knew that Aric's son tended their wounds. There he heard rumors of a Kushan last stand at Rajanpur. Days later, in that grim calm that follows the sack of a city, he slipped through the walls and into the palace to find his quarters looted but untouched by flames. After gathering what few possessions he could carry, he saw his father walking across the palace courtyard in Persian finery. For a moment, he considered revealing himself. But then, filled with revulsion, he found his way to the East Gate and took the road to Rajanpur. Having arrived in that ravaged city, he gazed about in exhaustion, uncertain where to begin to discover Calaf's fate.

"You're Ishmael, aren't you?"

Ishmael lifted his face to the silhouette of a large man standing over him.

"By the gods, it is you." As the man dropped into a squat, Ishmael recognized the uniform of an Arachosian soldier. "We met once—in Baktra. You were friends with my cousin. You're a physician."

"The festival at the fire temple."

"Yes!" The Arachosian slapped his knee. "He was drunk, bellowing like a demon, and you couldn't keep him from falling down. We helped you take him back to his tent."

"He's dead."

"I heard."

"I did everything I could to save him."

"So his comrades told me. But look at you. When did you last eat?" Ishmael shrugged. "Come."

The soldier led him through the city's Arachosian-occupied southern neighborhoods to his army's encampment along the Indus. When Ishmael noted that many Kushan-owned shops had reopened, the soldier said, "The Persians count on the people not caring who rules them as long as the caravans and river boats keep coming and going."

At the mess tent, by the time they finished eating, the few soldiers remaining were too far away to hear their conversation.

"So tell me, why are you here?" the Arachosian asked.

"I look for a friend, a Kushan soldier."

"Not many here. If they fought, most died. If they ran, they're far away."

"He was an officer."

"There are a few of those at the prisoner camp."

"Do you know who they are?"

"The only one I think you might know is called Barzin. I remember him from Baktra. He may know about your friend. Do you want to talk to him?" Ishmael could not contain his surprise. The Arachosian laughed and reached across the table to slap Ishmael's arm. "It's not a trap. I'm a night guard at the camp."

"You would do this for me?"

The Arachosian nodded. "For you—and for my cousin."

The moonless night gave Ishmael the cover of darkness as he crept along the barricade surrounding the prisoner camp. The sounds of several hundred men filled the air: talking, arguing, groaning, and an occasional guard's order. He came to a log leaning against the fence, the spot the Arachosian guard described to him. He sat and waited.

"Ishmael." Barzin's voice. "Are you there?"

He scrambled on hands and knees toward the sound. "Here—I'm here."

Barzin's fingers reached through a gap in the fence. "You—here. When I heard what happened at the palace, I feared the worst."

Kneeling, his forehead against the wall, he grasped Barzin's fingers. "Not many escaped."

"And my father?" Barzin asked.

"The general was imprisoned by the Persians but still alive when I left Peshawar. The emperor, too." Neither spoke for several long moments. Ishmael tightened his grip on Barzin's fingers. "You know why I'm here. Tell me."

Barzin hesitated then said, "Calaf's dead."

He released Barzin's fingers, turned about, and sat, his back against the wall. Barzin continued speaking, but Ishmael heard nothing but the sound of the back of his head striking the wall, over and over. He remembered rolling into a ball on the ground to Barzin's plea. *You must live. For him you must live.* Then nothing until the Arachosian guard shook him awake in the dim light of dawn.

"Come. You must not be found here."

He allowed the Arachosian to lead him away.

Peshawar

As in Baktra, Shapur ordered that religious sites be spared during the Persian army's sack of Peshawar. The decree had saved the lavish garden and rich exterior adornment of the Zoroastrian fire temple dedicated to the martyrs Yousef and Sanjar from the same plundering as the adjoining Kushan palace.

The courtyard doors opened, and a pair of Persian soldiers entered the temple garden, followed by Timur. Resplendent but disheveled in his imperial robes, he held himself erect but favored his right leg. His face was gaunt, the left side yellowish gray with a healing bruise. His hands were bound at his sides by a rope circling his waist.

Four soldiers followed. One moved to each side of their charge, the other two following. As they approached the temple and halted, the priest looked up from tending the altar fire just as Aric stepped out of the shadows to stand in the arched opening. He wore the black trousers and distinctive blue silk tunic of a Persian functionary. Aric felt Timur's eyes bore into him and suppressed the fear the emperor's stare had always engendered. He stepped down and turned to face the mosaics, looking first at Sanjar, then longer at Yousef. Slowly he turned around and stared into Timur's impassive face.

"Heroic. I remember you telling the craftsmen to portray them as heroic. They might even have looked like this had they lived. I know Yousef would have. He would have fought at your side against any foe, holding nothing back. He loved and trusted you as no other. And you thanked him with an executioner's axe." Aric searched Timur's face for a reaction and seeing none, he smiled. "You never believed I would someday avenge him, did you?"

Aric approached and gave one of the guards a downward signal with his hand. The guard grabbed Timur's shoulder and pushed him to his knees. Hands secured at his sides, Timur lost balance and began to fall, but the other guard caught and righted him.

"He must look at me." A guard grabbed Timur's hair and held his head back.

Timur's eyes narrowed. "What interest have I in the ravings of a traitor?"

Aric slapped the side of Timur's head.

Timur's lips moved into a smile. "You've wanted to do that for a long time."

Aric's face reddened. He spun about and stared at Yousef's image. When he turned again, his face again was composed. "I forgot my vow to avenge my brother until you destroyed the woman I loved, butchering her family before her eyes, then marrying her to that brute Baldev. By the time you finished using her and allowed me to marry her, her heart was closed to all but her hatred of you. Even so, I remained loyal, even as a Persian agent tried to recruit me and my own wife encouraged me to seek vengeance. But then you killed Demetrius. I'm amazed that you never suspected that I had betrayed you, even at Baktra when the Persians massed their attack against our weakest position. And by this winter, I had already given the Persians so much, why not the map to the Peshawar tunnels as well?"

"Villain!" The shout reverberated around the courtyard as Timur fought against the guards' hold. Aric stepped back until Timur ceased struggling. Timur's voice turned low and poisonous. "Your treachery killed Ishmael, burning alive your own son when your Persian friends torched the palace. How do you live with that?"

Aric leaned into his ear. "Ishmael was not my son." When surprise filled Timur's face, Aric laughed. "Ah, you didn't know, did you? Yes, I raised Ishmael as my own, but actually he was the son and heir of the raja of Srinagar. Surely you remember your grand design to use Sharina to seize his land and people. But before you had him murdered, Sharina conceived his child. Demetrius planned the deception when Sharina discovered she was pregnant. Even your queen kept it from you, hoping that Sharina might find happiness with me, a man who truly loved her."

The courtyard door opened, and a black robed man entered, followed by two soldiers carrying a scorched metal pot between them. The aroma of hot olive oil filled the air, and Aric smiled as Timur's eyes widened. The soldiers set the pot down before Yousef's mosaic, and the black robed executioner took his position beside the pot. A Persian general strode into the garden, his head tilted toward a light-skinned, fair-haired young officer walking at his side. The officer held back as the general approached Aric.

Aric bowed. "General Zab."

The general was tall and slender, his face undistinguished and inscrutable, his nose bent, his lips a neutral horizontal line, his eyes black orbs under thin brows. His words were quick and clipped. "Are you finished here?" Aric nodded. "Good. My aide, Captain Faraj, will accompany you now. Afterward he'll give you the final details for my report to Shapur on the occupation of Rajanpur. It must be completed and dispatched by first light."

Aric paused beside Timur. "I believe you've heard the Persians are superstitious about executing rulers."

At the courtyard door Aric looked back. Timur knelt before the Yousef mosaic as General Zab read the sentence from the parchment Aric prepared that morning.

Captain Faraj said, "The general goes next to Nozar. You haven't much time."

Aric followed the officer across the open passageway to the palace and descended the stone steps with Timur's screams filling his ears.

Nozar stood shackled to the wall of unfinished stone. Aric stared up into his face. "Fitting, don't you think, that you come to your end here, where my brother died?"

The general was relaxed, his gaze calm. "We were only boys, Aric, puppets in an old man's game."

"And that excuse comforts you?"

"A reason only. There is no excuse for what I did that led to your brother's death."

For a moment Aric looked away, unsettled by Nozar's dignified bearing. It had been easier confronting Timur.

Nozar spoke. "The emperor's fate?"

Aric responded with a smile. "Blinded and about to be bestowed on the Khyber's scorpions, snakes, and beasts as their new ruler."

"Yes, the Persian way. But for the sudden surprise of their entry into the city, I would have reached him in time, so he might die with honor at the hand of a friend."

"He deserves no honor."

"Aric, he is our emperor."

Aric could not hold Nozar's gaze and turned to face the opposite wall, where Captain Faraj sat in one of the execution witness chairs.

Nozar broke the silence. "Where is Ishmael?"

"Last seen fighting in the emperor's chambers before they were torched. Most were burned beyond recognition."

"You're unmoved," Nozar said.

"Why should I be? He wasn't my son." Nozar showed no surprise. "You knew this?" When Nozar nodded, he asked, "How?"

"Demetrius told me the day that Calaf rescued Ishmael from the river. It was before dawn while you and Flavus searched the canyon."

Aric did not hide his puzzlement. "Why would Demetrius tell you that Ishmael was the son of that raja? It would reveal his complicity in a plot against the emperor, along with Sharina and me. We all could've been executed if Timur found out. Ishmael, too. It doesn't make sense." In the silence that followed, Aric tried to read Nozar's face, but it was impenetrable. "Does anyone else know?"

"I told no one."

Aric remained perplexed. *What reason would Demetrius have?*

"Do you know the prince's fate?" Nozar asked.

Aric returned a distracted look until the question registered. "His boat capsized in the Indus before the battle at Rajanpur. He drowned."

"My son?"

"Barzin is imprisoned."

"Alive?" Aric nodded and Nozar continued. "If you speak for him and he is spared, you might find him helpful among foreigners." Aric recognized the quiet, measured voice the general used when advising the emperor.

The chamber's door opened, and General Zab entered, followed by the executioner. Captain Faraj rose from his chair.

Zab gave Aric a quick look. "You may stay, if you wish."

Aric shook his head. "I must prepare the Rajanpur report, sir."

"Go then."

Aric preceded Captain Faraj to the chamber door. He did not look back.

Khyber Pass

Timur lay naked face down in the dirt listening to the wagon wheels and horses' hooves. When he no longer heard them, he felt their movement through the ground, then nothing but the wind and the distant cry of an eagle. He extended an arm, feeling about the ground, then reached out with the other. He crawled about, fingers searching. The soldiers told him he was beside a high cliff.

He had been given the poppy to quiet his cries on the journey into the Khyber wilderness, but its relief had now faded. His head erupted in a spasm of pain. He rolled onto his back wailing, his face exposed to the sun's heat but never again its light. Another convulsion. He thrust his knuckles into blistered sockets and shrieked. Oblivion took him.

When he awoke, he was lying on his side. The air was warm, but the sun no longer touched him. He tried to open his eyes, then remembered. Each heartbeat delivered a throb of pain to his face. He felt something crawling on his jaw. When he brushed it away, he became aware of prickling about his body. With visions of scorpions he lunged to his feet, lost his balance, and fell hard. He threw himself around on the ground, hands furiously battling his attackers. He was on his stomach when he felt a stone bounce off his calf. A moment later another hit his back.

Ishmael remembered little of his journey from Rajanpur. *You must live. For Calaf you must live.* Barzin's words became his mantra as he placed one foot before the other. Joining a group of refugees at Peshawar, he had decided to go as far as Baktra. The chief fire keeper of the city's fire temple was a friend. Whether or not the athravan had survived the Persian occupation, Baktra was a place to start.

As the sun neared its highest point, Persian soldiers forced the refugees off the Khyber Pass road to allow the horse-drawn wagon to pass. Caught staring at the man in the back of the wagon, Ishmael felt a soldier's whip strike his head. He fell to his knees, stunned by the blow, but even more by Timur's burned, empty eyes. The numbness that had consumed him since leaving Rajanpur gave way to barely contained fury. Calaf is dead and Timur lives? Even blinded, the emperor drew breath. And what? Taken to Persia where he would live out his days in exile, a living symbol of Persia's might? Ishmael remained on the ground, seething as he massaged the side of his head, and held back as the other refugees resumed their trek.

Finally, he climbed to his feet, reclaimed his cap and pack, and jogged after his refugee band. At the top of the next hill he noticed that the soldiers and their wagon left the road and were moving up a wide flood plain. When he reached the spot, he stared at the dissipating cloud of dust following the soldiers. Lifting his face to an eagle's cry, he watched the great bird soar, wings spread to capture the Khyber's thermals, eyes scanning the terrain for prey. Lower in the cloudless sky, three vultures circled. Ishmael pulled off his cap and wiped the sweat from his eyes. The refugee group crested the next rise and disappeared. He tried to move, but his feet refused. He closed his eyes and opened his mouth but made no sound. His parched throat stung. When he lowered his face, the cloud of dust was returning.

He hid in a shallow depression as the Persians and their now-empty wagon returned to the road and disappeared toward Peshawar. He walked onto the flood plain. When screams shattered the quiet desert air, he adjusted his direction but continued at a deliberate pace.

He found Timur unconscious in a wide, flat gully. Dropping his pack, he drew close. His physician's instincts cried out that he tend to Timur's wounds. Instead he cursed. Timur stirred but did not awaken.

He walked to the gully's lone vegetation, a nearby scrub bush the height of a man. In its modest shade, he knelt and fixed his eyes on the ground. He pulled the chain he wore free of his tunic, and held Calaf's infant ankle band in his fingers. He could not deny the father of his friend a death vigil and some semblance of burial.

As the sun descended, the gully fell into shadow. Timur moved. Ishmael released the gold band and picked up a small stone.

Timur scrambled to his knees, arms outstretched. Another stone bounced off his shoulder.

"Who's there?" Another stone hit him in the chest. He moved forward then dropped to his hands and touched his forehead to the ground.

"Have mercy. I have fallen among bandits." Silence. He jerked back to his knees. "I am rich. Save me and you will be greatly rewarded." Silence. Panic ripped through Timur's chest. "I know someone's there!"

A stone hit the ground and bounced against his knee. He stifled a cry and waited. A warm wind gusted about him, kicking up dust. He doubled over in a fit of coughing and held his head in his hands. Each cough sent jabs of pain through his empty eye sockets into his skull. Finally he sat back on his heels.

"Torment me as you will, but before you leave, I beg you tell me where the cliff is, that I might plunge to my death before the beasts and vultures rip my flesh."

"What cliff?"

"The soldiers said there was—" *The voice.* Sudden recognition swept through him. "Ishmael?" He crawled forward, moved his head between Ishmael's knees, and wrapped his arms around his calves. "Here, you're here. I should never have doubted. It was foretold that you will rescue me."

"Ah, yes, *the young healer who saves the emperor.* My father paid your astrologer handsomely for that prophecy, certain it would persuade you to lift my banishment and return me to court."

Timur lifted his face. "But it must be true. Otherwise, why are you here?"

"Does it matter? Fate has delivered you to this place. Who am I to interfere?"

"Fate?" Timur's mind raced. "There is no fate. *Let us not blame fate for our fortune, be it good or bad.*"

Ishmael leaned to Timur's ear. "Interesting. You attempt to save yourself by quoting Demetrius, the man you butchered before my eyes? You who would kill me with your own sword? Who banished me to keep me from the only person I loved?"

"To protect my empire. Always to protect my empire."

Ishmael slipped from Timur's grasp and stood. "Now you will die for your empire."

The quiet, detached tone of Ishmael's words struck Timur's ears as if they were thundered. Timur reached out but grabbed air. "It can be *your* empire. We'll find the prince. He will avenge me, and you—yes, you—will stand at his side."

"Calaf is dead, you raving fool, along with your empire." Ishmael kicked the ground, sending sand and stones in Timur's direction, and finally raising his voice to a shout. "Dead!" He walked away.

Scrambling along the ground, Timur followed. He lurched to his knees.

"Then redeem the treachery of your parents!"

The footsteps continued to recede. He struggled to his feet.

"Demetrius would not leave me!"

The footfalls faded into silence.

"Ishmael!"

Baktra

Dawn's light had not yet reached into the narrow alley as the rear gate to the Azar-i-Asp, Baktra's great fire temple, opened the width of a man's hand. Ishmael recognized the robe of an acolyte. "I seek Orand."

"You will find food and clothing at the west gate."

Ishmael placed his foot in the opening before the acolyte could close the gate. "Please—tell Orand that Ishmael waits."

"The athravan is at prayer."

Ishmael extended a coin. "He will want to know his friend Ishmael waits." When the acolyte took the coin, Ishmael removed his foot and let the gate shut. He listened to the acolyte's slow footsteps as he crossed the courtyard beyond the gate, a courtyard where he spent many hours before the Persian siege of Baktra. Relief washed through him. Orand had survived and remained the Azar-i-Asp's chief fire keeper.

Ishmael heard quick footsteps, then the gate opened. An aged but robust man in the athravan's gray robes emerged, his arms outstretched and eyes filled with joy. "You live." They embraced. When Orand stepped back, he took Ishmael's arm. "But come. You must be tired and hungry."

Ishmael placed a hand on Orand's. "I don't journey alone." He pulled a rope hanging about his waist and Timur stepped out of the shadows, his hand clinging to the wall.

CHAPTER 25

PESHAWAR

THE RULER OF TUR SWEPT into the chambers of Peshawar's former governor, followed by his daughter. A short, barrel-chested man, the bearded Altoum wore a ceremonial version of the leather horse warrior uniform of his people. His weathered round face surrounded small dark eyes and a nose long ago flattened in battle. His graying hair was pulled back into a braid that fell to his mid-back. The expression on his face carried a menace contradicted by his high, piercing voice when he spun about to face Captain Faraj. "Where is Zab? He was to attend us when we entered the city."

Turandot placed a hand on her father's arm. Dark blue silk flowed about her slender body. Her hands, face and neck were powdered white, her lips and fingernails black, her almond-shaped eyes topped by plucked, black brows. She leaned into his ear, her voice a soft vibrato. "I'm certain no slight was intended." She gave Faraj a pointed glance.

The Persian captain bowed. "The general sends his deepest apologies and anticipates attending you at tonight's welcoming banquet."

Ignoring Faraj, Altoum turned on his daughter. "If Shapur's senior general doesn't show me proper respect, how can I expect theirs?" Altoum swept his arm in the direction of the apartment's balcony and the city beyond.

Turandot took her father's extended hand and brought his fingers to her lips. "Dear father, do not forget that Shapur has freed the Kushan people of their tyrant. Why wouldn't they welcome his choice as their new ruler?" She looked at Faraj. "Isn't that correct, captain?"

Again Faraj bowed. "It is as you say, my lady. Tomorrow all of Peshawar will join your father in celebrating his ascension to the Kushan throne."

Altoum glared at Faraj. "And my palace, when will I have my palace?"

"My lord, repairs to the palace's royal chambers near completion and we await word of your desired appointments."

Altoum uttered a curse and walked onto the balcony. Turandot studied the floor for several moments, then looked up and gave a sharp nod of dismissal.

"My lady." Faraj bowed and left the chambers.

General Zab stripped off his uniform, stretched with a groan of fatigue, then collapsed on the bed beside Faraj. He rubbed his eyes. "An awful little man."

"And my palace, when will I have my palace?"

Zab gave a deep laugh at Faraj's high-pitched mimicry of the new Kushan ruler. "Has anyone broken it to him that he will be called King of the Kushans rather than be given Timur's title of Emperor?"

"None, but surely Altoum realizes there can be but one emperor, and that's Shapur."

"One only hopes."

Faraj lay his head on the general's shoulder and tangled his fingers in his thick, black chest hair. "The Kushans will devour him."

Zab kissed Faraj's forehead. "Not with the daughter at his side."

"So the stories are true?"

The general rolled Faraj onto his stomach. "It's best not to become her enemy."

"I'll remember."

"You'd better." Zab slapped Faraj's buttocks and climbed onto his back.

CHAPTER 26

RAJANPUR

ARIC APPROACHED THE PERSIAN SOLDIER and displayed the medallion that hung from his neck. The soldier examined both sides of the bronze disc and motioned another soldier to open the blockade.

"The women?"

"At the back."

Aric passed through the gate and suppressed a gag as the stench of excrement and unwashed bodies assaulted his nostrils and stung his eyes. "Best breathe through your mouth and watch your step," the soldier advised as he closed the gate behind them. He acknowledged the soldier with a quick nod, then stared across the camp at hundreds of men. Some stood in small groups, but most sat or lay on the hard packed earth. Here and there he spotted the remnants of a Kushan army uniform. To his left angry voices rose and those on the ground scrambled out of the way of thrown fists and furious kicks. The Persian soldiers standing along the perimeter watched with disinterest.

Aric picked his way along the blockade wall to muttered curses. A leg rose to block his progress and he looked down into the face of a boy with an outstretched hand. A bandage covered the left side of his face. A guard struck the boy's leg with his spear butt, and Aric stepped over when the boy went limp.

As he approached the barricade that separated the women, he once again showed his medallion. The soldier gave him a brief smile. "I hope you find who it is you're seeking."

Aric returned the smile then passed through the gate. Only a few of the dozens of women looked at him as he scanned the enclosure. All but one looked away. She lay on her side several paces away. Her voice was weak. "Aric?"

He dropped to her side and lifted her into his arms. "Sharina." Tears filled his eyes. "It's over. You're safe now."

Barzin awakened to the Arachosian guard's boot against his buttocks and felt no impulse to strike out. They had broken him days earlier, beating him until only the longing for death remained, along with remorse at choosing capture over falling on his sword when confronted with the Persian army's final and decisive onslaught.

"Get up!" the guard snarled. Barzin barely got to his feet before the guard shoved him. "Move!"

Stumbling in the darkness his foot struck a prisoner lying on the ground. A grunt, nothing more. Then he bumped another. No sound, no movement. *Dead?*

The barricade gate opened. Torchlight blinded him. A trick? Walk through the gate to death as an escapee? Another shove sent him to his knees. He waited for steel to enter his back. He would not give them the satisfaction of his crying out.

A warm, soft hand touched his bare shoulder. He raised his head and seeing a familiar face scrambled backwards into the legs of the guard.

"Traitor," he growled.

The guard pushed him to the ground, his face in the dirt, the guard's boot on his back.

Aric knelt and leaned into Barzin's ear. "Within a few days, the Arachosian army departs Rajanpur to return home. The Persians will take over this prison camp. A most unpleasant prospect, you'll agree. But I give you a choice. Before your father died he urged that I save you, suggesting you'd prove most loyal in return."

"I'd rather die."

"Nobly said—and no doubt the Persians will enjoy obliging you—but let's be practical. I don't expect you to like or respect me. Hate me until your dying day—it doesn't matter—but pledge your loyalty to me as I will to you. Together we can survive these Persians. Return with me to Peshawar, and I will speak for you before the new court. Of course, they'll have their doubts, but over time I'm certain you'll prove your value."

Aric slipped a small metal object into Barzin's hand. Barzin knew without looking it was his father's most treasured possession, the oval bronze disk engraved with his mother's likeness.

"Decide now. Go with me from this place or return to the barricade to await the Persians." Aric stood, motioned the guard to move away, and then extended his arm. "It was your father's last request."

Barzin remained motionless. Choose life over torture and death for the price of loyalty to a traitor? Life over honor? A question with meaning only if he lived to answer it.

He brought the bronze disk to his lips then grasped Aric's arm and rose. "We will never be friends."

CHAPTER 27

JIDDA

FLAVUS TURNED HIS BACK ON the receding Arabian port city of Jidda and made his way across the deck of the Roman merchant ship to where Callista stood looking out over the Red Sea's choppy water.

"If the winds remain favorable, the captain says we should reach Myos Hormos in five days."

When he placed his hand over hers, she grumbled, "Ah, yes, what's five more days when we've been at sea for three accursed months. Remind me again how you talked me into this dreadful journey."

"Your great affection for me?"

"So, we are blaming Venus now."

"Well, Clementia hasn't worked."

Callista laughed. "What? You expected compassion from me after that storm along the Arabian coast almost sank us."

"Isn't she the goddess of tolerance, too."

"You're better with Coalemus."

"Who's that?"

"The god of stupidity. As if using Drusus to fake Calaf's abduction wasn't bad enough, now you abduct him yourself."

"I had no choice. He would have died at Rajanpur—or worse, been captured by the Persians."

"You should have left him to his fate."

"You know I couldn't."

"That damned vow to your Greek?"

"That and more. If Rome places him on the Kushan throne, I will rise in power with him."

"And why would Rome honor you with that prize?"

"Calaf will demand it, of course. He needs me."

"Have I missed something? He hates you."

"I will regain his trust." Callista's eyes went to the heavens. "What?" Flavus asked.

"Just praying to Jupiter that Moros never takes an interest in you."

"Who's that?"

"The goddess of impending doom." Flavus responded with a deep laugh. With a slap on his arm, Callista continued, "Barring her intervention, while you attempt to charm Calaf back into your good graces, you heard what that merchant in Jidda said about Emperor Decius."

Flavus was just as surprised as Callista had been to hear that Decius was dead, only two years after overthrowing Philip. He had asked around further and found out that the Senate had raised Decius's son to the purple while the Danube legions have proclaimed their general the new Emperor. Not a good time to be surprising his *frumentarii* associates with the brooding, angry prince of a fallen nation.

"Yes, it's not a good time to make an appearance," Flavus said. "That's why we now go to Antioch."

"Antioch? But you're ordered to Alexandria."

Flavus gave an exaggerated shrug and lop-sided smile. "Orders get lost in transit."

"I hope you don't expect me to join you. It's another ten days to Antioch. You will not get me on another ship."

"No ship."

"Then how?"

"We risk discovery if we travel through the port at Alexandria. We'll only go as far as Memphis. There we'll join a caravan."

A shocked look swept across Callista's face. "A month of camels? Absolutely not. Anyway, Drusus's friends in the *frumentarii* command don't believe he defected to the Persians and are convinced you're involved in his death. When you don't report at Alexandria, they will come looking for you."

"You worry too much. They're distracted by the succession and aren't paying attention to me. I'll keep a low profile until I know which way the imperial and *frumentarii* winds are blowing. When the time is right, I'll bring the heir to the Kushan throne before them. They'll forget Drusus quick enough."

"Calaf will bolt at the first opportunity." When he gave her a questioning look, she nodded toward Calaf, stripped to the waist, helping trim the ship's sails. "Aren't you concerned he's becoming such a good sailor?"

"He won't bolt. He needs me to reclaim his inheritance and find Ishmael. And who can do a better job than you to teach him how to blend into Roman life? He even likes you."

"You expect flattery will make me forget the camels?"

"Of course." Once again Callista's eyes went heavenward. "Which god do you pray to now?"

"Jupiter again, that Moros doesn't take an interest in me either."

CHAPTER 28
252 CE

PESHAWAR

SHARINA DID NOT REMEMBER WHAT happened at the prison camp at Rajanpur, nor Aric rescuing her. When she asked him about it, Aric answered with nothing more than, "That is past. Only the future matters now."

The past. She recalled Calaf's hands closing her throat until Flavus revealed to him she was his mother. Then Flavus freed her. *Thank Demetrius, not me.* Afterward she wandered day and night without thought of direction or intention. She was captured by soldiers, but too weakened to defend herself, she plunged into fortunate darkness until her eyes opened to the bump and roll of a wagon, her skin ablaze with fever, a woman bathing her face with cool water.

"She awakens," the woman called out. The wagon stopped, then Aric knelt beside her, his lips touching her forehead.

"I feared I lost you."

Eyes wide, her lips moved but no sound came.

"Shh. Rest. We're almost home."

When next she awakened, she lay on a bed in a sun-drenched room. When she raised herself, dizziness threatened to overcome her. Quick footsteps, and then hands took her shoulders and eased her head back down to the pillow.

"All is well, my lady," the woman said. Moments later Aric sat beside her holding her hands.

"Thirsty," she said, her voice barely a whisper.

He called out, "Bring water."

"Where am I?"

"You're home. The palace."

"Peshawar?" When Aric nodded, she asked, "How?"

"Later." He lifted her and brought a cup of water to her lips. "Slowly now."

Days became weeks and Sharina grew stronger, venturing from her room to walks in the palace garden. Aric often joined her. She walked apart, unresponsive and conflicted. She owed him her life, yet she refused the simple courtesy of taking his arm. He entertained her with stories of court life, yet she denied him a simple smile. He extended tenderness, she responded with disregard. And yet he persisted as if he believed kindness and gentle words would reach her. Years earlier when he offered to marry her and take her unborn child as his own, he said, "You knew happiness once. You will know it again." She called him a fool. And thus he remained, still dreaming of happiness and love, believing he would find them with her. *The fool.*

On one of their garden walks Aric recounted the fall of Peshawar, concluding with, "I gave maps of the city defenses to the Persians, allowing them to breach the walls."

"And thus you won the vengeance I sought." A bitter laugh escaped her lips. "He butchered my family, but you he slapped around."

"He killed my brother—he destroyed your life."

"My life, not yours."

"Yours has always been mine." He paused a moment then added, "In exchange for my help, the Persians agreed to help me find you."

"Surely you negotiated more than that from them."

"Nothing else mattered."

"You delivered Timur *and his empire* to the Persians for a woman who never loved you?"

Aric spun about, his expression furious, his voice tightly controlled. "Woman, never again will you mock my love."

Stunned Sharina stepped backwards and bowed. "No, my lord."

When she raised her head, Aric extended his arm. After a moment she took it, and they continued their walk in silence, her thoughts and feelings in disarray. Aric was no longer the timid and cowed man she once knew. She stole a glance at him. He stood taller, his limp less pronounced. Without looking at her he spoke.

"Ask yourself: why do the Persians show me such favor? I betrayed my emperor. Someday I might betray them. Exile me, yes. Kill me even. But no, I live freely in the palace. The royal physician cares for you." Excitement entered his voice. "To my amazement my search for you touched the new king's daughter. I suspect she knows something about love. She persuaded her father that an advisor from the old Kushan court would prove helpful to their rule and that my loyalty would be unquestionable if they helped me find you. She brought me into her inner circle."

"Fortune smiles on you, my husband."

"You are my only fortune."

He pulled her into his arms. When she did not relax in his embrace, he kissed her forehead and released her. Offering his arm again, she took it without hesitation.

A week later she invited him to her bed.

A year later she presented him with a daughter they named Jiya. One evening while watching Aric dote on the infant, Sharina said, "I've never seen you so happy."

He returned a smile, his eyes bright with joy. "When I look at her, what else can I be?"

Sharina knew the truth behind his words. *When I look at her, there is no past, no Yousef, no Timur, no Aric the traitor.* She stroked his cheek. "Then I'm content, my husband."

His smile grew wider as she knew it would. *I'm content.* It was the closest she ever came to saying she loved him, and she understood that for Aric it was enough. His reaction confused her, and in quiet moments alone she asked herself, *What do I know of love?*

The love of her family? That was but a distant memory, overshadowed by the cries to avenge their slaughter that filled her mind.

A mother's love for her child? Had not she turned Calaf into an unknowing instrument of retribution and annihilated love, hers for him and his for her.

Romantic love? She used men as they used her. A night of passion in return for a favor, all focused on a single end, the cold-blooded execution of revenge.

Of all the men she had, only Aric professed love, its innocence exposing the travesty of her life and creating insurmountable indebtedness. *I'm content.* What more could she give, she whose innocence died the moment her baby brother was ripped from her arms?

But what of Demetrius? His was a love given to her without condition, except that she forsake vengeance and seek happiness. But he did not carry her burden—

Her burden. After learning of Timur's death, her mind grew silent and in those moments before awakening she saw her father and mother, Ashu and little Tanay. Their bodies still and gray, their eyes lifeless, their mouths closed: a tableau of emptiness. Morning after morning they stood before her, ignoring her entreaties to tell her what to do now. Then the morning after she knew she carried Aric's child, only her mother stood before her, vibrant and smiling. "Come, let me teach you the Heart Sutra," she said. "It will help you in the days to come."

When Aric awoke, Sharina knelt beside the bed whispering, "Form itself is emptiness, emptiness itself form. Sensations, perceptions, formations, and consciousness are also like this."

She lifted her face. "Will you call a Buddhist priest to visit me?"

The Buddhist priest arrived every morning as Aric left their dwelling to walk to the palace. Most evenings he returned to find Sharina pensive and quiet as she sat with little Jiya before the shrine the priest had helped her create. Others he found their nurse caring for their infant daughter and Sharina in another room anxious and pacing or despondent and crying. Once she greeted him lighthearted and playful. He grew hopeful that her frequent despondency finally had passed, but the next morning he found her particularly agitated. When her mood was dark, he attempted to raise her spirits with a humorous tale from the palace, only to have her ignore him or tell him to leave her alone. One morning he sought reassurance from the priest.

"She carries heavy burdens that in time she will release," the priest said. "Only then will she find peace."

"Has she shared these burdens with you?" Aric asked.

The priest shook his head. "It must come in her own time. Be patient. She is on the right path."

Several weeks later Aric received a message from Sharina asking him to meet her at the Buddhist temple. When he arrived, the priest directed him to a private meditation room.

Sharina knelt upon a cushion facing a statue of a seated Buddha, its right hand raised, its left palm up in its lap. It was surrounded by glowing candles. She looked up as Aric entered and gave him a gentle smile. "The Buddha promises protection if one is courageous in the face of fear."

Aric knelt beside her. "What have you to fear?"

"My family's wrath at my failure to avenge them, the disapproval of a long-dead queen, the loss of your love at the truth."

He resisted the urge to take her hand in his. "After so many years you must believe that no truth can destroy my love."

Sharina was silent for a long while, her eyes closed, her lips moving. Aric had been raised a Zoroastrian with its emphasis on purity of thought, word, and deed. But there was nothing pure about vengeance. While he kept the outward signs of observance, he had begun to turn away as a boy when he discovered that Timur had executed his brother. His inner rejection had then grown with Timur's forcing Sharina to marry the Srinagar warlord and become complete when Timur killed Demetrius. As he waited for Sharina to speak, his eyes rested on the face of the Buddha and doubted that he could ever realize such serenity.

Sharina's soft and hesitant voice interrupted his reflection. "I did not conspire with the Persians."

"I never accepted that you did."

"I suspect that the accusations were fabricated by Flavus to prevent me from killing Ishmael."

Aric keep his eyes focused on the Buddha's face. "You were going to kill Ishmael?"

"Yes."

He fought to keep his voice steady. "But he was your son."

Her response was a whisper. "No, he wasn't."

Aric could not stop his sharp intake of breath. If not hers, then whose? As his mind raced for possibilities, her next words sent him reeling.

"Ishmael was the son of Timur." It was as if someone had struck him in the stomach. He struggled to remain silent as she continued, "When I became the prince's wet nurse, I saw an opportunity to avenge my family, and I resolved to kill him. But I could not take the life of an infant I had held to my breast. Instead, moments before the *chakor*, I switched him with my son."

He shifted his hands to the cushion to keep his balance. "Are you telling me I raised and loved the son of," he turned his face to her, "of that monster?"

"Yes."

"And Calaf was your son?"

Sharina nodded then lowered her eyes to her hands.

Fighting the growing agitation that swept through him, he stood and paced the tight confines of the room. Then he stopped, his voice a harsh whisper. "All these years you kept it from me."

"At first I was terrified at what I had done. Later I did not want to implicate you in my crime."

He leaned his back against the wall, his eyes on the ceiling. *Be calm. Hers is not the crime. The only villainy is Timur's.* He took a deep breath. His voice turned quiet and inviting. "Who else knows?"

"At the *chakor* Demetrius saw what I had done but did not betray me. I suspect he told Nozar to prevent Timur from harming Ishmael. He also told Flavus, who stopped Calaf from killing me by telling him I was his mother. And now I've told you."

"Calaf tried to kill you?"

"He discovered I planned to kill Ishmael."

"Why kill Ishmael?" he asked. "Wasn't switching them enough?"

"In the beginning, it was. But when the spirits of my family returned to haunt me, I knew my vengeance was incomplete. Only the death of Timur's son, in exchange for the sons he slaughtered, would quiet their cries for retribution. While knowing nothing of what I had done, his queen, obsessed with her own vengeful purposes, fed my need to punish Timur. When I was thwarted, all was lost. When Flavus freed me, he said, 'Thank Demetrius, not me.' It has taken me a long time to understand what that truly meant. Demetrius knew that vengeance had infected my heart and begged me to release its burden. But the dying cries of my family and Adelma's poisonous provocation deafened me to his plea. Until I had lost everything but my life. Only then did Demetrius's words reach me. Only then did I appreciate the gift my mother gave me when she taught me the Heart Sutra. I have at last begun to find peace."

Aric dropped to his knees and took her hands in his. "They are all dead now: Timur, Ishmael, Calaf. Never again will they disturb the peace you seek."

She placed her hand on his cheek. "And you? Will you find peace?"

"Your peace is mine, my love. I need no other."

CHAPTER 29
253 CE

ANTIOCH

UPON THEIR ARRIVAL IN ANTIOCH, Calaf lived with Callista and her companions Agatha and Kawtara in nearby Daphne on the slope of Mount Silpios, guardian of Antioch's eastern flank. Flavus hired tutors to teach him Latin and Greek, while Callista exposed him to the social rituals of Roman life. Flavus spent his time in Antioch, but Calaf often joined him for practice bouts at the army garrison's arena, followed by carousing at legionnaire haunts and visits to Flavus's favorite brothel. During these visits Calaf began to talk about his birthright, declaring he was still the heir to Timur and that nothing Sharina did changed that. He bombarded Flavus with questions about organizing resistance and fomenting insurrection. Calaf balked at Flavus's efforts to interest him in the Roman army, reminding him that soon he would be on the next ship back to Minnagara to reunite with Ishmael to take his homeland back from the Persians.

One afternoon at a chariot race in the Hippodrome, Flavus introduced him to Felix, a visiting Roman. Dressed as a prosperous patrician, he stood tall and thin, his head shaved bald, the dim scar of a blade across one cheek.

"Is Felix an army veteran?" Calaf asked afterwards as they walked through a quiet alley toward the Daphne Gate for the return to Callista's villa.

"Not army," Flavus answered, "but yes, a veteran of many battles. You may trust Felix as you would trust me."

"But I don't trust you." Calaf dodged Flavus's jab to his ribs and sprinted ahead, calling back, "Be grateful I like you." When Flavus caught up, Calaf faced him. "This Felix, he knows who I am?" Flavus nodded. "But you said no one must know."

"No one else does."

"Why him?"

When Flavus shrugged, Calaf did not press. *Most likely another frumentarius.* It did not matter. Before long Antioch would be a memory.

A week later Calaf sat with his Greek tutor when Flavus and Callista entered the courtyard. Callista signaled the tutor to leave. Calaf gave them a questioning look, and then jumped to his feet as Taj emerged from behind Flavus.

Flavus said, "Calaf, I'm sorry, but Taj brings word that Ishmael died in Peshawar when the Persians attacked the palace. They torched the emperor's quarters. He died in the fire."

Callista hurried to Calaf's side. When he resisted her embrace, she placed her hand on his shoulder. His eyes went to Taj.

"No urn? You don't bring him to me?"

"No bodies to—" Taj's voice faltered.

Flavus said, "The fire was too hot, the bodies unrecognizable."

"Taj knew about my infant ankle band, didn't he?"

"Yes."

Again, he looked at Taj. "Did they find it?" Taj shook his head. "Then he still lives. If it wasn't there, he still lives."

Flavus said, "Calaf, it was gold. It would have melted in the fire, and even if not, someone could have taken it later."

Calaf shouted, "He still lives!"

Calaf remembered stumbling from the courtyard but little else until he awoke in the hold of a merchant ship with Taj throwing a bucket of salt water over him. As he sputtered in protest, Taj announced that Flavus had secured them work as seamen sailing the Brindisi-Antioch trade route. Afterward, Calaf raged like a trapped animal in the hold for two days until the captain dragged him above deck and ordered him either into the rigging or the ocean.

Calaf looked at Taj. "Is he truly dead?"

"I'm sorry."

When Calaf moved to the ship's railing, Taj grabbed his arm. Calaf lashed out, "Why stop me?"

"Flavus will expect me to go in after you." Taj pulled him toward the rigging. "Up you go."

Calaf grumbled but began climbing.

CHAPTER 30

Shushtar

Ishmael opened his eyes to darkness. It had not cooled during the night. The still air lay atop his damp nakedness like a blanket. Nearby Timur snored as if sleeping deeply, but he no longer slept as other men did. At the slightest sound he would call out, alert as any cat, ever fearful that someone would break into the room to attack him. Each night Ishmael noisily dragged the stool across the floor before banging it against the door of the room he shared with the blinded one-time emperor. Then as he lit the frankincense and blew out the candle, the old man would yell, *The stool?* To which he always replied, *Yes, old man. Now go to sleep.* Most nights Ishmael awoke several times to Timur's panicked cries. In the beginning Ishmael would lie awake wondering at the terrors that awaited Timur outside that door, but now he did not care. His bed creaked as he sat up and swung his feet onto the plank wood floor.

"Boy!"

"I told you I go early today, old man." Ishmael felt around with his feet and snagged his sandals with his toes.

"Liu?"

"I'll send her in."

Ishmael finished dressing and pushed the stool away from the door.

"You could be emperor." Always the same daily farewell.

"Sorry, old man."

Timur gave a disgusted grunt, to which Ishmael laughed.

You could be emperor. It had begun two years earlier on the Khyber Pass road when Ishmael told Timur they headed for Baktra.

"No, we must return to Peshawar. You must help me take back my empire."

"Take back your empire? And I thought you were only blind, old man, not insane."

"If my people know I'm alive, they will rally around me."

"Fool—no one must ever know you're alive. Your life—and mine—are forfeit should anyone even suspect the truth. And your people? They're relieved to be rid of you." *As I was once relieved to be rid of you.*

"You're just a boy. What do you know? The yoke of Persia will be heavy. You will see—they will rally to me." Timur paused in thought. "And betrayal must be dealt with harshly. Upon our return you will bring me the head of the traitor Aric."

"You expect me to kill my father?"

"But Aric is not your father."

"Truth means nothing to you, does it, old man?"

"It is the truth. Aric revealed it to me before the Persians did this." Timur pointed at his face. "You are the son of Baldev, the last raja of Srinagar, who married your mother a short time before he died. Afterwards, I gave Aric permission to marry her. Had I known she carried the raja's child, she would have met an executioner's axe before you were born."

Ishmael's mind raced. The revelation made sense of his mother's indifference, even hostility, giving Timur's story a ring of truth.

"Think of it, Ishmael, as the son of the raja of Srinagar and, through your mother, the grandson of the raja of Minnagara, you are a prince in your own right. You *could* reclaim the Kushan throne on my behalf."

"That would have been your son's destiny, Calaf's destiny, never mine."

"But—"

Ishmael had grabbed Timur's head. "No more, or I swear I will abandon you where you stand."

A prince, not a servant. Calaf and I might have stood together as equals. Absorbed in this recurring thought, he touched the infant ankle band hanging from his neck before leaving the darkened room to be enveloped in candlelight.

Liu sat on her small cot, its bedding neatly folded and tucked. Draped over her lap, Ishmael recognized a robe he had torn. She smiled, set her sewing aside, and rose. She was already dressed for the day in a blue cotton tunic that reached her ankles. It was tied at the waist with a hemp belt decorated with painted beads of fired clay, a gift he gave her soon after their arrival in Shushtar. Small in stature, she was often mistaken for a young girl, but at twenty-eight she was ten years Ishmael's senior. A runaway from a Baktra brothel, she had sought refuge at Azar-i-Asp several days after Ishmael's arrival. She began sitting with Ishmael's blind companion—Ishmael said Timur was his father—while he assisted the athravan Orand with his duties in exchange for access to the fire temple's Zoroastrian medical texts. Orand had urged Ishmael to leave Baktra and continue his medical training at the Persian royal city of Shushtar, two months away by caravan, where Shapur had gathered the greatest medical minds of Persia, Greece and China.

"But I am Kushan. The Persians will not accept me."

"Many races thrive under Persian rule," Orand said. "Live quietly, and if anyone asks where you are from, tell a story of how your people were oppressed by the Kushans."

When Ishmael decided to go to Shushtar, Liu had begged to join him, offering to care for his father while he studied, and the three had been inseparable since.

Liu touched his arm. "You rested well?"

Ishmael shrugged. "No better, no worse."

Liu raised her hand to his cheek. "You should let me watch over him at night."

"But you carry the heavier burden already." Gently he lifted her hand from his face, and she returned it to her side.

"Laleh comes today."

"Good. He isn't as difficult after she's been with him."

Soon after they departed Baktra, while Ishmael was away securing food, Timur had groped Liu. When she told Ishmael about it later, she laughed, saying a hard knee to his groin calmed his ardor, while a promise to secure others for his needs assuaged his anger.

Liu added, "She demands a greater payment—after the last time."

Ishmael groaned, retrieved several coins from the pouch at his belt, and handed them to Liu. "Keep her happy, and tell him to behave or he'll go without." He shouted the last words, and a loud curse answered him from the other room. Ishmael and Liu exchanged smiles. He placed a quick kiss on her forehead. "It's good your gods reward patience." He felt her eyes follow him as he departed.

Outside in the quiet alley, Ishmael took a deep breath, leaned against the opposite building, and looked up at his second-floor dwelling. Not for the first time he asked himself why he allowed Timur's cry *Demetrius would not leave me!* to shatter his resolve to leave him to a cruel but just fate. A healer's compassion? A servant's inbred obligation? A last connection to Calaf? Often he wished he had heeded Calaf's plea to flee Peshawar before the Persian attack. Then he would have been at his friend's side in Rajanpur, freed with Calaf in death, instead of bound to a delusional blind old man and a woman who yearned for something he could not give her.

Today I will walk away. It was a resolution made each morning.

Go to sleep, old man. And broken each night.

Ishmael gazed at the sky. The day's first light had not yet appeared, so he would have time to bathe before reporting to the city's health group, which was responsible for preventing the spread of contagious diseases. That month another outbreak of intestinal disease had occurred due to contaminated water in the city's central reservoir, and he wondered if the group's lead physician might at last convince the city magistrate to relocate the camel herds away from the cistern's water source outside Shushtar's walls. It would be a simple solution but was challenged by a powerful landowner anxious about losing his lucrative grazing fees.

Ishmael's time with the health group was nearing its end, and he was eager to leave behind the unending job of keeping the sacred elements of water, wind, earth and fire free of contamination within the city. His magi assured him that his studies would next take him to the city hospital, where he would work under the noted surgeon Mani, a much-coveted assignment.

Ishmael emerged from the packed earth alley and began walking down the wider cobbled street that led to the Karun River. In the distance a dog barked. From within a nearby building a baby began to cry. A sudden breeze enveloped him in the smell of baking bread and his stomach grumbled. Then stepping aside, he made room for an ox cart loaded with sugar cane and called out, "An early morning, my friend."

The driver slowed the ox. "Market day. No carts allowed on the streets after the sun rises."

Ishmael patted the ox's rump. "How's your daughter?"

"No more ear aches." He tossed a broken stalk to Ishmael. "And no more crying at night."

"Good. If the juice of rue helped her, it's not serious. Keep some around. She may need more."

The driver gave a nod and flicked the ox's rump with his switch. As the animal lumbered forward, Ishmael began to chew on the cane stalk, its sharp sweetness filling his mouth. He called his appreciation to the driver before picking up his pace toward the river.

Like Srinagar, Shushtar was an island city, its river channeled to form a surrounding moat. A system of tunnels connected the river to private reservoirs that supplied water to the city's houses and buildings. These *ghanats* were also built to store and supply water during times of war when the main gates were closed. When Ishmael reached the river, he headed past the last *ghanat* opening, one of the few areas where bathing would not contaminate the city's water. Most people used the public baths, so this stretch of river provided a quiet refuge.

Ishmael undressed and slipped into the thick reeds that bordered the bank and laughed at the noisy eruption of waterfowl taking flight at his invasion. He found an opening in the reeds and disappeared underwater, reemerging moments later to float on his back. He reached for the chain about his neck and moved the infant ankle band so it rested on his chest. He stared up at the first streaks of dawn rising above the city's skyline as the current, a gentle eddy amongst the reeds, moved him about, the only sounds the river's flow and the cries of circling birds. He closed his eyes and thought how easy it would be to float past the reeds, letting the river carry him away.

"How is the water?"

Startled, Ishmael jerked, went under, and came up coughing and fighting to gain footing in the spongy riverbed. A man's laughter filled his ears. Ishmael got his feet under him, swept the water and his hair from his eyes, and looked toward the bank at a grinning, fair-haired Persian officer.

"Want company?" He didn't wait for a response before starting to undress. Ishmael gave quick looks up and down the river. The officer laughed again. "Don't worry. I checked. Just some fishermen downriver. Too early for anyone else."

Even in the dim light Ishmael could see the officer's erection as he slipped from the bank into the water. He said, "I've seen you before."

"Then you know I've been watching you." The Persian slapped his hand against the water, sending a spray in Ishmael's direction.

Ishmael grinned and ducked away, his flight short-lived as the officer leapt on top of him, sending them both below the surface. The officer was stronger but Ishmael more agile, allowing him to escape the Persian's attempts to subdue him. But what began as playful turned serious when the officer locked his arm around Ishmael's neck and held him underwater. When Ishmael broke free, coming up breathless and choking, the Persian grabbed his arm and spun him about to face the bank. Ishmael fell forward, his hands thrust into the soft, damp earth.

At first, Ishmael welcomed the officer's domination. His mood had turned dark that morning, and he wanted the distraction sex always gave him. Most often the man sought little more than sexual release. Not often enough, Ishmael perceived a desire for giving pleasure as well. Then there were the times when he sensed an absence of desire, replaced by something dark and explosive. It was rare that he misread a man's advances, but it was too late once he realized the Persian's playfulness had been a deception. A moment of alarm swept through him, checked at penetration by his own hunger. The officer's orgasm was violent but silent, a disconnection of body and voice that left Ishmael unsettled.

The Persian did not release Ishmael for a long moment, his uneven breathing and quick heartbeats pulsing through Ishmael's back. When finally he backed away, he pulled Ishmael around and gave him a playful cuff to the side of his face before falling backward into the water with an exuberant shout.

The officer climbed onto the bank first and extended his hand. "You look Kushan."

Ishmael stiffened as he climbed up beside the Persian. "Don't tell that to my Srinagaran family. We hate the Kushans."

"Your people are tough. They rebelled against the new Kushan king, and he's been unable to subjugate them."

Ishmael contained his surprise at the officer's ready knowledge of Srinagar, along with sudden anxiety about what else the officer might know or could discover. As he began to dress, he shifted the topic. "And you look Greek."

"My grandfather claims we descend from Alexander himself and gets angry when I suggest it's more likely one of his foot soldiers." He emitted an easy laugh before grabbing Ishmael's wrists and pulling his hands away from tying his trousers. "Stay."

"I can't."

The officer's grip tightened. "Your health group won't mind if you're late."

Ishmael's stomach turned. "What do you want?" He yanked his wrists from the Persian's grasp.

The officer raised his palms as if in appeal. "I wanted you, and I followed you to where you work, that's all. You—that's all I want."

"You've had me, and yes, my health group will mind if I'm late." Ishmael stepped back, tied his trousers, slipped his feet into his sandals, and grabbed his tunic and belt.

The still naked Persian stared at him. "I want to see you again."

Ishmael responded with a shrug, turned around, and climbed to the road. When he glanced back, the officer waved and called out, "Faraj!"

Ishmael hesitated a moment before answering with "Ishmael!"

As Captain Faraj entered Zab's chambers, the general rose from a table covered with stacked parchments and an unrolled map. Faraj searched Zab's face, but it was the general's slow, deliberate steps that forewarned him of his anger. The smell of wine was in the air, which was rare before midday, rarer when the general was alone.

Zab's thin lips curved downwards as he ran his fingers through Faraj's hair. "Wet—and stinks of the river."

"The night was hot, the water inviting."

The general stroked Faraj's cheek with the back of his fingers. "Surely not another soldier so soon after—" His words trailed into silence.

"No, a civilian, a young physician." He added a conspiratorial grin. "You'd like him."

The swift blow to his stomach angled upward, maximizing the impact. As Faraj doubled over Zab grabbed his hair and yanked his head back. Faraj tightened his jaw against the pain but could not control the watering of his eyes. He blinked, trying to keep the face glaring down at him from blurring. He waited for a kick to the groin. Instead the general thrust him against the wall and said, "Your soldier died last night."

"He shouldn't have resisted."

"Fool! I should have you castrated and presented as a gift to Shapur's number six wife. Did anyone see you with that soldier?"

"No."

"You are certain."

"Yes."

"Did he recognize you?"

Faraj clambered to his feet. "What's this about?"

"He was the grandson of Shapur's finance minister."

"How was I to know that?"

The general dismissed the question with a jerk of his hand. "Answer me, did he recognize you?"

"I don't know. I don't think so. It was dark."

"Even so, that probably doesn't matter. Your proclivities are well known, so even if he died never uttering your name, suspicion will reach you."

Faraj ran his fingers through his hair. "What'll we do?"

"I will deliver a eulogy at the grandson's funeral, then apprehend and execute his killer." He handed a parchment to Faraj. "As for you, here are your orders. You depart for Peshawar immediately."

Faraj groaned. "Why Peshawar?"

"It seems Princess Turandot has beheaded another suitor and our new client king in Armenia is enraged at losing his youngest son."

"What concern is that to us?"

"If you gave affairs of state half the attention you give to where you shove your cock, you'd know the importance of Armenia to our Syrian campaign against the Romans. Shapur demands an investigation before negotiating appropriate compensation for the king's loss."

"Why me?"

"What better investigator than an officer who has met Turandot and would benefit from increased diplomatic exposure. Away from the court."

"Must it be Peshawar?"

"What? You'd prefer Shapur's number six wife?"

CHAPTER 31

Peshawar

Built facing the palace tower containing the royal apartments, Turandot's amphitheater rivaled any Captain Faraj had ever seen. A wide stone stairway dominated the center of the raised stage, descending from a balcony that stretched across the tower's second level. At the top of the stairway a double door gilded in gold reached to the tower's third level. Monumental mosaic portraits of two standing women wearing royal garb faced each other across the stairway. The white face of one identified it as Turandot, but Faraj did not recognize the other. Below the stage at either end, massive wood gates provided access to the amphitheater. Set back at least forty paces, banks of stone seating rose in a semi-circle. Rising behind the back row were three spikes topped with stone replicas of severed heads, the originals long ago decayed and disintegrated.

Workmen were placing another replica on a fourth spike, representing the head of the youngest son of the Armenian king. Faraj walked before the stage, the height of the proscenium exceeding his own, and stopped before the steps that climbed to its midpoint. He looked up and imagined the intimidation a suitor must experience. Hearing a laugh behind him, he turned, shading his eyes from the sun's glare. A short, rotund figure descended the center aisle of the stone seating, balancing his uneven gait with a staff.

"Beware climbing those steps—unless, of course, you're prepared to lose your head." Aric stepped onto hard-packed earth of the orchestra and approached.

"Maybe my next visit." *Should I be so unfortunate.*

"But, as you are not of royal blood, that is correct, is it not?" Faraj nodded. "Then you would keep your head. She skins alive those impersonating a prince. Discourages the rabble from trying."

"And when is the suitor's identity known?"

"Afterward, of course. We wouldn't want to ruin the suspense for the crowd. Only after he fails her test and pleads for his life does she ask who he is. Turandot is strict about the tiniest detail."

Faraj gestured toward the newly installed spike. "So she did not know he was the Armenian king's son."

"How quickly we come to the reason for your journey." Aric placed his hand on Faraj's arm. "But forgive my rudeness. Refreshments first. Interrogation on an empty stomach is most disagreeable, don't you agree?"

As Faraj followed Aric up the steps, he lost and recovered his balance. The front of each step angled downward. *The tiniest detail.*

Faraj pointed at the mosaic facing Turandot's and asked, "Who is she?"

Aric gazed at the portrait. "Princess Lou-Ling, an ancient ancestor of Turandot's who was raped and murdered by a Tartar king. *A desperate cry rang out and down the generations that cry has found refuge in my heart!* Many in the crowd break into tears when Turandot intones those words before confronting the suitors with her riddles. But while Lou-Ling's death makes great drama, Turandot's vengeance is closer to home. When we have a private moment away from the palace, do remind me to tell you about Wei. But come, Turandot said she might join us."

"*Might* join us? Does she not realize I come at Shapur's personal request?"

"Of course, she does," Aric lowered his voice, "and I suggest you take no offense. Do not forget, you're in her kingdom now."

"Her kingdom? What about Altoum?" Faraj smiled recalling the Tur king's high-pitched cry, *And my palace, when will I have my palace?*

"Her father hunts and plays general and leaves ruling to her. All agree she's much better at it. Is your party taken care of?"

"The palace guard met us when we arrived and escorted my companions to their quarters."

"I understand an imperial diplomat accompanies you."

"Yes. He advises me."

Entering the palace, Aric led the way into a courtyard surrounded by a colonnaded walkway. Gulmohar trees bloomed in crimson. In the shade of one of the trees a servant stood beside a round table and three chairs with silk embroidered cushions and low backs. The table was set with bread, hummus, and mangos. As they approached, the servant poured wine in two of the three waiting cups. He was a muscular youth with a round face and the close-cropped black hair common to the soldiers of Tur. His white tunic was sleeveless and reached to his knees, emphasizing his athletic build and sunbaked skin. *This is no household slave.*

Aric took both cups, handed one to Faraj, and lifted his. "To the success of your mission."

Faraj returned the gesture. "And to your obvious success in the court of Tur."

They sat and Aric dipped bread into the hummus. "Yes, I have been most fortunate. At first there was little for me to do. Altoum deferred all things written to Turandot and she had her own scribe, a Chinese eunuch. As you may have heard, the people of Peshawar resisted Persian rule at first, violently at times. Turandot decided to seek the help of the court's only Kushan, and quieting Peshawar became my responsibility. I didn't see a way to achieve the impossible, and I despaired for my life until a prince from a tiny raj along the lower Ganges River appeared asking questions about Turandot." Aric lifted his cup for more wine. "Before then, Turandot's test took place in private before the king's council, followed by a quick beheading. We had all heard stories, but few had witnessed the proceedings. I suggested they make the test public, that it might capture the people's imagination and divert them from thoughts of rebellion. While that first ceremony was crude and the Ganges prince rather pathetic in his rage before losing his head, the people loved it."

Faraj sliced into a mango. "Rome has its bread and circuses."

"And Peshawar has its Turandot, heart hardened by the spirit of the innocent Lou-Ling, wreaking vengeance on all men through the destruction of these hapless princes. In less than two years, three more have come and met their fate, including your unfortunate Armenian. The crowd loved his youth and innocence. Sobbing and rending their clothing, women begged he be spared. At first we worried about a riot, but once he was separated from his head—please tell his father bravely so—those same women danced in ecstasy. It was a great moment. But the next prince may not be as sympathetic, so we'll pay prostitutes to do the sobbing and ripping of clothes—with more abandon, of course. We've learned that to keep the people satisfied, each ceremony must be more elaborate than the last."

"You have done well for yourself." Aric acknowledged the compliment with a smile. "Rarely does a traitor to the old ruler advance so far under the new." Faraj smiled as Aric's shoulders stiffened and color rushed across his face.

"The gods bless my decision." His words came as if spoken many times.

"As well the gods of Persia should."

They ate in strained silence until Faraj complimented the sweetness of the mangoes. Recovering his composure, Aric lifted his face in delight. "They come from my garden."

When Faraj motioned for more wine, he caught the servant's eye and they exchanged smiles. Returning his attention to Aric, he asked, "The woman you sought. Did you find her?"

"Yes, at the prisoner camp outside Rajanpur.

"She was?"

"My wife."

"Of course. Is she well?"

"Quite well, as you will see for yourself. Sharina has planned a quiet meal for us this evening." Aric beamed as he added, "She carries my third child."

"I cannot believe he's only now telling you." Both rose from their chairs. "You'd think he'd never been a father before." Nothing about the woman before him reminded Faraj of the Turandot he had previously met. Gone were the white powdered face and black lips and brows. Her slim body, enveloped in flowing yellow silk, moved with grace and sensuality, not rigid formality. Only her voice remained the same, words spoken as if in song. Behind her walked a Chinese man in a black silk robe, his bearing relaxed. The black leather bag hanging from his shoulder and ink-stained fingers identified him as her scribe.

"My lady." Aric bowed from the waist. Without expression Faraj lowered his head and said nothing.

Turandot swept over to Faraj, her face alight with a bright smile. "Very good, Captain, you've expressed your displeasure with us over that awful Armenian affair. Now let us relax and enjoy each other's company." She stroked his cheek with her fingertips. "We forgot how handsome you are." Before he could react, she spun about, and signaled the servant for wine. Aric and Faraj joined her as she sat. "Aric, you were speaking of Sharina. What a jewel." She turned to Faraj. "And he knows to treat her well or he will answer to us." Her smile was casual, her laugh easy.

"I'll never answer to you on that account." Faraj knew Aric was sincere, recalling the desperation of his plea after the fall of Peshawar: *I must find her.*

Turandot said to Faraj, "We received word of Shapur's great victory over the Romans."

"Yes, Barbalissos, then Syria."

"We understand Antioch welcomed him as a liberator."

Faraj frowned. "Without the Armenian army fighting at his side it may have gone otherwise. You are most fortunate the Armenian king did not receive word of his son's execution before Barbalissos."

Aric's reaction was quick. "You dare—"

Turandot raised her hand. "Aric, you forget yourself."

Aric lowered his face. "My lady."

"Captain, we too felt great distress at learning his identity."

"Yet you proceeded to execute him."

"The ceremony gave us no choice."

"A surrogate perhaps."

"He was too recognizable," Turandot replied. "The people would have known."

"So what?"

"Captain, does the Emperor appreciate his quiet border at the Khyber Pass?"

"Of course, he does."

"Then you might tell him that this ceremony is the difference between peace and rebellion on his eastern flank. It's also the reason he could ignore us, advance on Barbalissos and Syria, and enjoy the fruits of his labor at Antioch. Tell us, Aric, when can we expect our next suitor?"

"Wagers in Peshawar say four months. Betting in the outer provinces say seven, but they never show the same eagerness as the royal city."

"Hear that, Captain? They wager. They anticipate. As the days and weeks pass, their excitement grows as they wonder when and who. Rome teaches that a country occupied with spectacle does not look to rebellion. If we had spared the Armenian prince, we would have compromised the integrity of the ceremony. We assure you the people would have risen in outrage."

Turandot paused, and when Faraj remained silent, she continued. "Tell us, why do the princes come? My beauty?" She tossed her head with a laugh. "Maybe once, but no longer. Rather, they seek what we offer, the Kushan throne. A prize worth dying for? Of course, it is, particularly if the prince is not first-born in his own realm and has ambitions to rule. Might not one of these ambitious princes consider challenging our own Emperor Shapur's rule? Instead they come to Peshawar, where I dispose of them."

Finally Faraj spoke. "Then change the ceremony so you do not risk angering our allies."

Aric's face darkened, his hands became fists in his lap, but he remained still.

"Captain, what do you propose? No more beheadings? Princes must present proof they have their father's permission?"

"My lady, there must be a way to avoid future unpleasantness between you and the empire."

"We agree. So to demonstrate we are reasonable, we offer to consider any proposed changes that do not jeopardize the integrity or popular support of the ceremony."

"A reasonable place to start."

"We will give you a written script of the complete ceremony." Turandot glanced toward her scribe. "Tomorrow?" The scribe nodded. "Then for the moment we are settled."

Abruptly Turandot rose. As the two men stood, she motioned to the servant and turned to Faraj. "We trust you approve of him. During your stay he will be your personal attendant."

"That is most kind."

She touched the youth's chin. "We understand you are most agreeable."

His face flushed as he lowered his eyes. "Yes, my lady."

"Good." She patted the side of his face.

Turandot approached her scribe. "Wei, be certain to include our latest decisions regarding the Chinese gong."

"Yes, my lady."

Faraj pulled Aric from the busy market street into a quiet alley. "Are we far enough away from the palace yet?"

Aric smiled. Faraj showed admirable restraint since the moment Turandot spoke the name Wei. Deciding to toy with the captain's impatience, he nudged the captain in the ribs. "Not here," he said in a conspiratorial whisper. "This way."

When they reached a narrow stairway that climbed the city wall, a guard stopped them, but when Aric identified himself, they were allowed to pass. Aric looked back as they mounted the steps. "As a boy, I played up here with my brother. The wall was open to all then, but Altoum closed it during the first rebellion." When they reached the top, Aric raised his arm and pointed. "See the East Gate? And the roof with the red and blue canopy? That's my house. We could have an apartment in the palace, but Sharina prefers living away from court life."

Aric led Faraj to a spot midway between two sentries and resting on his arms allowed his eyes to wander over the patchwork of farms and orchards stretching far into the distance. Beside him Faraj leaned his back against the wall, facing the opposite direction toward the chaotic jumble of Peshawar's rooftops.

Faraj said, "Now tell me about Wei."

"First, you must hear about the questions Turandot asks her suitors." Faraj raised his eyes to the sky but nodded his assent. Aric continued, "In the beginning, before coming to Peshawar, Turandot crafted the riddles herself and did not divulge the correct answer until after her suitor ventured his solution. As you might imagine, this led to a problem the first time a suitor gave a credible answer that did not match the one she revealed. The suitor raged that she deceived them all by creating a riddle with two correct answers, but he was a prince of little consequence, so his appeal was ignored in favor of his head. But afterward Altoum ordered Turandot to give her riddles and their answers to the head priest to verify that each riddle had but one answer. To further distance her from the riddles, the head priest decided which of her riddles a suitor received, and though Turandot continued to present the riddles, he provided the correct answers. In Peshawar these responsibilities are assumed by the Council of Three Holy Men representing each of the city's great traditions: Zoroastrian, Buddhist, and Hindu."

"Then she truly risks the possibility a prince might answer all three riddles." Aric nodded. "And she would marry him?"

"She would have no choice. Either we have the grandest wedding in memory or a bloody revolt against Tur and its Persian masters," Aric's voice dropped to a whisper, "or a funeral pyre that will make Turandot a legend."

Faraj raised an eyebrow. "That's somewhat dramatic."

"She is anything but subtle."

"Then it's time I hear about Wei?"

"Yes, it is time," Aric replied with a laugh of pleasure at capturing Faraj's interest so completely. "As a young girl, Turandot was betrothed to the son of a Tur warlord, second only to the king in power. But she fell in love with Wei, the son of a Chinese merchant. When her betrothed heard of this, he flew into a rage and with two companions broke into her bedchamber and discovered the lovers. As his companions held Wei, her betrothed castrated him before her eyes. But before they could finish the job and kill him, Turandot's screams brought her father's guards. Caught between his love for his daughter and the dishonor she brought on him, Altoum sought a middle ground. Standing before his court he proclaimed that Turandot's betrothed also committed punishable dishonor by attacking Wei on royal property. He pardoned both dishonors, saving them from a sentence of death for their actions, in exchange for the warlord's agreement to an immediate marriage. Before the warlord could respond, Turandot took a dagger and held it to her stomach, crying that she would rather die by her own hand than marry a man capable of such brutality. The court's laughter, led by the warlord, quickly died as the blade drew blood. Like I said, anything but subtle.

"By the gods, if only I could have witnessed what happened next. She raised the dagger and pointed it at her betrothed. *I give you three riddles. If you solve them, we will wed. Fail and your head is forfeit.* Before his father could intervene, the arrogant fool rushed before her and agreed. Given the chance to reconsider and ignoring the counsel of his father, the youth remained firm. 'By her trial she will be mine,' he said. With the warlord's reluctant concurrence, Altoum decreed the trial would resolve the matter. To his credit, Turandot's betrothed answered the first two riddles correctly. When he failed the third, he went to his death without embarrassing his father further. I understand it was only a few months before another prince appeared before Altoum demanding *By her trial she will be mine.* In the meantime, Wei became her scribe and closest confidant."

Roaring with laughter Faraj slapped Aric on the back. "Your seduction is complete. Tell me truthfully, have you ever doubted any of it?"

"Why would I?"

"And that funeral pyre? Turandot and her beloved Wei joined at last in the flames?"

"Of course."

Faraj laughed again. "There's no arguing your instinct for survival, my friend. Lead the way. You said a meal awaits us under that blue and red canopy."

The night was quiet in the streets below. Even the ox-drawn cart made little sound as it moved over the cobbles. The stars were bright in the moonless sky, casting a soft glow over Sharina as she stepped from under the red and blue striped canopy to the rooftop wall. Except for the palace's tower, the house was higher than any building in Peshawar, a gift of Turandot to Aric, who now managed her hold over the Kushan people. Sharina placed both hands on her growing belly and smiled, not for the first time bewildered by her contentment. She moved her arms behind her back, a hand taking the forearm of the other, her eyes captured by the flickering torches atop the East Gate. Timur's memory flickered like that, behind her just out of sight, always walking away but forever present. She gazed down into the empty street. She was free of him but knew she could never be free of his memory. Content, even happy at times, but never free. The demands of vengeance leave a permanent mark.

She heard steps but did not turn. Aric came up behind her and stroked her hair. He wanted her to grow it long again, but she declined. *I will never be the woman I was.* He did not ask again, and for that she began to feel affection for him. He slipped his arms around her, his hands resting on her stomach.

"I'm sorry that took so long. Faraj insisted on another drink when we arrived at the palace. The young man the princess gave him seemed anxious. Someone must have told him about Faraj's proclivities. Even so, the boy will be better off if our Persian captain takes the bait."

"Will he?"

"Uncertain. Either way Turandot wins, but I know she'd prefer adding a spy to the imperial court."

"Faraj is dangerous."

Aric turned Sharina around and kissed her forehead. "I agree."

"And Ishmael?" she asked.

Over their meal Faraj had asked about their third child, having only met little Jiya. Aric took Sharina's hand and said, "We once had a son." She added, "Ishmael died defending Peshawar." After a polite show of condolence, Faraj mentioned meeting a youth named Ishmael in Shushtar. "A common enough name," Aric replied, to which Faraj added, "I thought him Kushan, but said he was Srinagaran. He studies to be a physician." Sharina called for more wine, and the conversation had moved to another topic.

Aric moved to Sharina's side and placed his hands on the rooftop wall. "Do I believe he lives?"

She nodded.

"I'm surprised, but it seems likely."

Sharina rested her head on her husband's shoulder and whispered, "I pray he lives and lives well." She felt Timur move deeper into the shadows of her mind.

Faraj rolled off the youth's back and climbed from the bed. When he returned, carrying two wine cups, the boy was sitting up. The bruises to his face and ribs from their first night were showing the first signs of healing. He had been tougher and more versatile than Faraj anticipated. It was unfortunate the grandson of Shapur's finance minister had not been as responsive. Faraj sat and handed a cup to the youth. "After bathing and dressing me, you will pack my belongings. I depart after watching the installation of Turandot's Chinese gong."

"Please take me with you, sir."

Faraj patted the boy's leg. "Betray a host's generosity? You forget yourself."

"She'll send me back. They will kill me like they killed—" His voice trailed off.

Faraj studied his face, saw fear, and recalled that the soldiers of Tur were extreme in their condemnation and punishment of sex among men in their ranks. "I'm sorry. I cannot interfere."

"But she wants you to take me."

"Then I will ask her."

"She will deny it."

"You try my patience, boy." Faraj stood. "Prepare my bath."

The new square platform stood a dozen paces from the middle of the amphitheater stage, rising half its height. It took eight workmen the entire morning to unpack and carry the massive Chinese gong onto the platform then maneuver it into place. Suspended from a black wood frame, the gong, forged of bronze and gilded in gold, was the height of a man. Four dragons circled the center disk, the point of impact and maximum sound.

Once the workmen stepped away, Aric walked around it several times, tracing his finger along its edge. He turned to Faraj. "It is exactly as Turandot commissioned it."

Faraj examined the dragons. "Each a different posture and expression. I have never seen its like."

"Just imagine it, Captain." Aric pointed at the top of the terrace of stone steps. "The suitor emerges there in the center, torches ablaze around him. He solemnly descends, the people around him urging him forward or crying to him to flee before it's too late. At the bottom he hesitates. That's the signal for silence. Believe me, the crowd will hush, the only sound their breathing as he ascends and takes the wood mallet in his hands. Three times he strikes the gong, three times he shouts the name *Turandot*. He steps back, the mallet raised above his head, and waits." Aric lifted his arm toward the balcony. "The gold doors part and she appears. The people erupt."

"I am impressed."

A broad smile filled Aric's face. "Then Turandot will be pleased." But Aric's smile disappeared and slowly he shook his head.

"What's wrong?"

Faraj followed Aric's eyes. Armed palace guards entered the amphitheater and approached the platform.

"Such a pity you did not agree to the boy's request that you take him."

"How did you know?"

Aric ignored the question and waited until the officer in charge joined them. "May I introduce Captain Barzin of the palace guard."

Barzin gave a crisp nod. "Captain Faraj, it is best that you come quietly."

Faraj's eyes snapped to Aric, who shrugged and walked away.

After being taken to his room and shown the mutilated body of the boy sprawled across the bed, an ashen-faced Faraj followed Barzin into the prison's execution chamber. Barzin directed him to stand before the rough-hewn stone wall opposite the double row of witness chairs. Chains hung from the ceiling behind him. The last time he had been in this place, they bound the Kushan general Nozar.

Barzin placed a guard on each side of him, their swords drawn at their sides. He ordered the other guards to position a table several paces before Faraj, then behind it one of the witness chairs. The guards took positions before the chamber door, and Barzin stood behind the chair, his stance relaxed, his arms behind his back, his gaze focused on Faraj.

"I did not kill the boy. He was alive when I left him." Faraj fought to keep panic from his voice but knew he was unsuccessful.

"Captain Faraj, your plea is of no concern to me."

A flash of anger replaced Faraj's panic. "Then what happens now?"

"We wait."

"May I sit?"

Barzin shook his head.

At first Faraj could not block the image of the youth's brutalized body. He tried to tally the chamber wall's blocks of stone, losing count when a guard shifted his stance or a trickle of sweat pulled his attention to his back or a sound outside the chamber sent a false signal of his ordeal's resolution. But soon it was his own fate that dominated his imaginings, intensified by memories of the tortures he witnessed at Zab's side. His bowels churned as his head began to throb to the quickened pace of his heart. He took deep breaths, and as he calmed, he marveled that those around him seemed unaware of his distress.

The guard changed. Bread and wine were brought to Barzin, which he ate and drank without a glance at Faraj. When the guard changed again, Faraj became alert. Tension filled those standing beside him. Barzin's stance was less relaxed. The guards at the chamber door now stood on either side of it.

The door opened.

It was Turandot, looking the way she did when Faraj first met her: skin powdered white and her lips, nails, and brows painted black. White silk flowed about her body hiding her feet, emphasizing the ethereal as she entered the chamber. As if her shadow, Wei followed attired in black. Barzin bowed deep and stepped back. Turandot stopped behind the chair, her eyes downcast, and waited for Wei to sit. He placed two folded parchments on the table. Barzin ordered the guards to leave the chamber, and removing his sword from its scabbard took a position beside Faraj.

Turandot raised her face, gazed at Faraj, and remained silent, as if tempting him to speak first and add breach of protocol to his crimes. Faraj acknowledged her with a brief bow of his head then returned her gaze.

"A most unfortunate affair." While soft, her voice carried the formality of royal to subject. When Faraj did not respond, she added, "You may, of course, speak."

"I did not do this."

"We know you did not." He knew his eyes betrayed his surprise. Turandot smiled then motioned to Barzin. "A chair for our guest." After Faraj was seated, she continued, "Unfortunately, the body was discovered by the imperial diplomat who accompanies you. The poor man was most shocked and mentioned suspicions surrounding the grandson of the Emperor's finance minister."

"That killer was apprehended and executed."

"Yes, that excellent news preceded your arrival. Shapur must be pleased with General Zab's swift justice."

"I'm certain he is."

"The diplomat seems most talkative. You must be concerned that an unfounded scandal might follow—even precede—your return to Shushtar."

"I am."

"Then you will be pleased to learn that he has been under my personal physician's care since discovering the boy."

"He has spoken to no one?"

Turandot shook her head. "You also will be pleased to learn the boy did not suffer during the mutilation. When his comrades came to collect him, they found him already dead by his own hand. He must have been most disappointed you refused his request."

"If I'd taken him?"

"For you, a diplomatic row likely culminating in a reprimand from an understanding general. For us, another spy in the Persian court."

"I assume you have another plan."

Turandot nodded. "The imperial diplomat has provided us with his account of finding the boy along with his speculations about your involvement." Wei rested his hand on one of the parchments. "You will sign a confession that you killed the boy. In exchange, we will invite the diplomat to witness our interrogation of the boy's comrades, where he will learn the truth of what happened."

"A guarantee of future cooperation."

"We do appreciate someone who understands such matters."

"What do you want from me?"

"First, you will do all in your power to convince General Zab that it is not in Persia's interests to interfere in our affairs."

"First?"

"Who knows what the future may hold, but you will find us most generous."

"And the confession?"

"It will stay safely hidden, and no word will reach Shushtar."

"What guarantee do I have?"

"Do you need more than our gratitude for your assistance, Captain?"

"Of course not." Faraj gestured to the other parchment that Wei had placed on the table. "And the second document?"

"Wei has kindly prepared your report concerning the Armenian prince."

CHAPTER 32
254 CE

Antioch

SITUATED IN A LONG VALLEY between two mountain ranges along the banks of the river Orontes, Antioch spread from its island center up the gradual slope of Mount Silpius, where vineyards and fig trees mingled with myrtle, oak, and sycamore. After years in the arid lands of the Kushans, Flavus relished Antioch's lush vegetation, the bracing Mediterranean wind, and waters so abundant that fountains decorated both public baths and the courtyards of most homes. He particularly enjoyed the town of Daphne, situated outside the city on a terraced plateau of cool forests, gentle breezes, and quiet temple gardens, where Callista rented a modest villa. Several days of relaxation awaited him.

Walking along the city's colonnaded main thoroughfare against the flow of farmers and herdsmen heading to market, he stopped a moment to watch workmen restoring a collapsed walkway atop the city's Wall of Tiberius. The previous week's earthquake also damaged the aqueduct but with its repair a priority, water flow resumed after only two days. Passing through the Daphne Gate, he took a deep breath, stretched his arms, and smiled. Normally he would have requisitioned a horse, but the spring day was clear and mild, perfect for the half-day walk and for time without distraction to decide how he would convince Calaf to fully align himself with Rome by joining the army. Felix, his *frumentarii* chief, tolerated no further delay.

After crossing a wooden bridge over the deep ravine of the river Phyrminus, flooded with a raging torrent from the previous night's storm, he entered an open area of rock strewn fields. A single glint of sun among the rocks interrupted his thoughts. Then another across the road. A robbery in daylight on a well-traveled pathway was not unheard of, but other than his sword he carried nothing of value. Abduction seemed unlikely, assassination more so. One does not survive among the *frumentarii* without making enemies. Ahead approached an oxen-drawn cart driven by a young boy. As a defensive position, it would suffice. Flavus pulled his sword, yelled for the boy to flee, and rushed for the cart. But as the boy jumped and ran, two armed men leapt from the cart and four more closed in from the fields.

He circled, sizing up each: well armed and battle hardened. "So many of you. Excessive, don't you think?" he called out.

One replied, "Our employer wants to be certain that Drusus is avenged."

"Ah, yes, the traitor killed by a mere boy."

The assailants attacked.

Seven voyages and a year and a half had passed since Calaf and Taj joined the crew of the Roman merchant vessel, and gradually Calaf had accepted Ishmael's death. He leaned against the stern, entranced by the dolphins leaping and somersaulting in the ship's wake, the sun reflecting off their silver backs. In the Mediterranean Sea the dolphins traveled in larger numbers than those in the Indus River. Their beaks were much shorter, and they were just as playful. *The dolphin favored you.* He smiled at the memory of Gadhi's words, and then sighed, closing his eyes and wrapping his hand around the bronze armband circling his bicep. *But, Ishmael, I never had the chance to show them to you.*

"Calaf!"

He turned, his eye first captured by the sliver of Syrian coast on the distant horizon beyond the ship's bow, then Taj's waving arms from the amidships hatch. Calaf waved back. "I'm coming!"

When he reached the hatch, Taj had already dropped back into the hold. Naked with straw sticking to his legs, arms and torso, Taj scowled up at Calaf. "I can't do this alone." He stooped over, retrieved a large piece of shattered pottery and tossed it up for Calaf to cast overboard. The previous night's storm had shifted the cargo and broken several ceramic olive oil amphoras. The captain ordered them to clean the mess before their arrival at Seleucia Pieria, Antioch's port.

After all the amphora pieces were discarded, Calaf stripped and lowered himself into the hold to the overpowering smell of olive oil turning rancid in seawater. By the time Calaf and Taj pulled themselves from the hatch, reeking of sweat and olive oil, the ship was within sight of Seleucia Pieria's lighthouse. Encouraged by the captain's shouts of "Get that stench off my deck," several crewmen jumped them and threw them overboard. Howls from the water and laughter from the ship accompanied their rescue.

Once the ship was secured to the dock and the plank positioned, the crew began unloading the amphoras of olive oil onto the waiting carts that would move the cargo to Antioch, a day's journey inland. A young port official appeared and announced, "I'm looking for Calaf."

When Calaf acknowledged him, the man maneuvered around the other crewmen as he pulled a small parchment from the leather bag hanging from his shoulder. The message was brief and in Callista's own hand.

Come, it concerns Flavus.

Calaf handed the parchment to the captain, who after reading it asked the port official, "How old is this message?"

"Six days, maybe seven."

The captain handed the message back to Calaf. "Go now. Take Taj."

Calaf sat cross-legged on the floor of the temple of Daphne and Apollo, a short walk from Callista's dwelling. Water cascaded nearby, providing a steady sonic background to the noisy chucking of a covey of partridges feeding beneath the shrubs surrounding the temple.

When he and Taj arrived at Callista's two days earlier, they were led to her private chamber, where she lay on her bed turned toward the wall. As she rolled over and slowly climbed to her feet, her ashen face told him the news before she spoke the words, "Flavus is dead."

With a cry Taj dropped to his knees, wrapped his arms around Calaf's legs, and shook silently. Calaf patted Taj's head and waited for Callista to continue.

"He was ambushed on the Daphne road on his way here. He was discovered near death surrounded by six dead assailants. Six attacked him, yet he still lived. He was alert enough to demand he be brought to me." Her voice broke into a sob. "His beautiful body mercilessly hacked. He had a wound across his skull that should have ended him."

As she spoke, grief and anger punctuating every word, Calaf remained motionless. He felt shock, of course. Invincible, larger-than-life Flavus—how could he be dead? Not only that, despite their differences Flavus had been his confidante and protector. Then gradually it dawned on him: he was relieved. *No longer am I a piece in his grand designs.* He felt a moment of suppressed exhilaration at his sudden and unexpected freedom.

Callista recaptured his attention when she said *Barbalissos.* On their arrival at Seleucia Pieria the battle of Barbalissos was the talk of Antioch's port. A Roman army of 60,000 butchered almost to a man by forces let by the Persian ruler Shapur, leaving Syria and its prosperous capital Antioch defenseless and open to invasion and pillage.

"Even his *frumentarii* allies paid scant attention to what happened to him," Callista said, not even bothering to wipe the tears falling to her disheveled gown, "too occupied by this new Persian threat to the Empire. And Antioch officials did little beyond cursory questioning and disposal of the assailants' corpses. Of course, I know they are distracted by the unrest in the city due to Barbalissos, but still it's a travesty," her voice trailed off to a whisper, "a travesty."

Calaf disentangled from Taj and embraced Callista, guiding her back to her bed where he sat on one side, offering whispered condolences, while Taj moved to the other, placing his head in her lap and softly crying. In the days that followed he went through the motions of grief to support Callista and Taj in theirs, all the while contemplating a new life opening before him, a life truly his own.

Voices interrupted his thoughts as two craftsmen entered the temple to resume the repair of a wall mosaic damaged in a recent earthquake. It depicted the goddess Daphne at the point of Apollo's capture, her legs becoming a trunk in the ground, her arms reaching to the sky as branches of laurel. *Desire forever out of reach.* That is how Callista summarized the tale, adding that its truth was confirmed every night in every brothel she ever owned. He looked down at the bronze armband and traced Ishmael's name. He took a deep breath to calm the ache filling his chest. *Desire forever out of reach.* Climbing to his feet, he went from the temple's cool shade into the hot glare of midday. The last vestige of the morning's clouds still hid Mount Silpios's peak.

Arriving at Callista's he found a richly decorated litter and six finely clothed attendants waiting outside. Two tethered horses eyed him as he walked toward the colonnaded entrance. Once inside he went to the room he shared with Taj and found him still lying on his bed. Since their arrival to the news of Flavus's death, he rarely left the room.

Calaf nudged him and Taj moved, giving him room to sit. "You once said to me, 'I know you loved Ishmael, but it's time to let him go.' Remember?"

"Our first shore leave—after we docked in Brindisi."

"Then you took me riding."

"You didn't want to go," Taj said.

"I didn't at first, and then I didn't want to stop."

Taj sat up, his face easing into a slight smile. "You were laughing."

"First time since—" When he hesitated, Taj squeezed his knee. After a moment Calaf said, "There's still plenty of daylight. We'll go riding now."

"But Callista looks for you."

"After I talk to her then. What's happening?"

Taj shrugged. "The captain's here."

"The captain?"

Taj nodded.

Calaf stood. "Let's see what they want."

“She said just you. They’re in the courtyard.”

“Then you go ready the horses.”

Taj touched Calaf’s arm. “We’re friends, aren’t we?”

“What foolishness. Of course, we are.” He cuffed the side of Taj’s head then dashed from the room, calling out, “Get the horses—I won’t be long.”

Nearing the courtyard, he paused before a candlelit niche. Freshly cut white jasmine blooms were arrayed around the simple bronze urn containing Flavus’s ashes. On a low table below the niche lay his sword, still stained with the blood of his assailants. When he offered to clean the blade, Callista became angry, shouting, ‘You would erase this last testament to his courage?’ The blade was turned so that the engraved name *Eberulf* was visible. Calaf smiled, wondering which gods had won his services in the underworld, those of Rome or those of his German homeland.

“Calaf.”

Callista stood at the courtyard entrance. She smiled and motioned him inside. Dominated by a reflecting pool stretching the length of one side, the courtyard was the most secluded area of the house. Beside the pool sat two men—Felix and the captain—facing each other over a table of bread, meats, and fruits. The captain stood.

“Calaf, join us. I believe you’ve met Felix.” *Trust Felix as you would trust me.* That is what Flavus had told him, but he had also said, *Use Rome, use me, but never trust us—never trust anyone.*

Felix raised his wine cup and gave Calaf a wide smile. “Sit beside me, my boy.”

Callista took his arm. “Come, Felix has brought us wonderful delicacies from this morning’s market, and I haven’t tasted better wine in ages.”

Felix pointed at a bowl of rolled betel leaves. “I even found a merchant selling areca nuts. They’re quite the luxury here. I do hope you’ll show us how to properly enjoy them.”

When Calaf resisted her gentle prodding, the captain said, “I know you’re distraught over Flavus’s death. We all are. But there are things we must discuss, and decisions that must be made.”

“What decisions?”

Felix motioned to the servant. "Wine, give the boy wine." Then to Calaf, "Hear what we have to say. Afterward, we will honor whatever you decide."

The servant extended a wine cup. Calaf shook his head before sitting on the edge of Felix's couch. Felix raised his cup, toasted Flavus as a trusted friend and valued colleague, then insisted that pleasure come before business. Over the meal the men did little talking, deferring to Callista's reminiscences of Flavus, interspersed with ribald brothel tales and her plans to return to Minnagara.

"The caretaker of my brothel has died, and there is a clamor for my return. Then there are those brutish Persians. I surely don't want to be here when they invade Antioch."

After the third time Calaf declined the offer of wine, Felix asked, "You do not care for it?"

"If I have decisions to make, it will be with a clear head. You're *frumentarii*." It was a statement, not a question. Felix nodded, as did the captain. "Callista, too?"

"Not officially, of course."

"Is Flavus really dead?"

Felix raised his eyebrows. "Flavus was right to tell us not to underestimate you. But, sadly, his death is not a ruse. We suspect he fell to those who never forgave him for Drusus's death."

"But I killed Drusus."

"True, but they held Flavus responsible."

"Because he used Drusus for my abduction."

"So he told you."

He nodded. "Do they target me?"

"I expect so, but we took precautions. Callista and her companions here in Daphne. Flavus whenever you went to Antioch. When you ran off after hearing about your friend's death, we found you drunk and incoherent below the aqueduct near the Daphne Gate. In your grief and anger you became a threat to yourself. I decided time at sea would keep you occupied, where I knew we could keep you safe from Drusus's friends."

Calaf went to the reflecting pool. A mosaic of Neptune riding his hippocamp-drawn chariot decorated its bottom, the god holding a trident, like the one Flavus taught him to use at Srinagar. "And what? Taj got the job of becoming my new friend."

"His job was to warn the captain should he suspect you were in danger. Nothing more."

"What does he know?"

"Only what he needed to. He's not *frumentarii*."

The captain stepped up and placed his hand on his shoulder. "I am Antonius, an officer of the Emperor's Praetorian Guard. My first love is the sea, so I welcomed the assignment. I now return to my duties. Two horses wait outside. I would like you to begin as my aide. Over time you will become an officer in your own right."

"Why?"

Felix raised his cup for more wine. "Come, sit again."

When he hesitated, Antonius squeezed his shoulder. "The decision remains yours." Callista gave an encouraging smile.

He looked at Felix. "Flavus used me. Why should I believe you are any different?"

"Because you have something to gain." Felix waited until Calaf returned to the couch. "Flavus told me you wish to reclaim your father's throne. You must realize the impossibility of success if you act alone with nothing but a band of insurgents. Persia will crush you, bringing the dynasty of your ancestors to an ignoble end. Rome does not want that to happen. When the time is right, we will want the Kushans returned to their former glory with you at their head. And Rome will do whatever is required to see that you succeed."

"When the time is right?" With a laugh he started to rise.

"You will regret not allowing me to finish," Felix said and Calaf settled back. "The Persians are gathering strength: their victory over the Kushan Empire, their assassination of our client king in Armenia replacing him with their own puppet, now their annihilation of our army at Barbalissos. But it will not last. We will avenge Barbalissos, just as we did Carrhae. And when we do, you will be there, triumphant on the Khyber Pass, containing Shapur's eastern border with Rome's support and gratitude."

"Why not show your support and gratitude now? What difference does it make?"

"Besides our weakened military and economic situation after Barbalissos, there's the question of your loyalty."

"My loyalty?"

"Surely you do not believe Rome will extend its aid to someone whose loyalty is unproven. Your time with Antonius will cement your ties to Rome and demonstrate the maturity and steadiness of purpose we know you possess."

He stood. "And you say the decision is truly mine."

"Yes, but I urge you to give serious consideration to how Rome can help you."

"I'm sorry, Rome has helped me enough." He bowed to Callista, then Antonius, and finally Felix.

Felix raised his hand. "There is one more thing that you might affect your decision." They locked eyes. "Ishmael lives."

Calaf fought to keep his face impassive, even as his stomach churned in outrage. Finally he calmed enough to speak. "You would use Ishmael to manipulate me? Even Flavus wouldn't go so far."

When he moved to rush from the courtyard, Antonius took his arm. "A moment more—please."

Felix reached into his toga, retrieved a small blue silk pouch, and extended it. "The wax mold was poor, but there should be enough detail to satisfy you."

Calaf untied and emptied the pouch. A clay replica of his infant ankle band fell into his palm. One of the two griffins, the words *son of Timur*, *champion*, and *people* were visible. He bit his lower lip against the sting in his eyes. He closed his fingers over the band and brought his fist to his chest. "This does not mean he lives."

"After Ishmael didn't agree to the plan to leave Peshawar with you, Flavus assigned an agent to him. That agent is with him still. I assure you he did not die when the palace fell to the Persians."

"Calaf," Callista said. "He speaks the truth."

"You knew?" She nodded. "And Flavus?"

Felix spoke. "We all knew."

"Taj, too?" Felix nodded.

Slowly Calaf rose, unsteady at first. When Antonius reached for him, he pushed his hand away. He moved to the reflecting pool. He opened his hand and looked at the clay band. *They seek to entrap me, but if he lives, nothing else matters.* He looked across the pool at the courtyard wall, painted with intertwining vines and flowers over a deep red background, not for the first time reminding him of the carpet on which Ishmael and he played as boys and then slept the last time they were together. He took a deep breath. "The band could have been taken from his corpse."

Felix stepped beside him. "The band was removed as he slept, and the mold made."

As he slept. Distrust fought hope as he tightened his hand about the clay replica.

"He is safe and continues his medical studies."

"Where?"

"That is not something we can tell you at this point."

"So that I remain compliant, doing your bidding?"

"I'd rather it be our working together toward a common goal, you on the throne of your ancestors."

"Then bring him to me," Calaf demanded.

"And lose what leverage we have over you?"

"That's blunt."

"I'll always be forthright with you. You cooperate with us, we protect Ishmael. It's as simple as that."

"So, I've no choice."

"No, my boy, you have a choice, but work with us and we'll watch over your friend until the time is right for him to join you—when at last you sit on the Kushan throne." Felix paused a moment. "Hephaistion to your Alexander?"

Heat rushed to his face. "You seek my cooperation, yet you bait me."

Felix took his elbow. "Bait you? No, my boy, I test you, as you will be tested time and time again." He pulled him back toward the others. "But today you have proven Flavus's confidence in you. I was certain you'd bolt, your impulsiveness getting the better of you." He waved at the servant. "Certainly you will enjoy the wine with us now?"

"But I haven't—"

"Of course, you have, my boy. And to demonstrate our gratitude, we will find a way to let Ishmael know that you too live. The poor man believes you died at Rajanpur."

Taj had not moved from the bed. Callista had told him they might be forced to tell Calaf the truth about Ishmael and urged him to leave the villa until Calaf departed. Taj refused. He would not take the coward's path.

Footsteps approached then Calaf's silhouette blocked the doorway's light. Taj raised his eyes and waited.

Calaf said, "When did you last see Ishmael?"

"After the Persians took Peshawar, heading toward Baktra over the Khyber with a group of refugees."

"So when you told me he burned to death in the palace fire, you lied."

Taj nodded.

"How many nights did I awaken hearing his screams in that fire? And you comforted me, my head against your chest, your fingers brushing away my tears, instead of ending my suffering with the truth."

"I wanted to tell you."

Calaf stepped into the room. "Then why didn't you? You said you were my friend."

"I am your friend."

With a howl Calaf threw himself at Taj, sending them crashing to the floor. Taj did nothing to protect himself, just stared into Calaf's rage-distorted face.

When Calaf's fist wavered. Taj took a deep breath. "Flavus made me vow to keep it secret."

Long moments passed as Calaf's eyes lost their fury. "You've played your part well. Too bad he isn't alive to reward you."

"It was terrible not telling you."

"But not terrible enough."

Antonius appeared in the doorway and cleared his throat. "We must leave, Calaf."

As Calaf climbed to his feet, Taj grasped his leg.

"I'm sorry."

"A true friend would have broken a vow so vile."

Without another word Calaf stepped past Antonius, who acknowledged Taj with a quick nod then followed.

Taj did not move, staring at the ceiling with eyes that did not see. Flavus was dead. Calaf lost to him. He was alone. His world shattered.

Kawtara appeared, touched his cheek, and whispered his name. When he did not respond, she left. A short time later Callista knelt beside him and stroked his hair. When his vacant gaze cleared, tears filled his eyes.

He whispered, "Calaf hates me."

"Do you blame him?"

He jerked at her unsympathetic tone. "But I was protecting him—and Ishmael."

"So you were told."

"Flavus wouldn't lie to me."

"Why not?" Callista asked. "You idolized him. Bigger than life, exciting, mysterious—you aren't the only one to fall under his spell. But he was no better than any man, perhaps worse than most."

"But you loved him. Everyone knew that."

"Yes, but I loved him for the man he was, faults and all."

Taj sat quietly for a few moments. "So he used me."

"Yes, just as he used me and many others, but it doesn't mean he wasn't fond of you. Learn from it and move on."

"But what about Calaf?" Taj asked.

"He will move on, too."

"Hating me."

Callista pushed him away. "You dishonor Flavus with self-pity. What's become of the boy Flavus took under his wing, seeing in him a young man worthy to follow in his footsteps? Did I believe you capable? No, all I saw was a charming—and highly profitable—brothel boy. But Flavus saw more in you, and you proved him right. Yes, you betrayed Calaf, convincingly, I might add. You regret it, as you always should or you'll become cruel. You must get past it, just as Flavus always did. Now compose yourself. Felix wishes to speak to you."

Nearing the courtyard Taj motioned toward Flavus's candle-lit niche. "A moment please."

Callista stepped farther down the corridor and waited. Taj bowed his head but his mind remained blank of anything divine. Only Callista's words absorbed him: *worthy to follow in his footsteps*. Lifting his face, he ran his fingers along the blade of Flavus's sword stopping at the engraved name *Eberulf:* the wild boar of his native land. One day his own sword would bear the same—once he felt he had earned it.

He approached Callista. "I'm ready."

She motioned him toward the courtyard. "He will speak to you alone."

Felix stood facing the courtyard's reflecting pool. "Tell me, Taj, what is the most important thing Flavus taught you?"

Sensing a quick reply was expected and necessary, Taj answered with the first thing that flashed in his mind. "Unquestioned loyalty."

"And now that he is dead, where does your loyalty lie?"

"With those who earned his."

"And who are they?" Felix asked.

"Callista."

Felix finally turned to face him. "Any others?"

The Roman's eyes were hard and searching. Like a hunter. He the hunted. *Eberulf.* He grew calm. "You."

"But you know little of me."

"Flavus once told Calaf to trust you as if you were him," Taj replied. "That is all I need to know."

Felix moved toward the couches, motioning Taj to join him. Taj sat across from him and waited as Felix poured wine. As they drank in silence, Felix's eyes studied Taj's face. Taj fought the urge to look away.

"You do not speak of loyalty to Calaf," Felix said.

"He was a job Flavus gave me, nothing more."

"Yet I understand you were very attached to him."

A sharp ache rose in Taj's chest. "I was."

"No more?"

"He turned on me."

"You betrayed him," Felix said.

"I did what Flavus expected of me."

"Yet it pains you."

"Of course, it does," Taj said, keeping his voice steady. "I am not Flavus."

"No, you're not, but then no one is or ever will be." Felix raised his wine cup. "To Flavus."

Taj raised his and whispered, "To Flavus."

Felix refilled their cups. "I have agreed to let Calaf send a message to Ishmael," Felix said. "I want you to deliver it and return with Ishmael's reply."

Taj's eyes grew wide. "But he's in Persia."

Felix smiled. "Not just any place in Persia. The imperial capital at Shushtar. A sight to behold I understand."

"But why me?"

"Who better? You proved yourself with Flavus's assignments. And because Ishmael knows you, you can assure him that Calaf is indeed alive and well. As if that's not enough, Callista says you know the agent Flavus assigned to watch over Ishmael. Her name is Liu."

"Liu is with Ishmael?"

Felix nodded. "It's almost a year since her last report, so you can return with that, too. Ah, I see amazement but no resistance. That must mean we can drink to your next assignment?"

Taj raised his cup.

"Excellent," Felix said. "You will return to Minnagara with Callista, and any communication between us will go through her. You must agree to two conditions. First, Liu's role cannot be jeopardized, so Ishmael must not discover she works for us. Second, under no circumstances do you tell Ishmael where Calaf is. The success of our venture depends on keeping them separated until Calaf takes the Kushan throne. You and I can have no misunderstanding about this."

"I understand the consequences of failing you, sir." When Felix gave him a questioning look, he added, "Flavus was quite clear that with the *frumentarii* there are no second chances."

"No, Taj, there are not," Felix said.

After Felix departed, Taj reclined on the couch and stared into the cloudless sky.

Flavus dead.

Calaf lost to him.

But Fate sends him to Ishmael.

A servant appeared with a fresh pitcher of wine. With a whispered thank you to Callista, he allowed the grape to bring its welcome numbness.

Storm clouds formed in the distance ahead while a thick fog bank obscured the Syrian coast. Taj tightened his cloak about his neck against the cold, damp wind buffeting the merchant ship. Callista emerged from below deck carrying the bronze urn containing Flavus's ashes. Agatha and Kawtara followed behind her. Once together, the four stood along the ship's railing, the only sounds the sea slapping the side and the ropes and sails straining against the wind. A lone seagull swooped before their eyes then disappeared over their heads. Callista turned to Agatha and lifted the top from the urn and handed it to Taj. Taking the urn from Agatha's arms, Callista held it over the water for several moments before turning it upside down. In silence they watched the wind billow the ashes away from the ship to disappear into the sea.

When the others moved to return below deck, Callista touched Taj's arm. "Please stay."

In silence they stared over the water. Several fin whales surfaced then disappeared, one slapping its tail, sending a stream of water into the air. Finally Callista spoke. "Did Flavus ever speak to you of Demetrius?"

"The physician?" When she nodded, Taj added, "Rarely but always with fondness."

"Did he tell you he made Demetrius a sacred promise to protect Calaf, Ishmael, and Sharina?"

"No," Taj answered.

"It's why he allowed Sharina to escape after Calaf tried to kill her," Callista said. "It's why he sent you to discover Ishmael's fate after Peshawar fell, and it's why he assigned you to watch over Calaf on the merchant ship."

"Why didn't he tell me?"

"Because he couldn't risk the *frumentarii* discovering his motives weren't purely Roman, and he wouldn't put you at risk for anything more than following his orders."

"Why are you telling me this?"

"Before he died, I promised Flavus I would." Callista turned silent, her eyes focused on the sea. Finally, she continued. "I thought him a fool, and still do, for his stubborn insistence on honoring his vow to Demetrius. Most likely he'd still be with us if he'd not meddled in the lives of those three. His death should have brought this madness to an end and voided my promise to say anything to you. But then you accepted Felix's offer to take Calaf's message to Ishmael."

Taj said, "Tell me what Flavus said." When Callista hesitated, Taj insisted, "Tell me."

"*Taj must complete what I cannot.* But I beg you, let this vow die with Flavus. Deliver Calaf's message, return with Ishmael's. Then go away. Go anywhere. Forget Calaf and Ishmael. They are not your responsibility. They never were. Salvage your life."

Seeing Callista's distress, Taj embraced her and kissed her forehead. "Flavus's vow is not mine to honor."

The ship lurched in a gust of wind, throwing them off balance. As he steadied Callista, he said, "You should join Agatha and Kawtara until the sea calms."

Callista nodded vigorously. "Neptune protect us, I hate such voyages," she grumbled and allowed him to guide her to the opening that led below deck. She placed her hand on his cheek for a moment, then descended the ladder.

CHAPTER 33

PESHAWAR

TAJ WALKED THE LENGTH OF the caravan forming outside the Khyber Gate. He spotted a merchant crossing a field of scattered wagons, waving his cap, the edge of his blue wool robe kicking up dust. Taj returned the wave and jogged up to the man.

The merchant gripped Taj in a hug then pushed him to arm's length. "When did you arrive?"

"Midday yesterday."

"And how fares that river scoundrel Kabir?"

"As ornery as ever, but he's grateful, as am I, at your hiring me on such short notice."

"Just don't forget his promise to include me in your deal with the Shushtar sugar merchants."

"If we reach a deal, count on it," Taj said with his widest smile.

It amused Taj that anyone, particularly this veteran caravan merchant, would think him capable of negotiating anything other than a tavern doorway, but Kabir had assured him, 'Act like you can, and people will believe you can do anything.' No wonder Flavus had valued this river merchant so much.

"So how long's the journey?" Taj asked.

"Two months if we're lucky. It's a bad time of year. Dust storms." The merchant turned around and pointed. "The red wagon's yours. All loaded.

Just need to hitch the team. Better move quick. You don't want the gray with the black mane."

Taj took off running toward the horse pen, the laughter of the caravan merchant echoing in his ears.

SHUSHTAR

Taj emerged from the public bath, the accumulated dirt of three months on the road from Peshawar cleansed from every pore, his curly black hair trimmed short in the style of Persian laborers, his trousers and tunic new but simple. His only luxury were camel leather boots, a gift of the caravan merchant. After passing through several alleys, he proceeded along a wide paved avenue, picking his way through a noisy market day crowd of people, carts, and animals, staying below the branches of the flowering silk trees that provided welcome shade from the hot midday sun. A bearded man standing on a box shouted about a god called Jesus, and Taj recalled a fervent Christian sailor who spent an entire voyage from Brindisi to Antioch attempting to convert Calaf and him. The thoroughfare came to a grand square dominated by a central fountain. Taj shielded his eyes and scanned the surrounding shops and taverns until he spotted the silversmith's sign, the shop that Liu's message had told him to find. He took a few steps before a hand pulled him to a quiet spot.

Liu embraced him then stepped back. "You're really here."

Taj's face spread into a wide grin. "Look at you, grown so mature and responsible."

She pulled him back into an embrace, her mouth to his ear. "Say that again, and you're dead."

"I meant young and beautiful." She squeezed him harder. "And strong!"

She relaxed her hold and laughed. "Didn't Callista teach you anything about how to charm a woman?"

"It's not her fault. She really tried." Then with an exaggerated smirk he added, "That must be why she only gave me to men." Liu directed an obvious glance toward his groin. Surprise filled Taj's face. "That, too?" He dodged Liu's jab at his ribs, grabbed her hand, and gave it a quick kiss. "I've missed you."

Liu stroked his cheek. "It has been a long time. You must tell me everything."

"Not here."

Liu took his hand. "Come with me."

The silversmith's second story room was small and dimly lit, its only window facing away from the square into a yard shaded by a massive gulmohar. They reclined on pillows in a corner away from the window.

"The last I heard you were in Antioch working for Flavus."

"I returned to Minnagara with Callista."

"Callista's back? At the brothel?" When Taj nodded, Liu place her hand over his knee. "Oh, please don't tell me she's got you working there again."

"Oh, no, that life's too long ago. Anyway," he said with a laugh, "you must admit I look more like a customer now."

Liu gave his knee a squeeze. "But what happened between you and Flavus? I thought you were working for him."

Taj turned serious. "You're certain it's safe to speak here."

"Yes, the silversmith can be trusted. Why?"

"I know you're Flavus's agent assigned to watch over Ishmael."

"You should not know this," Liu said. "What's happened?"

"Flavus is dead."

Her initial shock quickly turned to grim composure. "Dead? How?"

"Ambushed by a faction of the *frumentarii* loyal to Drusus."

"The one who betrayed Flavus to deliver Calaf to the Persians?" Taj nodded. "Did they kill Calaf, too?"

"No, he's safe in Rome."

"So the Romans still intend to use him in their fight against Persia," Liu said.

"Yes, and we now work for a senior *frumentarius* named Felix."

"Flavus's boss."

"You know about him?" Taj asked.

"Only that Flavus distrusted him."

"Flavus distrusted everyone, except maybe Callista."

"No, this was different. I believe Flavus feared him."

"That I cannot believe," Taj said.

"So why are you here?"

"Felix told Calaf that Ishmael is alive to get him to cooperate."

"But that wasn't the plan," Liu said.

"He also agreed to tell Ishmael that Calaf survived Rajanpur."

"Both will know that the other lives? Aren't they to be kept apart?"

Taj nodded. "Neither will know where the other is."

"They'll find out. You know they will."

"Not if we do our job."

As Ishmael left the hospital, he yawned and stretched, squinting into a mid-morning sun that bathed the sprawling square before him, home to the city's silk merchants. A caravan had arrived several days earlier, and the crush of buyers made crossing the square an unwelcome task after two days of little rest treating the injured and dying from a collapsed building that housed Arab workmen and their families. As he turned toward the warren of alleys that surrounded the square, he heard his name called, and shielding his eyes from the sun, he spotted a familiar Persian officer moving through the crowd toward him. For a moment he did not recall his name. Then he remembered him standing naked beside the river, fair hair wet about his shoulders, shouting *Faraj*.

The Persian smiled as he gripped Ishmael's shoulder. "You're no longer with the city health group." Accusation filled his voice.

"I left it five months ago."

Faraj ignored Ishmael's irritation. "I have a room nearby."

"I'm exhausted."

Faraj tightened the grip on his shoulder. "I want you now."

Ishmael wrenched himself free. "I'm exhausted."

"Tonight then." Faraj pointed at a nearby tavern. "I'll meet you there after sunset." Before Ishmael could respond, Faraj strode away.

Someone touched his arm. "I'd be careful with that one. I've heard dreadful stories about him."

Taj stood beside him, eyes focused on the Persian officer as he disappeared into the crowd.

Ishmael paced before the window of the silversmith's upper room and read the parchment a third time.

I am told that you did not perish when Peshawar fell.
If this be true, and your reply will confirm it,
know that I live to be with you again.

He touched the small drawing below the message. Two foxes, neck touching neck, heads turned in opposite directions, surrounded by a circle of arrows. Ishmael longed to shout his joy, but fought down the urge, for Taj sat on a pillow watching him. The drawing's arrows warned of danger to both of them. He recalled what little he knew about Taj from meeting him in Peshawar before it fell to the Persians: Minnagaran brothel boy turned emperor's servant with ties to Calaf's bodyguard.

Ishmael asked, "Do you work for Flavus?"

"Flavus is dead. But it's best we talk away from the window." Taj patted the pillow beside his. "Come, sit with me."

Ishmael drew the pillow away from Taj's, sat, and waited.

Finally Taj spoke. "You take the news calmly."

"I disappoint you?"

"I'm surprised, that's all." Taj shifted about. "The silversmith has wine. Do you want some?" Ishmael shook his head. Taj scratched his. "I bring you good news and—"

"The seal was broken."

"That was Felix's doing. I did not read what Calaf wrote to you." Ishmael raised his eyes. "Believe me, I didn't and never will."

"Who is Felix?"

"Calaf's protector."

"How did you find me?"

"You're important to Calaf, so the Romans tracked your movements here."

"Someone watches me?"

Taj looked away with a shrug.

"So we're to be kept apart with you delivering his messages to me," Ishmael said. "Why can't we see each other?"

"These are dangerous times. It is for your safety—and his."

"Felix told you to say that, didn't he?" When Taj nodded, he said, "I think we need that wine now."

When Taj returned carrying a pitcher and two cups, Ishmael paced the room. Taj sat and filled the cups. "I trust Felix. You can, too."

Ishmael dropped onto his pillow. "Where is Calaf?"

"I can't tell you."

"Does he know where I am?"

"No."

"Have you seen him?" Ishmael asked.

"I have."

"Is he well?"

"Yes, he is," Taj answered. "Felix told him you're also well and continuing your medical studies."

"When do you want my message to Calaf?"

"I leave with a caravan that departs in four days."

Ishmael drained his cup then said, "Tell me about Makli."

Taj's eyes grew wide. "You know about Makli?"

"Of course, I do," he lied, remembering only Calaf's plan for him to flee there. *A fishing village upriver of Minnagara. The fishermen know me and will hide you.*

Taj shook his head. "I don't think I should."

"It happened so long ago. What difference does it make now?"

"I—I—"

"You were there, weren't you?"

Excitement filled Taj's eyes. "But not when he killed Drusus. Did he tell you about the fight?" Ishmael gave an encouraging nod. "I'd seen Drusus at the brothel a few times. A brute, not anyone to meet in a dark alley, and thank the gods, he only sought women. When we got to Makli, the fishermen wouldn't stop talking about Calaf's impossible victory over him. I've never seen Flavus so angry as he raged about Drusus's treachery. Afterward I overheard him talking to Callista—"

"Callista?"

"She owned the Roman brothel in Minnagara where I worked. They were good friends. He told her Drusus betrayed him and ruined his plans." As if finished, Taj brought the cup to his lips.

"Anything more?"

Taj shook his head. "That's all I heard, but it was Drusus's friends who killed him."

"Romans killed Flavus?"

Taj froze then jumped up. "We need more wine."

A satisfied smile crept across Ishmael's face as he stretched out and closed his eyes. When Taj shook him awake, the next morning's light reached into the room.

Calaf is alive. The Romans have him and a Roman agent watches me. Taj seems loyal to the Romans, but might he be convinced to help him reunite with Calaf?

These thoughts flooded Ishmael's mind as he made his way home through the bustle of mid-morning Shushtar.

Calaf is alive.

Not long ago such news would have blinded him with a flood of longing and sullen frustration. Instead, Calaf's true message, the arrows surrounding the drawing of the foxes, made him focus on the dangers facing them, challenging him to find ways to overcome them. *Calaf is alive.* His relief and joy would only be realized in Calaf's arms. Until then, he would live, endure, watch, and be ready to act.

As Ishmael rounded the corner to his dwelling's narrow alley, Faraj stepped into his path.

"I waited." Faraj grabbed his arm. "You will not do that again."

"Who are you to—?"

"Handsome woman you live with. And the old man. Your father?"

Ishmael broke Faraj's hold. "What do you want?"

"You know what I want."

"Not here."

"Why not? I watched them leave."

"They're never gone long. Your place. Tonight."

"Don't disappoint me again or it will be the worse for you—and them." He waited until Ishmael nodded. "Same tavern at dusk."

"Same tavern."

Faraj stroked Ishmael's cheek before departing the alley.

Ishmael arrived at the tavern before dusk. He took a table near the entrance, a chipped wine cup in his hands, watching the room fill with silk merchants from the neighboring shops. His mood shifted between revulsion and arousal as he prepared to see Faraj again, his confusion disgusting him, especially now that he knew Calaf lived. It had grown dark outside when Taj appeared in the doorway then sat across from him.

"I'm expecting someone."

"He sends his regrets." Taj caught the serving girl's attention and pointed at Ishmael's cup. "It seems friends of yours convinced him to treat you with more respect."

"What friends?"

"Good ones."

Ishmael groaned. "I don't need your help. I know what I'm doing."

"It's what your Persian might do that worries me."
"But I've learned that he's well-placed in court."
"General Zab's boy?"
"Yes," Ishmael replied, "and my knowing him might prove useful."
"Assuming you don't end up dead."
"You forget I have much to live for now."

CHAPTER 34
258 CE

PESHAWAR

THE SEVEN YEARS SINCE SHARINA had been rescued by Aric from the Rajanpur prison camp had been unsettled for a time as she struggled to build a life not dominated by vengeance and court intrigue. But with their daughter Jiya's birth, Sharina's life shifted to the needs of her new family. Calaf, her son long gone, while rarely far from her thoughts, no longer loomed over her. Looking back Sharina hardly recognized in herself the person who sought the death of an innocent Ishmael to satisfy—to satisfy what? A young girl's anguish at being the only survivor of Timur's brutality against her family? Or the rage of Timur's queen Adelma against her husband, using her to exact a vengeance she could not or would not do herself? Sharina had obsessed over such questions, finally accepting what only mattered was that her mission of revenge had been thwarted and that the events that had delivered her to Rajanpur's prison camp were her redemption.

The spring had been unseasonably hot, cloudless skies offering no relief for the parched city. Few wildflowers decorated open plots, the buzzing of insects subdued. No breezes stirred, the scent of jasmine cloying in the heavy air. Dawn's hopeful orchid blossoms wilted by mid-morning, few surviving to dusk's shadows. The few people who moved about kept to the shade of alleys, avoiding the broad streets and open plazas, empty of the usual bustle of merchants and customers, who surrendered the midday heat for the shelter of their shops and homes. Aric led Sharina and their two children into the fire temple's courtyard. It, too, was deserted but not because of the heat.

Even though it was a symbol of Timur's rule, the Persians preserved the temple dedicated to the martyrs Yousef and Sanjar in deference to the city's Zoroastrians. However, to prevent its becoming a focal point of rebellion, armed palace guards manned its gate and patrolled its courtyard, which discouraged visitors. Within a few months, the Persians locked the gate. Those who noticed shrugged and moved on, and the temple was forgotten, except by the ancient priest assigned to maintain its flame and Aric, granted access to pray at the temple to his fallen brother Yousef. The courtyard's gardens lay barren, the ground parched, its gulmohar trees overgrown. Sharina guided the children to their shade and sat to watch them play, marveling that they seemed unaffected by the heat.

Jiya called out, "Look, look!"

Almost six years old now, Jiya stooped several paces before little Ashu. A few days earlier he began to walk. His pudgy arm extended, he held a stick in his hand and lurched forward into his sister's waiting embrace. He squealed in delight. Sharina smiled and motioned to Jiya. "Remember, play quietly."

Jiya whispered to her brother, "Shh. Father is praying." Ashu squealed again.

Sharina suppressed a laugh and turned her gaze to the lone figure kneeling in the sun before the mosaic of Yousef. Sweat dripped from Aric's beard and stained his cloak. She longed to lift him from his knees and sooth his torment, but there was nothing anyone could do when the ghost of Timur consumed him, as it once consumed her.

Sharina still dreamed of Timur but less often, and when she did, he was a distant, shadowy figure whose menace no longer gripped her. Her children filled her heart instead. She knew that Aric also dreamt of Timur. He no longer spoke of them—and she no longer asked—but in the dead of night as she held his shuddering, sweat-covered body, she felt the terror coursing through him. She knew that every day he spent in the court of Persia's puppet king reminded him of his betrayal, a vengeance that did little to lessen

Timur's hold on him. But now only in dreams did he do battle, but there was no triumph in dreams and no assuaging ghosts.

His dreams brought him to his brother's temple. She always joined him, sitting nearby, pondering why his vengeance succeeded and gave him no comfort, while hers failed and her demons fled, leaving her at peace.

CHAPTER 35
260 CE

Edessa

Calaf paused a moment before descending the barren western slope of the Roman Emperor's hilltop command post. Below him was Valerian's army of fourteen legions, the tents of almost seventy thousand soldiers arrayed in a precise grid that extended across the desert plain that lay before the city walls of Edessa. The sun neared the horizon, casting lengthening shadows throughout the increasingly active camp.

The weeks of scouting the terrain and the Persian opposition were over, as were the impassioned speeches, sacrifices to the gods, and announcements of good omens to bolster the morale of the troops. This evening the legions would begin moving into formation on the massive plain east of the command hill. If the auguries truly revealed what lay ahead, tomorrow would be the day that the Romans would finally avenge their past humiliations by the Persians at Carrhae and Barbalissos.

The plague that ravaged the army for months had finally subsided, turning stubborn despair into long pent-up enthusiasm, bolstered further by a Roman victory the previous week in a skirmish with the Persians. Calaf too was swept up in the excitement, even more so because he did not expect to be here. A different Praetorian Guard cohort had been slated to accompany the Emperor when he left Rome for Mesopotamia, but Calaf awakened the day of departure with orders to muster. When asked why, his unit's centurion—and his onetime merchant ship captain—Antonius answered that the Emperor would be safer with a new cohort. Calaf recognized the true meaning of his words. The *frumentarii* had uncovered another imperial plot, this one within the Praetorian Guard itself. Calaf had recently sent his latest message to Ishmael, in which the shapes and directions of the arrows surrounding the two foxes confirmed his continued presence in Rome. It would be months before Ishmael received that message, then months before a reply could reach Calaf. But it did not matter. For Persia lay ahead and he imagined a successful Roman campaign bringing him to the gates of the Persian capital at Shushtar—and Ishmael.

As Calaf approached the tents of his century, he recalled Demetrius's stories of Alexander's victories over the Persians and his boyhood dreams of one day fighting in such battles. Six years he had fought alongside the Romans, but none of those battles came close to an epic confrontation between two great armies. Until now, at Edessa. When the sun again appeared in the eastern sky, he would realize those dreams.

Calaf was surprised to find Quintus Volcacius Tiro, the oldest of their unit, standing before Antonius's tent. While his stance was relaxed, it was clear he guarded the tent, normally unnecessary within the encampment's safety. Calaf gave him a questioning look but Quintus only nodded as he parted the tent flaps for Calaf to enter.

Antonius sat at a small desk and looked up from an unrolled parchment. Calaf raised his arm in salute.

"At ease, Gaius."

Gaius Lucius Valens. A Roman name given to him by Felix, his *frumentarii* handler, to hide his true identity from Flavus's killers and to ease his entry into Roman life. Felix had introduced him as the son of a distant Greek relation who—to account for Calaf's dark skin—had married a Kushan woman.

Antonius rose and indicated his armor laying on his cot. "Help me, please."

Once again Calaf was surprised. During his difficult first years with the Guard, Antonius often requested his assistance with his armor but rarely since. He remembered those early days with fondness, a time when

Antonius would instruct, admonish, and encourage him. Calaf lifted the segmented metal plates over Antonius's head and began the tedious work of tying the multitude of leather straps that kept the armor in place.

"Quintus stands guard?" Calaf asked.

"Only to assure our privacy."

Calaf knelt to tie the straps about the centurion's sides. *Why privacy?*

Antonius said, "The Praetorian Prefect has called a meeting of centurions to assign units for the Emperor's protection during the battle."

"Will our century remain nearest the Emperor?" Calaf asked.

"I expect so. We impressed him during the recapture of Antioch."

"We saved his life."

Antonius smiled down at him. "That too."

That the Persians would leave agents behind upon their withdrawal from Antioch was expected. That one would get within striking distance of an Emperor surrounded by his elite bodyguards was not. Calaf had spotted a guard slowly moving out of position then noticed his sandals, the leather straps tied around his calves in the unique manner of the Persians who came to meet with his father. As Calaf moved to intercept him, he had waved his arm at Antonius with his thumb raised in the unit's *immediate threat* signal. Alert to the warning, several of his century companions moved with him. The guard lunged toward the Emperor, but Antonius blocked his path. Calaf brought the assassin to his knees, and his comrades swarmed over them both. As the assassin fell forward, he turned his dagger on himself, his death removing any possibility of determining whether negligence or treachery lay behind his infiltration of the Praetorian Guard ranks. Leaving nothing to chance, the Praetorian Prefect immediately moved Antonius's unit closest to the Emperor. To avoid attracting undue attention toward Calaf that might lead to his true identity, Antonius did not reveal Calaf's key role in saving the Emperor. But word had spread throughout the cohort, elevating him in the eyes of his comrades.

The armor completed, Calaf helped Antonius into the leather harness decorated with his military awards. As he reached for the helmet, Antonius stopped him. "I've assigned Quintus to you."

"I don't need—"

"I know you don't. But he has his orders and now so do you."

"Does he know who I am?"

Antonius shook his head. "All he knows is that he must protect you with his life."

"He didn't ask why?"

With a smile, Antonius cuffed Calaf's shoulder. "An order is sufficient for some." His lightheartedness faded as quickly as it arose. "There is something else. According to our scouts the Persian army only lightly occupies the hills to the south. It's a land of small farms and herdsmen. An itinerant Kushan would unlikely be noticed."

"What are you saying, sir?"

"If the battle turns against us, you must complete what you attempted at Portus."

Shocked, Calaf opened his mouth to speak, but Antonius silenced him with a look. "This is Rome's battle, not yours."

Calaf's voice was barely a whisper. "I will not desert, sir."

"And I will not reward your loyalty to me and to the Guard with death—or worse—at the hands of the Persians. If we succeed, I expect you in Rome at my side for Valerian's triumph. If we fail, go to your friend with my blessing."

"We will not fail, sir."

"Then you can raise a toast to my foolishness." Antonius clasped Calaf's forearms. "Consider it an order. Now I must meet with the Praetorian Prefect." He grabbed his helmet from the cot and hurried from the tent, leaving Calaf stunned.

Complete what I attempted at Portus?

Seven years earlier, six months after his arrival in Rome, he had received his first communication from Ishmael. As he decoded the drawing of the foxes and arrows in the message, surprise had turned to alarm. The Romans had been lying to him about where Ishmael was.

Stealing the horse was easy. The stables were lightly watched. The city gate easier. Lone Praetorian Guards often took the road to Portus to deliver messages. The attempt to board a ship without having booked passage, that brought his escape to an end. While infrequent, army desertions through Rome's port did occur. Having never encountered a desertion from the Emperor's elite corps, the harbormaster reacted to Calaf's appearance with caution, confining him under guard to a room beside his own office until he received instructions from Rome. Those instructions came in the person of Antonius, who thanked the harbormaster for his diligence and dismissed the guards before entering the room. Calaf saluted and waited as Antonius studied him.

"What were you thinking, Gaius?"

"Calaf, sir. If I am to die for desertion, it will be with my true name."

"If I hadn't intervened with Felix, you'd already be executed along with orders issued for Ishmael's death. Why did you try to escape?"

"Ishmael is not where you told me." When Antonius did not respond, Calaf continued. "Felix said he was in Minnagara where Rome has a strong presence and Callista watched over him like her own son. Now I discover he's in Persia. In Shushtar, by the gods, the damned imperial capital."

"How did you find this out? Only Felix and I knew."

"Does that matter?"

"For his safety, yes, and the success of our mission to put you on your father's throne, a mission *you* now jeopardize."

"And Ishmael's not in jeopardy? What if the Persians discover who he is?"

"I assure you he is in no danger."

"And you'd tell me if he was?"

Antonius ignored the question. "But into what danger have you placed him? Even if you had escaped, don't you realize we'd get to him first?"

"I expected you'd let us go."

"Fool! You know Felix better than that."

"What happens now?"

"You remain valuable to us alive."

"No, what happens to Ishmael?"

"Return to Rome, and he will not be harmed. Of course, only Felix and I will know that your time in Portus was anything other than official business. Also, you must marry."

"Marry?"

"Felix has decided a wife and children will help you develop more mature attachments and repair a loss of confidence in your stability and loyalty."

Calaf retorted, "But Roman soldiers can't marry."

"You forget you are not an ordinary soldier."

"Do I know her?"

"I believe so. Senator Avitus's niece."

"The younger?"

Antonius shook his head. "Felix thought an older woman more suitable."

Felix could not have paired Calaf with a woman more like Sharina, dooming the marriage from the start. Even Felix's attempts at mediation failed. So it surprised no one that after the birth of the twins, a boy and a girl, they separated. Calaf wanted a divorce, but Senator Avitus, having embraced the idea of his niece as the future Kushan queen and her son one day its ruler, would not allow it. But the issue faded with Calaf's frequent absences from Rome as Valerian campaigned in Syria and Asia Minor against Persia's marauding hordes. Shapur showed no interest in holding the lands he overran. Rather he looted then withdrew to find another vulnerability in Rome's defenses before looting again. As this exposed Rome's uneasy hold on its Eastern Empire, Valerian became obsessed with defeating Shapur, providing fertile ground for Felix's plan to create a new Kushan Empire on Persia's eastern border and as its ruler a Kushan prince with family ties to Rome.

Calaf stiffened at the memory of his children, having learned long ago that it was futile to dwell on his separation from them. He took a deep breath, still bewildered by Antonius's offer of his freedom, and stepped from the tent. Quintus stood waiting and gave him a curt nod. Together they climbed the Emperor's command hill to rejoin their eighty-strong Praetorian Guard century.

The next morning Calaf shielded his eyes from the first rays of the rising sun as he stood guard overlooking the broad barren plain, the thick dust kicked up by tens of thousands of Roman legionaries rising into the cloudless sky as they settled into formation. Above him the imperial throne and banner had been placed before the Emperor's tent, but Valerian had not yet emerged to take his place. Nearby stood General Successianus and his senior officers. Couriers on horseback carried his orders to the plain and returned with reports from his field officers.

Antonius appeared beside him. "So what do you see?"

Recognizing that Antonius was testing his knowledge, Calaf answered, "They're forming the square, which means our scouts have confirmed cavalry."

Antonius nodded. "We've determined that their forces consist almost entirely of horse archers and light armored cavalry."

"That puts us at a disadvantage, doesn't it? What few cavalry we have are untested in a major battle."

"It could, but we have numbers. Their army is barely half the size of ours. The Emperor and General Successianus are confident our infantry gives us a decided advantage." Lost in thought, Antonius gazed over the plain.

Calaf observed, "And yet you seem concerned."

"The plague took too many veterans. The field commanders will miss their experience and discipline, particularly on the front line. Then there's Shapur. He is not only smart but cunning as well. It worries me he's decided to engage us now. Why doesn't he wait to reinforce his ground troops?"

"He knows that the plague hit us hard?" Calaf ventured.

"Perhaps."

As Antonius moved away, the sun cleared the horizon. Horns sounded and Valerian emerged from his tent. He did not wear his usual military uniform but rather the white toga reserved for formal imperial appearances. Calaf wondered why until the Emperor stepped past his entourage, his toga now ablaze in the sun's rays. A roar arose from the troops on the plain, spreading up the hill as the Praetorians took up the battle cry *Ad victoriam*. A wide smile replaced Valerian's usual somber demeanor as he raised his arm. Another outbreak of cheers swept upwards. Suddenly General Successianus rushed to Valerian's side. Seeing the Emperor's smile vanish, Calaf turned toward the horizon. A cloud of dust now stretched across the far end of the plain.

"The Persians make the first move," Calaf said under his breath, determined to remember every moment of what was to come.

"Most likely the horse archers."

Calaf turned to Quintus, who stood several paces away, and said, "The sun is at their backs."

"And in our infantry's eyes." Quintus nodded toward the command tent. "The signal flags are changing. Watch the field."

The front lines closed ranks into a compact mass to face the approaching enemy while holding the square in the event they were surrounded, the usual Roman response to a cavalry attack. As the horse archers drew close, Calaf was surprised by their modest number, no more than five thousand, and since they posed no threat of encircling the Romans, he puzzled at the Persian strategy. A direct frontal assault seemed a suicide mission. A feint perhaps? He scanned the hills to either side of the plain, expecting to see additional Persian forces but none appeared. Shouts rose from the field as the Persian cavalry came within range of the Roman archers, who released a cloud of arrows into the sky. In response, the horsemen unleashed their fusillade against the well-shielded Roman front line. As the Persians began taking casualties they reined their mounts out of range, where they hesitated, visibly in disarray as if their officers no longer had control over them.

Quintus called out, "Our line grows restive."

Calaf shouted back, "They taste Persian blood."

"But they must not break formation."

The Persian horsemen began pulling back, one by one at first then in a complete rout. The Roman line reacted. In the midst of raised spears and loud cheers, Calaf heard commanders yelling to hold firm. The cheering grew louder. A ripple of movement shifted the formation forward, and then another. Within moments a wave swept along the line. Finally it burst, sending thousands of screaming soldiers in pursuit of the fleeing Persians.

The plague took too many veterans. The field commanders will miss their experience and discipline, particularly on the front line.

Calaf glanced at Quintus, who shook his head.

Above them Antonius shouted, "Close ranks."

Within moments Calaf and Quintus stood shoulder-to-shoulder, part of a wall of shields and spears three deep surrounding the Emperor's command tent and throne. Other Praetorian units shifted into tight positions below them.

By that time the Roman infantry stretched across half the plain. Many were tiring and slowing in their pursuit. The field commanders began to regain order and a front line began to loosely reassemble. The Roman cavalry sped up the flanks. Suddenly out of the dust of their flight the Persian horse archers reappeared sending their arrows into the Roman ranks. The surprised and still disorganized legionaries began taking heavy casualties.

Quintus nudged Calaf and nodded at the far ridge. Another cloud of dust, far greater than the Persian's first onslaught, rose into the sky and descended onto the plain.

Then there's Shapur. He is not only smart but cunning as well.

Calaf shielded his eyes from the sun and strained to see the new threat. The dust-thickened morning haze blocked his view, but then a smattering of shiny reflections appeared. "Armor," he whispered as anxiety gripped his stomach.

Some above shouted, "Cataphracts."

Calaf stared in disbelief as thousands of heavy cavalry emerged out of the haze. He had never seen anything like them. Armored head-to-toe and mounted on armored horses, they brandished long lances, swords, and axes. Due to the weight they carried, the Cataphract horses moved slower than those carrying the archers, but that only increased their menace. The horse archers shifted to the Roman flanks, leaving the front line to face the advancing Cataphracts. The legionaries formed pockets of resistance as the *cornicens* sounded their horns, rallying the centuries to their *signifers*, who carried the unit standards. But Roman arrows, swords and spears proved useless against the Cataphract heavy armor. The Persians began targeting the *signifers*. As the standards fell, panicked and disoriented Romans threw down shields and weapons and began running, only to be chased down and slaughtered, punctuating the din of battle with their death cries.

Calaf kept his eyes focused on the eagle-topped standards of the legions, and as they began to fall, tears of helplessness and rage blinded Calaf's eyes as he fought the bile rising to his throat. Several Praetorians below him began retching. By the time the Persian infantry began to descend upon the plain, the Romans were routed. Growing numb with shock, Calaf realized that there would be few survivors. He turned to Quintus. "Will they attack us on the hill?"

"Depends on whether they want to kill or humble the Emperor. I'd guess humble him, but I for one am girding myself to slay as many of the bastards as I can before joining my ancestors."

By midday the plain was deep in Roman bodies and blood. The Cataphracts and horse archers advanced to the bottom of the Emperor's hill but only attacked with taunts and curses as their infantry advanced across the plain to crush counterattacks and loot the dead and dying. As the sun reached toward the horizon, the Persians pulled back, taking the remaining daylight to recover their casualties. As dusk filled the sky, surviving Romans emerged from the plain's horror, stumbling and crawling over their dead and dying comrades. The Praetorians—except for Antonius's century, which continued to guard the Emperor—were ordered onto the field to find, organize, and care for the survivors. Calaf watched their torches move in a grotesque dance over the carnage, their approach greeted by cries of pain, anguished sobs, and pleas of 'Over here' and 'Save me.'

Calaf spotted Antonius walking among his men, offering a pat on the shoulder for some, a word for others. Finally he reached Calaf. "Come with me." When they reached a quiet spot out of range of the nearest torch, Antonius dropped into a crouch. As Calaf knelt, he noticed that Quintus had followed but stopped a discrete distance away.

When Antonius did not immediately speak, Calaf asked, "What happens now?"

"At daybreak the Emperor will send a messenger to Shapur suing for an end to hostilities."

"Will Shapur accept?"

"He's won a great victory, so there's no reason for him not to," Antonius answered. "There'll be demands, of course, but the Emperor will have little choice but to accept them."

"What kind of demands?"

"Most likely territory and gold. I won't be surprised if Shapur wants us to permanently remove our troops from the Armenian border and give him Antioch with its access to the Mediterranean. In return the Emperor will demand that we be given adequate time to bury our dead, after which we'll be given unrestricted passage to return to Roman territory."

"Like scolded puppies with our tails between our legs." Bitterness filled Calaf's voice.

"But alive to exact future vengeance." He placed his hand on Calaf's leg. "My order still stands, Calaf." Antonius's use of his Kushan name surprised him. "Join those helping the survivors. Quintus will go with you to vouchsafe your orders if you're challenged. The darkness will conceal your escape."

"What will you tell Felix?"

"The truth," Antonius answered. "Too many witnesses know you did not take the field."

"You'd survive Edessa only to die a *frumentarius* traitor by letting me go? You cannot expect me to accept such a sacrifice." Calaf stood. "I will not desert, sir. We march out together." He did not wait for Antonius's response, bolting past Quintus to rejoin his comrades guarding the Emperor.

When Quintus slipped beside him, he leaned close to Calaf's ear and whispered, "You're a fool, Valens."

"And you would have accepted such an offer?"

"In a moment."

The next morning Shapur accepted Valerian's call for an end to hostilities. By midday the Persians had erected a tent in a clearing a short distance from the Roman command post. Recalled from their duties tending the wounded, the Praetorian units took positions surrounding the hilltop.

Antonius gathered his men around him. "The Persians will not allow a full century to accompany the Emperor," he began. "General Successianus has ordered half our unit to form the Emperor's escort. The rest will remain on the hill to safeguard the Persian negotiation hostages. I will lead the escort. The hostage squad will report to Lucius, my second."

Expecting to be included with the escort, Calaf was shocked when Antonius assigned him to Lucius. But before he could react, Antonius pulled him and Quintus aside. "Shapur's son is one of the hostages. You will be his personal guards from the moment he arrives. The situation is volatile. The general fears a misguided act of vengeance. If anything happens to the boy, it could put the Emperor's life in jeopardy. Keep him safe."

"But I belong—"

"You belong where I order you, Valens," Antonius snapped. Then more gently he said, "Nothing remains certain until our boots march on Roman land."

Six Persian nobles and a small cadre of lightly armed soldiers accompanied Shapur's son. Halfway up the command hill they moved past Valerian, General Successianus and his senior officers, and Antonius's escort. An uneasy quiet settled over the hilltop as the hostages were directed to wait before the Emperor's tent. Calaf was surprised to see that Shapur's son was a mere youth, no older than fifteen years. The prince stood ramrod straight, eyes forward, a twitch of his lower lip the only sign of nerves. Calaf stepped before him and smiled. "It'll be over soon."

The youth's face remained immobile but his eyes darted to Calaf's. "You speak Persian."

Calaf nodded. "My name's Valens."

The prince glanced about as if looking to the nobles for guidance, but when none reacted, he said, "Akbar."

"Are you Shapur's heir?"

"No."

Expendable?

When the youth returned his focus to the distant tent, Calaf followed his gaze. Valerian's party neared the clearing, and a tall figure dressed in a brilliant blue robe with matching turban emerged from the tent. "Your father?"

"Yes." Sweat now beaded his forehead.

Calaf asked, "Have you been a hostage before?" When the youth shook his head, Calaf added, "You need not be concerned."

"I've heard stories," Akbar said.

Calaf smiled. "No harm will come to you or the others."

Akbar's lower lip began to tremble. Again he looked about. Again there was no reaction except stony silence from the other Persians. A sudden realization struck Calaf.

The negotiation hostages await their deaths.

He swung about. Valerian and his general and senior officers were entering the tent, followed by Shapur. The Emperor's escort remained outside. Behind him Akbar spoke, his voice barely a whisper and shaking. "My father said if we are unharmed, you will face capture not death." Distant shouts erupted. Calaf watched in horror as Persian soldiers rushed the Emperor's escort, driving them away from Shapur's tent.

Chaos swept through the Praetorians around him. Spears flew, bringing down several of the Persian guards who had accompanied the negotiation hostages. As the Persian nobles closed around Akbar, Calaf jumped into the growing melee, his arms raised and shouting over and over, "Kill the hostages and the Emperor dies." Beside him Quintus echoed his shouts, adding emphasis by brandishing his sword. Lucius moved the rest of his squad into a protective position around the negotiation hostages.

For a moment the other Praetorians hesitated. One of the centurions, his face red with rage, rushed at Calaf. "The Emperor's dead. Kill them."

"We don't know that," Calaf shouted back.

"Our first duty is to the Emperor," yelled Quintus. Then he began to chant, "Valerian—Valerian—"

Cries of 'Valerian' erupted throughout the Praetorian ranks until suddenly they were drowned out by howls of outrage. When Calaf looked toward Shapur's tent, the Emperor's escort lay unmoving in blood-soaked dirt.

Antonius.

All self-control now lost, Calaf spun about, his sword raised, and looked into Akbar's terrified face. Quintus grabbed his arm and said, "The Emperor lives."

Calaf looked. Valerian now knelt before Shapur. The sun caught a reflection of a sword threatening the Emperor's head. As Calaf forced himself to calm, the cohort's centurions silenced several defiant shouts. Calaf held his breath as all around him grew still. The next move would decide the fate of everyone on the hill.

Shapur waved his arm, and a line of Persian soldiers began moving toward them.

The senior most centurion stepped away from his unit and shouted, "Lucius, lead the negotiation hostages down."

CHAPTER 36

SHUSHTAR

ISHMAEL SAT ACROSS THE TAVERN table from Taj and read Calaf's most recent message. Ishmael lifted his face in a wide grin. "So, he remains in Rome."

"Give it to me." Taj grimaced as slowly and silently he mouthed the words. "He encourages you to continue your medical studies, says he's become adept with the bow and longs to see you. There's the drawing of the foxes and arrows. Nothing more. And nothing about Rome."

"He is, isn't he?"

"I can't."

"You always do."

Taj groaned. "Remember your promise."

"No one will ever know."

"All right, yes, he is." Ishmael motioned him to keep talking. "Felix's last message to Callista said the Emperor finally agrees to support Calaf's retaking the Kushan throne. Calaf will stay in Rome until the Emperor returns from his current campaign against the Persians. Felix will then accompany him to Minnagara to organize the overthrow of the Persian puppet in Peshawar."

"So Calaf will return soon."

"It seems so."

"You're a true friend."

Taj returned a shy smile before asking, "With Calaf returning, why remain in Shushtar?"

"What would I do in Minnagara?" Ishmael asked in reply. "Anyway, my physician training continues. A teacher from China has just arrived. Can you believe they heal with herbs and animal parts? If I leave now, I may miss something that could save Calaf's life someday. I'll leave when Calaf leaves Rome."

"How will you know that?"

Ishmael grinned broadly. "You'll find a way to tell me, of course."

Once again Taj groaned, and then changed the subject. "Is Faraj still obsessed with you?"

Ishmael nodded. "Fortunately, Shapur's campaigns in the north keep him away. But when he's here, he seeks me out or watches me from afar like I'm prey."

"Even the Roman soldiers garrisoned at Minnagara know the name Faraj and speak of his savagery on and off the field of battle. You must remain cautious."

"Of course."

Taj lifted his cup. "Then let's drink to a Roman spear finding that demon's heart."

Taj stood at the window of the silversmith's upper room. Crimson blossoms had turned the backyard's massive Gulmohar into a blaze of color.

Liu stepped behind him, wrapping her arms around his chest, her chin on his shoulder. "Something's disturbing you. Tell me."

"It's nothing."

"Tell me anyway," Liu insisted.

He hesitated, uneasy about sharing his growing doubts, then decided that if he could trust anyone, it was Liu. "Felix's last message. It prepares us for Calaf's return to Minnagara but makes no mention of Ishmael."

"Why should that concern you? It's always been the plan to keep them apart until Calaf takes the throne."

"Have you ever asked yourself why?"

Liu shook her head against his shoulder. "Why would I?"

"Because it's never made sense."

At that moment the silversmith entered. "Thought you might want some wine." Setting down the pitcher and cups, he pulled Liu into his arms and she nibbled his ear.

Taj laughed. "I think I've overstayed my welcome."

"No, no," the silversmith said. "I've an order to complete. Then we eat. Then I kick you out." Giving Liu's backside a playful slap, he added, "We have all night, right?"

"Right," Liu answered and gave the silversmith a quick kiss. "So go get your work done."

Once the door closed behind him, Liu poured the wine and handed a cup to Taj, her face turning serious. "Listen, Taj, it doesn't have to make sense. Just do your job, as I do mine. Our loyalties were to Flavus, not to Felix and certainly not to Rome. But soon our work will be done, and then we'll be free to move on with our lives."

"But there's something we don't know, something important. I feel it."

"Please, Taj, let it go. Whatever it is, what can you do about it?"

"I can make sure you're safe, along with Ishmael and Timur."

"What are you talking about?"

"When Calaf and the Romans move against Peshawar, all Kushans in Persia will be in danger. The Persians will round you up as enemies and spies. You know they will. As soon as Felix arrives at Minnagara with Calaf, I will find a way to help you flee Persia. If I can't, you must be ready with your own plan to escape."

"You're scaring me, Taj."

"I'm scared, too. Flavus would have protected us. But these Romans? They don't care about us or Calaf or Ishmael. We are all but pieces in the game they play to defeat Persia. If we don't act to protect ourselves—"

The silversmith's footsteps sounded on the stairs. Taj embraced Liu and whispered, "Consider what I've said."

The door opened. "Who's hungry?" the silversmith boomed.

"She is, and I'm on my way." Before either could protest, Taj dashed from the room.

CHAPTER 37

Edessa

No one forgets the sting of the yellow scorpion, nor the swelling that follows the poison through the body until the throat begins to close. Most survive the venom, but afterward few hide their terror at seeing the creature's upturned yellow tail. Even those least affected are known to die from multiple stings. But ask any Roman soldier and he will choose a scorpion's death over capture by the Persians.

Of the five-hundred-man Praetorian Guard cohort that arrived at Edessa, only thirty-two remained a week after Valerian's capture. With each dawn they marched into position near the tent of the Persian general Zab to stand in the blazing sun until it set. The morning began with thirty-four, but two collapsed. They lay lifeless where they fell, their throats cut by the officer in charge, Captain Faraj.

Calaf suspected others might fall before day's end, but they had learned not to fake incapacity in hopes of a quick death. Days earlier after seeing the first Praetorian's collapse and execution, another dropped to the ground. Faraj ordered him stripped and after examining his wounds declared him fit. Commanding he be tied to the ground face-up, Faraj walked the line of prisoners.

"Hide your eyes and his fate will be yours."

The Praetorian begged for mercy then wailed as whips ripped open his torso, groin and legs, his cries becoming screams when yellow scorpions were dropped into his open, bleeding wounds. Several around Calaf retched, but none looked away.

Later, the sun still sat high in the afternoon sun when Faraj emerged from the general's tent, silenced the tied-down soldier with a dagger across the throat, and ordered the guards to return the prisoners to the barricade. "Except that one." He pointed at Calaf. "Take him to my tent."

At dusk Faraj entered the tent and ordered the guard to unbind Calaf then wait outside.

"Your identification." Calaf removed a small lead tablet from a leather pouch hanging from his neck. "Read it to me."

"Gaius Lucius Valens, Praetorian Guard, age 24, birthmark right hip."

"Show me." Calaf lifted his tunic. Faraj nodded and Calaf returned the *signaculum* to the pouch.

"You remind me of someone, Gaius Lucius Valens. Who are your people?" Calaf did not reply. "Do not tire me, Valens, if not for your own life, then the lives of your comrades. Cooperate or one won't see tomorrow's sun."

"Greek. I was born in Alexandria."

"Your features are not Greek."

"My mother was Kushan."

Faraj went to the folding table beside his bed and held up a bronze armband. "You were wearing this when you were captured and adamant about keeping it. Why?"

"It belonged to my brother."

Faraj studied the inscription. "A brother named Ishmael? Who is honored for valor by the Kushan emperor?"

"To our father's distress, he followed his Kushan blood and died many years ago. Our mother gave it to me."

"Dead, you say. You're certain?" After Calaf nodded, Faraj shrugged then said, "You're not an officer."

"No."

"Yet your comrades defer to you. Why?"

"I don't know."

"For their sakes, and yours, it's best they continue to do so. All prisoners are ordered to Shushtar, where they will build a Roman bridge across a Persian river to honor Shapur's great victory over Valerian. You will be responsible for what remains of your Praetorian Guard. Should anyone go missing, you will choose a remaining one to die. Should you go missing or disobey me—" Faraj stroked Calaf's cheek "—they all die. Am I clear?"

Calaf nodded.

Faraj called out, and the guard reappeared. "Return him to the barricade—and an extra ration of food for his men, compliments of their new leader, Gaius Lucius Valens."

Calaf estimated that no more than two thousand Roman prisoners of war began the trek from Edessa to Shushtar, the only remaining of the seventy thousand that a confident Emperor Valerian led into Mesopotamia that spring. Weakened by wounds and the plague that ravaged the Roman army after its arrival at Edessa, many would not survive the march. At day's end Faraj culled the weakest to keep the Persian soldiers entertained. But he spared all Praetorian Guards and two nights rarely passed without the appearance of his guards calling the name *Gaius Lucius Valens.*

Calaf no longer offered resistance. He steeled himself the first time, knowing his men's lives depended on Faraj's satisfaction, but when faced with the reality of penetration, his courage vanished and he fought. Initially it seemed his struggle heightened Faraj's excitement, but in a breath arousal became fury. Two soldiers subdued him, and Faraj closed his hands around Calaf's throat, tightening his grip with each thrust. Calaf lost consciousness before it ended. Returned to his cohort, he revived bruised and bleeding to news that one of the men had been led away. They never saw him again. Calaf found that submission after brief resistance inflamed the Persian officer's passion, bringing the ordeal to a quicker conclusion with fewer bruises. Faraj kept his promise: no further men were taken.

In the days after their departure from Edessa his remaining men avoided him. Only Quintus looked after him when he returned from Faraj. This he did in silence until one evening he said, "They fear your fate should they be seen associating with you."

"Do they not understand I save them from that fate?"

"Of course."

"And yet they turn away from me," Calaf said.

"You allowed yourself to be taken like a woman."

"And they wouldn't if it would save others?"

"So they tell themselves."

"So rather than be dishonored, I should have died—and thereby sealed their fate?"

"A paradox, I grant," Quintus said.

"Yet you befriend me."

"There came a time when I too chose to survive as you do. Give them time."

Several days later one of the men fetched his food ration, handing it to him with a respectful nod. The next night two others tended to his bruises when he returned from Faraj's tent. Several evenings later they drew him into a circle sitting around a small fire. One sang, followed by another, then another. The songs were in languages Calaf did not recognize, but the longing in their voices spoke of homelands left behind. During a lull, their faces turned to him. The first song he remembered was a comic one in the Bactrian tongue. Ishmael had learned it as a boy from a camel trader. As Calaf began to sing, he added the face and hand gestures Ishmael created. Tentative at first, he relaxed when several of the men began to mimic him. He repeated the song giving his gestures Ishmael's exaggeration and exuberance. Smiles became laughter, drawing the rest of the cohort around them. Those not joining in the gestures began to stomp their feet and clap. After the fourth time he paused, but they demanded he sing it again. This time he attempted the lyrics in Latin.

One day the ostrich was asked to carry a load.
In reply it said, "I'm a bird."
When asked to fly,
The ostrich said, "I'm a camel."

Calaf knew the literal translation of the song's Kushan proverb made little sense, but that did not stop the men from joining in. Some picked up the tune and sang, others chanted the words, most gestured, and all laughed. The shouts of approaching Persian guards only made them raise their voices louder until the pain of spear butts joined the shouts. As the prisoners dispersed, defiant murmurs of *I'm a bird* and *I'm a camel* only stopped when the guards retreated.

PART 5

Nothing You Did Mattered

261 CE

CHAPTER 38
261 CE

MINNAGARA

THE LATE AFTERNOON SUN REFLECTED off the slow-moving Indus as Taj watched the Roman merchant vessel approach the Minnagara dock. After removing his cap and wiping the sweat from his brow, he leapt from the rear cargo roof onto the rowers' deck of Kabir's river boat. The Roman ship maneuvered toward an opening several berths away, steered by the two oars extending from the rear of the vessel. On the voyages between Antioch and Brindisi he and Calaf had manned such oars. 'You work together as if one man,' their captain once praised them. He sighed. Such memories still brought a moment of sadness.

"Another's arriving," he called out. "The fourth one today."

The aged merchant emerged from the cargo hold. "And the fourth time you've stopped work."

"But look at it. Have you ever seen a bigger one?"

"What? The gaping hole in my thatch roof? You'll never finish the repair by nightfall."

Taj's face broke into a wide smile. "When have I ever failed you, old man?"

"Careful who you're calling old. Don't forget who—"

With a sudden jerk Taj's attention shifted back to the Roman vessel, both hands now shading his eyes. As the ship turned about, a man came into view standing beside the massive carved swan's head adorning the stern.

Kabir came up beside him. "What is it?"

"It's Felix. He arrives without notice."

"Is Calaf with him?" Kabir asked.

Taj quickly scanned the others on deck, apprehension clutching his stomach as he recalled Calaf's last words to him: *A true friend would have broken a vow so vile.*

"No," Taj answered. "Maybe he's below."

"Go," Kabir said.

Taj felt something unseen rushing toward him. "But the thatching," he said, hoping the merchant would insist on his completing his work, giving him a reason to hold back to let what was unfolding become clear.

"Forget the thatching. Go now."

Taj jumped from the river boat's bow to the dock and arrived at the Roman ship's berth as Felix was instructing a crewman to deliver his baggage to Callista's brothel. With a wide smile of recognition and a quick stride, Felix descended the gangplank and grasped Taj's forearms with his hands.

"Apollo be praised, a friendly face after a long journey."

"I was working nearby." The Roman's exuberance unsettled Taj. "You've come from Rome?"

"By way of Antioch," Felix said with an exaggerated groan. "It's been four months since I left Rome."

Glancing toward the ship Taj asked, "Is not Calaf with you?"

Felix's buoyant expression did not change as he ignored the question. "We have much to discuss. But let's surprise Callista first. Lead the way."

Taj waited inside the open doorway of the brothel's private quarters as Felix pulled a speechless Callista into his arms.

"It has been a long time, my friend," the Roman said. "When I return to Rome, I beg you to return with me. Leave this backwater and come home to us where you belong."

Still in Felix's embrace, Callista gave Taj a questioning look. Taj shook his head and gave a shrug. Kawtara slipped past him carrying a tray with a wine pitcher and cups. When she departed, securing the door behind her, Felix's high spirits immediately vanished, replaced by a face turned grim and eyes exhausted. A silent tension filled the room as Callista poured wine and they sat facing each other.

Without preamble or further pleasantries Felix announced, "The Persians crushed us at Edessa. Our entire army is slain or captured."

Callista's fingers tightened around her wine cup. "The Emperor?"

"A prisoner," Felix answered.

Disbelief flooded Callista's face. "He lives? An Emperor captured? It's never happened."

Felix nodded. "I know few details. Survivors were still arriving at Antioch when I left. It seems Shapur lured Valerian to his tent to negotiate an end to the fighting and seized him."

Taj asked, "Where is Calaf?"

"The Emperor took Calaf's Praetorian Guard cohort with him, so he fought at Edessa."

"Is he alive?"

"If he is, he longs for death. The barbarism of the victorious Persian army is legend."

"But he might be."

Felix responded with a shrug. "He's no longer our concern. Ishmael is."

"But—"

Felix cut Taj off with a dark look. "Ishmael."

As Taj's eyes snapped to his wine cup, Felix placed his hand on Taj's knee. "Forgive my harshness. I know you were once close to Calaf, but we have no choice but proceed with Flavus's backup plan to place Ishmael on the Kushan throne."

Taj fought to keep his voice steady. "Of course."

Felix squeezed Taj's knee. "Good." He raised his cup and said, "I'm counting on you." With a nod Taj touched his cup to Felix's.

Breaking the brief silence that followed, Callista said, "So Ishmael will be brought here."

"Yes," Felix said. "We must prepare him to assume Calaf's place."

"And Timur?" Callista asked.

"Him, too. It's now even more important that the former emperor, maimed by Persian atrocity, publicly bless his champion and new heir."

"But what if Ishmael refuses to come?" Taj asked.

"Oh, he'll come. Calaf's next message will say that he waits for him in Minnagara. Of course, it will be forged, but once Ishmael's here, it won't matter. You and Liu will handle getting him and Timur out of Persia. But to deal with anything unexpected, I will accompany you. We must leave as soon as possible."

"Kabir prepares to go upriver to trade with the cloth merchants at Rajanpur," Taj said.

"Go tell him I'll make it worth his while to take us to Peshawar instead."

As Taj stood, Felix took his arm. "Your loyalties remain clear, do they not?"

"Most clear, sir. Your news, for a moment it stunned me."

"As it has for us all."

"How can he abandon Calaf like this?" Taj demanded.

Callista placed her hand over his mouth. "Shh, not so loud. No one must hear you."

They sat across from each other in Callista's chamber, knee touching knee, a single candle lighting the room, casting a clandestine glow.

"How can he?" Taj whispered.

"Because he—because Rome—cares about only one thing, an ally on the Kushan throne. This was always Flavus's plan should something happen to Calaf."

"So this is why they were kept separated?"

"Yes," Callista replied.

"But they haven't even tried to discover Calaf's fate. He may yet live."

"It doesn't matter," Callista said.

"It does to me. It will to Ishmael."

"Oh, Taj, you court danger with such thoughts. Let them go."

"I can't."

Frustration entered her voice, turning it harsh. "What you can't do is defy Felix. He will destroy you." When Taj remained silent, she continued, her tone softening. "I once told you to go away, to forget Calaf and Ishmael and salvage your life. I tell you that again. Leave here tonight. Disappear."

Taj rose and moved into the darkness the candle did not reach. *Disappear.* Often he had considered it. What could he do, one simple man? There could be no more fooling himself. Stepping back into the candlelight, he sat and looked into Callista's worried eyes.

"You are right." He watched her face relax and took her hands in his. "I do not mean to cause you such distress."

Callista smiled. "Sometimes you feel things so intensely it frightens me. What will you do?"

"I will make one last journey. I promised Liu to bring her home safely."

"And Felix?"

"I will do what's expected of me until Ishmael and Timur also are delivered out of Persia. Afterward, if he wants more, he'll have to find me."

As Callista pulled him into her arms, Taj was surprised how free and unburdened he felt.

CHAPTER 39

Edessa to Shushtar

Calaf jerked awake to a tap on his head. It was still dark. He shivered under the thin blanket that covered his shoulders but left his dirt-encrusted, callused feet exposed. Rolling over, he winced as a stone jabbed his back then whispered to the man kneeling beside him, "Dax is dead?" Quintus squeezed his shoulder and moved away.

Four dead in the last six days, this one from an infected wound, two from lingering effects of the plague, and one who fell from the road into a deep gully and struck his head. Only thirteen Praetorian Guards remained of the thirty-two who left Edessa a month earlier, and if the rumors were true, they were still another week's march away from Shushtar. Calaf knew that some would not survive the march but had not expected to lose so many.

Calaf rose and stepped around still-sleeping bodies, pausing to nudge two awake. Bearing pickaxes, Quintus approached with several Persian guards carrying torches. Calaf had been surprised by the decency of some Persian soldiers. At first he dismissed it as tactic to maintain order in a volatile situation. But then an officer named Javid slipped him fly-agaric on his way to Faraj's tent with the words, "Don't judge us all by him." The mushroom eased his ordeal, but the relief was compounded by the officer's unexpected kindness. Later, after the march's first cohort death, Javid allowed them to bury their comrade under guard rather than leave his body for the vultures. Afterward he pulled Calaf aside. "I spoke with Captain

Faraj. You may continue your rites but not as a pretext for escape." Calaf agreed.

By the time the shallow grave was ready, the entire cohort was gathered. After the burial, each placed a stone upon the packed earth while Quintus intoned a brief *nenia*.

Pour out tears, utter laments,
let all resound with sorrowful clamor:
Dead is a man with the heart of a hero.
No one was a match for his strength
all the world wide.

As they dispersed to prepare for the day's march, Quintus pulled Calaf aside. "I expect Dax is the last. The rest are too stubborn to die."

"That is good."

"There's talk they will free those who survive the building of the bridge."

"Anything to get us to work harder."

"So you don't believe it?"

Calaf shook his head and then making sure no one was close enough to hear, he asked, "The men know of my plans?"

"No one will betray you." Quintus paused before asking, "Then you are determined to do this?"

"Faraj said one more time before Shushtar then he's through with me. It'll be my last chance."

"But it means certain death."

"Only his death will be certain. The Persians grow tired of this march and have become lax. Faraj is too confident. He now orders his guards to leave the tent. Last time he had to wake them to return me, and he didn't even reprimand them. I can escape. I'm sure of it. But even if I fail, I will take this demon with me."

"But what about us?"

"The bridge, Quintus, they need you for the bridge."

"But Faraj—"

"He'll be dead."

"What if he isn't? After he's through with you, he'll come for us. Forget him, survive with us."

"No, he will die for what he has done to us."

"Let the Fates deal with him."

"I am his fate—as he is mine."

After Quintus shrugged and walked away, a moment of exhilaration swept through Calaf. Bound by a pledge that kept his cohort safe, forced to witness Faraj's cruelty on the march by day, compelled to endure degradation in Faraj's tent by night, he played the timid lamb, the emasculated eunuch.

But soon no longer.

Whenever Faraj passed on the road, Calaf was shoved to his knees by Persian soldiers, his face forcibly twisted upward to Faraj's piercing stare. The question was always the same: *Who are you, Roman?* Followed by the required answer: *Your servant, my lord*. Faraj would lift eyes of triumph to scan averted Roman faces before he rode away, kicking up dirt and stones. Then loudly whispering *I'm a bird, I'm a camel* the cohort defied anyone—Roman prisoner or Persian guard—to stare at Calaf as he climbed to his feet.

But soon no longer.

The lamb, a lion.

The eunuch, a warrior.

I am his fate—

as he is mine.

Pushed through the tent flaps, Calaf fought to hide surprise. Still in full uniform Faraj sat reading a parchment. The ground was bare, the rug rolled and tied. Instead of wine on the table there lay Ishmael's bronze armband, cleaned and polished, gleaming in the lamplight.

Faraj glanced up then returned to the parchment. "Bind his hands."

As a hemp cord tightened about his wrists, digging into his skin, his fingers tingling with numbness, he was relieved his arms were not secured behind his back. He spotted Faraj's scabbard and sword hanging from the nearest tent pole. *I need but one unguarded moment.*

Faraj stepped before him and stroked his cheek with his fingertips. "You disappoint me, Gaius Lucius Valens. I thought we had a bond." When Calaf did not respond, he raised the armband to Calaf's face. "The truth this time, and what happens next will go easier for you. Who is Ishmael?"

"My brother."

"Your brother who died?"

"Yes."

Faraj shook his head. "Who is Ishmael?" When Calaf did not answer, he said, "Very well, but know this could've ended differently." He called out, "Ramyad."

An officer entered and gave a stiff salute. "Sir."

Without taking his eyes from Calaf, Faraj said, "You may proceed."

Returning to the table, Faraj resumed studying the parchment. At first the only sounds were the usual clamor of the camp at night, the low rumble of prisoner voices, sentries calling out as they circled the perimeter, their mounts' snorting and hooves striking the hard ground, and soldiers talking and laughing. Suddenly discordant shouts rose above the din and then faded as if they never happened. A wail was silenced, followed by sobs. Faraj yawned and stretched his arms as dread ate into Calaf's stomach. The sobs grew louder until the sound of boots to flesh silenced them just outside the tent.

The flaps parted and soldiers threw Quintus to his knees. Blood covered his hands and arms, soaked through his torn tunic, but he had no wounds. His frantic, terror-filled eyes searched about, landing first on Faraj then Calaf. He held up his bloody hands and cried, "Dead—they're all dead."

Faraj began to clap. "A performance befitting your betrayal of your comrades."

"You never said anything about—" Quintus jumped up but the soldiers grabbed him, shoving him beside Calaf. He reached for Calaf's arm. "Believe me, he never said anything about the cohort." Calaf flinched at his touch but kept his focus on Faraj. *I need but one unguarded moment.*

Faraj stood. "Grave mistake, Gaius Lucius Valens, confiding in one who values survival above honor. I thought you were like him, but then he surprised me with news of your plan." He removed his sword from the scabbard hanging from the tent pole. "Unfortunate about your comrades, but one still remains." He paused then asked, "Who is Ishmael?"

Quintus whispered, "I'm a bird, I'm a camel."

Calaf shook his head.

Faraj said, "I thought not."

Faraj's sword plunged into Quintus's stomach. Calaf's guards loosened their hold as Quintus shrieked. Wrenching his arms free, Calaf threw them over Faraj's head and pulled him to ground. Faraj gagged as Calaf's fingers and the hemp cord cut into his neck. Other hands joined Faraj's, broke Calaf's hold, and hauled him to his feet. Choking through gasps for air, Faraj sprung from the ground, yanked his sword out of Quintus's writhing body, and planted the bloody blade at Calaf's throat. Their eyes locked.

"I would gut you where you stand."

"Do it!"

Faraj laughed. "Oh, you'd like that, wouldn't you? Your last breath as a vanquished but defiant warrior?" In silence he slowly wiped the sword clean of Quintus's blood against Calaf's tunic and returned it to its scabbard. "No, Gaius Lucius Valens, I give you a different fate. You will live whatever remains of your miserable life knowing that nothing you did mattered. Not surviving Edessa, not debasing yourself to save your cohort, not this pathetic attempt at vengeance." He picked up the bronze armband. "And not your hiding the truth of Ishmael."

"I will kill you."

"A delusion that will pass. Now, go ponder your failures as you bury your comrades." Then to the soldiers, "Take him away."

Lucius Salvius Rufus: quick with a joke.
Decimus Pomponius Severus: big and ugly but no one had a bigger heart.
Gnaeus Livius Ruso: devoted to his mother.
Numerius Servilius Aquila: the last to wake each morning.
Appius Marius Longinus: angry, always angry.
Aulus Sergius Victorinus: the shy poet.
Mamercus Norbanus Philippus: never stopped talking about the women he had.
Tiberius Tullius Tappulus: son of a merchant fallen on hard times.
Publius Minucius Rufinus: the Christ follower who prayed over each who had died.
Caius Aquillius Caesoninus: dreamed of owning a farm after this one last campaign.
Marcus Decius Malleolus: his singing helped you forget.
Quintus Volcacius Tiro: the survivor and betrayer.

Calaf placed each in the shallow mass grave, turning rage and despair into vows to avenge them.

But once the day's march began, as the sun breeched the horizon with its hot glare, as the dust kicked up by hundreds of feet filled his nostrils, as his muscles screamed their exhaustion, his mind and body descended into numbness. He did not speak, did not see the stares from Roman and Persian alike, did not hear their murmured accusations and snarled threats. Given water, he drank. Given food, he ate. One night he stumbled and slept where he fell. In those moments when his mind cleared, his thoughts reached for Ishmael but only Faraj appeared to mock him.

Nothing you did mattered.

The walls of Shushtar appeared at midday. Calaf did not even glance at them. By evening the Romans, randomly assigned to work groups, settled into designated areas within the fenced prison camp. Calaf shuffled behind his group then wandered about, uncertain where to drop his pack.

"Where is the prisoner Gaius Lucius Valens?"

Calaf spun about, his mind reawakened, his body taut. A soldier grabbed Calaf's shoulder and pushed him toward the mounted Persian officer. Calaf kept his footing, drew himself erect, and stared up at Faraj.

"What's he doing with the stone carvers? I ordered no tools of any kind. Move him. Now!"

Led away to a group of stone movers, Calaf was confused. Faraj did not look at him, did not gloat over him. No tools of any kind? It made no sense.

One by one the faces of his comrades appeared before him.

Lucius, Decimus, Gnaeus.

How am I a threat?

Numerius, Appius, Aulus.

If I am, why keep me alive?

Mamercus, Tiberius, Publius.

What does Faraj want?

Caius, Marcus, Quintus.

Then a final face.

Ishmael.

CHAPTER 40

Shushtar

Downriver a short distance from the Persian capital's wall Taj lay atop his bedding near the fire's dying embers. The night was warm, the moonless sky clear. He lifted the leather pouch that hung from his neck. Inside was the message he would give to Ishmael the next day with the lie that would propel Ishmael's joy as high as the stars only to send him crashing to earth upon his arrival at Minnagara.

"I know Ishmael. I've become his friend," Taj had said to Felix early in their journey. "He won't cooperate after you've lied to him. He will be enraged at the deception."

"Of course, he will. And who will he turn to? With Calaf gone, you'll be there to console him."

"But I work for you. I delivered the message. He will turn his rage on me, just as Calaf did."

"Not if he believes you too were deceived. Together you will burn in outrage at me, and then gradually you'll guide his thoughts to what Rome can do for him and for his people. Think of it, Taj, from brothel boy to the closest companion to the ruler of the Kushans. Who knows how high you will rise? You have seduced him, right?"

When Taj shook his head, an incredulous expression crossed Felix's face. "You tried, didn't you?"

"Of course," Taj lied. "His devotion to Calaf—" With a shrug he let his voice trail off. Yes, he had been tempted, but Calaf's cry *'A true friend would have broken a vow so vile'* always cooled such desires.

"Curious, but not a concern," Felix said. "Once we tell him Calaf is dead, he'll be vulnerable, giving you the opening you need to cement a close relationship with him."

Once we tell him Calaf is dead.

Taj kept his growing contempt for the Roman hidden over the three months they had journeyed together, first with Kabir on the Indus and then with the dozen men and horses Felix hired at Peshawar. But as the time drew near for their arrival at Shushtar, Taj began wondering how he could reach Ishmael before Felix did. He would tell him the truth, knowing that Ishmael would search for Calaf as long as there was a glimmer of hope he might be alive. And he would accompany him on his search to discover their friend's fate? If he helped Calaf reunite with Ishmael, his guilt over betraying Calaf would be washed clean. If Calaf indeed had died, Ishmael would never forget Taj's assistance, maybe even fulfilling Felix's forecast—*Who knows how high you will rise?*—but it would be on Ishmael's terms, not manipulated by his or Rome's deceit.

He knew he must act or forever let the moment pass. Taj rose from his bedding and pushed his bags underneath to simulate his body. Fortunately Felix, who lay beside him, did not stir. He was a sound sleeper. Taj slipped away and found the guard on watch with the horses.

"Who goes there?" the guard called out.

"Taj," he answered. "I can't sleep."

As Taj approached, the guard groaned. "After three straight nights on watch, that wouldn't be my problem."

"No sense both of us standing about awake. Let me finish your watch."

"Felix won't like it."

"Don't worry. It's my decision. He'll be fine with it."

"You sure?"

Taj gave him a gentle shove toward the sleeping company. "Go."

His heartbeat quickening as he waited, Taj did not move, listening as the guard settled into his bedding. Another guard stirred and coughed. Finally, he approached the tethered horses and finding his, saddled it, then walked it away from the camp before mounting.

He prayed that Flavus's *eberulf* watched over him.

Taj stopped pounding as the door opened a crack. Liu peeked out, blurry eyed, feet bare, wearing her sleeping tunic.

"What're you doing here?"

"Shh." He drew her into the corridor and closed the door. "Where's Ishmael?"

"You're not supposed to be here."

"That doesn't matter anymore. Where is he?"

"At the hospital."

"He's not there." He fought the urge to pound his fist into the wall.

"Taj!" She grabbed his head in both hands. "What's going on?"

"Where does he go?"

"Sometimes the river. End of the road beyond the alley."

"Be strong. I cannot go with you. Take the old man. You must flee now before it's too late."

"Too late for what?"

"Don't listen to him."

"Who?"

"Don't tell him I've been here."

"Taj, who?"

"Felix."

Taj rushed from Ishmael's dwelling and found Felix standing at the opening of the alley. Behind him were the hired guards and the horses. Taj backed against the building and glanced toward the alley's other end.

"You won't get far," Felix called out.

Taj dropped his shoulders and leaned his head against the wall as Felix approached. Liu emerged onto the narrow second-floor balcony. Her eyes searched Taj's. Slowly he shook his head.

"He's right, Liu," Felix called out. "Don't get involved."

A voice called out and Liu turned to look into the apartment.

"See to the old man. He's your only concern now."

Timur called out again, and she withdrew.

Felix stepped before Taj. "The message." Taj removed the parchment from the pouch hanging from his neck. Felix placed it into his own. He stroked Taj's face.

"You showed such promise."

He slipped the blade below Taj's ribs and thrust it into his heart. Taj cried out, slumped to the ground, his arms wrapped about Felix's calves as his body convulsed.

Above them Liu screamed.

CHAPTER 41

ISHMAEL FLOATED ON HIS BACK among the reeds. At the sound of his name he thought first of Faraj, returned from the war in the north. But as he stood, striving to keep his balance in the soft mud, he spotted a smiling stranger coming toward him from the river's frontage road. Warily he returned the stranger's wave and reaching the bank took his extended hand. Tall and thin, his uncovered head shaved bald, a blade's scar across one cheek, he matched Taj's description of Felix.

"Ishmael, at long last we meet. I am Felix, a friend of Calaf's."

"And Taj's *frumentarii* boss."

"Ah, he told you about me," Felix said.

"I insisted."

"Of course, you would."

"Why are you here and not Taj?" Ishmael asked.

"I wanted to bring the good news myself." Felix retrieved a folded parchment from the pouch hanging from his neck.

Ishmael studied the message, tracing the arrows surrounding the drawing of the two foxes with his finger. *A forgery.* He lifted his face and remained calm. "Indeed, this is good news."

"I expected more excitement."

"I promise you excitement when Calaf stands before me." Ishmael began to dress. "You will take me to him?"

"That's why I am here—to take you and Timur to Minnagara. I expect Liu's already packed and waiting for us."

"You know Liu?"

"Of course. She works for me."

So Liu is the Roman agent watching me. Ishmael fought to keep his voice steady in spite of the shock of Liu's deception. "Does she journey with us?"

"Yes."

"That is good. Timur has grown fond of her."

"As she has of you both."

Ishmael followed as Felix led the way to the road. "Will I see him soon?"

"Who?"

"Taj."

"No, he does other work for me."

"A good man. You're fortunate to have one so loyal." When Felix did not respond, Ishmael asked, "Is Calaf well?"

"Quite so."

"Yet he does not come for me himself?"

"And risk capture by the Persians?"

"Of course. I forget myself. The son of Timur must be cautious. When do we depart?"

"Immediately."

"A caravan?"

"No. We will move faster in a small party. I have hired men to protect us."

Ishmael followed Felix in silence. As they approached his dwelling's alley, he said, "The hospital—I can't leave without telling them."

"We'll send a messenger."

"But there's the care of my patients."

Felix stopped. "Persians?"

"Yes."

"The enemy?"

"Not to me."

Felix placed a hand on Ishmael's shoulder. "You have been among them too long." When Ishmael tensed and pulled away, Felix said, "Forgive me. Of course, you must make arrangements. I'll accompany you to the hospital."

Felix's men stood outside the dwelling with swords drawn.

"You expect problems?" Ishmael asked.

"It's always wise to be prepared."

As they climbed the stairs, they heard Timur's voice. "At last I return to my throne. They will welcome me with shouts of joy."

Liu called out. "Be silent or the Persians will discover our escape."

Ishmael entered the room first. "She's right, old man."

Timur's voice dropped to a whisper. "Ishmael, after all these years."

Ishmael kissed Timur's head. "Yes, we go home."

When Liu handed him his pack, he touched her cheek. "You've been crying." Her eyes darted to Felix, who leaned against the doorframe.

"Only with joy—finally we leave this dreadful place. Oh, I couldn't find Demetrius's parchments."

"Under my bed?"

"I didn't look there."

Ishmael went into the dark, windowless room he shared with Timur and pulled a small bundle tied with hemp from under his bed.

"Find them?" Felix stood behind him.

"Yes, they're here."

Outside Ishmael led Felix from the hard-packed dirt alley onto the cobbled main road where the market day crowd swallowed them. Merchants hawked wools and leathers outside multi-colored tents and fruits, vegetables, and melons from behind makeshift tables. Buyers pulled carts, mostly empty at this early hour, as boys chased each other among the stalls to shouted rebukes of merchants and buyers alike. When a street brawl erupted ahead of them, Felix took Ishmael's arm. With a scowl Ishmael shook free and pointed Felix toward a side street. When the Roman turned, Ishmael rushed the opposite way, dropping into the darkness of the underground *ghanats*. On hands and knees he crawled to the main artery that crossed the city. There he could stand, relieved that the water rose only to his calves. An occasional duct from the surface cast dim light against the tunnel wall. He found a ledge near a duct and sat. His breathing and heartbeat slowed, the rush of escape giving way to a snare of confusion.

What's happened to Calaf?

Remembering Liu's tears, he recalled the bundle of Demetrius's writings. For a moment, he sat puzzled because Liu knew he kept it under his bed. He pulled the bundle from his pack and found a message under the tied cord.

Felix killed Taj. Trust silversmith.

Ishmael dared not venture from the *ghanats* until darkness hid his movements, so he curled up on the ledge, his head resting on his pack, and stared into the tunnel's dimness.

Taj was dead. An ache ripped through his chest at the loss of a friend. Why would Felix do such a thing? That Liu knew both Taj and the silversmith added to his confusion. Taj had refused invitations to Ishmael's dwelling because the Romans insisted that no one know of their meetings. That is why they met most often in the silversmith's upper room. But if Liu knew the silversmith, would not Felix also? And be lying in wait for him to appear? And why the haste for him to leave Shushtar? The forged message likely meant Calaf did not wait for him in Minnagara. So where was he?

As the light from the overhead duct faded to darkness Ishmael crawled from the *ghanats*, determined to test Liu's trust in the silversmith.

When the silversmith opened the shop door, his eyes scanned the darkness behind Ishmael. "Quick." As Ishmael slipped past him, the silversmith locked the door and said, "Liu and your father—they're upstairs."

As the silversmith turned to lead the way, Ishmael grabbed his arm. "How do you know her?"

"We're lovers."

"And she and Taj?"

"Friends. They worked together at a brothel somewhere in the Kushan Empire."

Ishmael asked, "Minnagara?"

"I think that's it."

"What do you know of me?"

"You're a physician at the hospital."

"Nothing more?"

"No." Irritation filled the silversmith's voice as he shook free of Ishmael grasp. "Come."

They found Liu and Timur huddled in a corner of the upper room. As they entered, Liu uttered a gasp and rushed into Ishmael's arms. "You're safe."

Timur cried out, "Who's there?"

"Shh, old man, it's me," Ishmael eased out of Liu's embrace and knelt beside Timur.

"Assassins," whispered Timur.

Ishmael stroked Timur's cheek. "The danger's still great. Be silent while we plan our escape."

"Shh, yes, escape."

Ishmael rose to face Liu. The silversmith now held her in his arms. "All these years you deceived me."

"Flavus said I was helping you—and Calaf."

"Then help me by telling me where Calaf is," Ishmael pleaded.

"I don't know," Liu said.

"Don't lie to me."

"Trust me, I don't."

Ishmael gave a bitter laugh. "Trust you? You who work for those who keep Calaf and me apart."

"No more. Before my very eyes—Taj stabbed in the chest." She shook with a suppressed sob.

"Stop this." The silversmith stepped between them. "She is not your enemy."

Ishmael backed away and after a few moments asked in a calm voice, "How did you escape?"

"Felix never returned. His men gave up waiting, ransacked our place for anything of value, and left." She reached for Ishmael's arm. "Truly, I don't know where Calaf is, but Taj was searching for you. He was frantic."

"Felix gave me a message from Calaf," Ishmael said. "It said he's in Minnagara, but Calaf didn't write it."

Liu said, "Felix took it from Taj before he killed him. Taj must have known it was forged and wanted to warn you."

Ishmael began to pace the room, finally turning to Liu. "We will go to Minnagara. You and the old man will be safe there, and even if Calaf isn't there, Taj told me your brothel owner was a friend of Flavus. She may be able to help me begin my search for Calaf."

"Felix will surely continue looking for you," the silversmith said.

"Yes, so it's best that Liu and Timur journey separately from me."

The silversmith said, "In the next few days the caravan merchant who sells my wares leaves for India. I'll arrange for them to travel with him."

Ishmael knelt before Timur, who had dozed. He shook him awake. "You will go with Liu to Minnagara, old man."

"Minnagara? I conquered it once—" Timur's voice faded and his head dropped to his chest. "Minnagara," he muttered as he dozed once again.

Downstairs at the shop door Ishmael gave Liu a stiff embrace. "Thank you for your devotion to the old man."

"Please do not hate me," she said.

He gave her a sad smile. "I can't hate you." Then he kissed her forehead.

"Where do you go now?" she asked.

"To find Taj. He deserves better than an unmarked grave in a Persian field."

"The morgue?" the silversmith asked.

Ishmael nodded and disappeared into the night.

Avoiding more direct avenues, Ishmael moved through dark alleys to the city's morgue, located behind the hospital. Even though its thick walls kept the morgue relatively cool, they were no match for Shushtar's heat and humidity. As a result, unclaimed bodies rarely were kept more than a day before cremation. He did not know when Taj had died or if his body had been discovered. But if it had, it would be brought here, which would allow him to make proper funeral arrangements. He knocked on the morgue door several times before it creaked ajar. The attendant rubbed sleep from his eyes.

"We don't receive visitors until—"

"Arash, it's me, Ishmael."

With a grunt of surprise the attendant pulled the heavy door open. He held a torch and behind him the room was dark, the smell of death overwhelming. "Why are you here?"

"I'm looking for a young man, shorter than me, dark skin like mine."

"Arrived midday, knife wound to the chest."

"Can I see him?"

The attendant shook his head. "The priests came soon afterward and took him."

"Someone claimed him?"

Hearing footsteps he spun about. Faraj stepped out of the darkness.

"Seemed the decent thing to do for your friend." Two armed soldiers moved out of the shadows. Faraj took his arm. "It's best you come with me quietly."

"Where?"

"My quarters at the palace."

"Why?"

"You must ask?" Faraj's free hand stroked Ishmael's cheek. "After my gesture of respect for your friend, I expect you want to demonstrate your gratitude."

"And if I don't?"

"Oh, I believe you will." Faraj released Ishmael's arm and motioned to the guards, who searched Ishmael and his pack. "Now, shall we walk together or would you prefer my guards escort you?"

Ishmael moved beside Faraj.

"Very good. It's the first wise decision you will make this night."

Ishmael fought to keep control over the panic that had swept through him with Faraj's arrival. As he walked beside Faraj, his initial distress began to subside, replaced by a surprising calm and heightened vigilance. While rocked by the events of the day, he sensed the confluence of numerous paths, some still unknown. Faraj's connection to Taj leapt front of mind, but more unsettling was the Persian officer's confidence that he somehow controlled Ishmael's destiny. He touched the infant ankle band hanging under his tunic.

Upon their arrival at Faraj's apartment, a slave emerged, bowing deeply. "Clean water in the bath, sire. Wine is refreshed and candles lit."

"Then why do you wait? Go!" As she scurried away, Faraj motioned Ishmael to enter and turned to the guards. "Under no circumstances am I to be disturbed."

After securing the apartment door, he laughed. "Even my regular guards need reminding not to be alarmed by anything they hear."

The apartment was spacious but sparsely furnished, the only sign of luxury a tapestry hanging above a heavy wood table upon which were several rolled parchments and writing tools. The only chair sat before the table. Ishmael stared at the disheveled bed then at an ornately carved wood chest beside it.

Faraj pointed at an anteroom. "Do you wish to bathe first?"

Ishmael shook his head.

"Afterward then." He began removing his uniform, but when Ishmael did not follow his lead, he added, "I'd rather you not resist." Ishmael did not move as Faraj stepped out of his trousers. "You submitted once."

"Before I knew what you are."

Faraj shrugged. "You must know I could have taken you anytime I wanted."

"Why didn't you?"

"Waiting for the right moment. Ah, did you notice this?" He pointed to an angry scar on his thigh. "My latest. Got it at Edessa. Those poor Roman bastards never had a chance." He stepped to a small table near the door and lifted a pitcher. "Wine?"

Ishmael asked, "How did you know Taj?"

Faraj took his wine cup to the bed. He patted the mattress, but Ishmael moved the chair before him and sat, placing his pack on the floor. Faraj laughed. "The soldiers will think I've lost my touch." Ishmael remained silent. "Very well. Taj interested me because you interested him. Nothing more. We never met, never spoke. The silversmith told me of his arrivals and his meetings with you and that woman Liu. He also told me you went to the morgue tonight." Faraj smiled as Ishmael tightened his fists in his lap. "Taj's sudden appearance this morning surprised me. He didn't arrive with the caravan from Peshawar like he usually does. When I heard of his frantic visit to the hospital searching for you, I sent a soldier to your dwelling. He arrived in time to witness Taj's death. We apprehended his murderer just after you escaped him."

"You have Felix?"

"Ah, you react at last." Faraj drained his cup. "What do you know of him?"

"He's a Roman spy. As Taj learned today, he is not to be trusted."

"Any idea why he killed your friend?" Ishmael shook his head. "A Roman spy? Maybe I should delay tomorrow morning's execution for a more thorough interrogation. You could join me. Have you ever witnessed blinding with hot oil?"

Ishmael felt Faraj's eyes bore into him and fought to steady himself. "No."

"But you are familiar with the results, aren't you, Ishmael, son of Timur?"

"What're you talking about?"

Faraj rose from the bed to refill his cup. "Isn't it true you tell everyone the old man's your father?" When Ishmael did not answer, Faraj continued. "Imagine my surprise when I finally saw him and recognized a supposedly dead emperor. Who could have imagined that his son would find and rescue him? And even deliver him to his conqueror's imperial city. Truly unbelievable."

"Where is he?"

"He and the woman escaped. Soon enough they will be found."

"What'll happen to them?"

"That depends on you."

"Who else knows about me?"

"No one—yet. The reign of Tur over the Kushans becomes increasingly loathsome at court. Turandot's circus of princely beheadings has offended too many Persian allies. Soon Shapur's patience will reach its limit. When that happens, the Tur king and his daughter will fall, and I will step forward with you, a legitimate heir to satisfy the Kushan people, but loyal to Persia through the bonds you and I share."

"What bonds?"

"The bonds we forge this night."

"Because you believe me to be the Kushan heir? Forget it. He isn't my father. I was his physician. When I found him in the Khyber wilderness, I couldn't leave him to die."

"It doesn't matter. After people see Timur, they'll believe whatever we tell them."

"You expect me to agree to this?"

"Yes, and most urgently so. Now, you must see what I've found."

Faraj knelt before the ornate chest and removed its top. "My battle trophies." He lifted a split helmet from the chest. "The first man I killed in battle." Next, he retrieved a leather belt tooled with intricate designs. "Beautiful workmanship, don't you think? If you like it, it's yours." He tossed the belt on the bed. "I took this dagger from a dead Kushan at Baktra. The tip is broken but look at the beauty of the blade's engraving." When Ishmael did not reach for it, he cast it beside the belt. "Ah, here it is." Faraj lifted a bronze armband. Ishmael's stomach lurched as Faraj said, "Yours perhaps?"

Ishmael kept his face immobile as he rose from the chair. "I will have some wine now."

Faraj shouted in triumph. "It *is* yours! I knew there was a connection."

"A connection?"

"Between you and that Roman Valens."

"Valens?"

"Too late to play coy with me," Faraj replied. "Come, sit." When Ishmael joined him, he secured the armband around Ishmael's bicep. "My gift to you."

Ishmael wrapped his hand around it, its cool hardness clearing his mind. In a restrained voice he said, "I trust he died well."

"Died? Oh no. He lives." He traced Ishmael's jaw with his fingertip. "After Edessa many wanted him, but I kept him to myself. Otherwise I doubt he would have survived in the hands of soldiers still filled with blood lust. He fought me at first, but soon enough he learned the value of submission."

Ishmael struggled to remain outwardly calm, allowing only the bile that burned his throat to vent to his rage. "Where is he?"

"Here in Shushtar. He builds Caesar's Bridge with the other Roman prisoners. Unfortunately, it's dangerous work and many will die. I could arrange his transfer to a more agreeable position."

"In return for my cooperation?"

"No, no. Think of it as a partnership. You, the future ruler of the Kushans, and I, your most trusted counselor."

"Free him."

Faraj laughed. "Free a prisoner of war?"

"Free him, and I will do whatever you ask."

"I'm afraid you are in no position to bargain."

"But I must. He once saved my life. You are a soldier. You know my obligation. Free him, and I too will be free."

"And loyal only to me?"

"Only to you."

Faraj did not hesitate. "It will be done." He tried to push Ishmael onto his back, but Ishmael resisted.

"First I would see the signed order."

Faraj cursed, and then threw open the apartment door and shouted at the startled guards, "My scribe! Now!" He spun about and pointed at Ishmael. "You will never doubt me again."

Ishmael rose and stroked Faraj's chest with his fingertips. "His release removes all doubt."

Faraj grabbed Ishmael's wrist, twisting it until Ishmael grimaced. Eyes locked, neither blinked until the sound of quick footsteps stopped. The disheveled scribe stood breathless in the open doorway. A rumpled tunic covered his thin body.

Faraj barked, "You have my seal?"

The scribe held up his bag. "Of course, sire." He pulled the chair to the table and prepared to write.

Ishmael reached for the leather belt laying on the bed, at the same time pushing the Kushan dagger under a pillow. "You're right, the belt is beautiful."

"As I said, it's yours."

Ishmael asked, "Valens will have safe passage to leave Persia?" When Faraj nodded, he added. "The northern border so he can return to Rome?"

"As you wish."

While Faraj dictated, Ishmael tossed the belt to the floor, undressed, and sat on the bed. When the scribe finished, Faraj handed the order to him to read.

"Satisfied?"

Ishmael nodded. Faraj motioned to the scribe, who rushed from the room, pulling the door shut behind him. A wide smile filled Faraj's face, and taking the order, he tossed it into the open chest. "At first light, we go together to the bridge site to release him. Both of you must know the debt is paid. But first—"

Faraj threw himself at Ishmael. They wrestled to Faraj's triumphant laughter and Ishmael's quiet exertion. Faraj's greater bulk and strength gave him the advantage, and Ishmael quickly found himself on his back.

Faraj pushed Ishmael's legs up and positioned himself for entry. "At last you are mine."

Ishmael slipped his hand under the pillow and grabbed the handle of the dagger. With a single thrust the blade entered Faraj's side, plunging between his ribs. Faraj screamed in surprise and pain. His grab for the dagger threw him off-balance, allowing Ishmael to shove him onto his wounded side, forcing the blade deeper. He wrapped his legs about Faraj's hips to hold him down, and for the benefit of the guards, raised his voice in cries of passion, matching in volume Faraj's rage-filled thrashing. Face-to-face, Ishmael watched his eyes turn from disbelief to fury to panic. His shouts became gasps, his body stopped jerking, and blood drained from his mouth.

When Faraj grew still, Ishmael did not move until his own breathing and heartbeat slowed. Only then did he release the dagger's hilt and pull his hand free. He stood but had to sit again, his head between his knees, taking deep breaths, until his nausea and dizziness passed. When he looked up, he stared for long moments at the split helmet. Then dragging Faraj's body to the floor, he crossed the dead man's arms over his bloodied torso before placing the trophy of his first kill over his head.

Going to the anteroom he cleaned himself of Faraj's blood then dressed. He removed the dagger from Faraj's side, wiped it clean with bedding, and placed it into his pack along with Calaf's release. He turned to leave but stopped. He went to the table and picked up the two candles. He placed one on either side of Faraj's helmeted head.

Ishmael grabbed his pack, and without a backward glance opened the apartment door and spotted Faraj's guards at the end of the corridor. As he approached, one asked, "He sleeps?"

Ishmael gave a quick nod and began to walk past. A hand grabbed his arm and pulled him about. Ishmael kept his face impassive as the guard looked him up and down. The guard's face erupted in a broad smile, "If he tires of you, let me know."

Ishmael tossed his head toward the other guard. "Only if he's with you."

Their guffaws followed him down the stairway to the palace courtyard.

Calaf awoke to the river's thundering roar before the guards began their shouting. Even in the coolness of the night, he sweated with fever. A week into the march from Edessa such a fever had befallen Servius Flaminius Nepos, and he had succumbed within days. Calaf pushed the thought from his mind. *Not until my hands again are around his throat.* Faraj called this longing a delusion, but it carried great power, keeping him alive with the hope that the Fates would use him.

The prisoners were marched from the camp before sunrise. His work group began to sit around the boulders they would move that day when shouts of 'Valens' rose above the tumult of the river. Calaf's heart raced.

I am his fate—
as he is mine.

Ishmael stood in darkness catching his breath, ears alert to sounds of pursuit, the city wall at his back, the turbulent Karun before him. The morning before he had bathed in a peaceful, slow-moving river. He too was calm, preparing for a day like any other. At sunrise distant black clouds upriver had hugged the horizon, signaling the torrent that now raged before him. He wore a Persian uniform, taken from an unconscious drunken soldier he had stumbled upon in an alley.

For months cartloads of stone for the new bridge had arrived daily from quarries near Bishapur. When the Roman prisoners arrived, the sounds of hammer and chisel reached across Shushtar as they fashioned the rough blocks into the precise shapes demanded by the bridge engineers. Joining many curious townspeople Ishmael stopped to watch them work. At the time he did not know to seek a familiar face among the hundreds slaving in the hot sun. He had wondered if any might know of Calaf and decided to seek a position on the prisoner medical team so he might question some of them. That was then. Now he stood poised for rescue—or death. But if death, he would be at Calaf's side.

A growing commotion rose above the water's roar. Upriver, torches cut through the pre-dawn darkness, casting a glow across water and shore, silhouetting mounted soldiers flanking the line of prisoners. Some moved stiff with purpose, most shuffled, a few staggered held up by their comrades. Guards shouted their impatience at the procession's slow pace. Whips cracked above the din of groans and footfalls.

Ishmael waited until the guards began to dismount then strode toward the officer shouting orders. Spotting Ishmael's approach, he swung about with his hands on his hips.

"I was promised at least twenty more soldiers. You better not be the only one."

Thinking quickly Ishmael replied, "They're on their way, sir." Then handing him the release he added, "My orders are to bring the prisoner Valens to the palace."

"Only you?"

"Two wait at the wall."

The officer did not read the parchment, only traced its seal with a finger. "So Faraj wants him again. Poor bastard." He returned the release and called out, "Bring me Gaius Lucius Valens."

Shouts of 'Valens' passed down the line of prisoners, who were dispersing into smaller groups among the blocks of stone. Remaining outside the torch's light Ishmael waited. Finally a soldier approached leading a prisoner. Ishmael's heartbeat quickened. When last they parted, they were but sixteen years old. Ten years can change a man.

Calaf stepped ahead of the soldier and acknowledged the officer with a nod. "Javid." Barefoot and clad in a torn, knee-length tunic that may at one time been white, his body and face were thin, his black beard and hair long and tangled.

"Captain Faraj calls for you." Calaf showed no reaction. Javid reached into a pouch at his waist. "Fly-agaric?"

"Maybe afterward."

"This soldier will take you." Then turning to Ishmael he said, "The captain will expect him bathed. A clean tunic, too."

Ishmael moved into the light. "Understood, sir."

Only Calaf's sharp intake of breath betrayed surprise. Ishmael took his arm and led him into the darkness. Wordlessly they walked, their pace increasing with each step. They reached the wall as shouting from within the city interrupted the pre-dawn quiet. Ishmael grabbed his pack from the ground. "This way. Quickly."

They got past the city gate before soldiers on foot and horseback thundered through and headed toward the worksite. Calaf stumbled and fell to his knees. Ishmael reached under his arms to help him rise and was shocked by how little he weighed. His body trembled from fever. "The tunnels aren't far."

Struggling to stand, Calaf staggered against Ishmael, clutching his uniform. "No!" he gasped.

Frantic, Ishmael pulled Calaf. "We must hide."

"Faraj." Calaf began to cough and again collapsed, dragging Ishmael down. "Must kill him." Then he went limp and fell unconscious. Lifting him over his shoulder Ishmael rushed along the river's edge.

By first light as the Persian army's manhunt began in earnest, Ishmael carried the semiconscious Calaf through the city's *ghanats*, the only sound Calaf's moans punctuated by the words, "Must kill Faraj."

CHAPTER 42

EARLY THAT MORNING BEFORE DAWN General Zab had stood over the naked body of his dead lover. Although Zab knew that Faraj's end might result from a reckless sexual encounter, he had always hoped he would find death heroically on the battlefield. That is where he belonged, not slain on the floor of his palace apartment. And what sort of monster was this Ishmael that he would decorate his kill with the helmet of a vanquished foe and celebrate his deed with candles about his victim's head? Zab had knelt and lifted the helmet. Faraj's eyes were open, his mouth agape, the agony of his death fixed as stone. Zab had leaned toward his lover's ear and whispered, "You will be avenged, no torture spared."

Now he stood before the prison cell of a Roman, whom Faraj had arrested for killing a Kushan youth. Faraj had ordered the Roman's execution at dawn, but when the general heard that the Roman had been seen with Ishmael, he delayed the order. The cell door scraped against the floor as the dungeon guard pushed it open. In the sudden torchlight, the prisoner moved into a defensive crouch.

Zab ordered, "At ease. I come to talk."

The prisoner straightened and spoke in a firm, steady voice. "The boy deserved to die."

The general studied the Roman a moment. *A man used to command.* "Deserved?"

"He betrayed me to claim the Roman bounty for himself."

"A bounty for Ishmael? And who is he that the Romans want him?" Zab asked.

"Heir to the Kushan throne—the son of Timur."

"The son of Timur died at Rajanpur."

"A deception," Felix said. "The true son of Timur is Ishmael."

"You expect me to believe this?" Zab asked.

"What is important is that the Romans believe it."

"A desperate man will say anything."

"But if I speak the truth?"

"Even if you do, you allowed this Ishmael to escape."

"He will not escape a second time."

"Rather difficult when you are dead."

"Why kill me if I can deliver Ishmael to you?" Felix asked.

"My best men search for the killer."

"He has killed?"

"Yes, he murdered the officer who condemned you."

"Your men do not know Ishmael as I do," Felix insisted. "I found him once. I will again."

Zab studied Felix for several long moments before he said, "I understand this Ishmael helped a Roman prisoner called Valens escape. Do you know why?" Felix shook his head.

As Zab turned to leave, Felix said, "I can help you."

"Perhaps."

After the dungeon guard pulled shut the cell door, Zab ordered, "Proceed with the execution."

As the general emerged from the prison, a Persian soldier approached and saluted. "Reporting as ordered, sir." Given Faraj's appetite in men, his dark skin was not a surprise, but he was shorter than Zab expected. Clearly the loose-fitting Persian uniform hid his other attributes.

"Your name, soldier?"

"Shahed, sir."

"Walk with me." After a few moments of silence, Zab asked, "When did you become Captain Faraj's aide?"

"At Edessa, sir."

"The captain chose his men for their resourcefulness—and discretion."

"I trust I didn't disappoint him, sir."

"Not if you remained his aide for more than a week. He could be quite demanding." The soldier's face flushed, but he held Zab's gaze. "Did you know a Roman prisoner called Gaius Antonius Valens?"

"I did, sir."

"Well enough to recognize him again?"

"Yes, sir."

"Then I have an assignment for you. The captain's murderer helped Valens escape. I'm certain they fled together. Find Valens, and you'll find the killer. You will bring this Ishmael to me."

"Alive, sir?"

"Dead if you must, but deliver him alive and you'll find me more than generous."

"What about Valens?"

"If he interferes, kill him. If not, do whatever you want with him. He's unimportant to me." Zab reached into a leather pouch hanging from his belt. "Do you recognize this?" The silver signet ring was embossed with a lion's head.

"Captain Faraj wore it."

"It is my personal seal, and you will wear it now. With it you will secure whatever you require for the search. Keep your squad small to attract less attention. But once you've captured Ishmael, show the ring to the local garrison commander. He'll give you the troops you need to guard him for the return to Shushtar. You will also escort someone who's helped me in the past and is familiar with the Kushans, especially with one in the Peshawar court. I believe you'll find him most useful. Ah, here he approaches."

A richly dressed, bearded merchant strode across the courtyard at a quick pace, belying his imposing girth. He embraced the general without formality. "Zab, I am distressed at the news of your friend. And, of course, anything you need—anything."

"Thank you, my friend," Zab said. "In fact, I need you to go to Peshawar."

"Peshawar? Do you expect Aric is involved?"

"Seems unlikely but even if he's not, the killer may go to him for help. Also, there's a rumor that this Ishmael is the true son of the deposed Kushan emperor. Whether he is or not, he could foment rebellion, something our Peshawar ruler can little afford." Zab nodded toward the soldier. "This is Shahed. He will lead the escort." Shahed gave a quick stiff bow—Zab smiled—most likely to avoid an exuberant embrace. "Shahed, meet The Bear. You know Valens, he knows the Kushans. I expect you'll make a good team."

"You talk of Peshawar, sir," Shahed said. "Not north with the other searchers?"

"I've become certain the safe passage letter is a ruse. The fugitives are Kushan. Why would they escape to Roman territory? More likely they flee toward Peshawar and beyond. Any questions?"

"No, sir."

"And get yourself a new uniform, *Captain* Shahed."

"Yes, sir." With a wide smile and smart salute Shahed turned on his heel and departed to The Bear's hearty laugh.

Broken-tip dagger poised, Ishmael eased the heavy door ajar. The fire temple's pilgrim master, and his good friend, raised an oil lamp to his face and Ishmael pulled the door open.

"More water. Food and clothing, too," Aram said as he slipped past Ishmael into the tiny room and placed a jug and bundle on the stone floor. "How is he?"

Ishmael knelt on the mat where Calaf lay curled up on his side, moaning one moment, babbling the next. "Still delirious with fever. If it doesn't break soon—" Unable to finish he picked up the jug and poured water into a basin.

Aram loosened his cloak, letting it fall. "I'll help bathe him."

Calaf stiffened when they touched him, his eyes open wide but unfocused.

"They beat him badly," Aram said as they turned him onto his back. "No open wounds though."

Calaf's lips moved silently as Ishmael laid a wet cloth over his forehead and leaned toward his ear. "You will live," he whispered.

"Do you think he hears you?"

"As long as he knows I'm here, the words do not matter."

Suddenly agitated, Calaf began to writhe. "Nothing I did—nothing."

Calaf sees only Faraj's face, hears only his laugh, smells only his breath stale with wine. He tries to strike him but his arms do not move. He tries to run but his legs are rooted to the ground.

Nothing you did mattered.
Not surviving Edessa,
not debasing yourself to save your cohort,
not protecting Ishmael.

A voice. "Shh, you're not where you think you are." A touch. Soft. "I'm here with you."

Ishmael?

He shouts, "Ishmael!" But no sound reaches past his lips. Again, "Ishmael!" But he has no voice. Only Faraj's laugh fills his ears.

The foxes, one white, one gold, sit back-to-back surveying an open field from its highest point. Nearby a lion stalks an unsuspecting hare. A tiger circles a tree, its eyes never leaving a pair of yellow-bodied, blue-winged parrots. In the distance a leopard closes in on a fleeing antelope, while monkeys scramble to escape the claws of a dragon, its iridescent scales shimmering in the bright sun. An eagle, its massive wings casting a growing shadow over the foxes, swoops down from the sky. The gold fox leaps above his white brother.

At Calaf's cry Ishmael bolts upright.

Calaf is drenched in sweat. The fever has broken.

Calaf fell back asleep, awaking only once with arms flailing. Ishmael caught his wrists. "Calaf, it's me."

Calaf struggled a few moments more, then relaxed, allowing Ishmael to lift him into his arms. He whispered, "Faraj."

Ishmael kissed his forehead. "You're safe."

Calaf buried his face in Ishmael's shoulder. Ishmael rocked him, his tears joining his friend's. Soon enough, after his delirium had passed, he would tell Calaf that Faraj is dead. In the meantime, he cursed the gods for allowing Faraj but one death before departing life. A knife between his ribs, a moment of panic and pain, how could they offset the evil he brought upon Calaf and countless others? If the gods were just, Faraj now faced an underworld of unremitting agony and terror. But what if Demetrius and his Greek philosopher were right, that there is no afterlife? Then he must be satisfied with Faraj's face in his final moments, filled with blind rage at meeting his end not in glory on a field of battle but helpless and screaming on a blood-soaked bed.

Ishmael bathed the dried sweat from Calaf's body, relief loosening his tongue as Calaf moved in and out of consciousness. "You had me worried, but I asked myself, how could you come so far and not live? Impossible, right? Anyway, my mentor at the hospital says I'm the best he's trained, so there's no way you'd embarrass me by dying."

Calaf's eyes fluttered, then he mouthed the word *thirsty* with breath but no sound. Ishmael brought the cloth to his mouth, allowing a trickle of water to fall on his parched lips. Calaf sucked on the cloth for a few moments then turned on his side and grew still. Ishmael ran his fingers through Calaf's hair and sang.

Oh soul, torn by unbearable concerns,
stand up, defend yourself from your enemies,
outsmart them moving cautiously
through their ambushes.

"I learned it for Demetrius but never had the chance to sing it for him. But I've sung it for you many, many times. In quiet moments before sunrise while bathing in the river or after rereading your letters from Rome. I imagined you hearing it on a passing breeze. Silly, I know, but Aphrodite would do that for us, wouldn't she?" Without a pause, again he sang.

Immortal Aphrodite, beautiful-throned,
wiles-weaving child of Zeus, I beg you, Queen,
do not torment my heart with sorrow and pain
but come and help me again as you did before
when having heard my pleadings from far away
you left your father's golden palace
and yoked to your shining chariot swift, lovely sparrows
that brought you over the dark earth,
moving their thick-feathered wings
through the sky's bright ether.
Quickly they arrived; and then you, Goddess,
with a smile on your unaging face you asked me
what is wrong with me this time
and why I am calling you again
and what my wild heart wishes again.

"And I answered her, *My wild heart wishes you bring Calaf to me*, and she smiled upon my plea."

Calaf mumbled something. Ishmael leaned close.

"Camel."

Ishmael chuckled. "You'd ask Aphrodite for a camel?"

"I—I'm a camel—"

"Aha," Ishmael laughed then broke into the song.

One day the ostrich was asked to carry a load.
In reply it said, "I'm a bird."
When asked to fly,
The ostrich said, "I'm a camel."

Tears filled Calaf's eyes as he squeezed Ishmael's hand.

Ishmael awoke with Calaf sitting up, his back against the wall. When Ishmael reached over to touch his leg, Calaf smiled. "Not how I imagined our reunion." He ruffled Ishmael's hair then pulled him into his arms. Ishmael buried his face in his neck. Long moments passed in silence before Calaf eased back. "Where are we?"

"The city's fire temple. We're safe for the moment, but the pilgrim master takes a great risk hiding us. As soon as you're strong enough, we must leave."

Calaf reached for the gold circle hanging from Ishmael's neck. "All these years you kept it safe—but I—I lost—"

"I know," Ishmael interrupted and opened his pack. Calaf's eyes widened as Ishmael placed the armband around his bicep.

"But Faraj took it from me."

"He gave it to me before I killed him."

Ishmael expected relief, if not joy, at this news, but instead Calaf's body stiffened. "He's dead?"

When Ishmael touched his shoulder, he flinched. "Calaf, he can't hurt you anymore."

"Am I now a child you must protect?"

"I don't understand."

"He was mine to kill. Mine!"

Calaf turned away onto his side. Neither moved nor spoke. A tap sounded at the door, and the pilgrim master slipped into the room with a flask of wine and a tray of bread, dates and nuts.

When Aram nodded toward Calaf, Ishmael said, "Resting. What news?"

"The Roman has been executed, and General Zab's soldiers continue to tear the city apart looking for you. I've never seen anything like it."

"No one suspects we're here?"

"No one."

"Remember, even the slightest suspicion and we must leave."

After Aram departed, Ishmael said, "You must eat." Breaking the bread and handing some to Calaf, he ventured, "All that matters is that Faraj is dead."

"It kept me alive, the hope he'd die with my hands around his neck."

"But he died a horrible death knowing I would rescue you."

"How horrible?"

"A dagger between the ribs and squealing like a slaughtered pig."

Calaf responded with a slight smile. As they began to eat, he asked, "What Roman?"

"Felix—executed for murdering Taj."

"Taj is dead?"

"I believe he defied Felix by trying to warn me about this." Ishmael rummaged through his pack then handed Calaf the forged message. "Felix planned to take me and your father to Minnagara."

"Timur's alive?"

"Maybe I should start from the beginning."

"Maybe you should."

Calaf did not interrupt as Ishmael sat before him, detailing his life since they had parted ten years earlier at Peshawar. Ten years since they had laid together as lovers on the animal carpet of their boyhood and ten years since Calaf had been sent by General Nozar to quell an uprising at Minnagara and to pursue the traitorous Sharina. Only once did Ishmael hesitate, his voice breaking up as tears glistened his eyes. He stood and faced the wall for long moments before finally turning.

"At the prisoner camp at Rajanpur, Barzin told me you had died. I remember little after that until I ended up back in Peshawar."

Calaf said, "Taj spread the story that I had died, just as he told me you had died in the palace fire. But continue."

Ishmael knelt once again and recounted finding Timur left to die in the Khyber wilderness, his time in Shushtar with Timur and Liu, Taj's appearances with Calaf's messages, and Taj's death. Then he stared into his lap at his tightened fists and recounted the killing of Faraj.

When Ishmael stopped talking, sudden terror ripped through Calaf. He squeezed his eyes shut to blot out the specter of the smiling Faraj. Searing pain tore through his body. He couldn't breathe. With a cry Calaf lunged forward, his fists striking flesh. Unseen hands struggled to contain his blows. Only when he heard Ishmael's voice, distant at first but drawing closer, did he begin to calm. The hands released his wrists then arms wrapped around him.

"Ishmael?"

"I'm here."

"Faraj, he was—" Calaf muttered through quick, ragged breaths.

Ishmael stroked his head. "A vision, nothing more."

"So real—so very real."

Calaf steadily regained his strength as his appetite improved. The citywide manhunt lasted a week, but Ishmael and Calaf remained safe in the fire temple. As the pilgrim master expected, Zab did not wish to offend the head priest, so only ordered a perfunctory search of the premises.

One evening the pilgrim master reported that the search had moved out of the city and toward the north. Ishmael said, "Faraj's scribe will have reported that the release gave Calaf safe passage to the northern border with Rome."

"So we will head east to Peshawar?" Calaf asked.

Ishmael nodded.

Before dawn the next morning, Calaf and Ishmael reentered the *ghanats* and emerged a short distance downriver from the city.

Ishmael paused. "This is where I often bathed before dawn. I never felt closer to you than here."

"It's beautiful. Shall we?"

For a moment Ishmael considered it, but a sudden and noisy flight of water fowl out of the reeds deterred him. "We can't risk it."

First light found them on a path that hugged the Karun River's edge, out of sight of the wide road Shapur built to move his armies from the border with Armenia and Syria in the north to the Persian Sea in the south. At mid-morning they turned into a field of sugar cane bordering the river and headed toward the voices of laborers and the sounds of harvesting.

"Do you know this farm?" Calaf asked.

Before Ishmael could answer a young girl hurtled out of the stalks roaring and threw herself into Ishmael's stomach, sending both of them tumbling to the ground.

Ishmael cried out, "Beware Alya the ferocious lion!" He grabbed the girl's sides. "What? She's not ticklish!"

Calaf laughed. "Lions aren't ticklish!"

"They used to be. Save me!"

Calaf screeched and lifted the girl, holding her at arm's length to avoid flailing arms and legs. "Great eagle demon to the rescue."

With a growl the girl bared her teeth. With a cry of exaggerated fear Calaf released his hold. The girl dropped into a crouch, one hand pawing the air. "Is he friend?"

"Yes, he is friend," Ishmael answered.

The girl roared again then disappeared into the stalks.

Ishmael nudged Calaf with his elbow. "Great eagle demon?"

"Saved you from a most gruesome end, didn't it?"

Laughing they set off after the girl. Moments later the farmer blocked their path, motioning them to the ground. The girl crawled up behind him. "My laborers must not see you. Soldiers came looking for you."

"When?"

"Two days ago."

"Are they still nearby?"

The farmer answered with a shrug.

"Then we must keep moving," Calaf said.

"Is this the friend you spoke of?" Ishmael nodded, and the farmer gave Ishmael's knee a squeeze. "Listen—a caravan passes in a day or so. There's a merchant who buys my sugar cane to sell in Peshawar. He hates the Persians. He'll help you."

"We can't stay," Calaf said. "We put your family in danger."

The farmer dismissed Calaf's concern with a wave of his hand. "But for your friend I'd have no family." Then to Ishmael, "Remember the shack in the woods bordering my land?" Ishmael nodded. "Go there 'til Alya comes for you. Now quickly."

As they pushed through the cane stalks, Calaf asked, "What did he mean, he'd have no family?"

"Alya's mother died in childbirth. During last year's plague Alya was near death. I never left her bedside. She lived. Come, we must hurry."

The shack was no more than a lean-to covering a deep ditch. Ishmael examined the roof. "The region was once plagued with war. This was a refuge when the fighting drew close. The girl plays here now—says she saw a family of foxes using it last year."

Calaf came up behind Ishmael, wrapped his arms around him, and whispered, "Surely not foxes."

"So she said."

Calaf turned him around. Ishmael moved to speak, but Calaf covered his mouth with his hand. "I never knew when the pilgrim master would show up." He kissed his lips.

"I didn't know whether you—"

"I do."

Ishmael opened his eyes to light filtering through the lean-to's roof of branches. He was alone. Knowing what Faraj did to Calaf, Ishmael had resigned himself to love without sex, so was surprised when Calaf pulled off their tunics and drew him to the ground. Savoring the closeness he craved, Calaf's impotence did not bother him, but Calaf cursed, dressed, and crawled from the shelter. Ishmael fought the urge to follow, instead closing his eyes to a deep ache filling his chest. Memories swept through him of the brothel at Srinagar when he was forced to accept that Calaf would not love him as he desired. From that time forward Demetrius and his lover Torak often occupied Ishmael's mind, wondering if he, like Demetrius, could learn to share the man he loved with another. That Calaf would have women was certain, maybe even a woman he loved deeply. *Would there be a place for him in Calaf's heart then?*

When he opened his eyes again, Alya stared at him from the shack's opening. He smiled, and she withdrew. Pulling on his tunic he emerged to find Alya kneeling nearby. Without looking up she pointed at a bundle at her side.

"Brought food."

Ishmael sat and lifted her chin. Her eyes were red from crying. He stroked her hair.

"What's wrong, little one?"

"I hate your friend."

"Why?"

"Father says you go away with him—and I won't see you again—ever."

"Come here." Alya climbed into his lap and laid her head against his chest. "It's true I must leave."

"Take me."

"But your father needs you."

She wrapped her arms around him and squeezed. "But you're 'posed to marry me."

"I am?"

Alya nodded into his chest.

"When that day comes, you'll want a boy your age."

"No, I won't."

"You won't?"

"No!" Alya exclaimed.

"Then when you're old enough, we will decide."

"Promise?"

"Promise."

She kissed his cheek. At that moment Calaf returned. Alya jumped from Ishmael's lap to face him. "Don't let anything happen to him."

Hands on his hips, Calaf thrust his chest out. "Great eagle demon will protect him."

She shoved him backwards. "No, that's play."

Calaf dropped into a crouch and stared into Alya's eyes. "With my life I will protect him."

She held his gaze for several moments then smiled, and waving at Ishmael, she ran from the clearing.

Calaf dropped beside Ishmael. "What was that all about?"

"It seems I am to be married."

Calaf chuckled as Ishmael opened the bundle and handed him a wine skin. They began to eat. Ishmael said nothing, fighting the urge to ask if Calaf was all right.

Calaf broke the silence. "Actually, I am married."

Ishmael's stomach lurched. Not trusting his voice, he waited.

"The *frumentarii* arranged it. They said we must forge an alliance between Rome and the Kushans. A senator's daughter. She's in Rome with the twins."

"You have children?"

"A boy and a girl—must be two now. Septimius and Olivia. I wanted to name the boy after you, but she wouldn't have it."

"Do you love her?"

The moment the words were out of his mouth Ishmael wanted to pull them back, but Calaf's reaction was an immediate burst of laughter.

"Let's just say I'd rather be married to Sharina."

"That bad?"

Calaf turned serious. "To her I was beneath her, a barbarian to be tamed. That excited her at first, but then I resisted her attempts to mold me into her vision of a dutiful Roman husband. Within months it turned awful for both of us. Our fights became an embarrassment to the senator and his family, much to the chagrin of my *frumentarii* handler, whose solution was to keep me out of Rome as much as possible with my Praetorian Guard cohort on the Emperor's many military campaigns. But as far as Rome is concerned I died at Edessa. That makes her the widow of a hero lost defending the Empire. Her father is certain to parlay that into an even better marriage for her."

"But your children?"

Calaf was silent for several long moments. "There isn't a day that I don't think about them. But they're better off in Rome with their mother. Once I sit upon the Kushan throne, no one will keep them from me. In fact, I will send you to Rome as my emissary to bring them to me," a broad grin spread across his face, "without her, of course."

"Of course," Ishmael replied with a forced smile at the jest, resisting the temptation to ask if Calaf found his wife exciting at first, deciding he would rather not know. It was bad enough that thoughts of Calaf sharing the intimacy of marriage with this woman would now occupy his thoughts. What if she had not been like Sharina? What if he had loved her? Sudden pangs of jealousy consumed him, their intensity a surprise, forcing him to wonder how he could ever control, much less live with such feelings.

CHAPTER 43

FOUR WEEKS HAD PASSED SINCE they left Shushtar for Peshawar. The previous week sandstorms had slowed the caravan, forcing it to remain in an overcrowded caravanserai for several days, but the merchant who employed and protected them was confident they would make up the lost time, arriving in Peshawar within another five weeks.

Ishmael handed Calaf the reins of the sugar cane laden wagon and stretched before pulling out a cloth to wipe the sweat and dust from his face. Ishmael offered the cloth, but Calaf shook his head. When he reached for the reins, Calaf blocked him with a turned shoulder.

They rode in silence until Ishmael said, "You haven't spoken all morning."

"Nothing to talk about," Calaf snapped.

The previous night's nightmare had been the first in more than a week and one of the most intense. Calaf had consistently refused to talk about them, becoming almost violent the one time Ishmael pressed.

Ishmael placed his hand on Calaf's knee. "I only want to help."

"I know you do."

"You once told me everything."

"We were boys then," Calaf said. "It's different now."

"It doesn't have to be."

"But it is."

A stab of longing flowed through Ishmael. For ten years he had nurtured a memory of the man he loved only to discover that their time apart had changed him into someone he no longer truly knew. It was as if the Calaf with whom he had grown up was now hidden in a chest with a massive iron lock and no key.

Calaf and Ishmael sat alone in a quiet alcove surrounded by stored merchandise rather than in the warren of communal sleeping cells. It was rare that they had such privacy, but after hearing that Persian soldiers had searched the caravanserai the week before, the merchant had insisted they sleep with the cargo, saying, "It'll be easier for you to escape should they return." That day the caravan at last had entered the mountainous terrain whose passes would lead them to Baktra. Only the Khyber Pass would then remain before they finally reached Peshawar. Ishmael climbed to his feet and paced the confined space.

"You're restless tonight," Calaf said.

Ishmael was not sure why he had hesitated to reveal that Timur told him he was the son of a powerful raja not a lowly royal scribe. How Calaf might react filled him with anxiety. Might his being a prince change how Calaf looked at him? But knowing he must and taking a deep breath he finally blurted out, "Aric's not my father." He felt Calaf's eyes, probing and uncertain, bore into his. When Calaf remained silent, he asked, "Did you hear what I—?"

"How did you find out?"

"You know about this? That my father was the Srinagaran raja that Sharina was forced to marry?"

Calaf hesitated again, then looked away before answering, "Yes."

"Why didn't you tell me?"

"I learned it after we parted at Peshawar. Who told you?"

"Your father." Ishmael sat once again. "Aric taunted him with it before the Persians blinded him. Timur said if he had known Sharina was pregnant with me, he would have killed her, so they saved my life, too."

"They?"

"Demetrius and Aric. Your father even suspects the queen was involved."

A smile filled Calaf's face. "Imagine, you the son of a raja."

"Your father even decided I must avenge him and take back his throne."

Calaf's smile disappeared, reigniting Ishmael's unease. "We thought you were dead, but I told Timur that any hope he had of restoration died with you. I'm a physician, not an ruler."

"You didn't consider it?"

"Why would I? That was your destiny."

"And yours?"

"To stand at your side."

"Nothing more?"

"Listen to yourself. It's me, Ishmael. You have no cause to doubt my loyalty."

Calaf did not respond for several moments. "Of course." Then slowly his smile returned. "Srinagar."

"What about it?"

"That's where we shall go. It'll take time, years likely, but can you think of a better place than Baldev's home, your father's home, for the dawn of a renewed Kushan Empire? And I will be beholden to no one, not to Timur, not to Sharina, not to the Romans, to no one but myself. Yes, Srinagar. An easily fortified stronghold in the mountains, access to Ganges River caravan route, fierce warriors, and you, Baldev's son, my general. It's perfect."

Ishmael laughed. "Your general?"

"Of course, just as Nozar was to my father."

Ishmael shook his head. "I'm no leader of men. Rather, I will be your Demetrius."

"My Demetrius? What help can you give me as a physician? You must be Hephaistion to my Alexander, remember? He won great battles at Alexander's side. That too is your destiny."

"Have I no choice?"

With a wide grin, Calaf answered, "Why would you choose anything else?" He pushed back the sleeve of his tunic to reveal Ishmael's armband. "Anyway, you're battle-tested. Your men will follow you."

Ishmael lowered his eyes. *Headstrong as ever.*

Calaf plunged on. "Don't worry. You'll be a great general. I'll teach you all I know." His voice filled with excitement as he began recounting the strategies and logistics he had discussed with Flavus and had observed while in the Roman army.

As it always did when they were boys, Calaf's enthusiasm overcame Ishmael's resistance. Ishmael would do whatever he must to help Calaf reclaim his birthright. If Calaf needed him to be a general, a general he would become.

Calaf could not sleep. Ever since Flavus stopped him from strangling Sharina and he learned she was his true mother, he had agonized over what he would do if faced with telling Ishmael who they really were. And now that the moment had come, he was startled at how easy it was to lie to the one person he truly loved, aligning himself with Sharina's vengeance—*Ishmael is the son of the monster who butchered our family*—and Flavus's conspiracy—*Ishmael becomes your rival if he knows the truth.*

But how often had he heard Ishmael say that he was relieved that it was Calaf who would become emperor, not him? And whenever Demetrius told them the stories about Alexander, it was the friend Hephaistion that Ishmael wanted to be, not the king Alexander. Think of the pressure Ishmael would feel to fulfill a son's obligation to avenge the wrongs his father had suffered. Taking on the responsibilities of Timur's son was a burden Calaf had trained for and was prepared to assume. Ishmael need not take them on.

So not telling him would be a kindness. The truth could only ruin Ishmael's life.

PART 6

Rada Brothers

261 CE

CHAPTER 44

Baktra

After it was destroyed during the Persian siege of Baktra twelve years earlier, the caravanserai had been rebuilt larger and grander than any other between Shushtar and the Khyber Pass. Set against a red earth cliff several times the height of the building's two-story wall, its courtyard was open to the sky. The single entry portal was tall and wide enough to allow heavily laden wagons and beasts easy passage after crossing a four-arch stone bridge spanning the river that paralleled the road to Baktra, a day's journey away. The cacophony of hundreds of camels, horses and mules filled the courtyard. Chambers for merchants and their servants and merchandise lined the interior walls, along with shops to purchase supplies, a tavern for food and drink, and an elaborate bath of marble and mosaic that rivaled any city's.

As became their custom since joining the caravan two months earlier, arrival at a caravanserai found Ishmael unloading goods under the watchful eye of the sugar cane farmer's merchant, while Calaf scouted the building for any signs they were being pursued. As Calaf rejoined the merchant's company for the evening meal, he overheard someone say *Turandot.*

"That's a name I haven't heard in a long while," Calaf said as he settled beside Ishmael and reached for a flask of wine. With a laugh he added, "Is she still beheading her suitors?"

"In fact, we've just heard that a new fool has struck her gong and awaits her test," the merchant said. "That's why the caravanserai is so crowded. Everyone is heading to Peshawar for the spectacle."

"She'll really marry whoever answers her three riddles?" asked one of the merchant's crew.

"Only if he's a true prince," answered another. "She'll skin alive any commoner who would dare challenge her."

"I heard she has a lover," said a third.

"Her eunuch scribe," the merchant said. Groans of disgust swept through the company. "At least, that's the rumor. But I understand they're never seen apart."

Later, as Ishmael crawled beside Calaf for the night, Calaf whispered, "Did you know I was to marry Turandot?"

"I heard but didn't believe it."

"It was after Demetrius died. Our marriage was supposed to seal a Kushan-Tur alliance. Timur decided that together we stood a better chance against the Persians. But Turandot's father broke the treaty and sided with the Persians against us. The reward for his betrayal was the Kushan throne."

"You must not have met her." When Calaf gave him a quizzical look, he added with a chuckle, "Still have your head."

"Timur's astrologer assured us that my head would remain safely on my shoulders."

"And you believed that?"

"I had a choice?"

"I guess not," Ishmael answered and kissed Calaf's cheek. "I'm just glad you never had to face her."

The next morning Calaf was standing outside a supply shop when two merchants emerged in conversation.

"Persian soldiers search for a Kushan. Seems he killed an important Persian officer. There's a reward for anyone who helps them find him."

"Look around you. Kushans everywhere. Not like this fugitive is going to stand out. Forget it."

When they moved away, Calaf searched the caravanserai's courtyard and surrounding chambers. After finding a tavern girl who said she served a squad of Persian soldiers several nights earlier, he did not need to convince

Ishmael to leave the caravan to continue their journey over the Khyber Pass along the less traveled trails of herders and hunters.

Khyber Pass

They reached the highest ridge of the Khyber wilderness at midday and found an outcropping of boulders that provided shade. Unpacking a light meal of nuts and dried fruit, they ate in silence watching a lone eagle circling the rugged landscape, occasionally swooping toward the ground.

"Their patience amazes me," Ishmael said.

Calaf grinned, "More like you than me." Then he shouted as the great bird finally succeeded in its hunt, capturing a squirming hare in its talons. It released it from a height then recovered its now dead prey and carried it to a nearby peak to feed.

As they prepared to resume their trek, Ishmael said, "After the Persians took Baktra, they spent the winter on this ridge." Then pointing at the terrain below, he continued, "See where the caravan road disappears? Our army was camped near there." He paused a moment. "Do you remember Torak?"

"Demetrius's friend."

Ishmael nodded. "I had a friend like Torak. He was an Arachosian soldier. The Persians ambushed his patrol near here. I cared for him before he died."

"I'm sorry," Calaf said. "Did you love him?"

"I've only loved one man." Ishmael placed his hand on Calaf's cheek.

"What about Taj?" Calaf saw surprise sweep across Ishmael's face.

"What about him?"

"He slept with men."

"But not with me," Ishmael said. "He was a good friend, nothing more."

"I thought he was my friend—until I discovered he'd betrayed me."

Ishmael rested a hand on Calaf's shoulder. "But he died trying to help us."

"No, Taj betrayed us—betrayed us when he lied to me, telling me you burned alive when the Persians set fire to the palace. He comforted me in my grief all the while knowing you lived. If I had known the truth, Flavus could not have held me. No one could have stopped me from searching until I found you. But I never had the chance—because of him."

His eyes stinging, Calaf rushed from the shade of the outcropping. He sat on a boulder and stared out over the desolation of the Khyber, unable to calm the riot of memories and emotions sweeping through him. Ishmael emerged and joined him. Long moments passed, the only movement a hot breeze, the only sound buzzing insects.

Finally Ishmael spoke. "You loved him."

"He used me."

"But I never will."

"I know. It's not in you to use anyone."

Calaf looked into Ishmael's eyes, their faithfulness challenging him. For a moment he hated Ishmael, hated his love and devotion, hated that he was not like other men in their eagerness to use him to achieve their own ends. But that moment quickly passed, replaced by guilt. Calaf had already given up arguing with himself that it was a kindness to keep silent, that he was merely protecting Ishmael from the burden of being Timur's son. He no longer could deny that Ishmael deserved to know the truth. But Calaf had decided to live with the guilt of silence. While not a descendant of Kushan emperors, he was still of royal birth—a raja's royal blood flows through his veins. Raised to be Timur's heir, why could he not claim what had been promised him? He had surmounted all the obstacles the Fates had placed in his path: used by Sharina to exact vengeance, by Flavus, Felix and their Roman cohorts to achieve their designs for power, by the Persians to display their supremacy over Rome, by Faraj to satisfy his debased desires. Even if it was not his by blood, he had earned the right to Timur's throne.

But all that aside, could he truly forget that Ishmael had denied him vengeance? Calaf had vowed to destroy Faraj—for his men, for his degradation, and most of all to obliterate Faraj's taunt: *Nothing you did mattered.* But Ishmael had taken this from him. Then, adding to his disgrace, he needed Ishmael to rescue him. Ishmael had proven himself the stronger, the more courageous, the more relentless, the more determined, the more resourceful. The blood of Timur and his ancestors revealed itself in him. Ishmael was no pretender. Why should Calaf risk Ishmael's stepping between him and what was rightfully his?

Calaf patted Ishmael's knee. "Let's go." He pulled on his pack and led their descent of the ridge along a barely discernible trail.

Taking refuge on a boulder strewn hilltop, they watched a Persian army convoy moving west along the Khyber Pass road.

"Many happy soldiers down there," Ishmael said. "A year garrisoning in Peshawar is not a favorite posting."

"Peshawar isn't that bad."

"But it's not Shushtar."

Calaf gave Ishmael a mock look of horror. "You've not turned Persian on me, have you?"

"No more than you've turned Roman."

"Never." Calaf's grin shifted to a scowl.

"What?"

Calaf pointed toward the road. "A wheel just broke on that supply wagon. We've got to find another way around them, or we'll be spending the night here."

"If we cross to the next hill, I recall a flood plain on the other side. It'll speed our way around them."

"You *recall* a flood plain? I'm impressed."

"It's a place I'll never forget."

Before Calaf could ask him why, Ishmael moved away among the boulders. Keeping low to the ground, he led the way down into a narrow box canyon and up onto the next hill. Now out of sight of the Persians, they stood and gazed out over a wide flood plain, the only movement a meandering stream glistening in the sunlight.

Calaf slapped Ishmael's shoulder. "Just as you said. So what's so important about this place?"

"It's where they dumped your father to die after they blinded him."

"So this is where you rescued him."

"Yes, it was here." Ishmael searched the plain for the spot but, of course, many years of rushing water and changed vegetation had altered the scene. "I still can't believe I did it—after everything he did to us—to Demetrius—" To stop the tears that always stung his eyes at the memory, he rushed to descend the steep incline. The loose rock slipped from beneath his feet and unable to slow his plunge, he fell to his knees with a cry and tumbled forward down the slope.

"Ishmael!"

The vision erupts with an intensity that brings Calaf to his knees. He is no longer standing above the Khyber flood plain. He stands in the cool, mist-shrouded Srinagaran canyon watching Ishmael approach the fox den. Suddenly Ishmael is falling into the stream's raging torrent. Calaf breaks free of the arms restraining him and plunges into the icy water after him.

Pain tears through his calf as he limps into a circle of soldiers.

"I saved him, Father."

The blow to his head sends him to his knees. Reeling in pain and surprise he looks up into Demetrius's eyes, which beg him to remain still. But he stands.

His enraged father flings his wine cup across a table covered in parchments and shouts, "Nothing—do you understand—nothing—no one—neither friend nor servant—is more important than my empire."

When he turns to watch his father rush away, Ishmael stands before him, his tunic soaked in Demetrius's blood. Ishmael pulls him into his arms and whispers, "I love you," then plunges down the rocky slope toward the desert flood plain.

"Ishmael!"

Ishmael landed face-down at the bottom of the slope. After a moment catching his breath, he rose onto his hands and knees, coughing. When Calaf rushed beside him and began patting his back, he sputtered, "I'm all right. Stupid but all right."

"Can you stand?" Calaf asked.

When Ishmael nodded, Calaf helped him to his feet. "Looks like only a few scratches. Let's get you cleaned up."

After they undressed, Ishmael sat in the damp sand at the edge of the stream rinsing off his arms. Calaf sat before him in the shallow water doing the same for his legs.

"You're lucky," Calaf said. "Just a cut on your calf but it's stopped bleeding. Now lie on your back, your head over the water," He guided Ishmael's head onto his knees and began washing the dirt from his hair and face.

"That feels good," Ishmael said. "I should fall down cliffs more often." Calaf twisted his ear. "Ow!"

"You scared me."

"I didn't mean to."

Calaf leaned over and kissed Ishmael's forehead. "I know you didn't. I often think about Demetrius, too—and how, and why, he died. For that alone I would have left the bastard here to die."

"But he's your father."

Calaf eased Ishmael's head off his knees. When Ishmael shifted about, he found Calaf had stood, his back to him. "What is it?" Calaf's shoulders stiffened, but he did not answer. Ishmael moved behind him and touched his arm. Still Calaf did not turn or speak. Ishmael waited several long moments before whispering, "Another vision?"

Calaf slowly shook his head and said, "Timur—he's—" He did not finish. It was as if he had stopped breathing.

Ishmael waited, a shadow of unease creeping over him. He took hold of Calaf's shoulders and turned him around. "Tell me."

"Timur is not my father."

"What are you talking about?"

Calaf touched the infant ankle band hanging from the chain about Ishmael's neck. "This has always been yours."

Ishmael backed away. "No, it can't be," he whispered. But his memories leapt faster than his thoughts to a moment when he was seven years old and standing before Sharina. *Are you really my mother?* He stumbled but caught his balance. Calaf reached for him. He pushed him away and dropped to his knees. Calaf sat a few paces away. Ishmael picked up a stick and began drawing circles in the sand.

After several long moments, Calaf said, "I know it's a shock."

"Silence," Ishmael shouted, his eyes not leaving the ground.

Gar was to deliver your head to the emperor with a message from your mother. Nozar's words flashed across his mind, as they had many times since the general had spoken them. At last confusion gave way. If Sharina was not his mother, it is no wonder that she could coldly plot his death. How often had he deceived himself into believing she loved him? A mother must love her child, right? But he was not her child, so everything he had ever tried to believe about her was built upon a lie.

Without looking up, Ishmael asked, "How?"

"Sharina switched us after we were born, just before the *chakor*."

Ishmael shook his head. "Wasn't that enough to avenge the deaths of her family? Did she have to hate me so much she wanted me dead, too?"

"She hated Timur, and because you were his son, she hated you."

Ishmael laughed, its bitterness surprising him. "How long have you known?"

"After we parted the last time. Flavus told me to prevent me from killing her for plotting against you."

"Flavus knew?"

"Demetrius told him."

"Who else?" Ishmael asked.

"None that I'm aware of."

"Not even Aric?"

"Flavus insisted he didn't know."

Ishmael continued to draw, the circles in the sand now one atop the next, spiraling in a wide arc between him and Calaf. "Lavender—she smelled of lavender."

"Who?"

"The queen, my real mother." He reached for memories but found only disjointed fragments. He is sitting in her lap, held in her enveloping softness. He hears her laugh, deep and throaty, almost masculine. He tries to imagine her face but only sees her smile then feels her lips kiss his cheek. And the scent of lavender.

I had a mother who would have loved me. She took even that from me.

Ishmael lifted the ankle band from his chest to study the engraving. *Son of Timur, Prince, Warrior, Champion of His People.* He whispered, "So much now becomes clear." After pulling on his clothes, he retrieved his pack from the bottom of the cliff. When he returned, Calaf was dressing. Walking past Calaf, he called out, "The Persian soldiers should have moved beyond us by now."

When Ishmael awoke the next morning, his head rested on Calaf's chest. He had fallen into a fitful sleep with his back to Calaf, resisting Calaf's attempt to pull him into their usual slumbering embrace. But now he longed for it, nuzzling closer to Calaf's warmth in the chill of the high desert dawn. While he craved a lover's physical intimacy, he welcomed Calaf's desire for closeness at night, recognizing that Calaf's earlier impotence made clear that he had to be patient about anything more.

Upon leaving the flood plain few words had passed between them and none about Calaf's staggering news. While Ishmael appreciated not being pressured to talk, Calaf had shown uncharacteristic restraint in his silence, raising his uneasiness. Calaf had lived with the revelation for many years. *Why did he wait two months to reveal it to me?* His first thoughts had centered upon discovering he was Timur's son, but as afternoon turned toward dusk, he asked himself, *What's actually changed?* Yes, he had gained an unexpected birthright. Some might consider that important, but not him. That birthright belonged to Calaf, son or not. So nothing had changed for him. But what about for Calaf?

When Calaf stirred beneath him, Ishmael pushed himself up on his elbow. Calaf's eyes blinked open, then he pulled Ishmael back down.

Ishmael traced his finger around Calaf's stomach. "This doesn't mean I have to call you Ishmael, does it?"

Calaf laughed. "Don't you dare. After all, we were named after the switch, so our names are ours. But speaking of switching." Then in a lively whisper he chanted, "My love awaits me / crying herself to sleep / her heart broken—"

Ishmael pushed himself up again, wide-eyed. "—as I roam the world / searching for a stupid camel to love."

Both began laughing uncontrollably. Ishmael finally rolled away, struggling to catch his breath. "You—you remember."

"How could I forget our last *chakor* celebration? Sharina must have almost fainted when we made our grand entrance dressed as each other."

Ishmael feigned a high-pitched cry. "Oh, great emperor, it was a mistake anyone might make."

"To the dungeon, villainess," Calaf shouted.

"And take that mongrel son with you," Ishmael added.

Their gaiety came to an abrupt end.

After a few moments of silence Ishmael said, "If Timur had discovered what she did, he would have killed you."

"Most likely—and then declared you his son and heir."

Ishmael snickered. "What a disappointment for him."

"But why? You have proven yourself worthy."

"Of what?"

"To claim his throne for yourself. I can't believe it hasn't crossed your mind."

Before Ishmael could respond, Calaf climbed to his feet and went to relieve himself. Only after they had dressed and prepared their packs did Ishmael break their silence.

"You weren't going to tell me, were you?" Calaf did not look at him or answer. Ishmael's voice rose. "You decided to keep it from me?"

Keeping his eyes down, Calaf said, "I'm sorry."

Ishmael spun about, certain only that he needed to put distance between himself and Calaf. He reached a boulder and leaned against it, fighting to calm the anger that threatened to overwhelm him. As much as he had tried to deny it, the Calaf he once knew, the boyhood friend of shared secrets and complete honesty, was no more. What a fool he had been. Just because his feelings for Calaf had not changed, that did not mean Calaf's had not. The ache that filled his chest demanded to be released in a cry of despair, but he suppressed it. The crunch of footsteps drew close and stopped behind him. In the long moments that followed there was no sound, no movement. Even that morning's steady breeze had ceased.

Into that silence Ishmael asked, "Why?" It was barely a whisper.

"Flavus convinced me that you would become my rival if you knew."

"No." Ishmael spun about. "He convinced you I am just like him."

Calaf's eyes were glistening. "But you're not like him. I know it now."

"How could you have doubted me?"

"You're right, I never should have," Calaf said. He held Ishmael's gaze and added, "Tell me what to do or say to restore myself in your eyes. Whatever it is, I'll do it without question."

Ishmael took a deep breath and felt his anger subsiding. Remorse had never come easy for Calaf. "Tell me what you believe I want now that I know the truth."

"You've never wanted anything more of life than to stand at my side."

"Truly?" Ishmael pressed.

"Truly."

"Then I need nothing more."

Calaf took a step forward and waited. When Ishmael opened his arms, Calaf threw himself into his embrace. "I feared I'd lost you." After several moments, he added, "You're shaking."

"I was scared, too," Ishmael said.

"Then we will vow that nothing will ever separate us again."

Calaf rushed away. When he returned, he carried a pointed stick. They knelt side-by-side.

"Draw our foxes," Calaf said.

Ishmael smoothed the sand before them and created their foxes, back to back, facing the world around them. When he finished, Calaf took the stick and drew arrows, each aimed at the foxes.

"Now place your hand over the foxes, palm up."

Calaf clasped Ishmael's hand in his, intertwining their fingers. Ishmael expected that Calaf would proclaim something, putting their vow into words, but instead he said, "Think of the foxes." Then he closed his eyes. Taking his cue, Ishmael closed his, too. As he focused on their intertwined fingers, his mind grew quiet. Then an image came. Two fox cubs curled up together in a darkened den. Moments later Calaf's hand slipped from his, and Ishmael opened his eyes.

Calaf smiled. "You saw them?" When Ishmael nodded, he added, "Mine were running together."

"Mine were sleeping in a den. What made you think of this?"

"All these years, it's how I kept you close. I'd close my eyes and think of the foxes. I realized no spoken vow between us could be more powerful."

"Amazing," Ishmael said.

"What?"

"There's a mystic in you." When Calaf returned an awkward smile, Ishmael patted his shoulder. "But don't worry, I won't tell anyone."

Later that day they took refuge from the midday sun in a shallow cave and were eating a meal of dried fruit and nuts. Ishmael asked, "What changed your mind about telling me about my father?"

"When you fell down the cliff at the flood plain, I had a vision of you falling into the stream at Srinagar. Then you were standing before me covered in Demetrius's blood and telling me you loved me. I now realize you're the only one who truly has."

Ishmael smiled and gave Calaf a gentle jab in the ribs. "It's about time."

Calaf took Ishmael's arm and pulled him close, his lips to his ear. "I love you."

With a laugh Ishmael squeezed Calaf tightly. "About time for that, too."

As they emerged from the cave the next morning, Ishmael pulled Calaf into an embrace and kissed his cheek. "I knew it would be worth the wait."

"A real bed would be nice though."

Ishmael held him tightly for several long moments then eased himself apart. "But it's best we don't get accustomed to such times together." When Calaf gave him a quizzical look, he explained, "As emperor you must marry."

"Alexander married."

"So he did."

But Ishmael also recalled Demetrius's story that while Alexander's devotion to Hephaistion never wavered, he not only married but also took a Persian boy as his lover.

After two weeks crossing the Khyber wilderness they arrived in Peshawar, taking refuge in the abandoned tunnel outside the city's Khyber Gate where Ishmael hid with other refugees after the Persians overthrew Timur. As the sun began to set they wandered along the nearby stream where Demetrius and Torak once brought them as boys to bathe. The water level was low. Even so, as the day had been hot, they were surprised to find only a small number of men and boys sitting or playing along the banks. They found a spot away from the others, undressed, and lay in the shallow water staring into a cloudless sky turning toward dusk.

"It's hard to believe we're here," Calaf said.

"It's been ten years." Ishmael turned onto his side and placed his hand on Calaf's chest. "I left believing you were dead. I never thought I'd return."

"I always hoped I would—but not as a fugitive."

"Next time," Ishmael said and sat up to stretch. "And with an insurgent army behind your back. Too bad we don't have horses. We'd be in Srinagar in days not weeks."

Calaf remained prone in the water. "It's futile."

"What?"

"Srinagar. Raise an insurrection? Perhaps. But to defeat the Persians and take back the Kushan Empire?" Calaf shook his head. "I watched them defeat the Romans. They destroyed them. We'd have no chance against them."

"You're thinking too much." Ishmael splashed water at Calaf's face.

Sputtering Calaf lunged at Ishmael, who scrambled out of the stream laughing, just out of Calaf's reach. When Calaf did not pursue him, Ishmael returned to sit at the water's edge. He patted Calaf's knee. "There was a time when you would have chased me to the city gate."

"We were boys then," After a few moments of silence, he asked, "Will you stay at my side if I become a river merchant?"

Ishmael laughed. "You, a river merchant?"

"But if I am?"

"I won't even consider it." Ishmael pointed at the city. "You're going to sit on that throne."

Calaf nodded with a forced smile and returned to lie in the stream. Of course, Ishmael could not understand. He had not faced the might of Persia, nor its savage brutality. They had to accept that their dreams of his ascending the throne of a renewed Kushan Empire were nothing more than fantasy.

Unless he challenged Turandot and won. That seed had been planted at the caravanserai outside of Baktra, and it had grown with each passing day they drew closer to Peshawar. Foolhardy and desperate, it would most likely end in his death. Ishmael would assail him for his selfishness. *Die and I die*, he would cry. But what choice did he have? If he was to regain the Kushan throne, a destiny that had been his, and his alone, since his mother switched him with Ishmael, boldness was called for, even in the face of overwhelming odds. Ishmael would, of course, call it reckless. But the Fates had brought him this far. Had he not survived as a Persian prisoner of war, subjected even to Faraj's sadistic brutality? Odds be damned; he believed he could survive Turandot's test and claim the Kushan throne as her husband.

But if he did face death, it must be alone. Ishmael had already risked too much for him. He would no longer allow Ishmael's fate to be tied to his. Even if death awaited him, Ishmael must live.

CHAPTER 45

Peshawar

At sunrise Ishmael awoke to find that Calaf had shifted during the night and now lay against the tunnel wall covered by a blanket against the morning chill. Given that the roads were jammed with people crowding into the city to witness Turandot's latest suitor submit himself to her riddles that day, they had agreed that they would rest for several days before pushing onto Srinagar. Calaf had convincingly argued the likelihood that their pursuers would order the Persian garrison to set up roadblocks around the city, adding to the risk of travel until the city returned to normal.

Ishmael slipped noiselessly to the tunnel entrance. Scanning the terrain, he smiled. Several dozen paces away sat a fox, upright, still, but attentive, its ears flicking to each early morning sound. The fox turned its head to watch a second fox unfold from the ground, its rump raised, its snout between its outstretched front legs. The first gave a soft yelp before moving away. The second caught up and they disappeared over a rise.

Ishmael whispered, "A good omen."

He yawned, leaned his head against the wall, and closed his eyes. When he reopened them, the sun had reached its highest point. Turning toward the still sleeping Calaf, Ishmael called out, "Wake up. I'm burning up in here. Let's go to the stream and cool off."

Silence greeted him. Calaf did not move. Ishmael scrambled across the tunnel floor, ready to pounce, anticipating a bit of amorous wrestling.

Pulling the blanket, he revealed their packs, but no Calaf. At that moment, the blare of distant trumpets arose from the city.

"No!"

Ishmael's shout echoed in the dim confines of the tunnel.

The cemetery outside Peshawar's north wall was a quiet refuge from the disorder and clamor of the unruly crowds that had doubled the population of the city in only a few days. Encampments reached deep into the surrounding hills, but none invaded the solitude of grave sites and gulmohar trees. No doubt because of the patrol Captain Barzin placed on the perimeter a week earlier, after the old raja sounded the gong announcing his intent to challenge Turandot.

Barzin knelt before his mother's monument and stared into his palm at the oval bronze disc engraved with her likeness. It had belonged to his father, given to Barzin by the one who saved him from the Rajanpur prisoner camp, the very one whose betrayal led to his father's death. It was a painful irony that haunted his rise through the ranks in the palace guard of Persia's puppet ruler Altoum.

"My heart is heavy, mother. But then, it always is, isn't it?" He glanced at his wife's neighboring marker. "I know you wish me to remarry. A year is long enough: that's what you would say before arranging my marriage to your new daughter-in-law. She'd be young, strong, and able to bear many children, just as you were. But the gods have turned away from your prayers: with many grandchildren I was to bring joy to your old age. And to my father's: I was to follow in his footsteps, pledged to serve Calaf as he served Timur. Instead I grovel for scraps at the feet of our enemy."

With the crunch of approaching footsteps he went silent and waited.

"Counselor Aric asks for you, sir. He says it's urgent."

Barzin rose deliberately, returned the bronze disc to the leather pouch hanging from his belt, placed his palm against his mother's monument for several long moments, then his wife's. Taking a deep breath, he turned about, acknowledged his deputy's salute, and preceded him toward the city.

Sharina gazed into her father's smiling face. He stroked her cheek and kissed her forehead. With a jolt she awoke, her eyes searching empty darkness. She touched the kiss, the warmth of his lips still imprinted there. He had smiled. Always before, when he came to her, he did not smile, his visage forever somber, his eyes eternally sad. But this time he smiled.

She reached for Aric, her hand finding his side of the bed empty, only then remembering this day began early for him. Another suitor would face the princess's riddles. As Turandot's royal counselor he oversaw the ceremony's countless details. For days he was consumed with worry. This suitor was old and broken, a deposed raja from the south of India, his gait halting, his stooped shoulders resigned, only his eyes determined, captivated by the perverted glory of his head spiked atop Turandot's amphitheater. Over the years Aric had taught the crowd to expect passion, drama, spectacle; he taught Turandot to demand them. But as a suitor for Turandot's hand, this raja was a disaster. Dressing the suitor as a buffoon with garish silks, effeminate hat, oversized slippers, a parody of the raja he had been, Aric opted for pathos, hoping the crowd—and Turandot—would succumb to the tragedy of the old man's fall. If not, plants in the audience would provide whatever was necessary—be it suggestive dancing by women or fights among men, most likely both—to keep everyone entertained after the brief thrill of the beheading.

"Whatever happens, it's going to be forgettable," Aric had said the evening before. "Worse, few are wagering against Turandot at the bettors' exchange. She counts on those winnings to cover what this costs and won't be pleased about dipping deep into her personal treasury."

Sharina had hugged him. "You worry too much."

"This time it's different," he had replied.

Sharina rose from the bed, pulled a silk robe over her sleeping gown, and stepped onto the balcony. In the distance the palace tower caught the day's first light, distant pounding of workmen echoed around the buildings, mixed with the din of merchants hawking their wares, the street below already teeming with people, animals, and carts. It looked the same, sounded the same, and smelled the same.

But this time it's different.

She went to the day room and found her daughter Jiya sprawled out on her stomach on the carpet, her finger tracing the vines, moving from one creature to the next, naming each with a whisper. Her younger brother Ashu knelt beside her, repeating each name. It was a game Sharina taught them, just as she taught Calaf and Ishmael. When Sharina heard that the carpet survived the Persian sack of the palace, she had acquired it.

Jiya's finger rested a moment on the lion, and then on the hare, the wing-like leaves upon its back.

Ashu shouted, "Fly!" Then he spotted Sharina. "Fly, Mama, fly!"

Sharina knelt and placed her finger next to Jiya's. "That's right, Ashu. Fly!"

Together they traced the vines to lion, dragon, parrots, then came to a stop at the two foxes, one white, one gold, back-to-back, attentive to the swirl of life around them.

Not for the first time Jiya said, "They're my favorites."

"Mine, too," Ashu added.

Without warning tears stung Sharina's eyes. *My father smiled.*

"What's the matter, mama?" Jiya asked.

She stroked her daughter's hair, answered, "Nothing, darling," and then called for the children's governess. While awaiting her arrival, a servant prepared Sharina's hair, while another laid out a Chinese silk dress, deep green and embroidered with white irises, Aric's gift for her fortieth birthday last month. "Something Turandot herself might wear," he said when she opened it.

When the governess entered the day room, Sharina said, "I go to the ceremony."

Confusion filled the governess's face. "You never attend the ceremony, my lady."

"But today I will surprise my husband and sit in the space he reserves for me each time. Please call the litter."

Yes, this time it's different.

My father smiled.

CHAPTER 46

Barzin entered Turandot's amphitheater by one of the two massive wood gates that flanked the open orchestra, his deputy opening a path for him through the sparse crowd. The gates had opened at first light and by mid-morning the arena should have been jammed with spectators. He spotted Aric pacing about the stage and shouting at workmen to hurry the removal of scaffolding used to clean the two-story mosaics of Turandot and her ancestor Lou-ling on either side of the grand staircase. As soon as he spotted Barzin mounting the center steps, he rushed toward him, his limp more pronounced than usual, waving his arms at the half-filled seats.

"What if Turandot looks out and sees this? The old raja's head won't be the only one on a spike this day."

Used to Aric's pre-ceremony hysteria, Barzin answered in a measured, calm voice. "The city's overflowing. The taverns are emptying as we speak. Rest assured, when the ceremony begins, it will be filled beyond capacity."

"Order your men to fill it now."

"But I have them in place to control the—"

"Now!"

Barzin bowed. "Yes, Counselor."

Aric stormed away, and as Barzin stepped from the stage, his deputy asked, "Shall I deploy the men?"

"Of course not."

Barzin walked around the platform that dominated the orchestra's center and paused a moment to watch workmen polishing the massive Chinese gong used to announce Turandot's newest suitor. A woman's cry for help rose above the din of the crowd. Just inside the gate a surge of spectators was shoving past something blocking its way. More distressed this time, the woman again cried, "Help us!"

Barzin moved through the crowd, calling out, "Don't push, people, plenty of room. Slowly so no one gets hurt."

The woman was hunched over a cloaked old man, pulled down by the rope that bound them together at their waists. She looked up at Barzin. "He fell—the crowd—I couldn't get him up."

"Loosen your rope." When the woman stepped back, Barzin took hold of the man's shoulders and lifted him to his knees. "Can you stand, old one?"

The man's hands reached up for Barzin's face. "Your voice, can it be?"

Barzin now looked at the man's face, his stomach lurching at the sight of its scarred empty sockets.

"Nozar, is it you?"

Recognition brought Barzin to his knees. "My lord," he whispered as Timur's fingers hunted the contours of his face, "not Nozar but Barzin his son."

"A disguise, that is good." Timur lifted his head and whispered, "Liu, he is here, Nozar is here."

Barzin placed his hand over Timur's mouth. "Silence, my lord, danger surrounds us."

Timur mumbled, "Danger, yes, always danger."

Barzin pulled Liu down. "His mind seems—"

Liu lowered her voice. "He is here to announce his return."

"Come." Barzin led them to the stage's proscenium. "My lord, I must go prepare for your arrival. There is much to be done."

"I will surprise my foes, won't I, Nozar?"

"That you will, but success demands your silence."

"Yes—silence—dangers."

Barzin turned to Liu. "Stay here. Keep him cloaked and quiet. I will come for you after the ceremony." Then beckoning his deputy. "Under no circumstances leave them."

Barzin climbed the center aisle of the stone seating, nodding to his men, who stood at every fourth row to keep the passage open for the Procession of the Severed Head, the concluding rite of the ceremony. Fourteen heads rose above the amphitheater's back wall, the anguish of death in each face preserved in stone, testaments to the enduring attraction and horror of Turandot's trial. A fresh spike was already in place in anticipation of that day's suitor.

Barzin stopped midway up the aisle, twenty rows above, twenty below, and scanned the theater. As he expected, people were pouring in from the gates on both sides, pushing their way into the stands or filling the orchestra. Well-disciplined and experienced with the ceremony, his men kept the flow ordered and resolved any minor altercations. In search of the best vantage point to the stage the crowd grew thick along the entire width of the proscenium. Meanwhile, his deputy maintained a modest perimeter around his charges, his uniform enough to discourage interlopers. *Timur alive.* His eyes remained alert to the arena, but his mind refused to block out the face of his emperor nor the voice of Nozar the last time he saw him: *Saving the emperor from himself and preserving his empire, that is my life.* Did that charge now fall to his son?

A flow of green silk emerged upon the stage, arresting Barzin's eyes and clearing his thoughts. Aric crossed to his wife's side and with clear pleasure guided her to a place with senior members of the court. *Sharina here?* He could not remember the last time she visited the palace. Fortunately, from where she sat she could not see Timur, and Aric was too distracted by the ceremony to look into the crowd. But surely it meant something. Three avowed enemies, after all these years, mere paces separating them.

The blast of trumpets drew Barzin's attention to the palace tower rising behind the stage, to the second level balcony stretching across its width with its double doors gilded in gold. Before them the grand stairway descended to the stage. The crowd quieted. With a second blast of trumpets the ceremony began.

Released one by one by Aric at the edge of the stage and stepping to the beat of rhythmic drumming, the Council of Three Holy Men—Zoroastrian,

Buddhist, and Hindu—crossed the stage toward identical gilded stools on a raised platform beside the staircase, each carrying with outstretched arms a large rolled parchment, which contained a riddle and its answer. The Zoroastrian priest stumbled as he mounted the platform but was caught from falling by his Buddhist colleague, both their parchments touching the ground, sending a rush of murmuring through the crowd. Recognizing that it boded ill for Turandot and watching last moment wagers being made around him, Barzin shook his head. It would not be the first time a contrived omen increased the palace's winnings.

At Aric's signal the suitor entered next, flanked by four soldiers wearing the ceremonial black leather uniforms and helmets of Tur's cavalry. The old raja's ludicrous costume drew cries of surprise then shouted curses.

"He dishonors us!"

"Behead him now!"

"Feed him to the dogs!"

Barzin caught the anxious eyes of his nearest men and nodded. The sight and sound of swords half-drawn silenced all but a single drunk, who was removed, still shouting curses as the raja knelt on one knee before the grand staircase. His responsibilities completed, Aric moved to sit beside Sharina.

Only when quiet returned did the trumpets sound again. All eyes focused on the balcony's golden doors. Slowly they opened. King Altoum emerged, his thick body swathed in white silk. That Turandot convinced her warrior father to dress like a celestial god always amused Barzin, but the absurdity was lost on the spectators, whose awe was palpable. Preceded by similarly draped maidens, Altoum descended the staircase at a measured cadence. Reaching the last step he paused, then proclaimed:

People of Peshawar!
This is the law: Turandot the Pure
will be the bride of the man of royal blood
who shall solve the riddles which she shall set.
But if he fail in this test,
he must submit his proud head to the sword!

His role in the ceremony concluded, he then took his place opposite the three holy men on a precious jewel-encrusted throne, surrounded by his entourage of maidens.

Quiet whispering ceased. No one coughed. No child cried. It was as if the entire amphitheater held its breath. For Turandot now stood alone before the balcony's golden doors, sheathed in white silk, her long black hair hanging loose to her waist, her face, hands and bare feet powdered white, her lips, eyebrows and nails painted black, the only color a necklace of rubies about her neck falling low between her breasts. Her eyes lifted to the sky as she began to descend, her feet seeming not to touch the stairway. Midway her glide stopped. She turned to face the mosaic of her ancestor. Clear and strong her voice rang out.

In my homeland many thousand years ago, a desperate cry rang out,
and down the generations that cry has found refuge in my heart.
Princess Lou-Ling, my ancestress sweet and serene,
who ruled in silence and pure joy,
defying the abhorred tyranny of man with constancy and firmness,
today you live again in me.

The maidens surrounding Altoum raised their voices, joined by many in the audience.

It was when the King of the Tartars
unfurled his seven standards.

Before the chorus's echo receded, Turandot continued.

At that time—it is known to all—
war brought horror and the clash of arms.
My homeland was conquered and subdued
and Lou-Ling, my ancestor, dragged away by a man like you,
like you a stranger, in that cruel night when her young voice was stifled.

This time the audience drowned out the maidens' chorus.

For centuries she has rested
in her massive tomb.

Turandot lowered her head as if in prayer then turned toward her own mosaic likeness.

O Princes, who with vast caravans
from every corner of the earth
come here to try your lot,
I take revenge on you for her purity, her cry and her death.

She clutched her ruby necklace.

No man shall ever possess me.
Hatred for him who killed her lives on in my heart.
The pride of her great purity is reborn in me.

She raised her arm then pointed down at her suitor.

Stranger, do not tempt fortune.
The riddles are three, death one.

No one breathed, not even a child's cry broke the silence. Then, as if on cue, the audience coughed their held coughs, brushed aside tears, moved bodies rendered immobile by Turandot's grief and resolve. Barzin had seen her performance many times and her command over the amphitheater always amazed him. He began examining the crowd, but a quick flash of reflected sunlight jerked him back to the stage.

The raja's hand moved beside his leg.

Barzin plunged down the aisle into the crowded orchestra, pushing through startled spectators. By the time he reached the steps to the stage, taking two at a time, the raja was on his feet. With unexpected speed the raja rushed for the grand staircase. The cavalry guards hesitated, the king jumped up shouting "Stop him!" As screams erupted, Barzin reached the staircase and launched himself onto the raja's back, landing them both face down at Turandot's feet.

"My son. You murdered my boy!" the raja shrieked as Barzin struck his wrist, the dislodged dagger clattering against the stairway's marble until Barzin grabbed it.

A cavalry guard helped Barzin to his feet as another took hold of the assassin.

"Murderer!" The raja screamed, his face distorted by rage, his eyes crazed.

A third guard raised his sword to strike, but Barzin blocked his arm. "Not in her presence." Only then did he look up at Turandot. She stared back, a picture of tranquil poise, her powdered white hands placed one atop the other at her waist, her face expressionless, only her black eyes showing life.

"My lady, my men, not the cavalry guards, should remove him."

She nodded. As the raja was dragged away and the king ordered the cavalry guards back to their positions, Barzin addressed the princess in a low voice. "You must leave immediately. There may be another attempt."

"No, we must remain calm. The crowd must not panic. Motion to the audience that all is well, then order a gradual clearing of the staircase."

Barzin's men carried out the order and the audience quieted. Turning back to Turandot, he said, "He was not adequately searched, my lady."

"My father will deal with the cavalry's incompetence."

Barzin bowed. *Or treachery.*

A shout broke through the murmuring crowd. "Turandot!" Then others. "Turandot! Turandot!"

More joined until the theater thundered in an explosion of voices, feet stomping, and arms reaching to the sky, a cathartic moment erasing the letdown of no trial and no beheading. The shouts were silenced by the blast of trumpets. Turandot turned and slowly mounted the grand staircase. Led by his entourage of maidens, the king followed. The balcony's golden doors opened to receive them.

Barzin shook his head, once again amazed at Turandot's good fortune, then remembering Timur, he looked toward his spot below the stage, but his eye caught the determined stride of a man moving through the crowd toward the gong's platform.

Suddenly, another man rushed through the orchestra gate into the amphitheater, frantically pushing people aside.

"Calaf!" he shouted. "No!"

CHAPTER 47

CALAF LEAPT UPON THE PLATFORM, hefted the wood mallet in both hands, raised it above his head, and struck the gong. As the sound reverberated throughout the theater, he shouted, "Turandot!" At the second strike, Turandot spun about. Calaf's eyes bored into hers. "Turandot!" As he raised the mallet again, pandemonium swept through the audience, drowning out Ishmael's repeated cries, "Calaf, no!" The third joined the diminishing echoes of the second. Holding the mallet in one hand, pointing it at the top of the staircase, he thundered, "Turandot!"

When Calaf dropped his eyes from the princess, he found a wide-eyed Barzin staring at him from the stage. At Barzin's signal palace guards swarmed around the platform, holding back the surging crowd. Someone shouted, "Calaf!" Then another. His name became a chant rocking the theater. Barzin jumped from the stage and vaulted atop the platform, his back to Calaf's.

Barzin turned his head and called out, "A dramatic return."

"Surprised to find you here," Calaf shouted back, then moved to Barzin's side. "Your loyalty?" he asked, keeping his voice low so as not to be overheard.

"To you, my prince, as my father was to yours."

"Then your father would be proud," Calaf said. "You saw Ishmael?"

"Yes. I have your father and his companion, too." Barzin signaled and the perimeter of guards parted for his deputy, who led the three to the side of the platform.

Calaf asked, "Now what happens?"

Barzin glanced at the balcony. "If they follow custom, they will take you into custody and set the day for your trial. But the crowd has recognized you. If they don't proceed immediately, they'll likely have a riot—or worse—on their hands. How are you with riddles?"

Before Calaf could answer, the trumpets sounded and silenced the crowd. The king stepped to the top of the staircase, and the people roared in one voice as he began his slow descent.

Calaf said, "If I fail, get Ishmael away immediately. He's in great danger here."

"I will not leave your side," Barzin protested.

"After Demetrius died and Ishmael was banished, your father charged you to watch over him. I charge you now."

"But—"

"You refuse my command?"

"No, my prince."

"Then I would hear your promise," said Calaf.

"I will protect Ishmael."

"With your life."

"With my life," Barzin said.

Calaf shifted his attention to the stage where the king was completing his proclamation.

But if he fail in this test
he must submit his proud head to the sword!

Then Aric stepped forward. "Captain Barzin, escort Turandot's new suitor to the stage."

Barzin made a show of searching Calaf for weapons, then preceded him off the platform. As he passed his deputy, he whispered, "More men." The deputy nodded and slipped through the perimeter of guards. Calaf met Ishmael's anguished eyes and read the unspoken question,

"Why?" Voices whispered Calaf's name and hands reached out to touch him.

Barzin paused at the first step. "They angle backwards."

Despite the warning, Calaf wobbled as his foot reached for the second step, for the moment impressed by the trickery the princess employed to intimidate her suitors. Reaching the stage, he faced Aric.

"How unexpected, Calaf."

"Your worst nightmare, I expect."

"What? At last to witness your pride destroy you?" Aric asked.

"But should I live?"

"Ishmael might have a chance answering the princess's riddles—but you? You forget I taught you both." He signaled and a servant rushed from off stage carrying a black silk robe. "I apologize for its simplicity. Given more time I would have attired you appropriately."

Calaf refused the robe. "There was a time when you too dressed as an unassuming Kushan."

Aric's face reddened as he pointed to a spot at the base of the grand staircase. "Kneel there. Wait for her signal to stand."

"I will not kneel."

"But you must." Aric leaned close. "It is not wise to displease her."

"No."

Aric lifted his shoulders and raised his arms in an exaggerated flourish for the audience. Some in the audience laughed, while others recognized Calaf's defiance and cheered.

This time awed silence did not accompany Turandot's descent. A hum of murmuring filled the theater, punctuated by shouts of "Turandot" or "Calaf." While Calaf's eyes did not leave her imperious face, he noted hers remained focused on the people, as if only they mattered. Confident in her ability to stupefy her suitors with spectacle, rendering the most virile impotent, had she become an unwitting slave to her own creation? Had her suitors, no longer viable opponents, become mere players in an elaborate ceremony that she conducted?

Her voice momentarily broke through his thoughts. She faced the mosaic of her ancestor Lou-Ling.

In my homeland many thousand years ago, a desperate cry rang out,
and down the generations that cry has found refuge in my heart.

He recalled Flavus telling him, "Distraction is the gladiator's greatest foe, surprise his undoing." He remembered what he had learned at the fishermen's beach at Makli. He had ignored Drusus's taunts, remaining calm, studying how he moved, waiting for the opening that he knew must come. Drusus believed in his greater strength and experience and succumbed to a blade severing his throat.

Turandot now faced her mosaic portrait, her ruby necklace lifted from her breasts, clutched in her powdered white hand.

I take revenge on you for her purity, her cry and her death.
No man shall ever possess me.

It was an impressive act, orchestrated to move an audience to tears and disorient an unwary prince. With deep breaths Calaf fought to calm his racing heart. Turandot raised her arm and pointed her finger at him, for the first time her eyes meeting his.

"My prince, you tempt Fate. For my riddles are three while your death is but one."

With a voice strong and clear, Calaf laid down his own challenge. "My princess, your riddles may be three, but one life is all I need to prevail."

As the theater erupted into competing shouts of condemnation of his arrogance and support for his courage, Turandot's mouth lifted into a slight smile. On Makli's beach Drusus smiled such as smile.

Turandot remained midway on the staircase, her eyes on the audience, as she recited the first riddle.

It soars and spreads its wings
above the gloomy human crowd.

The whole world calls to it,
the whole world implores it.
At dawn the phantom vanishes
to be reborn in every heart.
And every night it is born anew
and every day it dies.

Her face remained uplifted, momentarily rankling him with her haughty confidence, diverting his attention until he saw the trap. He recalled Demetrius telling Ishmael and him the story of Oedipus answering the Sphinx's riddle and concluding with, "Oedipus did not fight the riddle. Rather he opened his mind to it." He told Demetrius he understood, but he did not—until now. *Every night it is born anew.* Once again he was a Persian prisoner, lying on the hard ground after a day's march, looking into the night sky. In those quiet moments, Ishmael always appeared to him, giving him—

"Yes, Turandot, it is born anew, and in my rejoicing, it carries me away." He paused, waiting. Only when her face lowered and her eyes met his did he say. "It is hope."

The Hindu priest rose, unrolled his parchment. "The answer is hope."

Shouts of "Hope" raced through the crowd. Barzin whispered to him, "It is rare that the first riddle is answered correctly."

"And the second?"

"No one since the first."

Turandot raised her hand, the audience went silent, and she descended several steps, this time her eyes never leaving his. Again, that smile. "Beware, my prince, for hope always leads to disillusion." After a dramatic pause, she delivered the second riddle.

It kindles like a flame
but it is not flame.
At times it is a frenzy.
It is fever, force, passion!
Inertia makes it flag.

If you lose heart or die it grows cold,
but dream of conquest and it flares up.
Its voice you heed in trepidation,
it glows like the setting sun.

A flame, not a flame. Grows cold and flares up. Contradictions defying explanation. Confusion pushed all thoughts aside. Cries from the crowd intruded, making it harder to focus.

"Don't despair."

"Speak, speak."

Then other voices filled his head. *I'm a bird, I'm a camel.*

One by one the faces of his comrades appeared.

Lucius, Decimus, Gnaeus.
Numerius, Appius, Aulus.
Mamercus, Tiberius, Publius.
Caius, Marcus, Quintus.

First in life. Then in death. Dragging each one to join his comrades in a common grave. *If you lose heart or die it grows cold.*

Turandot's voice tore him from the vision. "Anguish clouds your face, my prince. It is but fleeting for soon the executioner's axe will bring you comfort."

"No comfort can ease my anguish, Princess. Even in triumph, as it races hot through my veins, I cannot forget how cold and still it is in death. It is blood."

Turandot's face remained immobile. The Buddhist priest rose, unfurled his parchment. "The answer is blood."

Calaf closed his eyes as the crowd behind him roared, stomped their feet, and chanted, "Calaf, Calaf, Calaf."

Additional palace guards entered from both gates. Barzin's deputy guided Ishmael, Liu, and Timur onto the platform to protect them from the frenzied throng. Turandot's scribe Wei rushed forward, stopping beside the king's throne and bowing his head as if in prayer. Aric waved toward the balcony. Trumpets blared. When the crowd did not quiet, they sounded again. Finally, silence fell over the theater. Turandot descended, stopping on the staircase's lowest step. Calaf opened his eyes to a face still composed but from this close different, lines of age and fatigue showing through the white powder.

"Hope may be yours, my prince, but your blood will soon be mine." There was no smile.

Ice which gives you fire
and which your fire
freezes still more.
Lily-white and dark,
if it allows you your freedom
it makes you a slave;
if it accepts you as a slave
it makes you a king.

Behind him a hush swept the crowd. The only sound the beat of his heart. His mind blank, no image, no voice, no memory to awaken a solution, panic blurring the edge of awareness. Then Turandot was before him. Slowly she circled him and then stopped, her face in his.

"You turn pale from fear, my clever prince. Release the desperation that fills your heart. Accept that you are lost."

Again she circled him, again she stopped before him.

"Hurry, ice which gives you fire, what is it?"

Suddenly it was not Turandot before him. Sharina was at his feet, shaved head wearing monk's garb, seething with vengeance so intense it demanded killing Ishmael, an infant who once suckled at her breast.

Ice.

Turandot smiled. "Too late you discover that no man shall ever possess me." Her face *lily-white.*

Ice.

He returned her smile, watched her face freeze, and whispered, "You are the ice that makes me a king." Then raising his voice, he cried, "It is Turandot."

The Zoroastrian priest stood and from his parchment intoned, "The answer is Turandot."

As the theater exploded in a frenzy of shouting, chanting, leaping, and dancing, Barzin's men struggling to keep people from storming the stage, Turandot threw herself at the king's feet. Wei moved to her prostrate body, his expression distraught.

Her eunuch lover.

When he knelt and touched her hand, she did not resist the intimacy and returned a look of anguish.

Calaf felt the intensity of their suffering. *They do love each other.*

Turandot raised her face to the king, her voice defiant but breaking. "Noble father, do not throw me into the arms of this stranger."

The king's eyes revealed compassion but his voice was firm. "Our oath is sacred, my daughter."

"No, you cannot give me to him like a slave, dying of shame."

"But he offered his life for you."

"I will never be his. Never."

"You will not dishonor us." The king caught Barzin's eye and beckoned.

Barzin stepped forward. "My lord."

"The scribe Wei. Seize him."

Turandot rose to block Barzin's way. Then with a deep bow she said, "It will be as you command, my king."

"Then stand before me with the man who has won you fairly." As Altoum embraced Calaf, the crowd roared its approval. "Today you win the hand that was once betrothed to you, Calaf, son of Timur. Yes, I do remember. I expect our lord Shapur will not be amused to find the son of his past enemy again heir to the Kushan throne, but that is tomorrow's care. Today we celebrate your triumph. Let us retire to the palace where we shall plan your marriage festivities."

Calaf pointed at the gong's platform. "I request that my friend and his companions join us."

After a glance at the meanly-attired trio, Altoum responded in a low voice, “Might they be more comfortable in less extravagant surroundings?”

“I promised we’d not be separated,” Calaf said. “I trust you understand.”

“Then we too shall honor your vow.” Altoum signaled to Barzin. “Take them to the throne room.”

The king stepped before the grand staircase and waited as his retinue of maidens took their positions ahead of him. At the blast of trumpets the royal entourage began a measured ascent. When Altoum reached the midpoint, Turandot moved forward as if to proceed alone. Calaf stepped beside her and offered her his hand.

“Your arrogance—” she began.

He cut her off. “My right.”

She placed her hand above but avoided contact with his. “You may marry me, but you will never touch me.”

“It could be worse. I still have my head.”

The trumpets blared again, and together they climbed the staircase toward the gold doors leading into the palace.

CHAPTER 48

Aric collapsed on the couch in his palace chamber, his stomach churning with helpless rage. Unbelievably, Calaf now stood poised to retake the Kushan throne in the name of Timur. And not only that, the tyrant's true son Ishmael would stand at his side. Aric's betrayal of emperor and country and his subjugation to Persia's puppet king and his cruel daughter had all been for naught.

At a knock on his door he pulled himself to his feet. He would have been expected to proceed directly to the throne room and anticipated that a guard had been sent to find him. He girded himself for what would likely be his last assignment, Turandot's wedding to Calaf. Why would they need him after that? The end of Turandot's test took with it the source of any power and influence he had at court.

Upon opening the door, a familiar Persian merchant shouldered past the guard and threw his arms around the surprised Aric. With a swift backward kick, The Bear slammed the door closed on the guard and said, "You must be distraught beyond words, my friend."

"You—here—" Aric sputtered, stepping back out of The Bear's embrace.

"Of course, I'm here, where I've always been when you've needed me. Terrible business, this Calaf solving the princess's riddles. And then to see him in the company of that fugitive killer."

"What fugitive killer?"

"You haven't heard? I thought word would have reached Peshawar by now. Ishmael murdered Captain Faraj." The Bear pulled a frayed parchment from his cloak. "Here is General Zab's order for his arrest and return to Shushtar to face justice. And given the rumor, I couldn't have caught up with him at a better time to help you."

"What rumor?"

"That he, not Calaf, is the true son of Timur."

"It's not a rumor."

"Ah, what great news, my friend. While there's nothing I can do to help you with your Calaf problem, once Ishmael is in Persian custody consider the Kushan royal line finally at an end. The vengeance you've sought all these years will at last be complete. But we must hurry before Ishmael realizes we've hunted him down. Take this arrest order to King Altoum. He knows that Zab has great influence in Shapur's court and will welcome an opportunity to show his loyalty, particularly given that his daughter's marriage will likely generate diplomatic unpleasantness. I managed to restrain the Persian garrison from storming the palace. Instead soldiers are moving into position around the palace as we speak. I will join them now and wait outside the front gate to receive Ishmael."

Aric rushed down the palace corridor, elation replacing his earlier despair, and slipping into the cavernous throne room, he remained in the shadows of its massive columns. At the far end, raised upon a dais, the king sat upon the throne, seemingly content. And why not? His daughter's test had finally come to an end, and while it had placated the populace for many years, its potential for disaster always lurked below the surface. All it would take was another Persian ally, like that Armenian king's son, to lose his head and Shapur would likely see the king parted with his, too.

Beside the throne, Turandot reclined upon her black silk draped divan, the ever-present Wei hovering behind her. While her posture proclaimed calm, her hand gripped the rubies at her neck so intensely that Aric wondered that they had not crumbled into dust. Her situation might be hopeless, but her immobile face, hidden behind a mask of white powder, hid a will that would not easily bend. Aric smiled, knowing that he would soon give her what she needed to escape the fate Calaf had forced upon her—and great would be her gratitude to him.

Behind the dais the Council of Three Holy Men huddled together, congratulating each other on their good fortune at Calaf's triumph. The pageantry of a royal wedding required that each be involved, and the king, of course, would pay handsomely for their services. But soon enough Aric would turn their self-satisfied solemnity to teeth-gnashing chagrin.

A muffled groan diverted Aric's attention to the side wall where Ishmael's companions knelt. A woman, her clothing caked in dust, silenced the old man and pulled his hood more securely over his face. He suspected that she had been beautiful once, but life on the road had taken its toll. For a moment, he wondered how she would manage without Ishmael at her side but quickly waved the thought away. What concern was she or the old man to him?

Aric's eye traveled further along the wall to where Captain Barzin stood, alert to all around him. Rescuing him from the Rajanpur prison camp had been a good decision. Even though he refused any attempt at social contact, Barzin had remained loyal to him at court. But with Calaf's return, anxiety tugged at Aric's consciousness. Where would Barzin's loyalty lie once Aric set in motion the downfall of Calaf and Ishmael? Aric counted on Barzin being a survivor above all. It was unlikely that he would risk his position at court, particularly given that he had just solidified that position by thwarting the attempt on Turandot's life.

Finally, Aric shifted his gaze to Calaf and Ishmael, standing together before the king. At something the king said, Calaf threw his arm around Ishmael's shoulders and Ishmael responded with a smile, jolting Aric with memories of the boy he had raised as his own son. Laughing at his quick wit and high spirits. Feeling pride at Ishmael's quick grasp of language and writing and his hope that he would follow in his footsteps. Comforting him when he cried 'Why doesn't my mother love me?' Doubts flooded his mind. How could he send him to his death? Relieved that no one had noticed him, Aric moved behind a column and leaned his head against it.

Hadn't fate given him another opportunity to avenge Timur's brutality? How could he stand idly by in the face of what Timur had done to Sharina, even if she now inexplicably acted like she had found peace? And did not the blood of his slain brother cry out that he act? How could he ignore the many times he had stood at the Martyr's altar before battle, the gloating Timur gazing down at him as he forced him to recite the prayer that extolled his treachery?

Yousef and Sanjar,
Raised to Ahura Mazda as martyrs
To the glory of Lord Timur.
May their courage and deaths
Be celebrated forever in the hearts of all men.

Aric dug his fingernails into the column. What of Sharina and his children? Any attempt to rescue a Kushan fugitive from Persian justice would raise questions at court about his true loyalty. And would not Turandot turn against him now that he was of no use to her? Might not he and his family be exiled—or worse?

Resolution took hold of Aric and with it came calm. He was not responsible for the fate that awaited Ishmael in Shushtar. Persian troops surrounded the palace, making any attempt at escape futile. While he might feel remorse for the boy he once knew, that boy was now a man who had killed. The consequences were Ishmael's to face, just as Aric must protect himself and his family from the consequences of a foolhardy attempt to interfere.

Aric stepped away from the column just as Sharina entered the throne room from a side entrance. Turandot rose and taking Sharina's arm guided her to the divan, where they began to talk. Aric cursed to himself, knowing it would be better if his wife was not there to witness what he was about to do. But it could not be helped. Anyway, she would not challenge him before the court.

After Barzin helped him settle Liu and Timur along the throne room wall, Ishmael had paced like a trapped animal, reliving the moment when he had watched in horror as Calaf struck Turandot's gong. Outrage had swept through him. How could Calaf risk his life—no, their lives—in such an impulsive and futile quest? But his anger had been short-lived as helplessness in the face of the inevitable outcome threatened to overwhelm him. But the inconceivable happened. Calaf had prevailed.

When Calaf entered the throne room, he was alone. He had changed into a simple robe of red silk edged in embroidered gold. Spotting Ishmael, a wide smile spread across his face. Relief should have propelled Ishmael into Calaf's arms, but he did not move. Their eyes met. Calaf hesitated, and his smile vanished. Rather than continue toward Ishmael, he knelt before Liu and Timur.

"It's Calaf," Ishmael overheard Liu say to Timur. She took Timur's hand and placed it on Calaf's face. Timur's fingers hunted the contours of Calaf's forehead, nose and mouth.

"I once knew a Calaf, didn't I?" Timur muttered uncertainly, then brightened and whispered, "Nozar is here."

Calaf looked at Liu. "Nozar?"

"He believes an officer who helped us is this Nozar."

"You're a brave woman to care for him."

Liu replied, "Ishmael says it's only because I'm as stubborn as he is."

After a polite laugh at the jest, Calaf rose. Ishmael stiffened, keeping his arms at his side. Calaf approached. "Please don't be angry."

"You abandoned me."

"You would have tried to stop me."

"Of course, I would," Ishmael snapped.

"Nothing could have stopped me," Calaf hesitated a moment before adding, "even you."

A deep ache swept through Ishmael's chest. Finally, he said, "I know."

"And I would not risk your life, too."

"Do you think that matters to me?"

"It should," Calaf retorted.

"If you had failed—" Ishmael could not finish.

Calaf reached for him, and Ishmael did not resist as Calaf pulled him into his arms. "But I didn't."

After several long moments Calaf attempted to ease from the embrace, but Ishmael tightened his hold. "You terrified me."

"It's over now, and we're safe."

Ishmael stepped back. "But I'm still a fugitive."

"Nothing will happen to you. My victory assures that," Calaf said. "But until all is resolved, look to Barzin. I've charged him to protect you."

At that moment the king entered the throne room with Turandot, followed by her black-robed scribe and the Council of Three Holy Men. A few moments later Sharina appeared. After settling into their places on the dais, Altoum called for Calaf and him to approach.

With a nod at Ishmael, Altoum said to Calaf, "Tell us about your friend."

"We were born days apart and grew up together in this palace. Despite long separations our friendship grew stronger. He rescued me from a prisoner of war camp, allowing me to stand before you today. He fought bravely in the Kushan army and has completed his physician training in Shushtar."

Altoum glanced at Turandot. "Persian educated. Most impressive, don't you think? We always have need of good physicians."

The princess studied Ishmael for a moment before answering, "Yes, my lord."

Aric moved out of the shadows. It had been nine years since Ishmael had watched Aric strut across the palace courtyard in his new Persian finery, the stench of Peshawar's destruction—and his betrayal—permeating the air. Whatever Aric had gained by aligning himself with the Persians, the years had not been kind to him. The bounce in his step was gone, replaced by a heavy, uneven gait. Gray pallor and deep lines dominated a face that once seemed eternally youthful. Eyes that used to sparkle with contained mischief now surveyed the world with the wariness of the hunted.

The king acknowledged Aric's appearance with an impatient nod before continuing, "Now, Calaf, introduce us to your friend's companions."

All eyes shifted to the side wall where Liu and Timur knelt. Liu looked about nervously.

The king called out, "Come, come, we welcome you."

The rope tying Liu to Timur slowed their way across the room. When Barzin approached and attempted to untie it, Liu stopped him.

"He will panic if separated from me." Then she whispered to Timur, "Keep hidden, not a sound." Timur responded by pulling the hood tighter over his head. As she crossed the room, Liu kept her focus on Ishmael. He gave her a smile, hoping to reassure her. When she knelt, she pulled down on the rope and Timur dropped to his knees beside her, losing the grip on his hood. It slipped from his head, revealing his sightless eyes and scarred face.

Ishmael turned at Aric's gasp. Sharina, whose face mirrored Aric's shock, quickly moved to Aric's side and took his arm. But Aric shook free, bowing first to Turandot then to the king. "My lord, I have news that may affect our business here."

"Proceed, counselor."

Aric removed the frayed parchment from his cloak. His hand shook, and his voice faltered a moment before he declared, "General Zab orders the arrest of Ishmael and his return to Shushtar for the murder of Faraj, captain of the Persian army. Persian soldiers wait at the palace gate for us to turn him over to them."

Instinctively Ishmael reached for the broken tip dagger under his cloak, escape his first impulse. Barzin stepped closer and shook his head.

Calaf cried out, "You betrayed your emperor and country and now betray Ishmael?" He lunged toward Aric, but Ishmael restrained him.

"No, Calaf," Ishmael said. "All is in motion. It must play out."

"Wei," Altoum called out. The scribe took and studied the parchment. "It is the seal of General Zab, my lord. The instructions are clear. We must comply."

Calaf shook off Ishmael's hold. "You must not do this, my lord. Ishmael killed Faraj to save me. Release him to the Persians and you send him to his death."

The king asked Ishmael, "Do you deny the charge?"

"I do not."

Altoum remained silent for a moment before he addressed Calaf. "Your marriage to my daughter will enrage the Persians, maybe even to the point of armed conflict. I cannot afford to antagonize them further by refusing to return your friend to face judgment for an act he admits doing."

"But I owe him my life."

"An honorable sentiment, but you must understand that while I will defend your right to marry my daughter, I can go no further. Take what you have courageously won. Your friend must go to whatever the Fates have decided for him."

"No."

"You dare defy me?"

"No—but I will not allow my friend to die."

"You have no choice."

"But I give you one: my claim for Turandot's hand in exchange for Ishmael's freedom."

Ishmael grabbed his arm and whispered, "What are you doing? The throne's within your grasp."

"Not without you at my side."

The king demanded, "What is this game you play, Calaf, son of Timur?"

"None, my lord, but does it not concern you that the people shout my name with such passion?"

"You dare threaten us?"

"I dare nothing, my lord. I only seek Ishmael's freedom. Help us escape from your kingdom, and we will leave you—to your games."

Turandot pleaded, "Agree, Father, you must."

Altoum silenced her with a look and turned to Calaf. "You take a great risk placing us in such a quandary."

"But, my lord," Aric called out, "there is no quandary. Calaf is not who he claims. He is not the son of Timur."

Into the shocked silence, Turandot spoke first. "Father, if this be true, his triumph does not stand, and no accord is required."

Wei added, "My lord, death is the test's penalty for impersonating a prince."

Altoum raised his hand and addressed Calaf. "How do you answer this charge?"

"I am the heir of Timur."

"But not his son," Aric said.

Sharina stepped beside Aric. "Be silent, woman," he demanded.

"I cannot." Sharina acknowledged Turandot with a nod, the king with a deep bow. "I have something to say, my lord." When the king motioned her to speak, she began. "When I was twelve, my noble father was taken from me, deceived and cut down by an emperor's treachery, my brave, sweet brother Ashu at his side. The emperor's soldiers butchered my mother, ripped my baby brother from my arms, his head thrown against the marble floor, saving me as a prize for later political gain.

"My young heart turned cold, my ears heard only their dying cries, my eyes only searched to avenge their cruel deaths. The emperor married me to the raja of Srinagar then murdered him to seize his land and people. Unknown to the emperor I conceived the raja's son and would have been put to the sword but for the love of Aric, who claimed the child as his own. The emperor's own son was born within days of mine. Side-by-side they slept; together they suckled my breasts. All the while the spirits of my family demanded as vengeance the lifeless body of the prince. But in my weakness I did not heed their cries, and the infant lived to become a man.

"With the passing years, my resolve grew strong to end the clamor that demanded his death as redemption for theirs. But my plot was thwarted. All was taken from me, even the voices of my family abandoned me. Despair and death were my only companions, until Aric appeared, rescuing me a second time. The voices did not return, leaving a silence my husband and children came to fill. Hate and vengeance no longer hardened my heart."

Sharina knelt before Timur and lifted his scarred and sightless face. When she placed her fingers on his cheek, he took her hand.

"Do I know you?"

"It matters not. It is only important that I know you. Be at peace." Then looking at the king, "If it please my lord, I will make arrangements for them."

Altoum said, "It will be as you wish."

Sharina rose to find Aric before her. "You dare stand against me?" Raising his hand to strike her, he hesitated before throwing himself at Timur, grabbing his neck in his hands.

"Liu—help," Timur cried out, his arms flailing, struggling to get away.

Barzin grabbed Aric's wrists, breaking his hold. "Counselor, you forget yourself." Liu pulled Timur into her arms to calm his whimpering.

Sharina cried, "Aric, stop. Would you make your children fatherless?"

Aric twisted about to face the king. "Do you not know who he is?"

"Of course, we know who *he was*. We also know what he has become: a blind, feeble old man of no consequence." Altoum did not take his eyes from Aric. "Do not try our patience further. Allow your wife to continue."

Sharina took Aric's trembling hands in hers, "A moment more," and stepped before Calaf and Ishmael.

"While I could not bring myself to take the life of the infant prince, I could not ignore the cries of my family." She reached for the chain about Ishmael's neck and pulled the gold infant ankle band into view. "It is proper that you wear this, for it was the gift to you from your father the emperor when you were born. I can never atone for taking it from you and giving it to my own son. As a result, both of you carried burdens no one should have been given." She touched Calaf's cheek. "That you have chosen Ishmael above all is my redemption and greatest joy." Then she embraced Ishmael. "Before she died, I confessed to Adelma that you were her son. If she were here, I know she'd tell you how proud she is of the fine young man you've become. But at this moment her pride could never exceed mine." She pulled his face to hers and kissed his forehead.

Turning to Altoum she said, "At the ceremony of *chakor* the two before you were declared *rada* brothers, confirming the sacred bond that exists between unrelated infants nursed by the same woman. Calaf and Ishmael are inseparable, as they have proven time and again, most recently before you this day. One is the heir, one the son. Kill one, you destroy the other. I implore you to consider this as you pass judgment, my lord."

Silence fell over the throne room as Sharina rejoined Aric.

Calaf squeezed Ishmael's hand and whispered, "Can you believe what just happened? She just saved your life."

Ishmael heard the words but they did not register. His eyes grew moist and his lower lip shook. It was as if Sharina's neglect of him as a boy and her attempt to kill him were suddenly washed clean, all in the name of his hunger for a mother's love. He wiped his eyes and studied her, looking for some sign of artifice, but saw only calm resolve.

The king thrust his arm toward Barzin. "Captain, secure the hall. No one leaves or enters." At Barzin's signal, palace guards filled the throne room, stationing themselves along the walls. Altoum then motioned Turandot and Wei to join him with the Council of Three Holy Men behind the dais.

Ishmael strained to hear their deliberations, but they kept their voices low. At something the Buddhist priest said, the Zoroastrian and Hindu priests became agitated.

"He likely counsels compassion," Ishmael whispered to Calaf. "The others reaction doesn't bode well for us."

"Trust me. The king will rather deal with the Persians over an escaped fugitive than Timur's heir marrying his daughter. The tunnels under the city wall—I helped build them—they'll get us past the Persian troops. I'll demand horses to speed our escape."

"But if all else fails, remember it's a long journey to Shushtar," Ishmael said. "I will escape."

"Too great a risk. I won't allow you to face the Persians alone."

"But you have the throne in hand," Ishmael pressed.

"You killed Faraj to rescue me. You expect me to abandon you?"

Ishmael conceded with a nod. "And I will kill again to save you." He nudged Calaf. "Something's happening."

The priests and Wei stepped away, and the king spoke alone with Turandot. After nodding, she turned to face the wall as the king returned to the throne. Turandot did not move for many long moments. Finally she turned around, cast a consoling glance at Wei, and solemnly mounted the dais, each step deliberate, poised for maximum effect. Ishmael marveled at her instinct for drama. She stopped beside the throne and slowly gazed around the hall, her body erect and tense, her white powdered face impassive. Only after looking at everyone else did she shift her focus to them.

"I have seen many die for me, Prince Calaf," she began. "I despised them all, but you raised my fears. In your eyes shone the light of heroes. In your eyes I saw the proud certainty of victory. And I hated you for it. But you have revoked your well-earned triumph to save a friend, to honor the love that binds you together. There can be no hate for that. Of course, we are deeply moved by Lady Sharina's plea. Despite that, we find ourselves in an impossible situation." She paused as if deeply troubled before continuing. "The people now expect—no, they will demand—our marriage. Wagers are being settled as we speak. Your surprise victory has made some a great fortune, winnings they will not wish to relinquish. If there is no marriage, riots will threaten our rule—and Persia's. The rules of the trial are quite specific. The only alternative to our marriage is your death for misrepresenting who you are. Therefore, you must choose. Marry us and Ishmael returns to Persia and his fate—or die by public execution and we will free Ishmael to continue his flight from justice."

Without hesitation Calaf answered, "Then I choose death."

Ishmael spun Calaf around by the shoulders. "You will not sacrifice yourself for me."

"But I can't live knowing I caused your death by bringing you here." He kissed Ishmael and called out, "Barzin, get him safely out of the city."

Reeling in shock Ishmael did not resist as Barzin pulled him away. But then he broke Barzin's hold. Life meant nothing to him without Calaf. Dropping to his knees he pulled the dagger from his cloak. His eyes locked on Calaf's, he mouthed the words "I love you" and plunged the blade under his ribs, angling it toward his heart. He gasped, fighting the pain that radiated throughout his body, knowing that the dagger must go deeper to reach its mark.

"No!" Calaf rushed toward him.

Ishmael fell forward, landing upon the dagger's hilt, thrusting the blade up into his chest. The pain blinded him, his mouth opened, his head filled with his cry. He heard Liu scream. Then he felt himself gently turned onto his back. His sight cleared as Calaf pulled him into his arms, Calaf's voice sobbing, "No—no—no."

Sharina rushed forward, dropping to her knees, calling to the king, "A physician. My lord, call your physician."

Ishmael reached for Calaf's cheek and gave a weak smile. "No physician can help me—I knew where to send the blade." He coughed blood and clutched Calaf's robe.

Sharina touched his face and began stroking his hair. "Mama," he whispered.

"I'm here," she answered.

Then looking up into Calaf's face, Ishmael said, "No vengeance—do not let vengeance destroy you." As Calaf began to rock him, Ishmael murmured, "How far have I walked," recalling his song of love from atop Peshawar's wall many years earlier, watching as Calaf departed for Minnagara with Barzin's forces: *How far have I walked with your name in my heart, with your name on my lips?* He began to convulse.

"Don't leave me," Calaf cried.

Ishmael clasped Calaf's hand. "I will never leave you." Then intertwining their fingers, he leaned toward his ear. "Think of the foxes." He closed his eyes.

The foxes are running together.
Calaf's white surges ahead with Ishmael's gold nipping at his tail.
Then with a bark the gold takes the lead.

Sight and sound faded as calm enveloped him. Only the warmth of Calaf's arms holding him remained. Then one last breath.

Ishmael's fingers had tightened about Calaf's, and then relaxed. Calaf held the vision of the foxes a moment longer before looking at Ishmael's face. His mouth rested in a slight smile. He was gone. Calaf opened his mouth, but no cry emerged. Rage rushed toward the emptiness that now consumed his chest.

Sharina touched his cheek. "There will be time for grief later. Everything depends on what you do next. Your future, the future of your people, all that Ishmael gave his life for." Into the turmoil sweeping through him, she answered his unspoken question. "Do what Ishmael would want you to do."

He fought the urge to howl, 'What? No vengeance?' How could there be no vengeance for what had been brutally taken from him? For what Ishmael had suffered? Ishmael's last request or not, how could vengeance be denied him? All would understand. All would expect it—and see the justice in it.

After passing Ishmael into Sharina's arms, Calaf rose. Uncertain but knowing this was not a time to be distracted by emotion, he turned about in a circle, striving to calm himself with the slow movement. Barzin, his face in agony, now stood protectively over Ishmael and Sharina. The three priests stood together near the throne room's side door. Palace guards now encircled the king, who studied Calaf with keen interest. Resisting an officer's attempt to restrain her, Turandot had stepped off the dais. Her hand covered her mouth, her gaze intent upon the cradled body of Ishmael in Sharina's arms. Wei knelt a few paces away, his raised face never leaving hers.

Calaf came to a stop before Aric, who stumbled backward, catching himself from falling. Staring into Aric's terrified and wretched face, Calaf realized that this was not the same man with whom he and Ishmael had grown up. Revulsion spread through Calaf, edging aside his rage. He slowly shook his head, his eyes never leaving Aric's. "A warning that the Persians had found us, that would've been sufficient. We may not have survived an escape attempt, but you would know, and Sharina with you, that you did all that you could." He stepped closer and watched Aric's face blanch. "But you have nothing to fear from me. Your black heart destroys you beyond anything I might do."

Into the silence that followed came Timur's feeble voice. "Liu, what's happened?" Liu drew him close, comforting him with soft whispers.

Calaf stepped toward them. "Tell him, Liu, that his son Ishmael is dead. Tell him that with Ishmael's death the vengeance he called upon himself is at last concluded. Tell him—no, tell everyone that Ishmael loved—" Unable to finish, Calaf dropped to his knees before Sharina and stroked Ishmael's cheek.

Think of the foxes.

After reopening his eyes, he rose, resolute and calm.

To Barzin he said, "Watch over them."

To the king he bowed.

Then he stepped before Turandot. A single tear stained her powdered cheek. He traced its path with a finger. "Ice no longer, my princess?"

Her voice was barely a whisper. "Wei would have made Ishmael's sacrifice to save me."

Looking down at the kneeling scribe, Calaf motioned for him to rise. "I will not stand in the way of your love. I only ask that you pledge your allegiance to me."

Calaf watched surprise sweep across Wei's face. Wei and Turandot exchanged quick glances before Wei firmly replied, "I so pledge."

After Wei stepped back, Calaf waited until Turandot's eyes looked into his. Softly, for her ears only, he said, "To finally bring us together the Fates have dealt me a cruel blow, one you need not face. Do not defy them further, for Wei will never have cause to fear me." He offered her his hand, and after a brief hesitation she took it. His face firmly set, he gazed about the throne room, lowered his eyes for several long moments to Ishmael, and then looking up, he lightly squeezed Turandot's fingers. "Come, our people await."

POSTSCRIPT

17 DECEMBER 1959

I FIRST MET FRANCO ALFANO, the composer who completed the unfinished opera *Turandot* after Giacomo Puccini's death in 1924, when I interviewed him on the eve of *Turandot's* first post-war performance at the Arena di Verona in 1948, the year the incomparable Maria Callas sang the title role five glorious times. A colleague two years my junior got the prized assignment of interviewing Callas, while I found myself relegated to interviewing a composer who—while prolific in his own right—was only known for completing a master's work. Moreover, a close association with Mussolini during the war had not helped his reputation.

As it turned out, the interview evolved into something more than I expected. The allocated single hour became six, and I departed with more stories than I could ever fit into a thousand-word article. His questions about my personal life left me with a sense that I too had been interviewed, but most intriguing were several hints he made that the story behind the creation of *Turandot* was more than anyone knew.

In September 1954, one month before Alfano's death, the San Remo newspaper republished my *La Repubblica* review of that year's return performance of *Turandot* at the Arena di Verona. Within a few days an attorney contacted me to relay that Alfano wanted to speak with me.

The attorney's letter arrived as I made plans to travel from Rome to San Remo for a live concert by Maria Callas and Beniamino Giglil—and a long-overdue assignment to interview the diva. I arranged an additional day in San Remo and arrived at the office of Alfano's attorney early that morning. He informed me of Alfano's terminal illness, adding that my visit went against the advice of his physician and wishes of his family. When I asked why Alfano wanted to see me, the attorney replied that he did not know any specifics, but after the visit he would give me a package and pointed to the corner of his desk. It was wrapped in faded brown paper and tied with twine.

As the attorney drove me to the composer's residence—the mysterious package concealed in the attorney's black leather briefcase resting on the Alfa Romeo's back seat—he explained that his father, also an attorney, received the package from Alfano a week prior to the 1926 premiere of *Turandot* at La Scala. Alfano swore his father to secrecy, a secret then passed on to him. When I pressed for further information, he told me he knew nothing more, that the rest I would have to hear from his client.

Ushered into a small library with windows overlooking the Mediterranean, I found a nurse hovering about a figure seated in a brown leather wingback chair. As she moved aside I recognized a frail version of the man I had interviewed six years earlier. Another woman approached and introduced herself as Alfano's wife. As she guided me to her husband, I overheard the nurse say to the attorney that her patient had insisted upon meeting me seated, not bed-ridden. His hair, now thinning and gray, was neatly combed back to reveal a broad, ashen forehead, and his glasses rested atop a nose made larger by the gauntness of his face. But his smile transported me to our earlier encounter. I took his extended hand carefully, but he surprised me with a firm grip. In a voice that belied his illness both in strength and volume he ordered all but me to leave the library. His wife made a feeble attempt to remain, but a look from her husband sent her with the others. Alfano began by asking me a few questions about the previous evening's concert: Yes, Callas had been in excellent voice. No, sadly she did not sing Puccini. And, yes, the concert was recorded for "those infernal machines." Then Alfano turned to the reason for my visit.

After the attorney and I left the Alfano residence, he drove me to the train station for my return to Rome. I asked him to drop me off at a nearby café, where he lifted Alfano's package from his case and slipped it into mine before departing. Espresso and cigarettes at hand—and thankful for my trained journalist's ear and memory—I put to paper the words of Franco Alfano, words that I now share for the first time.

"For thirty years I have kept Puccini's secret, the truth about *Turandot*—a truth suppressed by his family—who feared it would ruin the Maestro's reputation and by extension the family's income from his works—and by the great conductor and Puccini's close friend Arturo Toscanini, who feared the potential scandal that might engulf the circle of composers and conductors that surrounded Puccini.

"I'm sure you've heard the story that Puccini had a premonition of his death before departing to Brussels for experimental radiation treatments and that he met with Toscanini and begged him, 'Don't let my Turandot die.' He did not, however, say this to Toscanini—he said it to me. In fact, Toscanini fought against Puccini's true vision for *Turandot*; it was I who fought for the Maestro's wishes.

"You have to understand that Puccini's prior successes rested on his ability to depict love as a destructive force. For proof, you only have to listen to *Madama Butterfly* or *Tosca*. When he initially considered retelling the folk tale of Turandot, a man-hating princess who finds love in the kiss of an unknown prince, he thought he could at last represent in music a vision of transcendent, transforming love—a goal that always had eluded him. It eluded him still, that is, until he turned his attention to Calaf, the unknown prince, and the companion to Calaf's father, the exiled and blind Emperor Timur. You know this companion as Liu, who, filled with love for Calaf, sacrifices her own life to save the prince from certain death. Of course, Puccini found this irresistible, and this servant's sacrifice became his central vision for *Turandot*, turning the primary tale of the ice princess consumed by an insane fear of love into mere backdrop to the true love story within the folklore: the tragic love of a prince and a commoner.

"I will never forget the afternoon the Maestro took me into his confidence and played his revised score for me. I sat awestruck by the depth of feeling, which was beyond anything I'd ever heard. He intended to present his revised *Turandot* to Toscanini upon his return from Brussels. His unexpected death meant that no one except me knew that he had changed the

Adami and Simoni libretto and scored the role of the prince's great love as a man not a woman, as a tenor not a soprano.

"When I showed the Maestro's family and Toscanini what Puccini intended, they were appalled and fearful. At first they accused me of forgery—and worse—until reluctantly Toscanini acknowledged that the manuscripts were true and confessed that he had thought his efforts to turn his friend from 'such folly' had been successful. With the Maestro's plea ringing in my ears I became a passionate champion within Puccini's inner circle, but in the end they silenced me—a silence cleverly engineered by Toscanini to feed my unbridled ambition: the commission to complete the unfinished *Turandot.* I ignored the Maestro's final request and sealed the betrayal that is my greatest shame.

"I believe you to be a sensitive man, someone who will value and protect this most important truth of *Turandot*, that the character everyone now knows as Liu is not as the Maestro intended."

I vividly remember how the dying Alfano's face lost the animation of the previous thirty minutes. His eyes closed and his breathing slowed to the point that I became concerned. I went to the library door and had barely opened it before the nurse and Alfano's wife moved past me as if I were not there.

The package that the attorney had slipped into my briefcase contained Franco Alfano's meticulously copied version of the score Puccini entrusted to his father when Puccini departed for Brussels. It also contained Alfano's copy of the Persian Turandot tale, annotated with Puccini's notes and plot ideas. Alfano's accompanying notes conceded that the Puccini family destroyed both originals—and the only unequivocal proof of his story.

I subsequently approached the descendants of Puccini and Toscanini, but when I told them I wished to publish the story, they turned me away with threats of legal action.

Many times I have sat at my piano and played (and yes, sung) the aria *Signore, ascolta!*—but not as Liu, a woman remembering the smile of her only but unattainable love; rather it is as Ishmael, a man who has known the love of his prince and cries out his helplessness at its approaching loss.

My lord, hear me!
Oh, hear, my lord!
Ishmael can bear no more,
his heart is breaking!
Alas, how far have I walked
with your name in my heart,
with your name on my lips?
But if your fate
tomorrow be decided,
I shall die on the path of exile.
Ishmael will lose his Lord,
the remembrance of his arms, his lips.
Ishmael can bear no more!
Ah!

Is this Puccini's last gift to opera? Or is Ishmael Alfano's creation, a troubled composer's last grasp for operatic immortality in the hallowed shadow of his Maestro? I ponder such questions without finding answers.

Reluctantly I conclude the time is not right for Franco Alfano's story. The fears of thirty years ago persist to this day, and outrage would still consume the sublime beauty of the tenor version of *Signore, ascolta!* I will keep Franco Alfano's package hidden and carefully preserved. Perhaps a time will come when the opera world will be ready to celebrate the love of Ishmael for his Calaf.

Ranuccio Farnese
Rome

ABOUT THE AUTHOR

AUTHOR, MOSAIC ARTIST, AND PHOTOGRAPHER Deak Wooten is a graduate of the University of California at Berkeley and has studied creative writing at Stanford University. He began writing fiction after retiring from a career in health care benefits consulting.

Giacomo Puccini's *Turandot*, a favorite opera, and his interest in ancient Roman and Persian history came together to inspire his second novel *Calaf and Ishmael*. His first, *Eyes of the Stag*, was published in 2011. His various projects are described at www.deakwooten.com.

Deak lives near Palm Springs in California's Coachella Valley with his husband, Paul.

Made in the USA
San Bernardino, CA
22 September 2018